"I will not keep you much longer." Queen Scalia paused, calling out to a servant in the next room before taking another delicate sip of her wine and continuing. "But before you go, you must see my cats."

"Your cats?"

Nodding, she said, "I'd like your opinion of them."

That sounded odd. What did it matter what I thought of her pets? And what kind of cats would they have here—saber-toothed tigers?

On that thought, the door opened and they entered—but they weren't cats—at least, not in the ordinary sense. They were tall male humanoids—undoubtedly more of Scalia's "exotic slaves." Separately, each one would have been stunning, but together, they took my breath away—would have taken *anyone's* breath away. I was just glad I happened to be sitting down when I saw them for the first time. Staring in awe at their naked, masculine beauty, I had barely managed to resume breathing when one of them turned his startlingly blue cat's eyes on me and, no doubt noting my open-mouthed expression, lowered his eyelids ever so slightly and sent a roguish smile in my direction.

THE CAT STAR CHRONICLES

ROGUE

CHERYL BROOKS

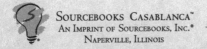

SOURCEBOOKS CASABLANCA™
AN IMPRINT OF SOURCEBOOKS, INC.®
NAPERVILLE, ILLINOIS

Published by Sourcebooks Casablanca, an imprint of
Sourcebooks, Inc.
P.O. Box 4410, Naperville, Illinois 60567–4410
(630) 961–3900
FAX: (630) 961–2168
www.sourcebooks.com

Library of Congress Cataloging-in-Publication Data

Brooks, Cheryl.
Rogue / Cheryl Brooks.
p. cm.—(Cat Star Chronicles; #3)
I. Title.
PS3602.R64425R6 20094
813.'6—dc22

2008041432

Printed and bound in the United States of America.
QW 10 9 8 7 6 5 4 3 2 1

Dedicated to all brothers everywhere.

Chapter 1

As you might expect from a planet where the intelligent species were reptiles, Darconia was hot, dry, and lacking in natural beauty—unless you happen to be fond of rocks. Lots and *lots* of rocks—as far as the eye could see, and then some. The palace was built of stone, as were all of the other buildings in the capital city of Arconcia, which made you feel only slightly cooler once you were inside.

"Should have listened to my mother," I muttered. "You're much too timid, Kyra!" she had said. "I can't even imagine you traveling alone." My father's comments had been similarly discouraging. "No point in compounding one mistake by making another," he had said. Not having an artistic nature himself, he hadn't approved my choice of music as a profession. "And when you get there, they'll walk all over you, just like everyone else does!" Mom had thrown in for good measure. But I'd found the courage somehow, and here I was! And what, I thought to myself, was a humble piano teacher from Upper Sandusky doing so far from Earth, about to be introduced to a lizard queen in a remote corner of the galaxy?

For that matter, when was the last time you heard of *anything* interesting happening to a piano teacher? I mean to the teacher herself, not one of her students who went on to find fame and fortune as a result of her outstanding musical instruction. Think about that for a minute. Have you—ever?

Well, I certainly hadn't, so when I ran across an ad for teaching the daughter of an offworld queen, I was intrigued. So what if the locals were all reptilian? It still seemed preferable to teaching the sons and daughters of no one in particular here at home. Interstellar travel had long been common, but I'd never been offworld before, and the idea of space travel appealed to me. It was a chance to see other worlds and other species, because if my information was correct, Darconia was a *very* long way from Earth.

Maybe the fact that none of the musicians I knew— even those who participated in the galactic music scene—seemed interested in the job should have been the first clue that I should have avoided it myself. But sometimes, you just have to go with your gut instincts, and my gut was telling me to go for it. If nothing else, it would look good on my resume—I mean, my student would be a *princess*, after all—and if I ever wanted to get beyond teaching at the primary school level it might be helpful.

I'd been teaching for all of the ten years since I left college armed with a degree in music education. The offers to teach at the university level hadn't exactly been pouring in, largely due to the fact that I'd never gotten up the courage to apply for that level of job—and I had yet to teach anyone who was even minimally gifted. Despite having been hailed as a promising new talent in my own school years, I hadn't built up enough of a reputation to attract any really good students, and since I was going nowhere, I figured I might as well go nowhere somewhere else—if you catch my drift.

I had no love interest to leave behind, either. Love and I were virtual strangers, and though I'd been through the usual series of unsatisfactory relationships most girls experience, there had never been one that I truly regretted having lost. I guess I should have known that giving piano lessons wouldn't put me in the way of meeting many eligible bachelors, but that never occurred to me when choosing my life's work.

I doubted that I would find true love in my new job, either, but I would at least get a taste of what life was like on different planets, and that sounded romantic enough. I'd done some research—though the information I'd found was a bit sketchy—and it all sounded fine to me. Darconia was a relatively peaceful planet and, although having royalty in power rather than an elected government seemed a bit backward, the fact that the Queen wanted her child to learn to play piano spoke of at least some degree of culture.

The strange thing was that while keyboard players weren't uncommon on any world, the ad had specified that the Queen wanted a well-qualified, young, and unattached Terran female. That was me. Why the requirements were so limited was a mystery, but I decided that a Queen could afford to be as choosy as she liked.

None of that mattered on the morning I waved goodbye to my parents and embarked for Darconia. I was leaving Earth for the first time, and no matter what happened, it was exciting! It was raining heavily, and my flight was delayed due to technical difficulties—but I was young and resilient and not particularly superstitious. My fellow travelers and I waited for what seemed like hours before the ship was finally cleared for takeoff, but at last we were on our way.

Once the ship was in space and we were free to move about, all I heard from just about everyone was, "*Where* did you say? Darconia? Never heard of it." It was no surprise that *I'd* never heard of it before, but the fact that it was unknown to most other travelers was unnerving.

I rechecked the database at my earliest opportunity and assured myself once again that, yes, Darconia did exist, and, no, I was not making a huge mistake by going there to work. I made a holocopy of the documentation—even showing it to a blue-skinned showgirl from Edraita who had been initially impressed when I told her that I would be teaching a princess, though, according to her, Darconia was such an out-of-the-way planet that even royalty didn't count for much. Later on, I learned that everyone—and not just the showgirls—on Edraita was notoriously snobbish.

This particular woman was tall and shapely with a brilliant mass of red hair, which contrasted nicely with her blue skin—and since her chief manner of dress seemed to be strings of beads of various shapes and sizes, I can assure you that she was blue all over. While her jewelry didn't cover enough of her to leave anything to the imagination—or keep her particularly warm—the jingling noise it made as she moved did encourage you to look in her direction, and once you did that, it was difficult not to stare.

Her name was Nindala, and we were as different from one another as two women could possibly be. She was confident and sensuous, while I was timid and would *never* have walked around wearing nothing but beads!

Despite our differences and her inherent snobbishness, Nindala and I became friends during the trip, which lasted nearly six weeks for me, though only about half that time for her. She was joining up with a troupe of acrobatic entertainers who were performing throughout the quadrant. I learned a lot from Nindala; for example, did you know that the men on Salurna Zebta have two penises and always have two wives? One for each cock, she explained. I tried, but I couldn't imagine what kind of evolutionary twist would account for such a variation. I mean, males wouldn't suddenly sprout a spare just because the women of their species outnumbered them two to one, would they? I came to the conclusion that this must have been the result of an extremely popular mutation, or it was genetically engineered at some point in the planet's history—though such practices were generally frowned upon.

I met another nonhuman traveler by the name of Garon, who overheard me telling Nindala where I was headed and tried to discourage me from ever setting foot on Darconia. When I tried to pin him down, all he would say was that he didn't care for lizards—which was possibly because with his pale, translucent skin, bulbous head, and glowing red eyes, he looked like a grubworm just waiting to become lizard food. I told him I didn't care what they looked like as long as they didn't stink or eat their food while it was still alive and wriggling. I also hoped that their hands were similar to those of humans, or I was going to have one helluva time teaching any of them to play the piano.

This particular man—at least, I assumed he was a man, although it was difficult to tell—also informed me that if

I was looking to start a family, Darconia probably wasn't the best place to do it, since Darconians were egg layers and therefore couldn't crossbreed with mammals. When I replied that I wasn't looking for love—and had yet to find it on a whole planet full of mammals—Garon seemed skeptical. Given my previous track record, it would have been just my luck to fall in love with a lizard, but since I tended to prefer men with hair and skin, rather than scales, this was doubtful.

Nindala seemed to think that I'd be very popular on her planet, though I thought it was due to the fact that I would have been an oddity there, especially if all the women were as stunning as Nindala. She disagreed, saying I was more attractive than I gave myself credit for, and, what was more, that my lizard-hating friend had been hitting on me.

"Oh, surely not!" I exclaimed. "He's much too alien for that!"

Nindala shrugged, a gesture which caused her bare blue breasts to bounce slightly. Informing her I had no intention of having sex with some slimy little alien grubworm, I left it at that—not mentioning the fact that I'd rarely had sex with anyone else, either. "Garon was probably looking at *you*, anyway," I said ruefully. Even without her exotic makeup and bizarre hairstyle, I was sure all of that blue skin would have stolen any glances which might happen to fall in my direction—and not just those of the male gender. I found it difficult not to stare at her myself, and I had no homosexual tendencies whatsoever.

"No, Kyra," she disagreed firmly, "he was not."

"Then I guess I should have left home years ago," I declared. "I might have been the toast of whatever planet he's from. I don't suppose you know what it's called, do you?"

"No," she replied, "but I have seen his kind before."

"And he's definitely a he?"

"Oh, yes," she replied knowledgeably. "The females have blue eyes. *That* one is male."

I nodded absently. I didn't really care one way or the other, but it was nice to know that it had at least been a *male* alien who'd been hitting on me—if that was what he'd truly been doing.

With the possible exception of a meteor shower to liven things up a bit, the rest of our journey progressed without incident. To pass the time, Nindala did some remarkable things with my hair—she was fond of really big, spiky styles, though they suited her hair texture much better than mine—and taught me how to put on makeup the way she did. I doubted I'd ever have much use for it, but Nindala disagreed, insisting that I might want to entice someone someday, and that it would be useful to know how. I didn't want to hurt her feelings, but I really didn't think I'd be trying to entice anyone on Darconia.

My first look at a Darconian did nothing to change my mind. As we drew nearer to their planet, we picked up several of them in the neighboring star systems. Garon's assessment had been correct, for looking at those downsized, snub-nosed versions of the *Tyrannosaurus rex*—though with broader shoulders and longer arms—filled me with no more desire than would your common, garden-variety gecko. Nindala's efforts to improve my allure would be wasted on their planet. I did not find them attractive in any way, and the prospect of having to fight off amorous lizards was enough to make me wash the makeup off my pale face, restore my dark hair to its customary braid, and consider wearing a very concealing cloak.

When at last Nindala disembarked, she promised to look me up if she ever made it to Darconia. She seemed to think there was a possibility that her troupe could add another planet to their tour of the quadrant, if she could get their booking agent to comply.

"If we do come, I promise to look for you at the show," she said. "But from the stage, it is difficult to see."

"Well, you shouldn't have too much trouble picking me out of the crowd—any crowd," I said dryly. "After all, it's a pretty safe bet I'll be the only non-reptile on the whole planet."

As it turned out, I was wrong about that.

Chapter 2

THE HEAT WAS OPPRESSIVE, BUT IT WAS A DRY HEAT, AND I wondered if there was enough water on the whole planet of Darconia to keep me alive. I learned later that this was only the desert sector and that there were other, more verdant areas, but you certainly couldn't tell it from where I stood on the landing platform at the spaceport. I consoled myself with the fact that there were at least some mountains in the distance to break the monotony of the horizon, but the rest was a sea of rocks.

The scenery may have been drab, but the lizards of Darconia were quite colorful, with scales ranging in hue from yellow all the way to purple. Like Nindala, they didn't wear very much—which made sense for a lizard living in the desert. But I did wonder how you could tell the Queen from the others; without royal robes and a crown, she would look no different from her subjects.

The best I could tell, most of what the Darconians wore was utilitarian—belts or harnesslike straps around the upper body, etc. They did have a decorative aspect: some adorned themselves with jewels, while others wore badges of a sort. I had no idea whether this had a particular significance or if it was simply a matter of personal preference. I hoped that someone would explain all of this to me, and I was counting on an extensive orientation period. My biggest fear was that I'd make some sort of cultural faux pas on my very first day, and I realized that I should have insisted on a visitor's information packet to go along with my boarding pass and letter of introduction.

By the time I left the ship and had walked the short distance to the cavernous spaceport building, I was already welcoming the opportunity to get out of the sun. Waiting in the shadows while the crew dumped the luggage from our flight in the middle of the stone floor, I let everyone else get theirs first so I wouldn't have to dig for mine, and then just stood there wondering what the hell I should do next. The words, "Take me to your leader," popped into my head, but I suspected I would have to go through all sorts of underlings before I met with the Queen, if, indeed, I ever saw her at all.

Pomp, formality, and proper etiquette weren't the sort of things I normally had much use for, but I'll have to say that a letter from the local queen is a darn good thing to have in your hand when you land on a strange planet, and the huge teeth of the locals made me wonder if the Queen's seal of approval was the only thing that kept me from being eaten alive. Darconians had lower jaws that opened much wider than mine did; the guy who came to inspect my letter could have gotten his jaw around my whole arm—perhaps even my leg. My only consolation was that they walked upright and didn't slink around like snakes or crocodiles—and they didn't smell particularly bad, though they did have a characteristic odor.

This one certainly looked official, with lots of little carved stones stuck to his breastplate, and I was pretty sure he was male because no female of *any* species would ever have consented to be that ugly—or that big. I'm fairly tall, myself, but this guy towered over me, the top of my head only reaching the middle of his chest. He spoke the Standard Tongue with a slightly raspy voice, clipping off his words in a brusque manner that led me to assume he was no diplomat or official greeter, but was either a member of the police force or the military.

Not knowing the proper etiquette for meeting someone on Darconia, I wondered if I should have bowed or saluted or something, but he took my letter without preamble. Having perused it briefly, as though to confirm what he'd already expected, he gave it back to me with a hand whose fingers would have spanned nearly two octaves on any keyboard instrument in the galaxy.

"I am Wazak, Chief of Security for the palace," he said. "You are the teacher, Kyra Aramis. You will accompany me now."

Nodding dumbly, I reached down for my bags, never dreaming of saying no for even a moment. I couldn't imagine that there would ever be any problems with crime or breaches of security with him around, because one look at Wazak was enough to make anyone want to walk the straight and narrow forever. It occurred to me that I ought to have offered to shake hands with him, but I had an idea that his grip would have ended my career as a pianist.

"You will not touch that!" he said sharply, and for a moment there, his hand seemed to edge toward the holstered pulse pistol that hung from his belt.

I glanced around briefly to see what important piece of official property I'd inadvertently touched, and, not seeing a thing, I looked up at him with as blank an expression as I possess, and asked, "Touch what?"

"That," he said, pointing to my luggage. "They will see to it."

I nearly jumped out of my skin as I realized that I was now being flanked by two more Darconians, not as big as Wazak, but still quite imposing. They picked up my heavy bags with no more effort than it would have taken me to pick up a silk scarf, and despite the heat, I found myself shivering. There went faux pas number one, and I hadn't even left the spaceport!

Wazak started off, and I followed him with all the cheerful demeanor of one who was marching off to be fed to the lions—or, in this case, the lizards. Then I went from wondering if they were going to eat me to what they might be intending to feed me in order to fatten me up a bit before grinding me to a pulp with those teeth. I hoped it wasn't animals or insects. Call me squeamish if you will, but I didn't think I'd care for crunching on beetles or crickets, and I never *had* eaten meat. Plants were what I preferred, but all I saw were a few bristly-looking things sprouting between the cracks in the rocky pavement— nothing green anywhere. The wiggling grubworm image ran through my mind again, and I shuddered with revulsion, but I didn't see any of them, either. What *did* they eat? I didn't dare ask Wazak. Aside from the fact that he didn't look like the type you'd ask "What's for dinner?" something told me that I wouldn't care for his reply.

Something else occurred to me: they didn't wear clothes. What was I going to do when mine wore out? I'd have to take really good care of them, or I'd end up wearing nothing but belts and jewelry like the natives. It was hot enough that I wouldn't freeze to death, but still, I didn't think I'd care for it.

I looked at Wazak's back (it was the largest and most eye-catching thing in sight), noting that his breastplate was held in place with strips of some kind of leather. I had almost gotten to the point of deciding that I could wear a dress made out of that when I realized that the leather had scales; without anything else to eat, these lizards might have to eat each other. Stricken with a sudden wave of nausea, I wondered just how much I'd have to pay for a return ticket to Earth.

Wazak led me out to an open-sided hovercraft of some kind, and there were two other vehicles that served as our escorts—each carrying three well-armed guards. It seemed like awfully tight security for a piano teacher, though I *had* come a very long way at considerable expense, and it probably made sense to keep me out of harm's way—at least until I reached the palace. It was also possible that this was simply a ceremonial escort, but, of course, I didn't ask.

Along the way, I was heartened by the sight of a camel-like creature being led down the street, carrying a large pack on its back. I say heartened because, if there was one animal like that, there were bound to be other, lesser creatures that the lizards might use for food. I was sure I could have eaten meat if given no other choice, but it seemed to me that something farther down the food chain had to eat plants, so maybe we could eat the same thing. I chuckled to myself, wondering what the Queen would say if I were to come tripping into the palace requesting Camel Chow for dinner.

I spotted a few non-Darconians on the streets—though none that looked particularly human—and some of them were wearing long robes made of a rough, white fabric to protect themselves from the burning sun, which made me feel much better with respect to the clothing issue, too.

Looking over at Wazak, I decided that I could get used to the scales eventually, but the fact that the Darconians put me in mind of carnivorous dinosaurs didn't make me very comfortable with them. They even had tails! I told myself that I was being silly; they were intelligent beings, and as such, it shouldn't have mattered if they had three heads, but I was still uneasy. I might have been less so, if Wazak had been a bit chattier, but he kept his eyes on the street and surrounding areas as though assassins lurked around every corner.

As we moved deeper into the city, an odd thing happened: buildings and streets abruptly gave way to open ground, and I began to see more plant life, and also understood why the city had been built there. It was an oasis, and, as in any desert, water is worth more than just about anything, even to a lizard. Off in the distance at the center of the fields, I could see what had to be the palace. It made sense to have the crops and trees grown near the source of the water, but it was still the reverse of any city I'd ever seen, and, with no room to expand, the layout certainly limited the amount of land available for growing crops, though the operation appeared to be fairly intensive. If there was a square centimeter of wasted space, it wasn't apparent from the road.

I could understand the way the city was mapped out now, and I wished I'd been able to get a look at it from space. The farms were in the center, encircled by a single road from which the other streets stretched away from the heart of the city like spokes on a wheel. To further reduce the amount of land wasted by putting streets through, there appeared to be only one road to the palace—appropriate from an ecological standpoint, though an escape route might have been useful in case of attack.

Still, the armed guards notwithstanding, Arconcia seemed peaceful and prosperous. The buildings had been a bit more seedy-looking out near the spaceport, but improved in quality as we moved through to the heart of the city. It was possible that we were simply passing through the nicer end of town—which would make sense, since it was the only direct route from the palace to the spaceport—but all in all, it was an attractive city. Everything I saw was made of stone, too, and stone carving seemed to be the decorative touch of choice.

At this point I noticed that while I was finding the scenery interesting, the locals all seemed to think I was pretty darned interesting myself! Since the vehicles we rode in were open, any of the passersby could see me quite plainly, making me wish I'd been wearing a big hat, as much to protect myself from their inquisitive stares as from the sun. To my surprise, Wazak seemed to notice this and commented on it.

"They have never seen a human before," he said. "They are… curious. Do not let it disturb you."

"I would be, too, I suppose," I agreed. "Curious, that is—" I added quickly—"not disturbed."

He nodded as though he understood, and I decided to take advantage of his efforts to reassure me by asking a few questions.

"Um, Wazak," I began timidly. "Is there anything special I should know before we get there? You know, like certain things I should or shouldn't say or do?"

I thought he waited a long time before he answered me, and just about the time I decided he wasn't going to say anything at all, he replied, "Queen Scalia is tolerant of breaches in etiquette."

He didn't say anything else. So much for being chatty. I tried again.

"Is there a rule book of some kind that I could read?"

Wazak shook his head. "No," he replied, "but you are to be an honored guest in the palace, not a servant or a slave."

"Slave?" I echoed. "You mean you have slaves here?" I found this difficult to believe. I mean, I'd never read any mention of such a thing in the descriptions of Darconia I'd found.

Wazak hitched his tail beneath him before he answered me. I wondered if sitting on it was the reason for his discomfort, or if it had been my question which disturbed him. Avoiding my eyes, he said, "Not many. The Queen is a… collector."

"A collector?" I repeated. "Of what?"

"Exotic slaves," he replied. "She finds the different species fascinating."

"Well, I can understand that," I said reasonably, "but why do they have to be slaves?"

Wazak might not have known many humans before, but he did seem to know an expression of horror when he saw one, and he hastened to assure me that the slaves were well treated and not used for drudgery, though they did have certain duties to perform. But even so, he didn't seem to care for the idea any more than I did.

"The Queen has also encouraged other species to settle here because of that fascination," he went on. "She enjoys the… diversity." The way he said it led me to believe that he didn't particularly enjoy "diversity" himself, though it did explain the aliens I'd seen on the streets, and possibly my own presence, as well.

"Is that why she wanted a human to teach her daughter the piano?"

"Perhaps," Wazak said evasively.

"But I'm definitely not a slave?" I was pressing the point more than I needed to, perhaps, but I wanted to make absolutely certain of this before we went any further. "I get paid, right? And I don't have to stay here if I don't want to?"

"That is correct."

While this was comforting, it was also what he would have said in any case.

"But I'll live in the palace?"

"Yes," said Wazak. He seemed to be getting rather testy by this time, but I figured I was safe enough, since presumably the Queen would be upset if her security chief slugged the new piano teacher on the way to the palace. He might try to intimidate me, but I was pretty sure he wouldn't kill me.

"And where are the slaves?" I asked. "Will I see them?"

"They are quartered in a special area of the palace."

That would be the jail part, I decided. The part with bars on the windows and locked doors so they couldn't escape. "Special?"

"It is more suited to the requirements of their species."

This was sounding even worse, more like a zoo than a prison. "Don't they try to escape?"

"They are not… unhappy."

By which I suppose he meant that they *were* happy, though I doubted it. I couldn't imagine anyone *ever* being happy about being a slave!

"Really?" I tried not to sound overly skeptical, but it was difficult.

"As I said before, they are well treated, and they are… protected." Wazak seemed to be getting more irritable by the second, for the tip of his tail was now tapping the side of the car in much the same way that an impatient person will tap their foot. He obviously didn't care to discuss this any further.

"Like pets, then," I said in an effort to sum things up quickly.

I wasn't sure if the concept of having pets was familiar to him or not, but he nodded anyway. As we were approaching the palace by this time, I was momentarily diverted by the view, so I left it at that.

To say that the palace was ornate would be a serious understatement. It appeared to have been constructed from something like marble, while the lesser structures were made of a type of sandstone. With its gleaming, domed roof, imposing pillars, and multitudes of arched doorways lavishly decorated with floral carvings, it made the Taj Mahal look like a quaint little cottage.

"Nice place," I remarked dryly.

Wazak's facial expressions might have been more subtle than a human's, but if my eyes didn't deceive me, what was on his face was essentially a smirk. However, he didn't take the opportunity to brag, and when he did speak of the palace, his tone was merely informative. "It is built of a type of stone called shepra, which is highly prized. It is quarried in the mountains near here, along with other precious stones."

His gesture indicated the mountains I'd seen on the horizon. I almost let out a snicker, because if that was what he called "near," I wondered what he would consider to be distant—halfway around the planet? I also wondered how many slaves it had taken to haul the shepra across the desert and then build the palace. A vision of Hebrew slaves building the pyramids of Egypt—same weather conditions, too—popped into my head.

Wazak seemed to be reading my thoughts, for he added, "And it was not built by slaves, and not strictly for the Queen. It was built as a monument to our people."

He seemed to be quite proud of that fact, though he didn't come right out and say it. As I gazed at the structure, I concluded that while it might have been intended as a tribute to the Darconian people, it was also a monument to beauty. Perhaps living in a barren desert had made them appreciate beauty all the more, making it as highly prized as the shepra—or the water.

And music!—what could possibly be more beautiful than that? Now I understood why I was there: to bring more beauty to an otherwise harsh and desolate world. And I would do it, too, because if they weren't all tone deaf, these people were going to love Mozart. And Brahms. And Beethoven. Maybe even Bach. I just hoped the kid could play.

Chapter 3

MY OTHER HOPE WAS THAT THEY UNDERSTOOD JUST HOW much water a member of my species would require to survive in such a climate. I seriously doubted that they bathed in water as we did on Earth, and I'd have been willing to bet that they didn't drink two or three liters of fluid a day, either. Their scaly skin probably didn't perspire; it was more likely they were similar to other reptiles and stayed out of the sun to avoid getting over-heated. Aside from the fact that there wasn't much else around to use, this was surely the reason they favored stone as a building material—good insulation.

The heat was unrelenting, and even the breeze cre-ated by the movement of the hovercars didn't help very much. My mouth was dry, and I could already feel the skin on my face beginning to tighten up and burn. Being pale even by human standards, I doubted that I would last a day out in the desert, even with adequate water. I knew I could survive with a lowered water content in my body, but it would take some time for me to adapt. I ought to have tried to drink less on the journey here, but this was one of the finer points about life on Darconia that I hadn't anticipated. I'd read that there were des-erts, but I hadn't known I'd be living right in the middle of one of them! Maybe that was why the job had been posted on Earth; we were too far away to know many of the details. Now that I was here, I was wishing I'd paid a little more attention to the fine print—and I might have, if there'd been any.

When we stopped at an entrance to the palace, Wazak actually helped me out of the hovercar. I suppose his irritation with all my questions was overborne by the need to observe at least some of the niceties, and as before, his two sidekicks carried my luggage.

Once underneath the portico, the temperature seemed to drop about ten degrees, and I heaved a sigh of relief. I couldn't even tell that I'd been sweating—the air was so dry that it evaporated immediately—until I brushed a hand across my arm, and it felt slightly gritty with salt.

"You will require some refreshment," Wazak said stiffly. "This way."

I found myself following him again, and as his buddies disappeared with my stuff, I wondered if they would go through it and confiscate all of my clothes. This was a palace, after all, and perhaps there was a rule I didn't know about: "Thou shalt not wear more clothing than the Queen," or something of that nature. I also wondered if shoes were permitted. I had worn some of my nicer shoes—they were an iridescent turquoise and had the virtue of matching my dress—since I thought it was possible that I'd be meeting the Queen. Now I wished I'd worn slippers instead, because the way my footsteps were echoing off the walls, I sounded like a herd of elephants strolling through the corridor. Wazak, on the other hand, was barefoot and the soles of his feet made a soft slapping sound as he walked. I figured he must have had calluses about an inch thick on the bottoms of those feet—walking across a bed of hot coals would have been no trouble for him at all. That was one way to keep the slaves from running off; just keep them barefoot and they wouldn't step a meter beyond the palace walls.

I was glad Wazak had mentioned refreshment, because I was getting pretty hungry by then, on top of being thirstier than I'd ever been in my life. I had no idea if it was dinnertime or lunchtime or what, but if this was how hot it was in the early morning, I would be remaining inside the palace for the entirety of my stay.

As if he'd known what I was thinking, Wazak announced: "It is time for the evening meal. You will be dining with the Queen."

"What?" I squeaked. "Right now? Don't I have to change clothes or pass through a weapons sensor or anything?" Perhaps I needed to be vaccinated against something, too. Or I might need to be decontaminated. After all, I might be carrying a germ that would wipe out the entire population. They didn't know.

Wazak stopped and turned to face me. "Do you have a weapon?"

"Well, no," I admitted, "but I thought you'd want to be sure…" My voice trailed off as I looked up at him. He certainly was imposing! Asking Wazak questions while sitting opposite him in an open vehicle was one thing, standing toe-to-toe with him was quite another. No one in their right mind would have followed him into the palace carrying so much as a pen knife.

Wazak didn't reply, but if he'd had eyebrows, one of them would surely have risen before he turned and started off down the hall again. I hoped the natives weren't all as unfriendly as he was, though I thought if I spent more time with him, he might warm up a little. It was possible he was trying to intimidate me on purpose, just to make sure I didn't cause any trouble in the future. Imagine that! Me, a troublemaker!

"Will the Princess be having dinner with us, as well?" I asked, trotting to catch up with him. "I—I'd like to meet her."

"Perhaps," was Wazak's noncommittal response.

I closed my lips firmly. *Oh, just shut up and follow him, Kyra! Keep quiet and stay out of trouble!* Which shouldn't have been difficult for me, since I'd never been in any kind of trouble in my life. My record was clean— no felonies, no misdemeanors, no minor infractions of the rules. I'd never even gotten a parking ticket.

I tried to focus on where we were going and where I had been. After the open portico, we were now passing through a maze of corridors, which all looked alike. This was probably another way of keeping the slaves safely inside, because even if they did get loose, they'd never be able to find their way out. Maybe there was a code in the carvings on the walls. Hell, there could have been numbers and signs plastered all over them, and I wouldn't have known what they meant! If I was ever left on my own, getting lost was a certainty.

"Should have listened to my mother," I muttered to myself. I wished I had Nindala with me for moral support. We would have been whispering behind Wazak's back, making fun of his tail or something, which would have eased the tension.

I tried to imagine what Nindala would have to say about Wazak and nearly bit my lip trying not to laugh out loud. I could almost her musing, "Do you think his penis is as ugly as his face?" I couldn't have said at that point, for, despite his lack of so much as a loincloth to cover the area where one might normally expect to find a penis, there didn't appear to be one. I decided that Darconians were probably one of those species that kept their tool drawn up inside until it was needed, but without Nindala around, I doubted I would ever find out. After all, I was lucky ever to have seen a *human* penis; what chance did I have of finding one on a lizard? Aside from that, I didn't want anyone to get any strange ideas, because I was pretty well convinced that having sex with someone like Wazak would be fatal to a Terran.

I was watching his tail sway back and forth, so I noticed when Wazak's swagger became more pronounced. Looking ahead, I saw that we were approaching a large set of carved doors, which were flanked by two guards who looked a lot like Wazak but had a different style of breastplate—more ornate than his and more polished, as though they'd never seen actual combat. Queen's guards, I decided. This was it.

The guards stiffened slightly, but Wazak waved them aside and pulled the doors open himself. I had a new thought: if there was a queen and a princess, shouldn't there also be a king? I couldn't remember anyone ever mentioning one, and while the room I entered contained two Darconians, one much smaller than the other, neither of them were nearly as large as Wazak, which led me to believe that I was now facing the Queen and her daughter.

Smaller than Wazak and not quite as ugly—though she wouldn't have won a beauty contest on any planet except, perhaps, her own—Queen Scalia had enough jeweled necklaces draped around her that she wouldn't have required clothing, even if she'd been human. She could have had mammary glands hidden under there somewhere, but, as an egg layer, she wouldn't nurse her young anyway. It was quite possible that I had the only tits on the whole damn planet.

Since I couldn't even swear Wazak had a cock, maybe the overt differences between the sexes had to do with color, because they *were* different: Wazak was an iridescent green with yellow highlights, while the Queen and her daughter were both a shimmering mixture of green and purple. I remembered seeing a few on the street who had a bluish tint, though, and decided that this characteristic corresponded to hair color in humans and had nothing to do with gender.

The room wasn't particularly large, but the table at which the Queen and the Princess sat was quite beautiful, made of that same marble-like shepra stone and polished to a high sheen. There were windows at the far end looking out on a grove of trees and the farms beyond. It was relatively cool there, and though the room wasn't lit with any conventional light that I'd ever seen, there was some kind of glowing stone set into the ceiling. It must have been in the corridors, too, for I hadn't seen any torches, yet the windowless hallways had been well lit.

"Welcome to Darconia, Kyra Aramis," she said. Her accent wasn't as thick as Wazak's, and she spoke the Standard Tongue quite clearly. "I am Queen Scalia, and this is my daughter, the Princess Zealon, your student."

"I'm very pleased to meet you," I said. I wasn't sure if I should have added a "Your Majesty" or a "Your Highness" to that or not. No doubt I would be informed. I smiled and bowed slightly toward the Queen and then to Princess Zealon, who, though she had coloring similar to her mother's, wore much less jewelry. "Will you join us for dinner?" the Queen asked.

I was starving, but the table was empty. No doubt the food was still squirming in the kitchen. "Yes—" I broke off there, not knowing quite how to address her and blurted out: "Um, what should I call you?" before I could stop to phrase it more delicately.

Zealon giggled, but Scalia was a bit more tactful. She stared at me for a moment. "I have given you my name," she said. "Have you forgotten it already?"

"Well, no, I haven't, but, on Earth, queens are usually called something else when you're actually speaking to them."

"How odd," she remarked with a questioning glance at Zealon. "Such as?"

"Your Highness or Your Majesty for queens," I began. "Your Grace for a duchess, My Lady for lesser nobles. Of course, there haven't been any queens for some time now, and I only know that much from reading books. We don't have kings anymore, either," I added, hoping that last statement would prompt her to tell me about her own king, and it did.

"We do not often have male rulers here," Scalia said. "Their tempers are too volatile." She gazed past me, looking at Wazak for a long moment. "We queens have only consorts."

"No king, then?"

"Only if a queen does not produce a female child," she said with a nod toward Zealon, "and it is rare that they do not." She paused for a moment, possibly considering my original question. "You may call me Queen,

Queen Scalia, or Scalia," she said with a casual wave. "It matters not. Which name do you prefer?"

"I—I'm not sure I…"

Zealon giggled again, and Scalia silenced her with a wave of her hand.

"*Your* name," Scalia said. "Kyra, Aramis, or Kyra Aramis?"

"Oh, you mean me," I said, feeling very stupid. "Kyra."

She nodded, first at me and then toward Wazak in what must have been a dismissal, for he left us, closing the door behind him. Motioning for me to take a seat at the table, she said, "We will have food then, Kyra."

Someone must have been listening on the other side of the door just behind her, because it swung open immediately, and some odd-looking aliens came in with laden trays—mostly fruit, thank God! I wondered if these were some of her "exotic slaves." One was squat and toadlike, but instead of hopping, it had legs that bent oddly at the knee, making it waddle a bit. The other was tall and spindly with long fingers that appeared to have suction cups at the tips, like an octopus. With round, bulbous eyes and a fishlike mouth, he was pretty ugly, but if his fingers were any indication, he must have been an outstanding waiter—I doubted he ever dropped much of anything. I also noted that, like the Darconians, neither of them wore any clothing. Having set down the trays, the taller one asked Scalia if she needed anything else.

She denied needing anything further, but looked at me, smiling slightly—at least, I thought it was a smile—and asked, "And you?"

"A really big glass of water," I gasped.

Princess Zealon laughed out loud. "You see, Mother," she said gleefully, "I told you so!"

"Yes, you did," Scalia said with a nod.

Mystified, my gaze darted back and forth between the two of them. "What?"

"My daughter has been studying humans since we decided to look for a teacher on Earth," Scalia explained. "She said that water would be the first thing you would ask for, and she was quite correct."

"I'm glad I could live up to your expectations," I said graciously. "So, tell me, Princess, what else have you learned about humans?"

Zealon sat up a bit straighter, as though preparing to recite a poem. "You are mammals, not egg layers, so you have hair, rather than scales, your skin burns in the sun, so you wear clothes, and you are omnivorous, but if you eat meat, you cook it first."

"Well, that just about sums it up," I said, silently thanking God that at least *someone* had done her homework, and I would never be offered wriggling worms for dinner! "Very good, Princess. Later on, I'll have to ask you some questions about your planet, because when I did my research, I wasn't able to find out very much."

Scalia smiled—I was sure this time, though in all honesty, it looked more like a grimace—as she patted her daughter on the head. "Zealon will be able to answer all of your questions, for she is quite intelligent. She will make an excellent queen one day."

I was glad I had Zealon to talk with, because I had always felt so much more at ease with children. They generally don't bother to hide their feelings; if they like you, you'll know it, just as you will know if they don't. It is so much more difficult with adults, who are often deceptive, no matter where they come from.

"We're getting a McDonald's next year," Zealon said ingenuously. "Then we'll be just like every other planet in the quadrant!"

"Ah, yes, progress," Scalia said with a sigh. "Zealon has encouraged me to seek a franchise, though I'm not quite sure what manner of food they will serve here. I understand that they sell meat sandwiches made from cow flesh," she said with obvious distaste. "We do not have cows."

"Oh, I think any kind of meat will do," I said. "And it doesn't have to be meat, either; what they serve usually depends on the local cuisine. You can make hamburgers out of just about anything if you try hard enough."

Scalia nodded. "We are striving to become a more open, cultural society. This, along with the influx of other life forms, has been my wish for some time now, though there are those who oppose it."

"And that's why I'm here, then?"

"Yes," the Queen replied. "It is my wish to improve the music education of our young, beginning with my own daughter as an example."

"So," I said, turning to Zealon, "what do you think of all of this?"

"I want to learn to play well," she said firmly. "I will do my best."

"I can't ask for more than that." Having the desire to excel was half the battle when it came to training young musicians. I wondered how well she'd be able to read music, which put me in mind of something else. "Do you all speak Stantongue? I know many worlds have adopted it as their official language, but have you?"

"Oh, yes," Scalia assured me. "For many years now. It is one of the best ways to encourage trade."

"Well, that and having something to sell," I conceded.

"Our stones are sought after by many," said Scalia, "but we have only just begun to market them to other worlds."

This made me wonder if she had traded some of the rarer ones for her exotic slaves. If she was interested in progress, she was probably going to have to abandon her rather barbaric hobby in favor of something more universally acceptable, like collecting coins.

I tasted some of the fruits and found them to be quite edible. Everything was either in its natural state or sun-dried; if anything had been cooked, you couldn't tell it, and the water, as well as the food, was served at room temperature. No one had cut up the fruits and vegetables, either, so if you wanted to eat something peeled or chopped, you had to do it yourself. I watched Scalia and Zealon carefully, noting which ones they peeled before eating and tried to follow their example, but I would have given a lot for a little salad dressing—along with some ice. Apparently "cuisine" of any kind would have been lost on them—even something as simple as a fruit salad. Of course, the food required no energy to prepare, which, on a world that seemed to have very little in the way of combustible fuel lying about, would be a definite plus. The new McDonald's should prove to be interesting.

They did, however, serve what Scalia told me was a locally produced wine, which I found to be delightfully sweet and fruity, but deceptively potent.

After dinner, Scalia sent Zealon off to bed, telling her that she needed to rest well before embarking on her new career as a concert pianist. I seconded that and was then left alone with the Queen, who wasted no time in introducing a new topic for discussion—one which she probably considered unfit for young ears, just as the wine was for young palates.

"Tell me about your human males," she said, as the little toad-slave poured out more of the wine. "I understand that they are very... desirable."

"You're asking the wrong person," I said candidly. "I'm single, remember?"

She nodded. "Yes, I knew that, but tell me, are they less volatile than our males?"

"I doubt it," I replied. "They get into trouble all the time. Of course, women do, too, so I can't really say that men are the root of all evil." I took a sip of the wine—it would have been impolite not to—but I'd have to watch how much I drank of it, or I might find myself out of a job.

"Is it true that there is a sexual reason for everything they do?"

I almost laughed aloud, because Nindala had asked me a similar question. "Not necessarily," I replied, trying to seem impartial. "I doubt if human males are that much different from any others—no more than the women are, anyway—but I haven't traveled much before this, and I came straight here, not stopping along the way. I probably should have," I added, "but I was anxious to arrive."

"As I was to have you here," she said graciously. "But you are tired, I am sure."

"A little," I admitted. "It's been a long trip, and I'd like to get some sleep. I'm sure I'll have a busy day tomorrow."

"I will not keep you much longer." She paused, calling out to a servant in the next room before taking another delicate sip of her wine and continuing, "But before you go, you must see my cats."

"Your cats?"

Nodding, she said, "I'd like your opinion of them."

That sounded odd. What did it matter what I thought of her pets? The little toad creature was told to fetch the cats, so I had a little time to think. Okay, if this was a desert planet with intelligent life forms that looked for all the world like dinosaurs, what kind of cats would they have here? Saber-toothed tigers?

On that thought, the door opened again, and the two cats entered—but they weren't cats, at least, not in the ordinary sense. They were tall male humanoids—undoubtedly more of Scalia's "exotic slaves"—and they certainly were exotic! Separately, each one would have been stunning, but together, they took my breath away—would have taken *anyone's* breath away, even Nindala's. For myself, I was just glad I happened to be sitting down when I saw them for the first time. Staring back at them in awe, I had barely managed to take another breath when one of them turned his startlingly blue eyes on me and, no doubt noting my open-mouthed expression, lowered his eyelids ever so slightly and sent a roguish smile in my direction.

And I had an orgasm.

Scalia probably thought I'd choked on my wine, but that wasn't it at all! I felt a fire begin to burn deep inside me when I first laid eyes on him, and his smile sent me over the edge. I'd never felt anything quite like it before in my life—nor had I ever seen anything to compare with him.

"They are my most prized possessions," Scalia said. "Very beautiful, are they not?"

I'm not entirely sure what I said in reply, but it was affirmative, though undoubtedly inarticulate.

Scalia smiled. "I hoped you would like them."

I took another sip of my wine—actually, it was more of a gulp than a sip—and asked, "W—where did you find them?"

"The slave traders in this region know of my penchant for interesting specimens and brought them to me," she replied. "You would not believe what I had to pay for them! The trader said that there had been a bounty placed on them, which, of course, meant that I was required to pay about twenty times that amount in order to get them—and also to keep him quiet as to their whereabouts! Apparently, someone holds a grudge against their kind and set out to exterminate them entirely—which would have been most unfortunate, as I am certain you will agree."

I think I nodded, but sitting there trying to imagine a whole planet full of these guys nearly made my uterus go into another spasm. I decided that a group of jealous men must have gotten an army together and plotted against them, for certainly no female in the known universe would have gone along with such a scheme. I mean, Scalia was a lizard, and even *she* liked them!

"But they are safe here," she added firmly. "They are kept under lock and key at night, and no one beyond the palace walls knows they exist. And, unlike my other slaves, even my daughter has never seen them."

The fact that they were both entirely nude except for jeweled collars around their necks and genitals might have been one reason Zealon had never been permitted to see them. She was much too young for such things, though I didn't think that anyone under the age of—oh, I don't know, a hundred, perhaps?—could look at them and not be affected.

"These two are brothers," Scalia went on, as though she were truly talking about a pair of pet cats who happened to be littermates. "I would dearly love to breed more of them, but they are a mammalian species and will not cross with our kind. Nor are they… aroused… by our females."

Which, of course, made me wonder whether or not they liked humans. I, for one, certainly liked *them*, especially the one who'd smiled at me. The other one didn't seem terribly pleased to see me—not quite scowling, but certainly not smiling.

As they had positioned themselves on either side of Scalia's chair, across the table from me, I had an excellent view of them both. They didn't seem particularly shy, either, not minding a bit that I couldn't take my eyes off them. The blue-eyed one was fair-skinned with the most spectacular hair—jet black with a thick streak of white running through it near his temple—hanging to his waist in perfect spirals. The other also had black hair which curled to his waist, but with a similarly placed orange stripe, green eyes, and more tawny skin. They both possessed upswept eyebrows and pointed ears, as well as vertical pupils that seemed to glow slightly. The green-eyed one yawned just then, revealing a mouthful of sharp white teeth with canines that looked downright dangerous. All in all, they put me in mind of Earth's tigers—the one Bengal, and the other Siberian—but they had body hair more like that of human males, not the fur you would expect to find on a cat. Neither of them had beards, but I wasn't close enough to determine whether or not this was natural. Both were tall, broad-chested, and lean, with smooth, rippling muscles and perfectly proportioned limbs. It was no wonder Scalia had paid a fortune for them!

All of this possibly wouldn't have mattered if they hadn't had one other notable attribute: they were both hung like horses. A crass description, perhaps, but it was accurate, nonetheless. Unfortunately, they were not, as Scalia had mentioned before, aroused. The mere thought of what they might look like if they *were* aroused made my mouth go dry, and I attempted to take another sip from an empty glass.

"My guest needs more wine," Scalia said, crooking a finger toward the Siberian tiger.

Nodding, he collected a flask from the sideboard and came around the table. When he leaned over to pour the wine, his cock was just below my eye level, but as my eyes were slightly downcast, I had an excellent view of it. Among other things, I noted that the jewels on his genital cuff were every bit as blue as his eyes. Scalia, it seemed, was not the slightest bit color-blind and had paid attention to detail when decorating her slaves.

"Thank you," I said hoarsely.

"You are very welcome," he replied. "It is my pleasure to serve you."

His deep voice was like melted butter and, even though polite, his choice of words had me envisioning all manner of pleasurable things—none of them having *anything* to do with food or drink. I couldn't help but look up at him, and, when our eyes met, he smiled again and blinked slowly. Then I watched, fascinated, as his nostrils flared with a deep inhalation—and his smile intensified, as did the hot blue of his eyes.

"Oh, excellent!" Scalia said in hushed tones.

Yes, he is! Excellent, perfect, amazing, unbelievable—and just about any other superlative you'd care to use. Still gazing up at him, I felt as though I were about to melt into a puddle and slide off my chair. Honestly, if I'd ever felt a more overwhelming sense of desire for any other man in the galaxy, this one would have made me forget it.

I felt something wet drop onto my hand. Glancing down to see if I was, indeed, melting, I saw what Scalia had undoubtedly been referring to, for the tiger's penis was now fully erect. As thick and long as a well-endowed human's would have been, it also had a wide, scalloped corona at the base of the head that was obviously there for one reason only: to give the greatest possible pleasure to any woman fortunate enough to be penetrated by it. Looking closer, I noted that the clear fluid that had fallen on my hand appeared to be coming, not from the opening at the apex, but from the starlike points of the corona.

I tried to swallow and couldn't. I looked up at him again with what must have been an expression of raw hunger mingled with guilt written clearly upon my face. In return, what I saw on his face was the most open invitation to partake of anything I'd ever seen. His mesmerizing eyes beckoned, his full lips promised sensuous delights beyond my wildest imaginings, and his provocative smile assured me of his knowledge of every possible way to drive a woman wild. He was offering himself to me—completely—without saying a word.

Unfortunately, just as I was about to take a taste of him, I suddenly remembered where I was. We were not alone, and he was a slave who belonged to the lizard queen sitting across the table from me. Reaching awkwardly for my wineglass, my sleeve slid across the head of his cock, soaking it with his fluid and drawing a barely audible groan from him.

Trying desperately to ignore his reaction, I looked away from him and saw that Scalia was watching us intently, but she had her hand on the Bengal tiger's thigh, stroking him, though without any erotic response on his part whatsoever. I would have thought that such a pornographic vision right across the table from him would have been enough to stimulate him, but apparently, it wasn't.

Then I remembered the blue-eyed tiger inhaling as though he was taking a whiff of me. It was something to do with scent, then—though it was surprising that I was clearheaded enough to figure that out at the time. What was also surprising was the fact that my "scent" hadn't reached the other man, because if the way I was feeling was any indication, it had to have been pretty heavy on the sex pheromones.

Breaking the silence, the Queen's voice was now brisk and businesslike. "You will require a personal attendant during your stay with us," Scalia said. "I believe he will suit you very nicely."

"Who, him?" I gasped. As I sat staring at his cock, I decided that if anyone could "suit me," it would have been him, but he was far more… *man*… than I'd ever so much as touched in my life! He could turn me to mush in a heartbeat—and, of course, in that state, I'd never play piano again… "Oh, but I don't really need—" I protested, before she cut me off with an imperious wave of her hand.

"Yes, you do," she said firmly. "You are new to this world, Kyra. He will be able to help you… adjust."

Adjust. What an interesting choice of words! He probably could have helped me adjust to just about anything—even daily torture—if only he were to hold my hand for the duration. And speaking of hands, I wondered if I'd be able to keep mine off of him when we were alone together. Having been within a hair-breadth of licking his cock just moments before—and in full view of two other people, I might add—I thought I'd probably have some difficulty with that. I also wondered if he'd go running to Scalia to complain if I did something of that nature—or what he would do if I didn't.

To be honest, I doubted that I needed a servant of any kind, though due to the scarcity of water and fabrics, it was a given that there wouldn't be any easy way to wash my clothes. I wondered if my bed would have sheets on it, or if I'd be sleeping on a bed of stones or sand. Hopefully, Zealon had done some homework in that area as well.

My tiger was still standing next to me, flanking my chair just as his counterpart did for Scalia—quite slave-like behavior, despite his persistent erection—and it occurred to me that he might like to have some say in the matter.

"What about you?" I asked, looking up at him curiously. "Do you think I need a personal attendant?"

"Absolutely," he replied, his luscious lips curling in a smile. "There are a great many things I can do for you."

I'll just bet you can, I thought grimly. "But do you *want* to?" I said aloud. For some reason, I felt it was important that his service to me be voluntary. Not that he wouldn't have done whatever he was told to do by his owner; after all, he *was* a slave, though a very valuable one. What would happen if he refused? I doubted that Scalia would punish him—doubted that she ever had, for neither of them had a mark on him, nor did they have the cowed expressions of people who were habitually abused or bullied. In fact, they appeared to have been well cared for, if not cosseted, by their owner—truly more like cherished pets than slaves.

"I can think of nothing I would like more," he assured me.

"Because you have been told to." I said this not as a question, but as a statement.

He seemed uncertain about how to reply to that, glancing at Scalia out of the corner of his eye as if for direction, but she gave him none that I could see.

"Because you smell of desire," he said finally. "Being near you pleases me… and I have no doubt that I can please *you*."

"An honest answer," Scalia asserted. "You may believe what he tells you. They are both very truthful."

I nodded. "Yes, I can believe that much," I said. This man undoubtedly could please the most stone-cold woman imaginable, but I secretly wondered if it was my desire which pleased him, or if any woman's desire would do.

Sighing deeply, I relented, knowing that while I might regret my decision in the end, if I refused, I'd regret it even more.

"It is settled, then," Scalia said to my tiger. "You may escort Kyra to her rooms." Turning to me, she added, "Your quarters have been adapted to suit human needs. I believe you will find them to your liking."

"I'm sure I will," I replied, "but, if you don't mind my asking, how are you going to keep him a secret if he's with me? The Princess, or someone else, may see him."

"We will take that risk," Scalia said with conviction. "I believe it to be worthwhile."

And her word was law. After all, she *was* the queen.

Chapter 4

SCALIA MIGHT HAVE SPOKEN WITH ALL THE CONVICTION of a reigning queen, but it was with a great deal of trepidation that I followed my new "attendant" to my quarters. I'd never had anyone do much of anything for me—had never needed to—and I wasn't sure how to deal with him. It was hard enough for me to ask someone to pass me the salt, let alone anything of a more personal nature. How in the world was I going to ask this incredibly attractive, naked man to wash my socks? I hoped he was really good at being a slave, because then I wouldn't actually have to tell him to do anything; he would identify what needed to be done and do it.

While his aptitude for slavery remained to be seen, the one thing I could see was that it was much nicer following him down the hall than Wazak—very nice naked buns and no tail. And his hair! It was so shockingly beautiful it made me want to bury my face in it. I found myself thinking about what it would feel like to have those curls draped across my skin and shivered, despite the heat. I felt a little light-headed, too, and thought perhaps I hadn't drunk enough water with dinner—or had drunk too much wine...

I tried to think of something else. I remembered hearing that it could get very cold in the desert at night, but the sun hadn't been down long enough to make much of a difference in the temperature yet. What if my bed was made of that shiny stone? What if there were no sheets, and I woke up freezing to death in the middle of the night? And for that matter, how did you turn off those glowing stones? Was it even possible? The more I thought about it, the happier I was that I had him to help me—whatever his name was. I would have to ask him at some point, but would he become as annoyed as Wazak if I asked too many questions? For that matter, what would he consider to be too many? How was I going to sleep with so much on my mind?

I took a deep breath to steady my nerves. I had been in space for six weeks, and now I was on a completely different planet—with a big, naked, male tiger for a companion; it was understandable that I would feel a bit rattled. I would adjust—and he would help me—it was simply a matter of time. And what was I there for? Oh, yeah, right… piano teacher. I'd even forgotten that part—which had been practically my whole life up until then.

Reminding myself that I was disoriented, a little drunk, and that the mere sight of a man smiling at me had set off an orgasm the likes of which I'd probably never experience again—unless I actually… but no, it didn't seem like a good idea. Sex with a slave? I shouldn't do it! It was, I don't know… unethical, perhaps? Still, the idea of having a love slave wasn't *all* bad. He'd seemed pretty willing, hadn't he? Even said that being near me gave him pleasure?

My mind was in turmoil, but my new attendant continued to lead the way as though it was perfectly natural for him to stroll through the palace wearing nothing but a collar every day of his life—which, I suppose, he did.

It was a new experience for me, however, because the further we walked, the more fascinated with his buns I became. They were perfect, and I couldn't take my eyes off of them—wanted to bite them, slap them, squeeze them like ripe peaches, and—

"Ah, my darling, blue-eyed slave!" a teasing female voice called out. "You have found a new lover?"

Looking further down the corridor, I could see that we were being approached by what I assumed was a Darconian woman—she was wearing beads, anyway—who stopped right in front of my tiger and ran a sensuous finger down the center of his chest.

"I see that I have been replaced," she lamented. "What a pity!"

Gazing up at her with a look that would have melted a glacier, my tiger lightly caressed her cheek. "If I could truly mate with any Darconian, Cernada," he said suavely, "I promise, it would have been you."

"Oh, but I am certain that the Queen would not allow it!" Cernada said, laughing. "Beware of this one," she warned me. "His tongue is as smooth as water flowing over shepra stones. You may *think* he is yours alone, but he is not." Cernada ran her fingers through his curls as she continued on past us with a throaty chuckle.

Dumbfounded, I stared after her, watching her tail swing back and forth as she sauntered off down the hall. It shouldn't have surprised me that there would be other Darconian women besides the Queen who had the hots for him, but for some reason, it did. And what on earth would the two of them do together if he couldn't—

I felt a tap on my shoulder and must have jumped about a foot. "Your rooms are this way, Kyra," he said with a sweeping gesture in the opposite direction. "I'm sure you are tired and in need of your bed."

I gaped at him for a long moment before my brain finally restarted. "Oh, yeah, right... bed. I *am* pretty tired." I took one more look in the direction Cernada had taken and asked the only question on my mind that didn't involve sex. "So, tell me: are their scales smooth, or rough?"

"Smoother than you might think," he said with a knowing smile. "And they are also slightly cold-blooded." His smile broadened as he added, "They like to sleep with something warm."

The look he gave me suggested that he might have been the warm "something" that Cernada liked to sleep with. Scalia had said that the slaves were locked up at night for their own protection, but his comment had me wondering if it was possible to check one of them out for the night—sort of like a library book.

He turned and started off down the hall again, and I followed just as before, but with so much more on my mind, it was a wonder I could spare the conscious effort to move my feet. We hadn't gone much farther when he stopped in front of a set of doors so suddenly that I ran into him from behind, because I wasn't paying attention. I may have gotten my wish to have my face buried in his hair, but it wasn't exactly the way I'd had in mind, and I didn't even have the presence of mind to grab his buns to keep from falling!

"I'm so sorry!" I exclaimed. "I didn't mean to—"

Turning, he put a hand on my shoulder to steady me. "There is no need for you to apologize."

"But—"

"I am a slave," he said quietly, "and though I have rarely been mistreated, my feelings are seldom considered."

"Well, I can't *not* consider them, just because you're a slave!" I protested vehemently. "You're—you're a living, breathing, thinking being! I can't just ignore your feelings!"

He regarded me for a moment with a thoughtful expression and then said, "I believe you mean that."

"Well, of course I do!" I exclaimed. "This is all just so—so weird! Slavery doesn't even exist on my planet! It isn't something I've ever dealt with before." I realized then that it had been a mistake to let myself get so upset. Breathing hard and feeling stranger by the second, I gasped, "And what the hell is your name?"

I didn't faint, exactly, but I came pretty close, for the corridor darkened just then, and I began seeing spots where moments before there had been none.

Slipping an arm around my waist for support and pushing the door open, he said, "You need to lie down. The heat is affecting your brain."

"Oh, is that what it is?" I mumbled. "Funny, I thought it was you."

It was dark in my room—if this was my room—and I couldn't see his face very well, but I heard him chuckle softly.

"What's so funny?" I demanded.

"*You* are," he replied.

"You know something? You don't act like a slave. I mean, slaves aren't supposed to laugh at their masters, or flirt with the ladies, are they?"

"I was not born a slave," he said. "Perhaps that's why I behave differently."

"Really?" I murmured. "How did you end up here, then?"

"At the end of the war in which my planet was destroyed, several members of my unit were taken prisoner. We were to be executed, but an enterprising fellow thought he could make a few credits by selling us, instead. My brother Trag and I were lucky enough to be bought by Scalia."

"Lucky?"

He laid me down on the bed before answering me. It wasn't made of stone, and it even had sheets on it—sheets that felt smooth, almost like satin. Rolling onto my side, I sighed with relief. Now if I could just get some more water…

"We are both still alive," he said, "and slaves are seldom treated as well as we have been."

"Well, if you don't mind wearing nothing but a collar." I thought for a moment and added, "Make that *two* collars."

He laughed again, saying: "We prefer it that way. We don't like to wear clothing any more than the Darconians do."

"Mm-hm," I murmured. "Well, you look very nice without it. Some guys wouldn't."

"Thank you."

He was so close that I could feel the heat radiating from his body and his breath, warm on my cheek. His lips couldn't have been very far away, either—his full, succulent, kissable lips. My own lips tingled with anticipation; I wanted to kiss him so badly… I had to change the subject before I did something stupid.

Clearing my throat with an effort, I said, "So, you're

going to look after me, then? Wash my socks and comb my hair?"

"I'll do anything you wish for me to do," he said. "Anything at all."

"You shouldn't say that," I warned him. "You might not like what I wish for."

"I doubt that," he said, his amusement evident in his voice. Obviously, he didn't consider my "wishes" to be much of a threat.

"What do *you* wish for?" I asked curiously. "Freedom?"

"I *have* wished for that in the past," he replied thoughtfully. "But now, I'm looking forward to serving you in *any* way I can."

Give up the chance for freedom to serve a woman? *That* didn't sound like anything a man had ever said to me before, regardless of what planet he hailed from— though, of course, I'd never met a slave. "Aw, you're making that up," I protested.

"No," he said, his voice deepening slightly. "Aside from freedom, my life here has lacked only one thing."

"And that is?"

With his reply, his voice dropped a full octave, sending tendrils of desire curling around my heart. "Love," he replied. "And I believe you are the one who will change that."

"Me?" I gasped. He might have been suggesting the very thing I'd had on my mind ever since laying eyes on him, but at the same time, the idea scared me a little. I'm *such* a wuss… "B-but I might not stay long here long," I sputtered. "I may not be able to toler-ate the heat, the Princess might not be able to play a note on the piano—anything could happen!" I paused,

groping blindly for some plausible excuse. "And, besides, I wouldn't want to be the one to break your heart.
You know me: old love 'em and leave 'em Kyra!"

This was an out-and-out lie, and, if his chuckle was
any indication, he knew it. He was so close that the soft
glow of his eyes shone right into mine. "Go ahead and
do it, Kyra," he urged in a deep, rough voice. "Break
my heart."

What I saw in his eyes scared me even more. It wasn't
just passion or desire, it was hunger: a desperate, all-
consuming hunger.

"You want me to break your heart?" I whispered
nervously.

"Loving you would be worth a broken heart."

I wasn't sure, but I had an idea he could stomp the
hell out of mine, and it would be worth the pain. Perhaps
he was desperate enough to feel the same way.

"The men of my world were warriors out of neces-
sity," he went on, "but we were made for love. It is
our purpose—one which has been denied throughout
the years of our enslavement. The Darconian women
may find us attractive, but their scent doesn't arouse us,
and if the scent of a woman's desire is not present, we
cannot mate."

"That's odd," I croaked. "Human men can mate
with"—I paused for a moment to think about that, before adding,—"anything."

"Is that so?" he said with surprise. "We cannot. Our
women were always very reluctant, and to bring out the
scent of their desire, we had to… *entice* them."

Swallowing hard, I said glibly, "Well, if you don't
mind my saying so, I think you got it right; you guys are

irresistible." I saw a change of topic and grabbed it like a lifeline. "So, are there any of your women left?"

"Perhaps," he replied with a shrug, "but our enemies were very thorough."

"Jealous husbands?" I suggested.

"Maybe," he said. The glow in his eyes increased again. "Tell me, Kyra: would *your* husband be jealous of me?"

I had an idea that any husband I might have had would have killed him just for looking at me like that. "He might—if I had a husband, that is." The tension broke then, and I dissolved into giggles. "'Once you go cat, you never go back,'" I chanted. I was getting downright goofy—it must have been the wine, or the heat, or something—but suddenly, more than anything in the world, I wanted him lying there beside me. The Darconians weren't the only ones who liked a warm body to sleep with—and his was one of only three warm bodies within dozens of light-years, including my own. It struck me then just how alone I was. The Darconians were far more fearsome than he and his brother could ever be, and that realization gave me the courage to say something I ordinarily wouldn't have. "Would you lie down with me?" I asked. "Just for a little while."

Obviously, he really *would* do anything I asked of him, because the bed promptly dipped beneath his weight as he settled in behind me. Within seconds, the heat of his body sent blood rushing to my erogenous zones like a flood. I tried to focus on something—anything—else. It was strange to think that a short while ago, I hadn't even known he existed, and now, here he was in my bed with his arm draped over me, and I still didn't know his name.

"You look like a Siberian tiger," I said impulsively.

"Tiger?" he echoed curiously. "And what is a tiger?" His voice was gentle and teasing, like a caress, and I felt its effects all the way to my toes. Oh, yes, falling for him would be *so* easy; resisting him would be *so* hard…

"A species of big hunting cats," I explained, doing my best to keep my tone brisk and informative. "They live in a place on Earth where it's cold and snowy, and they're black and white striped and have blue eyes. At least, I think their eyes are blue," I said, my brain still a bit fuzzy. "I'm not sure."

Picking up my braid, he brought it to his face and sniffed as though he was inhaling the sweet scent of a rose. "And do you *like* tigers?" he prompted.

"They're very beautiful," I replied, "but also very dangerous. Like you."

His throaty chuckle nearly set off another orgasm. "But I am not dangerous," he protested.

"No? Perhaps not right now, but I think you could be. Very dangerous." As I lay there drifting for a while, I noticed that my head was swimming less since I'd lain down, but I still felt odd, though it might have been because he was spooned up against me so intimately. His fingertips were tracing patterns on my hip, sending scores of tingles racing up and down my spine. As he snuggled closer, I felt his other hand began to tease the stray tendrils of hair at my temple, and his breath was tantalizingly warm on my neck. My body began to tremble with a level of desire that was impossible to ignore.

Inhaling deeply, he whispered, "You smell of desire, Kyra—a scent I had nearly forgotten."

I didn't have to ask what that scent did to him, because I could feel the thick hardness of his cock pressing against my backside. He seemed to be capable of moving it, too, for it left a trail of moisture behind as it swept back and forth. I'd never heard of a man with so much control of his cock, and all I could think of was what it would feel like to have him moving inside me…

Of course, what I *really* should have been thinking about was what would happen if I messed around with one of the Queen's slaves! Cernada had said that the Queen would not permit it, so if I ever did anything of that nature I'd probably be beheaded, or at the very least, banished from the palace! Was he worth the risk? For that matter, was any man worth that risk? Generally speaking, they were nothing but trouble. What was I thinking to ask him to lie down with me? I had to get him out of my bed—or at least find something else for him to do… "I'm so thirsty."

"I'll get you some water," he said promptly.

I missed his presence beside me almost immediately. "Hey, um, Tiger," I called out. "You still haven't told me your name."

"You may call me Tiger, if you like," he said. "There are few who can pronounce my name." I could hear him pouring water into a glass. From a pitcher, I thought glumly. So much for running water…

"Tell me what it is tomorrow," I suggested. "I'll be thinking more clearly by then, and maybe I can say it."

"Maybe," he said. "Here, drink this." Sliding an arm beneath my shoulders for support, he held the glass to my parched lips. The water was blissfully cool, and I felt it coursing through my body when I swallowed it, but the feel of his arm around me was enough to turn that water to steam. He even smelled good, and though I couldn't actually identify any specific scent—it was more like inhaling his essence—it made me want more. In the faint moonlight, I could just make out the sparkling stones on his cock ring and wished there was enough light to see him clearly.

To my surprise, the light suddenly became brighter, as though a cloud had moved aside, fully illuminating his thick shaft. It was every bit as hard and shining as the stones he wore, and the syrupy fluid was still oozing from the scalloped corona of the head. I'd never even *dreamed* of a man like this, let alone ever had one at my disposal. *Oh, God!* He was going to get me into so much trouble... Groaning miserably and murmuring my thanks, I sank back into the bed and wished for darkness to return. I was better off if *I couldn't* see him... Maybe I was imagining things, but the room instantly grew darker.

"Would you like me to help you remove your dress?" he asked, sounding more seductive than helpful. "It would be best if you did not sleep in it."

"Mmm, yes, I would like that very much," I said before I could stop myself. Regaining control of my tongue, I added, "But then again, I might like it a little *too* much. Maybe you should go on to bed yourself. I don't know what time it is here, but it must be getting pretty late."

I didn't know her very well, but somehow I didn't think Scalia would like the idea of me getting naked with her fancy, expensive slave boy—especially after what Cernada had said. Though as gorgeous as he was, surely Scalia should have known what might happen if she assigned him to me. Or perhaps she had… I reminded myself that she *had* seen my reaction to him, as well as his reaction to me. Scalia didn't seem at all stupid; she had to have known. Maybe he was a perk—something to make me want to stay, rather than deciding it was too darn hot on Darconia for a human being to tolerate—but I wished she'd been more specific about what I was allowed to do with him.

"It's so hot here," I muttered. "Is it always like this? I mean, does it ever cool off or rain?"

His tone of voice changed along with the subject, going from seductive to informative in the space of a heartbeat. "The desert does cool at night," he said, "but the palace walls keep the internal temperature fairly consistent, so I don't think you'll get cold. It hardly ever rains here, but there is more rainfall in the mountains."

Somehow I doubted that it would be enough to sustain any kind of forest; those mountains had to be as stark and barren as the rest of the desert. "Have you ever been there?"

"The mountains? No," he replied. "But I have seen the storms from the palace windows."

"Never get out, do you?"

"No."

"Do you want to?"

"Sometimes," he replied warily.

"Well, maybe I'll take you out to see those trees around the palace. If they ever let *me* out, that is," I added.

I was getting very sleepy—either that, or breathing in his aura had a relaxing effect. I was nearly asleep when I remembered something else I needed to ask him. "How do you turn on the lights?"

"Do you want them on?" The seductive edge to his voice returned.

"Well, no, not right now. I just wanted to know how to do it."

"That is how they operate," he said. "You have only to think that you need light, and they will illuminate."

"Can they tell if I'm lying?"

"No."

I opened my eyes. It was pitch-dark, and I thought I could use a little light. I wanted to see his eyes again, anyway, though they seemed to glow all by themselves. Slowly, the stones in the walls and ceiling began to glimmer. "That is so cool!" I exclaimed. I looked up at the one on the ceiling and wished for it to grow dim— and it did. This was obviously what had occurred when I'd wanted to see his cock. I'd have to be more careful about what I wished for. "How do they do that?" I asked, making them brighten again.

"No one knows," he replied.

"Must be a market for them."

"I believe they are a great source of the wealth of this region," he said. "Along with many other useful stones."

"I wonder how many Scalia had to sell to buy the two of you? It must have been a lot."

Tiger smiled at me and shook his head. He didn't know the answer to that.

Looking up, I stole a peek at his eyes—eyes the same shade of blue as an eastern sky just before dawn: serenely beautiful, but at the same time, absolutely breathtaking.

"You were worth every credit," I murmured. "Tell me, does Scalia like your eyes?"

"Yes," he replied. "And she is very fond of our hair."

"So am I," I sighed. "I've never seen anything like it. It's so beautiful."

"As are you," he said gently. "Go to sleep now."

So, my handsome tiger thought I was beautiful, did he? Wasn't that nice? It would be such a comfort to remember that when the guards dragged me off to the gallows for even *thinking* about consorting with one of the Queen's pets. I could almost feel the trapdoor giving way beneath my feet as I drifted off to sleep.

Chapter 5

I AWOKE THE NEXT MORNING WITH BLAZING SUNLIGHT IN MY eyes and the heat of the day only just beginning. Still in my dress from the day before, I remembered that I hadn't had a bath, or brushed my teeth, or even washed my face, and with all the sweating I'd done the day before, I felt pretty grungy. I got up to have a look around, thinking that if this room had been specifically designed to house a human, there must be something there to pee in. I chuckled to myself as it occurred to me that the bathroom, like the lights, might suddenly appear whenever I had a need for it. Now, *that* would be a neat trick!

Not so, as it turned out. It was a bit archaic, perhaps, but essentially what had been provided for me was a chamber pot in a small alcove next to the doorway between this and an adjoining room. I smiled, thinking that Scalia's information must have been outdated, for such articles hadn't been in general use on Earth for about a thousand years. As I had suspected the night before, there was no running water, either, the chamber pot being about half-filled with sand. There was, however, a pitcher full of water and a basin on a stand beneath a mirror that hung upon the wall. My luggage was nowhere in sight, but when I opened a drawer that fitted neatly into a recessed area of the wall, I found that all of my clothes had been carefully folded and put away.

The room itself was large, open, and airy, with no glass or screens on a pair of windows that looked out onto a garden in full bloom. I could see both the desert and, if I leaned out and looked to my left, the mountains in the distance. It already looked hot enough out there to scorch the soles of my feet—whether I had shoes on or not. Fortunately, it was much cooler in my room, and I found that I could walk barefoot without any trouble, the stone floor even feeling slightly chilly, making me glad that there were soft rugs on the floor by the bed.

The bed frame was made of a highly polished wood, as was the cushioned bench set beneath the windows. Looking up, I saw that glowstones formed a spiral pattern on the high ceiling, which was liberally decorated with carved stone flowers. Near the window sat a table and chairs, both made of the same wood as the bed. I wondered if the wood was local or imported—given the climate, I was leaning toward imported. Overall, the decor of the room made me wonder where Scalia's information on humans had come from, because it had a vaguely historical feel to it—almost as if I'd been set down in the middle of an old novel about a governess taking up a new post and finding her rooms to be far nicer than she had expected—or was accustomed to.

Passing through an open doorway into another spacious room, I stopped short, nearly having another orgasm, for there, perched elegantly on a dais, was a grand piano. And not just *any* grand piano—unless my eyes were deceiving me, what stood before me was an antique Steinway. Where Scalia had found it was anyone's guess, but it had been manufactured on Earth, God only knew how many hundreds of years before. Sitting down on the bench, I ran my fingers over the keyboard and found it to be in perfect tune, with a rich tone and a light action on the keys. It was love at first sight.

It had been weeks since I had played, and I hadn't realized until then just how much I'd missed it. Playing a sonata at random, I noted that the acoustics of the room were absolutely perfect—as if I were in a grand concert hall—and as the music swelled, filling the air with sound, I so lost myself in it that I didn't hear anyone enter. When the last notes died away, Zealon applauded behind me—an odd sound, coming from those reptilian hands.

"Oh, that was so beautiful!" she said reverently. "Will I *ever* be able to play like that?"

"Someday," I said, turning to face her. "Provided you practice enough."

"Oh, I will!" she assured me. "I'll start today!"

"Sounds good," I said, "but let's wait until after breakfast, shall we?"

"Breakfast?" she echoed. "What's that?"

I stared at her in disbelief. "You know, the morning meal? What you eat after you first get up in the morning?"

"Here on Darconia we only eat once a day," she said. "In the evening."

My stomach let out a loud snarl. "Humans eat more often than that," I said, my eyes undoubtedly growing round with horror. "Is there anything I can get at this hour? I'm starving!"

Having said that, I heard a sound coming from the other room. Frowning slightly, I got up from the piano and peered through the doorway. My tiger was in there—still wearing nothing but his two jeweled collars, by the way—setting out platters of food on the table from a heavily laden tray.

I cast a withering look at Zealon. "Very funny," I said dryly. "You had me going there for a minute."

Zealon doubled over, cackling with laughter. "I'm sorry!" she gasped. "But I love the way your face changes."

"Those are facial expressions," I said loftily. "And this one," I added, narrowing my eyes and thinning my lips, "signifies marked disapproval."

"I'll try to remember that."

"See that you do."

Following me to the door, Zealon let out a squeal of delight. "She's given you Tycharian?"

"What do you mean?"

"Him," she replied, pointing at Tiger.

"You *know* him?" I asked, a good deal astonished.

"Of course I do! Mother doesn't think I know he exists, but we're good friends, actually."

Tiger gave her such a look! "You are not supposed to reveal that," he said sternly. "To anyone."

"Oh, it doesn't matter if Kyra knows, does it? She won't tell."

"Well, the Queen did say when she assigned him to me that it was 'worth the risk' that you might meet him," I mused. "So it probably doesn't matter, but do you mean to say you've been sneaking off to make friends with the slaves?"

"They aren't really slaves, you know," Zealon said ingenuously. "Just special servants. Pretty lucky, actually, because they aren't allowed to touch the chamber pots."

"And what else aren't they allowed to do?" I remarked sarcastically. "Leave of their own free will?"

"Oh, they could if they really wanted to," she said, sounding as if she truly believed this. "Mother would never stop them, though she says it would be dangerous for any of her slaves to leave, because they are all either hunted or endangered species. She keeps them locked up at night for their own protection, but I think they *like* working here. I mean, it *is* a palace."

She was so naïve, it was downright comical. "Zealon, would *you* like being locked up at night? Even for your own protection?"

She looked up at me soberly. "But I am," she replied. "A princess is as much a slave as they are. We just get locked up in different rooms."

Perhaps she wasn't quite so naïve after all. "Touché," I said softly. "Okay, then, now that we know we're all stuck here living in a palace whether we like it or not, why don't you two 'slaves' join me for breakfast? Unless you've already eaten, that is. I think I'd like some company."

Tiger looked surprised. Zealon's jaw dropped. "What's the matter?" I asked. "Is that going too far?"

"I… don't know," Zealon said. "I've never done that before."

"Which part? Having breakfast with me, or with him?"

"With him, I think," she replied uncertainly. "Anyway, I've already eaten."

I nodded, thinking she'd ducked past that one pretty effectively. So, he wasn't really a slave, was he? It certainly seemed that way to me. "Well, then, do I have to eat all of this by myself?"

Tiger shook his head almost imperceptibly. Zealon shrugged, a gesture that looked odd on a lizard—a bit like watching a live cartoon character.

"I have other lessons this morning," she said. "So I couldn't stay, anyway. I just came in when I heard you playing."

"When are you free for your first piano lesson?"

"Not until after midday," Zealon replied. "I'll come back then."

"That'll be fine," I said with a nod.

The Princess waved her good-bye and left us. I went over and sat down at the table, taking a good, long drink before I did anything else. Tiger was still arranging the dishes and seemed to be taking an inordinate amount of time and care to do so.

"So," I ventured. "What was that name again? Tycharian?"

"Yes," he replied, his voice sounding wooden and neutral.

"I seem to be able to pronounce it without too much trouble. Why were you being so mysterious last night?"

He'd been keeping his eyes on his work but turned to face me then. "I wanted to hear what you would call me if you didn't know my name."

"Any special reason for that?"

"You did not call me 'slave.'"

"I think I see your point," I said. "And, no, I didn't call you 'slave,' but I *did* call you Tiger, which is a type of animal," I added ruefully. "That's not much better than calling you 'slave,' is it?"

"But tigers are not slaves, are they?"

"Well, no," I admitted, "but you do see them locked up and on display in zoos from time to time. That doesn't sound very good, either."

He seemed to think differently. Perhaps he liked the idea of being a tiger. "You may call me whatever you wish," he said finally. "Tiger, Tycharian, Tychar, or even Ty, which is what my brother, Trag, calls me." A mischievous little smile touched his lips. "So, tell me Kyra: would you prefer to have breakfast with a slave, or with a tiger?"

Returning his smile, I said warmly, "I'd much rather have breakfast with you, Tycharian." Gesturing toward a chair, I added, "Have a seat, and if the Queen doesn't like it, she can fire me."

"I don't believe she will."

"Like it, or fire me?"

Tiger looked uncomfortable for a moment. "Fire you," he said. "She has told me to see to your needs as much as I am able. You are my exclusive… assignment. She wouldn't object to us sharing a meal together."

"Really?" It seemed surprising to me that she would give him up entirely, though she *did* have two of them. Perhaps I wouldn't be executed for sleeping with him, after all. "Well, what if I need something during the night? Since you slaves are locked up—for your own protection, of course," I added, "who do I call if I get sick or something? Or do I get locked up, too?" I hadn't gotten up to try the door last night, but that didn't mean it hadn't been locked.

"Scalia didn't say specifically, but if you're locked in, perhaps it is because she feels that you need protection, as well."

I pondered this for a moment, remembering the armed escort from the spaceport, and consoled myself with the fact that at least Scalia hadn't asked Wazak to make me his "exclusive assignment." "Do I really need protecting?"

"Even slaves hear tales of unrest within a country," he said carefully, taking a seat across from me.

This sounded interesting. In an attempt to make the question seem casual, I bit into an odd-looking piece of fuzzy green fruit that reminded me of a kiwi. Tasted rather like one, too. Spitting out the fuzzy peel, I savored the sweet flesh. "What sort of unrest?"

Following my lead and helping himself to some fruit, Tychar said, "Whenever there is change, there is also unrest."

"True, but do I have anything to do with the changes?"

"You are an offworlder, teaching music to the Princess," he replied. "That could be seen as a radical change."

"Music?" I echoed in disbelief. "Radical?" I was about to deny having any radical tendencies whatsoever, but then I remembered my music history: musicians had been on the cutting edge of radicalism for a very long time. Funny how I'd never considered classical pianists as being radical, but, given where I was at the time, perhaps we were. "Well, yes, I see your point." Sighing regretfully, I added, "Guess we won't get to go on that vacation to the mountains, then. Honestly, if I'd known I'd have to stay cooped up all the time—even in a palace—I'm not sure I would have come."

"You'll get used to it," he assured me. "I have, though I *do* get restless sometimes—and my brother, Trag, is even less contented."

"I didn't think he seemed very happy last night," I remarked. "In fact, I don't think I ever even saw him smile. You were the much more likable of the two."

Tychar shrugged noncommittally. "Trag is a good man, but he doesn't like it here."

"And you *do*?"

His lips curled into a delightfully devilish grin. "There was a time when I rebelled against being a slave, but no longer. I have a new job as your personal attendant," he said. "And I think I will… *enjoy* my job."

The way he was smiling at me, I almost believed him. "You're very sweet."

"Ah, but you haven't tasted me yet," he countered, still smiling. "How can you know?"

The thought of tasting any part of him made my heart skip several beats. "That's just a figure of speech, Tychar," I said briskly, choosing to ignore the innuendo. "It only means that you're very nice and thoughtful, not that you actually taste good."

Regarding me with heavy-lidded eyes, he said, "You may find that I'm even sweeter when you've tasted me."

I happened to be chewing on an exceptionally juicy bit of fruit at the time, but my mouth went dry anyway. "You taste sweet?" I asked hoarsely. "That's funny, I would have thought you'd be salty."

He blinked slowly, seductively. "That depends on which part of me you taste."

I choked slightly as I tried to decide which part of him would be sweet. Perhaps there was more than one… "Tychar?" I said when I could talk again.

"Yes?" There was an eager lilt coloring his voice as he looked at me expectantly. He was getting to me, and he knew it. I couldn't see his groin from where I sat, but I'd have bet his cock was already rock hard. "It's much too early in the day for that sort of thing."

His full lips stretched into another smile. "But I am locked up at night."

"Which is a damn good thing, if you ask me!" I declared. "It's bad enough having to sit across the breakfast table from a naked tiger, trying not to—"

He leveled a knowing look at me. "If you feel desire for me, Kyra," he said reasonably, "then why do you resist? Is it because I'm a slave?"

"I'm—I'm not resisting anything," I protested weakly. "I just don't think Scalia would like it if I went around tasting her slave boys."

"So it *is* because I am a slave." I thought he seemed disappointed in me—as though he'd thought I'd be more liberal in my thinking, perhaps.

"Someone *else's* slave," I amended. "I wish Scalia had been a little more specific about what she wanted you to do here. I mean, attending to all of my needs could be a pretty broad range of duties, and I'm sure there are a few 'personal services' that she'd much rather you didn't provide."

I'd done my best to couch the idea in obscure terms, but he still knew exactly what I meant. Looking at me directly with his brilliant blue eyes boring into mine, he said evenly, "Perhaps she wishes for us to mate."

"Mate?" I squeaked. "Oh, surely not! We're not even of the same species, Tychar! How could we mate?" It was a stupid question, and I knew it, because there was absolutely no physical reason why we couldn't, though whether we were *genetically* compatible remained to be seen.

"She wanted a human woman to teach the Princess to play the piano," he said with a nonchalant shrug. "Perhaps she was told that a human would be able to mate with one of us."

I thought that was a bit of a stretch, but I'd heard stranger notions. "Well, she *did* say she wanted to breed more of you," I conceded. "But are you saying that this is the reason she hired me?"

"I'm sure it's not the only reason," he admitted. "She is very anxious for the Princess to learn your music."

"Now, wait just a doggone minute! Did she actually *tell* you any of this? It seems sort of… well, I don't know what you'd call it." I was stunned into silence. Part of a breeding program? That was worse than being a slave—downright dehumanizing, in fact.

"Kyra," he said gently. "She has not said this, and you do not have to do anything you do not wish to do. You are not her slave, as I am."

I nodded, but my suspicions had been aroused, and Scalia would have had a difficult time convincing me she'd never had any intention of using me to breed more of her precious tigers. It wasn't that I didn't *want* to mate with him, as he put it, because in actual fact, I couldn't think of anything I'd like more, but I sure as hell didn't want to do it as part of some lizard queen's bizarre hobby! It made me mad just thinking about it. Then an even more chilling thought occurred to me.

"What would she do if I had a child? Take it from me? Sell it into slavery?"

"She has said nothing of the kind," Tychar said soothingly, "but I don't believe she would take your child. She may only want to see if it's possible. She was very distressed when she learned that our race was nearly destroyed. She seems interested in preserving it."

"So I'd be rescuing an endangered species, huh?" I said, unable to keep the irony out of my voice. "Well, then I guess I should just quietly submit so you don't all become extinct."

An already upswept eyebrow climbed even higher. "If we were to mate, Kyra," he said confidently, "I would hope you would do more than merely 'submit.'"

"You mean you'd want me to enjoy it?" I would have been lying if I'd said I'd particularly enjoyed it in the past. In fact, quite frequently sex had left me feeling cold and ever so slightly used. However, something told me that it would be different with him—a *lot* different.

He nodded. "And I would like it very much if you could love me," he said quietly. "I have been Scalia's slave for nearly twenty years, and in all that time—"

"Twenty years!" I exclaimed. "How old *are* you?"

"Forty years, perhaps," he replied. "The length of a solar cycle is different on each planet."

"Well, you certainly don't look it. Of course, if you don't ever go out in the sun, you wouldn't age as quickly."

Tychar looked at me as though I'd lost my mind. "My species is very long-lived, and I have not yet reached my prime. My age is insignificant."

"Maybe," I said uncertainly. "But twenty years? Do you mean to say that it took Scalia that long to come up with this crossbreeding scheme of hers?"

"There is no scheme," he insisted. "At least, none that I am aware of, but in all that time, her slave traders have never brought her any Zetithian females."

"Zetithian?"

"Trag and I are natives of the planet Zetith," he explained.

"Never heard of it."

"It was very distant," he said, "and it no longer exists."

I sat staring at him for a long time. If any of my suspicions were true, they were already quite enough to make me feel used, manipulated, conned, coerced, and tricked; now he was playing on my sympathy and sense of duty. He was making it seem as though if I didn't mate with him, I'd be responsible for the extinction of an entire species—which was a hanging offense if I'd ever heard one. It seemed unlikely that Scalia would be so underhanded as to get me here under false pretenses and then spring something like this on me, but you never know with queens. The promotion of the greater good doesn't always go over so well with the individuals directly involved.

"Tell me something," I said finally. "Just how long have the two of you been hanging around here wearing nothing but fancy cat collars?"

"We have always worn them."

I thought he phrased that a bit oddly because it didn't truly answer my question, though his accent led me to believe that Stantongue wasn't the first and only language he'd ever spoken. Perhaps he'd misunderstood me. "And what else did you wear?" I believe I was tapping my foot at that point, much the way Wazak had been tapping his tail the day before.

He hesitated, but when it came, his answer seemed truthful enough. "We sometimes—though not always—wear clothes, though we wear them less now than we did in the past because the Darconians don't. We have... acclimated," he said, adding, "It's hot here."

"No kidding?" I said dryly. "I hadn't noticed. So, what you're saying is that your style of dress—or lack thereof—wasn't just for my benefit."

"No, it was not."

I hoped he was telling me the truth, because if he wasn't, I would have been a bit miffed with my new employer. "Well, I certainly hope not, but you've got to admit, it seems a little fishy. I mean, Scalia flies me clear across the galaxy, scares me half to death with Wazak, gets me drunk, and shows me her two incredibly sexy naked tigers—and *then* tells one of you to take care of all my needs! The surprising thing is, if I understand you correctly and you haven't smelled anyone's 'desire' in nearly twenty years, that you didn't take advantage of the chance to break that dry spell last night. I mean, you missed a golden opportunity there."

"It would have been glorious," he said—and I had no doubt that he was being perfectly honest. "But it wouldn't have been right. You were too... vulnerable."

"And you'd rather I be fighting mad?"

"It would be more like mating with one of our own females," he admitted with a quirky little grin. "They didn't always like to mate—or admit that they wanted to."

"You mean you had to take them by force?"

"No, as I told you before, we had to be able to smell their desire and be... enticing."

"Enticing? How?"

He leaned back in his chair, crossed his arms over his chest, and, with a frankly seductive smile, began to purr.

"Oh, I might have *known* you could do that!" I said acidly, feeling a sudden urge to throw one of those fuzzy kiwi fruits at him. It had been hard enough to control the rising passion that was coursing through my body, and now he was purring! "Okay, you're right. You look good enough to eat."

His smile broadened, revealing his sharp fangs. "Then eat me."

A lightning bolt of desire sliced through me, and I nearly had to bite my tongue to keep from gasping. I wanted him so badly that I could almost taste him from where I sat. Clearing my throat and making a vain attempt to change the subject, I asked, "What else can you do?"

His glowing blue eyes held my gaze for a long moment before he spoke. "I can give you joy unlike any you have ever known."

I stared back at him, my mouth agape. Such a boast should have made me respond with skepticism, but quite frankly, I believed him. My "Oh, really?" came out sounding high-pitched and silly, and if his expression was any indication, he wasn't exaggerating or teasing. No, he was perfectly serious.

Nodding slowly, his purring grew even louder.

"Tychar," I said evenly. "You're going to have to stop that."

The purring ceased immediately.

Then it hit me. He wasn't going to do a damn thing more than be enticing unless I specifically asked him to. He hadn't been a slave for twenty years and not learned a few things about staying out of trouble. The reason he hadn't done it the night before was because—stupid me!—instead of asking him to make love to me, I'd told him to go to bed! Obviously it had to be my idea, but I wasn't altogether sure I could say it.

"Look," I began, "it's nothing against you, but I think I'd like to get used to being here for a while before I start fooling around with anyone—and it doesn't matter to me whether you're a slave or not. What matters most is the fact that I only met you yesterday. Just… give me some time." I took a deep breath and settled on a new subject—one that surely wouldn't involve any more purring. "Meanwhile, why don't you show me around this maze so if there's ever a fire I can find my way out. I'm not sure I could even find my way back to where we had dinner last night. Or should I *not* know?"

If he was disappointed, it didn't show, for he merely shook his head in reply. "There are some areas where I am not permitted, but I will show you as much as I can."

"Great!" I said, blowing out a pent-up sigh of relief. The trouble was, he was just plain too much man for the likes of me; I wasn't sure I could handle him and still remain sane. He'd already said he wanted me to taste him, eat him, and love him—hell, just looking at him was overwhelming enough. "But first I'd like to clean up a bit. Where does one go to take a bath around here?"

Tychar looked pretty clean and smelled wonderful— and he wasn't a lizard—so I figured he'd be the best one to ask.

"I believe that keeping you clean is one of my duties," he said, his seductive little smile suggesting that he would consider this particular duty to be one of his greatest pleasures.

My throat dried up again. "I think I can probably take care of that myself," I said hoarsely. "All you have to do is tell me where."

"You don't have to *go* anywhere."

"But there isn't a shower or a bathtub in here," I protested. "I know because, trust me, I've looked! There's no running water, either, and the only water I've got is obviously intended for drinking purposes."

"Water is scarce on this world," he said, "and isn't used for bathing."

"Well then, what do you do to stay so clean?"

Rising from his seat, he went over to where the pitcher of water stood and picked up a towel. "You clean yourself with this."

"No water?"

"No water."

I found this hard to believe, but, still, his hair looked fabulous. Then again, perhaps the Zetithians didn't excrete oils through their skin—or perspire, either. Maybe they just panted like dogs whenever they got too hot. "You use this method yourself?" I asked doubtfully, not truly believing it was possible.

He nodded. "It may take some time to become accustomed to it, but it's quite effective."

Still a bit skeptical, I took the towel from him. Upon examination, it appeared to be fairly ordinary, but when I rubbed it against my arm, something odd happened. I could feel a subtle magnetic pull on my skin. I looked at the cloth again, noting that it obviously had gotten something off me because there was now a smudge mark on it.

"That's amazing!" I exclaimed. "What makes it do that?"

"It's woven from fiber called scrail, which is derived from a local stone," he replied. "It seems to have a strong affinity for oils and dirt."

"So, basically, you can clean anything with them."

"Yes," he replied. "And when exposed to direct sunlight, the fibers repel the dirt and oils and the cloth can then be reused."

This was as interesting as the glowstones—and probably just as valuable a commodity for offworld sale, which started me wondering about what else they might have to sell. The deserts of Earth once sat upon rich oil deposits; perhaps the same thing was true on Darconia. Remembering how much wealth the sheiks had amassed as a result of that oil, I decided that if Scalia was as rich as that, I might have to think about asking for a raise. Of course, I would only *think* about it…

"What do they use for power here?" I went on to ask. "I mean, something was running those hovercars! Oil, fusion, fission, solar, or what?"

"They have another stone for that."

I might have guessed as much. It seemed that they had a rock for just about any purpose you could name, and it wouldn't have surprised me to find that some were edible. "You know, it seems as though Scalia's sitting on a veritable gold mine here," I remarked. "No wonder she could afford to bring a piano teacher all the way from Earth! I'm surprised she couldn't get a better one."

He seemed surprised by this remark. "You are not a good teacher?"

"I didn't say that—not exactly, anyway—but there *are* better instructors out there. It's just that she was too specific about her other requirements."

"In what way?" he asked, curious now.

"Well, she wanted someone who could not only teach piano, but who was also a relatively young, unattached female. At the time I didn't think that was so significant, but—" I broke off there, thinking that if Scalia wanted to breed more Zetithians, I might be just the thing. Of course, I could have pointed out to Scalia that if she wanted me to have kittens, she would have to wait; I was on an extended-release form of birth control, and I'd taken a pill a month prior to my departure from Earth. It would take a while to wear off. I hadn't brought any more of them along with me because—call me careless and irresponsible if you will—I hadn't thought that having sex with anyone on a world full of lizards was even a remote possibility. The sad fact is that I hadn't particularly needed it even when I took the damned pill. It was simply time to take one, so I did.

But taking another good, long look at Tychar, I decided that if you could cross a horse with a donkey, you could probably cross a human with a Zetithian. I'd known people on Earth who were alien crossbreeds, and their parents had appeared to be even more different than the two of us. It was not beyond the realm of possibility that we could have children together.

Tychar must have seen the wheels turning inside my head. "But?" he prompted.

"Nothing," I said quickly. "Forgot what I was going to say." Hesitating a moment, I added, "Oh, I remember now; the better teacher thing. It's just that with so many stipulations, it tends to limit your choices."

He nodded, but with a slight lift to his brow. He wasn't going to come right out and accuse me of lying, because my reply had been plausible, but he knew that I hadn't been entirely honest with him, either. Scalia had said that the Zetithians were both very truthful, and, apparently, also pretty good at spotting a lie. I just hoped I didn't have to tell him any.

Any *more*, that is. I'd already told a small fib when I declined his offer to keep me clean. It wasn't that I *couldn't* handle it myself, but my mind was still reeling from the thought of him touching me anywhere, let alone in some of the more intimate places. Would he actually want to do that, or, for that matter, would I actually *let* him? Maybe he could just do my back.

He seemed to be thinking along the same lines, because during the subsequent conversation, the scrail cloth had somehow wound up in his hands, rather than mine.

"Let me help you with your hair," he said, returning to the original subject. "I would advise you to use one cloth for your face and hair and another for the… rest of you."

This last bit was said with a noticeable twinge of regret. So, he *did* want to get his hands on me—which wasn't too surprising, given the rest of the morning's events. I tried to imagine what it would be like to just lie down and let him do as he wished—which led me to imagine another situation—one in which *I* was the one cleaning *him*. To slide my fingers through his hair, to rub his back, polishing his skin until it glowed, to towel off that stiff erection, to massage that perfect ass…

I was recalled to my surroundings when Tychar moved to stand behind my chair and began massaging my scalp with the cloth. He was only touching me with his fingertips, but from the way he was purring, he might as well have had his hands all over me. I hadn't realized how tense I was—the muscles in my shoulders were as tight as coiled springs—but soon relaxed completely as a result of his soothing touch.

Tilting my head back to rest against his chest, he ran the cloth over my face and neck, pausing to linger on my lips. I could feel him purring, and the vibration both tranquilized and tantalized as his hands reached ever lower, moving in a circular pattern over my chest and shoulders. My dress was sleeveless with a scooped neckline in the front and back, and he took full advantage of the amount of skin it exposed.

Just when I thought he would go too far, he retreated, the cloth muffling the sound of his purring as his fingertips teased my ears. Then, with a casual flick to my earlobes, he left me, dropping another cloth in my lap.

"Do your feet last," he suggested just before the door closed behind him.

Chapter 6

HAVING PERFORMED MY MORNING ABLUTIONS WITH NOTHING but a towel, I then took a tour of the palace escorted by my tall, dark, handsome, and very naked tiger. He was telling me plenty of things about the palace, but I'll admit to only hearing about half of it, for he was much too distracting for me to be able to absorb much in the way of information.

It took quite a while to get through the tour because it seemed as if every Darconian we passed had something to say to Tychar. He may not have been known to anyone on the outside, but those who lived and worked inside the palace seemed to know him quite well—and all the ones wearing beads seemed to think he was the greatest thing since sliced bread. We saw Cernada again, and after a brief dalliance that had her laughing delightedly, she went on her way, this time patting him on the butt instead of running her fingers through his hair.

"That happen often?" I asked once she rounded a corner.

"All the time," he said. "Though she is my most dedicated admirer. The rest seem to be afraid to touch me. I think Scalia may have warned them to keep their hands off."

I felt my heart drop to my navel. Scalia had given me no such warning, but *still*. "Did she… say anything about me?"

Exhaling with a soft, rumbling purr, he said, "Those rules don't apply to you, Kyra."

"W-why is that?" I stammered.

"Unlike the other women in the palace, she has assigned me to *you*," he reminded me, "and I am to see to your *every* need." The look in his eyes and the emphasis he placed on the word "every" sent my imagination tearing off on another sexual rampage. Tychar seemed to guess the nature of my thoughts, for his purring grew even louder, and the tone of it deepened seductively.

"And… if one of those needs was to… touch you?" I ventured.

His lips curled into a smile. "Then you may touch me all you like."

My throat tightened uncomfortably, but I managed to say: "You're sure about that?"

"Yes, I am," he said with a slow nod. As if to prove that the reverse was also true, he brushed my cheek lightly with his fingertips, sending delightful little thrills racing over my skin.

"How sure?"

"Very," he replied. Noting that I remained skeptical, he added, "I know, because I asked."

"You asked Scalia?" I said incredulously. "When?"

"While you were… cleaning yourself," he replied, his expression one of apparent regret for not being allowed to finish the job. "And she said I was to do *anything* you told me to."

I couldn't even begin to imagine going up to the Queen and asking her if I could have my wicked way with her cherished slave! Tychar was obviously more courageous than me—or more determined to get what he wanted.

In an effort to downplay the innuendo, I said jokingly, "Even if I told you to jump off the roof?"

Leaning down so closely that I could feel his warm breath tickling my ear, he purred: "But you wouldn't do *that*... would you, Kyra?"

"No, you're right," I said lamely. "I wouldn't." I wouldn't want to do anything to prevent him from staying right by my side for the rest of my life. Now that I knew I had the Queen's permission, I wanted to feel every square inch of him and reached up to touch his cheek the same way he had touched mine.

"You don't have a beard, do you?" I said, finding his skin surprisingly smooth.

"Beard?"

"Facial hair," I replied. "Most human males develop it when they reach sexual maturity."

"That must feel very odd."

"Never liked it much, myself," I admitted. "When you shave it off, it leaves a rough stubble, and when you let it grow long, it tickles."

"You are speaking from the woman's point of view, then?"

"Well, yes, I suppose so."

"So when you kiss a human male, it is... unpleasant?" He seemed pleased with this idea—as if it gave him a slight advantage.

"Well... it could be."

"It doesn't hurt *or* tickle to kiss a Zetithian," he assured me, his eyes glowing with the desire to prove he was telling the truth.

I stared longingly at his lips, wanting to find out for myself. "W-what about the fangs?" I asked hoarsely.

His smile broadened, revealing them fully. "They don't hurt or tickle, either—unless I bite."

"You... *bite*?" I said meekly.

"I will if you want me to," he replied. "Would you like that—or would you prefer to bite *me*?"

As we were standing in the middle of a well-traveled corridor, all this talk about touching, kissing, and biting had me wondering why I'd ever left my room—or wishing I had as much guts as Cernada did. Choking back the gasp the thought of biting him evoked, I cleared my throat audibly and said: "Um, shall we get on with the tour?"

I got the distinct impression that Tychar wasn't fooled for a moment, but all he did was lead the way as I'd requested.

Finally, after we'd been down the five-hundredth corridor and seen the Great Hall, the Grand Ballroom, as well as the kitchens, the administrative offices, the Security Chief's office (Wazak was out to lunch, I believe), and the schoolroom where Zealon was engaged in studying geometry, I asked Tychar to take me somewhere to sit down, explaining that the heat was affecting me again. While this was probably true, I was also a bit footsore—aside from the fact that I wanted him to stop because every movement of his naked, muscular body was so fluid, so graceful, so *hypnotic*...

"This way," he said, motioning me toward yet another unexplored corridor. "It's the most beautiful part of the palace."

The guard posted there obviously knew Tychar, if not me, and waved us by. As I followed him through a set of doors even more ornate than those opening to the Great Hall, I was struck dumb by what lay behind them. To say that it was the most beautiful part of the palace was putting it mildly—it was probably the most beautiful place on this and several other planets. As we were enveloped by the unexpectedly humid air, riotous, tropical growth met my eyes, along with flowers of every shape and hue, carved stonework, and—I could hardly believe my eyes—cascading water. Some type of glass or plastic—the first I'd seen on this planet—formed the walls on three sides, as well as the roof. I say three sides, but it was actually more like part of a bubble, for the walls and ceiling were rounded, a perfect sphere broken only where there were doors cut into the glass. Beyond those doors I could see a walled patio that seemed to be sitting on top of the portico that encircled the palace. Fully half of the patio was sheltered from the sun by a domed roof, which was supported by columns crafted from the gleaming shepra stone. And, as if all of that weren't enough, the view of the distant mountains from where I stood was nothing short of spectacular.

"And I thought there was a nice view from *my* window," I said with awe. "What *is* this place?"

The corner of Tychar's mouth twitched into his signature smile, and his eyes sparkled with mischief. "The Darconians call it The Shrine of the Desert," he replied, "but it's actually the slave quarters."

"Oh, you've *got* to be kidding me!"

"No," he assured me. "This is where they lock us up at night."

Words like harem and seraglio leaped into my mind, even though the room wasn't filled with beautiful women. In fact, the best I could tell, we were all alone there. "Well, you certainly can't say you haven't got a nice room," I remarked, "even if you do have to share it." I stared longingly at the fountain, watching as water spilled from a bouquet of stone flowers carved high in the stone wall to be captured in a large basin of highly polished shepra. It was undoubtedly against the rules, but all I wanted to do was to jump right into it and just sit there and soak for a couple of hours. "Where does the water come from?"

"Underground," he replied. "This is the oasis source."

"Oh, surely they don't run *all* the water in through here, do they?" I found it hard to believe that anyone in their right mind would do such a thing. The slaves could have barricaded the doors and cut off the water supply to the whole city. Surely Scalia had thought of that when she decided to house her pets there.

"No," he replied. "This is only a small portion of the water that flows from the spring."

"And where do you sleep?"

"Anywhere we like," he said. "We have pallets that are put away during the day. We may sleep inside or out, according to our own preferences."

"And you, where do you sleep most often?"

"Out there," he said, with a gesture toward the patio. "I like to look up at the stars."

And dream of escaping to them one day—even with the knowledge that there were few of his kind left, that his homeworld had been destroyed, and that he might be hunted down for the bounty on Zetithians were he ever to leave this sanctuary. He *must* have dreamed of freedom, even though he might have had nowhere else to go.

"What was Zetith like?" I asked impulsively.

"Much like this room," he replied. "Green, beautiful, warm, and with many plants and trees—though in some places there was open grassland."

"What happened to it?"

The sparkle in his eyes disappeared, as did his smile. "We were at war," he replied grimly, "and during that time, an asteroid struck it, destroying the entire planet."

I tried to imagine what it would have been like to hear that the Earth had been obliterated while I was off gallivanting through space and couldn't do it. Tycharian and his brother were alone and adrift in a universe with nowhere to call home. To lose everything in such a way would be so devastating that I doubted very much whether it would matter to me if I lived or died—or was sold as a slave…

"I'm sorry," I whispered. "I can't even begin to imagine how you must feel."

"I try not to dwell on it."

He was thinking about it then, of course, for the sadness emanating from him was almost palpable, and I felt tears stinging my eyes. "I'm sorry I brought it up," I said. "Please forgive me. I won't mention it again."

He nodded briefly and gestured toward a bench near the fountain where a flowering vine bloomed, forming an arch overhead. "You said you wanted to sit down," he reminded me.

Blinking back unshed tears, I took a seat on the bench, telling myself firmly that Darconia was not the place for tears. Crying was simply a waste of water— and I needed all I could get.

Taking a cup from a niche in the wall by the fountain, Tychar dipped it into the basin and brought it to me.

"To drink from this cup is reputed to bring good fortune," he said. "May it find you, as well."

"It hasn't done much for the slaves who live here, has it?"

"We are all alive and well," he said reasonably. "How much more can anyone wish for?"

"You said you wanted love," I reminded him. "Have you forgotten?"

"No," he replied. "But I was speaking of the other slaves, not just of myself." He smiled, but his gaze conveyed a different emotion. "I have drunk from this fountain many times, but my good fortune was long in coming."

"You say that as though your good fortune had already arrived," I observed. "Has it?"

His eyes softened. "Yes, Kyra," he said. "It has. *You* are my good fortune—a beautiful woman for me to love and who will love me in return."

I already felt weak, but what he was saying made it even worse. I needed to drink a lot more water if I was ever to hold my own with him. Taking a long sip, I could almost feel the water giving me strength and thought that perhaps the fact that water is necessary for life was the only good fortune it could bring—enabling you to go on living long enough to give good fortune the opportunity to seek you out.

Good fortune. To love and be loved. The words kept running through my mind, repeating over and over again. What better good fortune could there be than to love and be loved? I was already alive and well, with work that I enjoyed, so the pursuit of happiness was all that remained, and I had an idea it was standing right there in front of me. I had only to reach out and take it—or ask for it.

Tychar interrupted my thoughts, taking the cup and returning it to its niche. "Come, Kyra," he said. "It is time for the midday meal."

He was holding out his hand and I placed mine within it. It was a simple, polite gesture, but as we touched and he pulled me to my feet, I wanted to go the rest of the way, into his arms to hold him, to kiss him, and to love him. But I knew he wouldn't do anything unless I asked him to. I stared at his lips, feeling an overwhelming desire to taste them. I wanted to kiss him so badly, and all I had to say was, "Kiss me."

Apparently, I had, because he leaned down and touched my lips, whisper soft, warm, gentle—and sweet. Not like sugar, but with a sweetness that went far beyond that. No one had ever kissed me that way. It was as though he was trying to tell me just how long he'd waited for me, how he'd almost given up hope, and that if his happiness could be anything, he wanted it to be me. I sank into him then, my body flooded with desire, and for one blissful moment, I thought that perhaps, just perhaps, at some point, I could even ask him for more.

"Having fun?" another voice said mockingly.

Pulling away from Tychar, I saw that it was his brother Trag, and if my tiger was gentle and loving, this one was just the opposite, for his green eyes were ablaze with a barely suppressed anger, bordering on hatred.

My first thought was to make a run for it, but I had no idea where to go. We were in a part of the palace that I knew was well away from my own rooms, but I had no clue how to get there from where I stood.

"So, the little teacher lady is consorting with the slave boys, is she?" he snarled. "That's funny, I wouldn't have thought it of you."

What he didn't know about me would have filled a ten-zillion gigabyte memory chip, but at the time, I was too stunned to point that out to him. If I'd thought Scalia would be irked that I'd kissed one of her slaves, her displeasure was nothing when compared with his. I stuttered something in protest, but he cut me off.

"Scalia certainly knew what she was doing when she brought you here, didn't she? Just look at him," he spat out with a scornful glance at Tychar. "His cock's so hard, it's a wonder he can even walk."

Evidently, unlike his brother, Trag wasn't all that taken with human females. He was so different from Tychar—it was almost as if the difference in their coloring also reflected a difference in temperament. Even his speech patterns were different—less formal than Tychar's—and his voice had a biting sarcasm that seemed to tear chunks out of my flesh. I was about to stammer out some feeble excuse or other, but then I realized that I was being chewed out by a slave, and, to be quite honest, it got my dander up.

I wanted to tell him to shut up, but decided on a more subtle strategy. Glancing up at Tychar, I smiled grimly. "Does he talk to the Queen that way?"

Tychar laughed, saying, "She likes his fierceness, but no, he doesn't, and he should not be speaking to *you* in that manner, either." He followed that up with a glare at Trag, which promised retribution at some later date.

Trag backed down slightly, but with a bit of a snarl.

"You're only angry because she preferred me to you," Tychar went on. "Admit it."

"She could have had both of us," Trag growled. "Scalia wouldn't have cared."

I stared at him in disbelief. His anger had nothing to do with who I was or where I came from, but was simply due to the fact that I'd chosen his brother instead of himself! *Typical male...* "Humans are monogamous," I interjected quickly, then had to add, "most of the time." Actually, I'd never had the option of being anything *but* monogamous, and the thought of being able to have both of them was making me a bit weak in the knees. "Besides, all I *did* was kiss him," I pointed out. "It wasn't like we actually did anything—" I paused, searching for the right words, but Trag cut me off.

"Oh, you'll mate with him," Trag said hotly. "It's just a matter of time. Every woman he's ever met has wanted him—he's so damned smooth—you just wait and see. It'll happen, and I'll get left out in the cold—again!"

"I am not to blame for your misfortunes," Tychar chuckled. "And I had no part in Scalia's decision."

"No?" Trag said mockingly. "Scalia must have had *some* reason for picking you over me. Did she owe you a favor, or what?"

Tychar smiled roguishly. "*You* never have learned how to deal with the women of this world—or any other—have you?"

"Yes, I have!" Trag hissed. "I've had women in lots of places!"

"Spaceport brothels," Tychar scoffed. "Women who flatter you only because you pay them."

I stood there, watching helplessly as sparks seemed to fly between them, thinking that Scalia had better do something soon, or her two cats were going to kill each other.

Then it occurred to me that they were fighting over *me*. I'd never been fought over in my entire life, and now these two incredibly hot studs were about to duke it out for the chance to be my love slave! My knees turned to jelly, and I staggered back to the bench and sat down heavily. I felt quite faint and was getting hotter by the second, my skin growing slick with sweat and my hands clammy and trembling. "You guys stop that," I said, surprised that I had the strength to get the words out. It's funny how excessive heat can take you from romance and passion to unconsciousness in the blink of an eye. Obviously, I couldn't let myself get too emotional during my sojourn on Darconia, or I was going to be fainting on a regular basis. And what was it you were supposed to do when you felt faint? Put your head between your knees?

I tried it, but to be quite honest, it didn't seem to help very much. I would have given a queen's ransom for a little ice at that point, but I had an idea that they'd probably never even *heard* of ice on this boiling cauldron of a planet. I was thankful to be sitting down, but with nothing but hard stone surrounding me, I was bound to crack my head open on something if I did happen to faint. With my vision rapidly growing dim, I noted that the two tigers were still all but spitting at each other.

"Forget it, guys," I said weakly. "This heat's gonna kill me before I ever get the chance to 'mate' with anyone."

One of them started toward me—I believe it was Tychar—but that's about all I can remember. I never found any lumps afterward, so I don't think I fell, but my head was still spinning when I came to. It took me a moment to realize that while I was still sitting on the stone bench, I was now being supported between the two of them.

"She's too weak," Trag was saying. "She isn't strong enough to be your mate."

"But just *smell* her, Trag!" Tychar exclaimed. "The scent of her desire is even more intoxicating than that of our own females!"

"No," Trag disagreed. "You've only forgotten. She's not Zetithian, Ty, and as I said before, she is weak."

It sounded like Trag had a bad case of sour grapes, because not long before, he'd been talking about a threesome, and now he seemed to be trying to talk his brother out of mating with me altogether! Of course, when he'd said I was too weak for Tychar, he hadn't exactly excluded himself. I wondered what the difference was; they both seemed to be similarly equipped, but perhaps Tychar was a wilder ride than Trag. Even so, I wasn't about to let him talk Tychar out of anything—at least, not yet. I might have been barely conscious at the time, but I'd been feeling plenty of desire before we were interrupted, and, aside from that, I was curious. That "I will give you joy unlike any you have ever known" remark had me downright intrigued.

"Weak, am I?" I grumbled. "And how many times did *you* pass out before you got used to this horrible climate?"

Trag didn't reply, but Tychar laughed out loud. "You will adjust," he said firmly. "As we did."

"If I live long enough," I said grimly. "You know, I think this tour of the palace should have waited a couple of days. I feel like I ought to stay in bed for a while."

At the mere mention of my bed, they were both on their feet instantly, and Tychar gathered me up in his arms. Trag got me another drink from the fountain, and before I knew it, I was being carried swiftly back to my room.

Having just kissed him, being held against Tychar's chest while he carried me was almost enough to make me pass out again, but I did my best to remain conscious enough to enjoy it. I wanted nothing more than to curl up with him forever—along with a big pitcher of water and a bucketful of the juiciest fruits and vegetables this dry rock of a planet could produce—and was about to say something to that effect, when Wazak intercepted us in the hallway.

"She is injured?" Wazak asked brusquely. It was a wide corridor, but as big as he was, he effectively blocked our path

"She was overcome by the heat," Tychar explained.

"This should not be allowed," Wazak said sternly. "See that it does not happen again." With a glare which was undoubtedly meant to be intimidating, he swept on past us, his tail waving behind him.

"Whoo-hoo!" I exclaimed softly when we were out of earshot. "Good thing you didn't slug me when you caught me kissing your brother, Trag! You'd have been locked up in the real jail for that, and then the only sex you could ever have would be with a lizard named Grunge."

"That's about all I can get as it is," Trag muttered ruefully. "Not that I'd want it." He blew out a pent-up breath. "Are you *sure* you wouldn't like to bed down with both of us?" he asked hopefully. "I didn't really mean it when I said you were weak."

"I'm sure you didn't," I said, "but right now, I don't think I'm up to bedding down with one man, let alone two! Besides, that would be too… promiscuous—or greedy!—which, as a general rule, I am not. "

"I'm sure you aren't!" Trag said hastily. He seemed to be regretting his earlier show of temper. "It's just that I—" He paused there and gave his hair a yank in frustration. "Oh, shit! I blew it, didn't I?"

"Probably so," I agreed, though the thought of having both of them was beginning to grow on me. I thought it best to change the subject.

"Hey, tell me something," I began. "How come you two talk so differently? I thought you were brothers, but you don't even have the same accent."

"I wasn't raised on Zetith," Trag replied. "I lived with our uncle, who owned a space freighter, which he taught me to pilot. We spent a lot of time in space—and in spaceports, too, so I learned a few things the guys back home *didn't*—and I was on my way back home to find a mate when I got caught in the middle of the war."

"Tough luck," I remarked, hoping to sound reasonably sympathetic.

"Yeah, it was," he agreed. "And as for the way Tychar talks, I think he only hangs on to that Zetithian accent because all the women around here seem to like it—sounds really suave, you know? I've *taught* him the right way to talk—and he does most of the time—but sometimes he holds onto the old ways a little too tight."

"Nothing wrong with that," I said, "though he seems to be a little bit more progressive than you are in other ways. After all, *he* hasn't held it against me that I'm not Zetithian!"

"I don't think he does, either," said Tychar.

Following his downward glance, I saw why. Trag's cock was every bit as hard as Tychar's had been all day. "I haven't had a hard-on in twenty years!" Trag declared. "Almost forgotten what it feels like. None of the women around here smell good to us at all, but Tychar was right, because you smell absolutely fabulous."

Tychar grinned knowingly. "I told you so."

"Sorry, Trag," I said meekly. "Didn't mean to get you all hot and bothered."

"Oh, I'm not complaining," he assured me, "it's just that I have an idea it's not gonna do me a damn bit of good to have one unless Scalia shows up real quick."

"The Queen?" I exclaimed, aghast at the notion that Scalia would consort with her slaves. It seemed rather medieval of her—though perhaps no more medieval than having slaves to begin with.

"She wants to have sex with anything that has a cock," Trag said roundly. "But we couldn't do it with her. Pissed her off a bit, I think. Been fucked by lots of the others, though."

"So it *is* a harem!" I exclaimed. "I thought so!"

"Harem?" Tychar said curiously. "I don't believe I've ever heard that word before."

"It's an old Earth custom in desert countries," I explained. "The Sultan, or king, would have a whole bevy of females to choose from. They were kept locked up in a seraglio, which, by all accounts, was very similar to your quarters. Same idea, it's just that Scalia's put a slightly different spin on it."

"She still likes us, even if we can't fuck her," Trag said. "It makes her hot just looking at us, and that stiff one Tychar got last night wowed her but good."

"She did seem rather pleased by it," Tychar remarked, dropping a kiss on the top of my head. "As was I," he added.

Of course, it was nothing when compared to the effect the mere sight of him smiling at me had had on me—and I think I would have noticed if he'd ejaculated, because it was bound to have been a rather spectacular explosion after twenty years—but I didn't see any need to tell him that. Not yet, anyway. He already seemed to be taking enough "liberties" as it was, since I hadn't asked him to kiss me again, though perhaps I only needed to ask him once. Not that I would ever complain; he could kiss me all he liked, just as long as I didn't pass out again.

"Not to change the subject, or anything," I said, "but how long *did* it take you guys to get used to the heat? These fainting spells could get old in a hurry."

"Not long," Tychar replied. His lips brushed my ear as he added in a voice that promised a myriad of sensual delights, "And in the meantime, I will take *very* good care of you."

"You just need to take it easy for a few days," Trag advised. "Spend a little time on your back."

"Very funny," I said. "You know, your brother is an absolute riot," I said to Tychar. "And to think, you've had to put up with him for twenty years! How did you stand it?"

Tychar rolled his eyes. "I have *no* idea."

"Well, if you guys don't mind, I believe I will spend some time on my back, *but*," I went on as Trag started to snicker, "if either of you have any ideas about climbing on top of me, I wish you'd save them until I'm feeling more up to it. Just being in the same room with the two of you is bad enough."

"Hey, man, I think she likes us," Trag said, nudging Tychar.

"My, but you're a cocky little bastard," I remarked. "Especially for a man who's been essentially impotent for so long."

"But I'm not anymore," he pointed out, wrapping his hand around his dick and giving it a hard squeeze. "I might not ever get to use it, but at least I've got one, and the way I see it, we both have an equal chance."

"Really? And why is that? Tychar is the one assigned to look after me, not you."

"But that doesn't mean I can't find lots of reasons to visit," Trag argued. "I can be as charming as he is, you know."

Somehow I doubted that. Tychar had made a very good first impression on me, and Trag was running a distant second at that point.

"You're probably a lot of fun," I said reflectively, "but I still think I like Tychar better. He's absolutely charming." Of course, I could have added adorably sexy and impossibly handsome to that, but I didn't want to rub it in.

"It's the blue eyes, isn't it?" Trag exclaimed. "Always with the eyes! I tell you, if I've heard it once, I've heard it a thousand times! 'Oh, his eyes are so blue!' Makes me want to throw up every time Scalia says it!"

"She has *never* said that!" Tychar protested. "At least, not that I've heard."

"Of course you wouldn't!" Trag snarled. "She doesn't say things like that to your face; she tells me!"

"Do you really think she likes him better?" I asked Trag.

"I'm *sure* she does," Trag said irritably. "Everyone always *has* liked him best! I can't figure it out. All the other women around here seem to like him better, too—they're always flirting with him and telling him how wonderful he is. What's so wrong with green eyes, anyway?"

"Did I say it had anything to do with his eyes?"

"Well, no, but—"

"He smiled at me, Trag," I said gently. "You stood there looking like you wanted to scratch my eyes out."

"Well, okay, you're right about that much," Trag admitted. "It's just that I thought Scalia wanted to show us off to one of her friends, that's all."

"Don't like being an oddity?" I ventured.

"Something like that," he replied.

We arrived at my room, and Tychar laid me down on the bed while Trag went off to get some more water. I drank as much as I could hold without getting sick and then tried to rest, but it's hard to relax when you've got two tigers prowling around your room.

Tychar sat beside me with his arm draped lovingly around my shoulders while he fed me fruit from a crystal bowl. His apparent intent was to get some food into me, but he was driving me wild by barely touching my lips with each bit he offered me—just being that close to him was enough to inspire some of the most erotic thoughts I'd ever had.

When I couldn't hold anymore, he moved to the foot of the bed to massage my feet. Having a man give me a foot massage has always been a particular fantasy of mine, but just how he knew it I didn't know and didn't care, because it felt *wonderful*.

As I lay drifting in a haze of sensuous delight, Trag busied himself with checking out the contents of my wardrobe, which he considered to be quite inappropriate for the local climate.

"You need to wear less," he advised. "These long, flowing dresses of yours trap the heat too much."

"Maybe," I admitted, "but that's what I wear most of the time at home. I didn't bring much else."

"Well, we'll have to figure something out," he insisted. "The trouble is, there aren't many people around here who are any good at making clothes."

"Don't you have something else to do at this hour?" Tychar asked innocently.

"Want to get rid of me?" said Trag.

"Yes, I believe I do," Tychar agreed.

"Hey, I'm smiling, Kyra!" Trag insisted, showing his teeth. "Don't I look… you know… enticing?"

"You look more like you're about to bite me," was my honest reply. "When he smiled at me I—" Then I remembered that I hadn't intended to mention what happened when Tychar smiled at me, but I didn't need to, because Trag supplied his own reason.

"Yeah, you turned to mush or something," he said ruefully. "I know, I saw it, too."

"Trag," I said gently.

"What?" he all but barked at me.

"I'm sorry." And I meant it, too. He wasn't as charming as Tychar, perhaps, but he had his good points. I might not have fallen for him on sight, but I *did* like him.

Trag stopped short at the foot of the bed. "Yeah, well, so am I," he grumbled. "Story of my life. I guess Scalia knew what she was doing after all—but if you ever change your mind…"

"I'll know who to ask for," I said promptly.

"Well, yeah—and just be sure you don't ask for Refdeck," he advised. "He's a slimy little bastard— even if he *can* fuck Scalia." He said that as though he wished he'd been able to do it himself, and—who knows?—perhaps he did. "She likes him pretty well."

"Refdeck? Slimy? You mean the little toad guy?" I asked, aghast.

Trag nodded, though I, for one, couldn't see him with Scalia. I mean, if she rolled over on Refdeck, she'd probably kill him. I lay there trying to imagine the position they'd have to get in to do it with any degree of safety and couldn't come up with one. Then I decided it was one of those details that I really didn't want to know anyway. Tychar massaging my feet was much more pleasant to contemplate, but then I remembered that he was a slave, too, and the fact that no man had ever done anything like that for me before who *wasn't* a slave made me want to cry again—which was a bad idea, since I was already hot and dehydrated.

Still, I reminded myself that looking after me was a job that at least one other of Scalia's slaves seemed to want rather badly. But it was all so strange and confusing—my brain probably wasn't working very well, aside from the fact that a lot had happened— especially when you consider that I'd only been on Darconia for less than a day and had yet to give even one piano lesson.

I groaned, rolling over in bed. "This is all just too weird! I shoulda stayed home," I lamented. "What was I thinking?"

I felt Tychar's hands grow still on my feet. "Are you saying you don't like it here?"

From his tone, I could only assume he was taking it personally. He might as well have asked if I didn't like *him*. "That's not what I meant," I said. "It's just that I'm not an adventuress by any stretch of the imagination, and it's a miracle I've made it this far without turning tail for home. I mean, I've never even been out of the *country*, let alone the world! And now that I'm here, one minute I'm feeling pretty good, and the next I'm passing out on the floor. And, let's face it; you guys are just too much for a little ol' piano teacher from Upper Sandusky."

"Maybe," Trag said as he looked down at me rather wistfully. "But if you'd just say the word, we could make you *so* glad you came."

"I'm sure you would, but—"

Tychar let go of my foot and crawled toward me on his hands and knees like a tiger stalking his prey. "I, for one, am already glad you came," he purred. "And I promise you, Kyra, you will *never* want to leave Darconia."

The look in his eyes was enough to assure me that he was telling the absolute truth. I might have been too much of a chicken to do anything about it at the time, but I believed him, too.

Chapter 7

WHEN ZEALON CAME BACK FOR HER LESSON, I WAS ASLEEP with Tychar curled up at the foot of the bed, purring contentedly. This time, I drank as much water as I could hold and *then* got up, but my skin was still gritty with salt. That was the trouble here; I was hot as hell and was undoubtedly sweating as a result, but it evaporated so quickly that I didn't even realize it was happening. I figured if I just kept drinking no matter what, I'd be okay, but I was probably losing more than just water…

Still, the Zetithians had survived this climate for a long time, and they seemed to be fairly human, at least from a metabolic standpoint. I was to learn that the Darconians became rather sluggish with cooler temperatures, and were, therefore, much more active in the heat of the day, but I knew that to survive, I was going to have to develop the siesta habit. Tychar, for one, seemed to think that a nap in the middle of the day was an excellent notion, and since he had only me to look after, he didn't need to do anything but sleep whenever I did. Zealon thought it was rather odd, though.

"You're sleeping *now*?" she exclaimed but kept her voice down so as not to wake Tychar. At least she was that considerate of him, even if he was a slave. "Are you really that tired?"

"You don't know the half of it," I replied. "It's going to take me a long time to adjust to this heat. It's not so bad morning and evening, but the middle of the day? Forget it! Give me a nice, climate-controlled building every time."

She looked at me curiously, as though unable to decide if I was being serious or not.

"My internal clock needs resetting, too."

"What do you mean?"

"Back home we call it jet lag, and even though jets are a thing of the past, the basic principles still apply. When you travel from one time zone to another, it takes a while to get used to it. I guess you could call it space lag in this case, though."

Zealon nodded, but I had an idea she was just humoring me. Perhaps lizards weren't affected by such things, though it was doubtful that she'd ever traveled much.

"He looks pretty when he's asleep, doesn't he?" she remarked with a gesture toward the foot of the bed. "I've never seen him sleeping."

"Never seen him eat anything either, have you?" I said with a touch of sarcasm. Then it occurred to me that I should watch my mouth more carefully—after all, she was a princess—but she'd have to learn to watch what she said to a groggy human, too.

"No," she conceded. "Does he look pretty when he eats?"

"Not really," I said. "Well, no more so than anyone else does."

She appeared to think about this for a moment. "You don't approve of my mother having slaves, do you?"

"No," I replied. "It's wrong on a multitude of levels. If your mother wishes to bring Darconia into the mainstream of galactic society, she needs to rethink that."

"But their safety…"

"There are other ways of protecting people besides keeping them locked up as slaves," I pointed out.

"But are you going to refuse to have Tycharian as your servant? I know I wouldn't."

"No," I replied. "I'm not going to refuse, though I probably should—and just on principle alone. But your mother was right; I do need someone to help me out. He had to carry me back here after taking me on a tour of the palace. Funny thing is, I've never considered myself to be a weakling, but this heat is sapping the life out of me."

"I hope you can become accustomed to it," she said, and her sincerity was evident. "It's… nice having someone here who's been to other planets and isn't one of us. Mother says she enjoys the diversity of having off-worlders here, and I tend to agree. I hope to learn more from you than how to play the piano."

"Well, you're not going to learn even that much if I don't get up and teach you," I said, making the gargantuan effort just to sit up. "Come on, then. Let's see if you can play, shall we?"

We left Tychar where he was, and I fought the urge to throw a sheet over him, but decided he was probably warm enough. And Zealon was right; he did look pretty when he was asleep.

I sat Zealon down on the piano bench, and unlike a concert pianist who *wore* tails, she actually *had* one. It looked like something out of a bizarre dream to see her sitting there, running her odd fingers over the keys.

"Now, the first thing to be able to find is middle C," I began. "Right here," I said, striking a key, "to the left of this set of two black keys. Everything else revolves around that point." I showed her how the fingering worked, giving each of her fingers a number designation—fortunately, she had four fingers and a thumb, or we'd have had to redesign a lot of things.

I set her to practicing scales, just like any other student, and noted that while she was dexterous enough, the pads of her fingertips were almost too large to avoid striking more than one key at a time. But she had a decent reach—better than mine, though not as much as Wazak's would have been had he played. He probably could have played a duet with himself!

After standing over her for a while and offering a bit of praise and encouragement, I left her to practice and drifted over to the window, which had a seat beneath it like the one in my bedroom. I sat gazing out over the trees, thinking to myself that beings were much the same the galaxy over, they only looked different.

But what would it be like to be intimate with an alien? I couldn't imagine why Scalia would want to have sex with a toad, and while Refdeck might be *able* to do it, why would he want to, either? The only male Darconian I'd had much contact with thus far was Wazak, and when I looked at him, desire for sex was absolutely the very *last* thing on my mind, and I doubted that he felt any desire for me, either. They were too different from humans—unlike the Zetithians, who were quite similar, save for a few superficial differences.

And the tigers certainly were, to use their own description, enticing! And that line about giving me joy unlike any I had ever known—was that a standard line which had been used on females of their species down through the ages, or had Tychar come up with it himself? Trag hadn't said it word for word, but even though he hadn't been raised on Zetith, he'd said something similar, like he knew something I didn't. I couldn't imagine how much different sex could be with them as opposed to another human, but I had an idea that my curiosity might get the better of me at some point—and this was aside from the fact that they were both irresistible. I will admit here that any sexual relations I'd ever had before had usually not come about as the result of my own instigation, nor had the episodes been frequent or particularly pleasant. I had an idea that with Tychar, it would at least be memorable.

Still, the ethics of my current situation were troubling to me. I was so strongly attracted to him, but I wasn't sure just what it would take to forget my reservations and get me to take the plunge.

If I spent enough time on Darconia, I knew that I would become accustomed to the climate, as well as its inhabitants—Tychar and Trag, included. It was only natural that I'd be curious, if not intrigued by them. It was simply the novelty of having sex with someone different—and sex with an alien was just about as different as you could get—which was probably why Scalia did it. It wasn't love and perhaps not even lust. Just curiosity.

I wasn't quite so jaded—at least, not yet—because I was still holding out for love, and while Tychar *claimed* to be looking for love, Trag only seemed attracted to me because of my scent. Of course, what it all boiled down to was that they were both highly sexual beings who hadn't gotten any in the past twenty years. I couldn't say that for myself, but I *had* gone my entire life without a grand passion. It could have been that I simply didn't have it in me to ever let myself experience such things, but when I played a Mozart concerto, I got an inkling of the way it was supposed to feel, and I knew that I never had.

Giving Zealon a few more instructions, I left her briefly and then looked in on Tychar, who was now awake and in the process of making my bed—yet another thing no man had ever done for me. A discordant note from the other room provided the likely reason that he wasn't able to sleep, but I also noticed that he was humming the scale and grimacing whenever she missed a note. Obviously, he was no stranger to music, which made me wonder about the music they might have had on his own world. How many songs, how much history, how many souls would be lost with the destruction of an entire planet? Every culture had its own unique music. When I thought of the hundreds of musical pieces that I had ever played, and the multitude of others that I had only heard, I felt an overwhelming sadness for all of those songs of Zetith— love songs, ballads, symphonies, silly little children's ditties, raunchy drinking songs, reverent anthems, even funeral dirges—all that might have been lost, never to be heard again. The loss of the people, themselves, was tragic enough, but their entire culture—all that they had learned, had worked for, had lived and died for—was lost as well, and it saddened me beyond belief.

Tychar looked up just then, and seeing my tragic expression, he must have assumed that it was Zealon's less than beautiful efforts at the piano which were responsible.

Chucking in amusement, he said, "Her playing is not so bad, Kyra. She will improve."

"I know," I said quietly. "It isn't that." Actually, it was thinking about him that was making me sad, but it wasn't something that I felt I could admit at the time. "I heard you humming," I said instead. "Do you enjoy music?"

"Yes," he replied. "But not Darconian music."

"I haven't heard any," I remarked. "Is it really that bad?"

"I don't believe you would call it music," he said with a glimmer of a smile. Noting my look of surprise, he added, "I heard you playing this morning. Darconian music is very… different."

"You liked what I played, then?"

"Yes, I did," he replied. "You play very well."

"Thank you," I said, the warmth of his smile causing me to blush. My playing had been praised before, but for some reason, it meant more coming from him. "Do you—" I paused as I considered the best way to ask, but decided that there was no easy way. "Do you remember any songs from your own world?"

He nodded, but gave me no clue as to how he might feel about sharing them.

"Would you sing them for me sometime?" I went on. "I'd like to hear them."

He looked at me curiously, as if not quite sure why I would ask, but I thought I saw a trace of suspicion there, too. "I don't remember them very well," he said evasively.

"Well, just think about it, then," I said. "I'm not going anywhere—at least, not for a while. You know where to find me."

Tychar left the bedside and crossed the floor to where the pitcher stood, pouring out a glass of water which he then brought to me, his own expression carefully neutral. "You did not drink when you arose," he said.

"What? Oh—no, I suppose I didn't," I said, momentarily confused. "No, wait a minute, I did, but you were still asleep. Thanks for reminding me, though, because I sure don't want Wazak fussing at me all the time!"

"He was not fussing at *you*," Tychar said, borrowing that distinctively Terran expression from me, though I doubted he'd ever heard it before. "He was fussing at *me*."

"Humph! Like it was all your fault." I took the glass anyway and took a long drink, only then noticing how thirsty I was.

"Your welfare is my responsibility," he said in a wooden voice.

I took another sip and decided to find out why he was acting so stiff. "Is something wrong? You changed the subject just now," I said, scrutinizing him closely. "Why?"

A variety of emotions washed over his feline features before he seemed to withdraw further into himself, his eyes not quite meeting my own. "I am… uncomfortable discussing what I remember of Zetith," he said.

Only then did I recall our earlier conversation. "And stupid me, I forgot I wasn't going to mention it again!" I said ruefully. "I'm sorry, Tychar, I—I wasn't thinking! But you know, even though music might be one of the more painful things to remember about a lost world, it's also one of the more meaningful things to try to preserve."

He appeared to consider this, but then winced as Zealon hit another sour note from the adjoining room.

"You've obviously got a good ear," I remarked. "Can you sing?"

He shrugged in reply, as nearly everyone does when asked that question. No one ever thinks they can sing—even some highly paid professionals.

"Well, what if I teach you some Earth songs," I suggested, "and then we'll see about the songs of Zetith."

He nodded briefly and went on with his work. He would do whatever I told him to, of course—would sing every song he knew if I demanded it of him—but I thought it best to let it be his idea, rather than mine. And since we'd be together for the greater part of each day, there would be plenty of opportunities for me to encourage him to change his mind.

Meanwhile, I thought Zealon had gone on long enough for a first lesson, so I sent her on to do whatever it was she normally did at that hour, but, surprisingly, she elected to stay there in my room. I thought it was a bit odd, but perhaps it was simply because she was lonely.

"Ever go out?" I asked her. "Or is a princess stuck in the castle all the time?"

"Takes an armed squadron for me to go out," she grumbled. "The closest I ever get to freedom is sneaking off to visit the slave quarters."

"I think that's just about the best example of irony I've ever heard," I said dryly. "But it *is* a nice place. Tychar took me there this morning," I added.

"Yes, it is beautiful," Zealon agreed. "And you're right, it's pretty ironic that I would feel free in one of the most secure areas of the palace, but that's the way it is. Maybe it's because Mother doesn't want me spending time with her slaves—or even to know they exist—but it's about the most fun I ever have."

"A touch of rebellion always adds spice to a young person's life," I conceded. "But surely you aren't alone *all* the time."

She shrugged. "I see a few people from outside sometimes—we get the occasional visitors from other planets, which are becoming more frequent nowadays—but I don't get the chance to spend much time with others of my own age."

I nodded. No wonder she seemed so mature! "And slaves, guards, and servants are all you've got as companions?"

"Yeah, I guess so."

"But not like having friends of your own, is it?"

"No, but I've learned lots of interesting things from them. For instance, did you know that Trag used to be a pilot on a space freighter?"

"No, I didn't."

"Well, he was," she declared. "Says he can fly anything."

Tychar was on the other side of the room, dusting the furniture with a scrail cloth, but I heard him make an odd sound. I couldn't tell if he was laughing or had choked on the dust he was raising—though there didn't seem to be much of it in the air, since scrail was pretty effective at trapping dirt.

"Care to comment on that, Tychar?" I asked.

"Trag might have been able to fly anything twenty years ago," he replied. "But I doubt if that would be true now."

"Technology *does* change," I agreed. "But the basic principles would stay the same, wouldn't they?"

"Possibly," he conceded.

"And you were a soldier, weren't you?" Zealon ventured. Tychar nodded his reply, and she went on. "So if someone handed you a pulse pistol, you'd know what to do with it, wouldn't you?"

"It's true that I was once a soldier," he said warily. "But that was a very long time ago."

Looking at him then, I'd have had to say he didn't look as if he'd ever been one. Oh, sure, the strong-looking muscles were still there, and there was something about the way he carried himself that suggested it, but, let's face it: he had hair down to his waist, was nude except for his two jeweled collars, and he was dusting my room, for heaven's sake! He looked fabulous, of course, but certainly not like any soldier I'd ever seen. Still, looks can be deceiving.

Tychar must have noticed me staring at him, because his eyes met mine just then and, lowering his eyelids ever so slightly, sent a suggestive little grin in my direction— which hit me right between the thighs and made me wish that Zealon would disappear so I could spend the rest of the afternoon playing with my new slave boy. That smile of his did the strangest things to me! I decided I would simply have to forbid him to smile at me anymore, but that would mean depriving myself of one of the few perks that went along with this job. Living in the palace and having plenty of free time was okay, and the Steinway was a dream, but I had an idea that once I'd learned my way around and wasn't fainting all the time, it could get pretty boring. So far, having Tychar and Trag around was what had made it interesting. I'd have to do a lot of piano playing myself or develop some other sort of hobby; otherwise, I'd be as lonely as Zealon. This was possibly why Scalia had hired me to begin with—not as a subject in a breeding program, but as a companion for her daughter. Still, she'd given me Tychar…

My mind wandered a bit. Zealon had changed the subject and was now chattering on about the piano and how much she liked playing it. I nodded absently, because what I was thinking about was playing a different instrument entirely. In my mind, I was exploring Tychar's body, massaging his back and shoulders, pinching his buns, running my fingers through his hair—and that was just the back side of him! Rolling him over, I would find even better parts: his lips, his eyes, and, of course, that incredible cock. I imagined lying on the bed between his legs, licking and sucking and pumping it with my hands until he came in my face. I could almost feel the heat of his thick, luscious semen as it hit me right in the mouth and ran down my chin. Then it occurred to me that this was probably the part of him that would taste sweet…

All at once I became aware that Zealon had stopped talking and was now looking at me expectantly. She'd obviously asked me something and was just as obviously expecting an answer—and I had no idea what the question was.

"Forgive me," I said quickly. "My mind must have wandered—crazy from the heat, I guess. What did you say?"

"I said, how long before I can play a real song?" she repeated.

"Sooner than you might think," I replied. "There are lots of short little songs that will help you learn."

"What about the one you played this morning?"

"I hate to disappoint you, but you won't be playing that one anytime soon. Sorry."

"Oh, I'm not," she said, actually seeming to be rather pleased by this. "That just means you'll have to stay here until I do."

Like I said before, she was lonely.

We talked for a while, and she told me I'd be having dinner with the Queen again. But they had other guests, so it wouldn't be just the family.

"Who is it?" I inquired. "Do you know?"

"Oh, just some government people," she said dismissively. "Nobody special."

Nobody special. That may have been true, but they were undoubtedly people who weren't supposed to know about Scalia's harem, so we probably wouldn't be served by any of the slave boys—at least not the two tigers, since their existence seemed to be one of the more closely guarded palace secrets. Scalia probably had other Darconian servants on hand for such occasions, which meant that I'd be the only offworlder in a room full of Darconians—and they all looked pretty much alike. So far Wazak, Scalia, Zealon, and maybe Cernada were the only ones I could identify on sight. There were always some about, of course, but if I'd ever seen the same ones twice, you couldn't have proved it by me. I'd have to start paying more attention to them and look for differences in size, coloring, speech patterns, etc. Of course, if none of them ever introduced themselves, I might have to come up with my own names for them. The best I could tell, most of them weren't what you'd call gregarious—unless they were flirting with Tychar. It was no wonder Scalia liked her slaves so much.

Zealon left us then, promising to see me at dinner, and I was alone with Tychar again. Fortunately, he wasn't smiling, because if he had smiled at me again—or made a move of any kind, I think I would have been on him like white on rice. At least that would give me something to do with my time, but I really did need to get in some piano practice. I was only speculating, of course, but Tychar looked as if he could keep me busy for hours on end—days, even. I wondered just how I would go about asking him to do that—I was such a wuss, after all. Getting him to sing for me was going to be tricky enough.

I left him to his work and went into the adjoining room and sat down at the piano, playing little melodies at random and thinking that perhaps I could try my hand at composing again. I'd done a little bit over the years, but hadn't finished anything as yet—nothing good, anyway.

Pulling my music tablet out of my bag, I set it up for a blank score. I thought I'd start off with a song or two, work up to a sonata, and then I might even attempt a symphony. God knows I'd have plenty of time…

I'd been playing for a short while, but was no closer to coming up with anything worth saving than I'd been when I began. I needed some inspiration, though the piano itself should have been enough. How many worlds had it been to, how many different species had played it, and in what style? If only it could speak…

It was rather dusty, I noticed. Besides rocks, dust was another thing they had in abundance on Darconia. Even in the middle of an oasis, there was dust. I suppose it blew in from the desert all the time, because there always seemed to be a breeze through the windows, which was nice, but it must have carried a lot of desert along with it. The piano must have been cleaned right before I'd arrived, because it had been gleaming that morning, but was now coated with a thin, slightly gritty film.

Tychar came in and began to work on cleaning the music room. Using a dust mop made of scrail cloth, he went over the floor quickly—like he'd done it a million times. After twenty years of doing light housework and not much else, he must have been bored stiff! He'd said he wanted love, but did he also long for adventure? Tychar might have claimed to have adjusted better to being Scalia's slave than Trag had, but just living out your life with nothing much happening had to wear on you after a while, and I began to see why he'd thought being assigned to me would be such a good thing. I was simply something new, a new person to be around and get to know. I was a diversion to him—he'd said being near me pleased him—and the reason for that was fairly obvious. Being sexually aroused after a twenty-year dry spell had to be a noteworthy event.

Having finished with the floor, he asked, "This will not disturb you?" before he began cleaning the piano.

"No," I said ruefully. "It won't bother me a bit. I'm just fiddling around anyway. I thought I might try to write something new, but so far, I haven't come up with a damn thing! You go right ahead—you can even whistle while you work if you like, I don't care. Actually, that might even help."

"Whistle?"

"Yeah," I replied. "You know—" I didn't know the Stantongue word for it, so I had to demonstrate, whistling the first few bars of Beethoven's "Ode to Joy."

"That is very interesting," he remarked. "I don't believe I've ever heard anyone make such a sound."

"Oh, come on!" I protested. "Surely you can whistle, Tychar! Anyone can do that!"

"Can you purr?" he countered with a wry smile.

"Well, no," I admitted, "but you've got—let me see your tongue. Open your mouth."

He did as I asked, sticking out his tongue. He was nothing if not good at following orders. Unfortunately, the words "lick me" ran through my mind just then, and I gasped as a bolt of desire hit me full force.

"Is something wrong?" he asked, noting my odd reaction.

Swallowing hard, I shook my head. "Well, it looks just like mine," I said, trying to regain my composure, "and you can purse your lips. I bet you could do it if you tried. It just takes practice."

"Perhaps you could purr if you tried," he murmured. "It's done with the muscles of the throat and neck."

I watched him carefully, but when I tried it, I couldn't even begin to make the same sound. Chuckling softly, he ran his fingers down the side of my throat. "It is done here," he said. "And it only requires *practice*."

His touch was gentle but sent waves of delight coursing throughout my body.

"You have such lovely skin, Kyra," he purred. "Soft, beautiful…" As he leaned closer, his lips brushed my neck, leaving a trail of heat in their wake, and his purring grew louder. "I will try again," he said.

"To do what?" I asked hoarsely.

He held his reply until his hot tongue had blazed a trail from the base of my neck to my ear, pausing to tease the lobe with the tip of his tongue before blowing gently.

"*Whistle.*"

I'd never known teaching someone to whistle could have such erotic consequences. "You aren't really whistling," I argued, trying to push him away but failing miserably. "You're just blowing. I think you need to practice more."

"I believe I would rather make you purr," he said. "It is more… pleasing than whistling."

"Well, maybe. But you still haven't taught me how," I reminded him.

Tychar shook his head slowly. "I said I would *make* you purr, not teach you how."

Being unable to phrase an articulate reply, my "Oh," came out as more of a moan.

"You would like this?" he asked. The purring sound deepened along with his voice. "I will give you joy."

Which no doubt translated to "I will fuck you senseless" in any other language—something that I wasn't sure I was quite ready for. I shook my head in an attempt to clear his "essence" from my senses. "Okay, so you can't whistle," I said briskly, pushing him away with a surprisingly firm hand, "but I know you can hum! You were humming while Zealon was playing. So hum something."

"You are very persistent," he observed, but complied with my request.

It was an interesting sort of hum, because he was still purring, which added a bass note to accompany the melody. It was an interesting melody, too—one I was sure I'd never heard before. Touching the intake pad on the tablet, I managed to catch part of it. "That's a very pretty song," I said when he stopped. "Would you mind going through it again?"

He didn't reply but began the song again. This time, I got all of it. "Tell me if this is right," I said, playing it back from the notes on the pad.

"Yes," he replied. "That is correct."

"Are there words to it?"

"Yes," he said. "But they are Zetithian. You wouldn't understand them."

"Would you sing it, anyway?" His reluctance was almost palpable, and I wondered if he was put out because I'd pushed him away, or because I was insisting that he do something he preferred not to do. "I could give you something to make it worthwhile, I suppose. Would you mind? Please?"

"As you wish," he said with a sigh. He seemed resigned to the idea, but when his expression changed from a show of reluctance to something more devious, I thought I'd better be careful. "But what will you give me?"

"Oh, I don't know," I muttered. "What do you want?—that I can give you, that is. I haven't got much, you know. Just some clothes, my music, and—"

Catching a glimpse of that provocative smile of his, I realized I'd fallen right into a trap, and it was perfectly obvious what he was going to say even before his lips opened to speak.

"Kiss me," he said. "I will sing every song I know if you will do that—one kiss for each of them," he added with another lip-curling smile.

Remembering the last time I'd kissed him, I had an idea that if I were to do it again, we might never get to the songs—which was possibly his intention.

"You drive a hard bargain for a slave boy," I grumbled. "You're sure you wouldn't rather have something else?"

His smile broadened. "There are many things I would like from you," he said. "But I believe they are worth more than songs."

It didn't take a space engineer to figure *that* one out! "Kisses will do, then," I said, capitulating before the bargain became any more complex. "Do you want payment in advance?"

Tychar looked puzzled. "In advance?"

"I mean before or after the song?" If he asked for it before, like I said, he might never have to sing a note.

"After," he replied, though the way he said it made me think that he still might be taking advantage of me somehow, but I couldn't see it.

Slightly suspicious, I ran through a short intro, and he began. His singing voice was a rich baritone, even more arresting than his speech, but the words were strange. Despite the fact that the Standard Tongue was essentially a mish-mash of words compiled from many different languages throughout the galaxy, I didn't recognize a single one in the song he sang. Obviously, Zetith had been too remote to contribute anything as the common language had developed over the past several centuries. It was small wonder that he had such an odd accent.

Improvising an accompaniment, I let him continue— apparently, there was more than one verse—and his voice seemed to grow stronger and more confident as he went on. I enjoyed listening to him. He might have been singing about anything at all, but not knowing what the words meant didn't seem to matter to me, and I felt myself becoming more drawn to him than ever. Perhaps it was a love song, and he was telling me about a lost love, a love he'd found, or the one he hoped to find. I might never know, because I was sure that a translation would have cost me more, and I already owed him a kiss…

That he was anticipating said event was quite evident, because his cock seemed to get bigger and harder as he went on with the song. When he sang the final note, more of that fluid began dripping from the ruffled corona. I watched out of the corner of my eye as it slid from him and stretched, gleaming, to the floor. My mouth went dry once again, and this time, it had nothing to do with a need for water, because I could feel exactly where all the moisture had gone; I was sitting on it.

"That was beautiful," I whispered.

"So are you," he said.

I raised my face to give him his due, but he had other ideas. Putting a hand on my shoulder, he moved closer, positioning that dripping cock mere centimeters from my lips.

"Kiss me," he said, pulling me closer.

"Why, you sneaky little—!" I exclaimed. "I *knew* there had to be a catch!" Not really, though, because at the time, I couldn't think of many things I'd rather do than to kiss him there—perhaps it would be sweet, just as he'd said.

Pressing my lips to his hot shaft, I found that it wasn't sweet at all, but was slightly salty, and I couldn't help it; I licked him quite thoroughly, just to be sure. If his soft sighs of pleasure meant anything, he was obviously enjoying the kiss, but his reaction was *nothing* compared to mine. Everything below my navel caught fire, and I was immediately wet enough to douse a flaming building. I felt him send out a little jet of fluid against my tongue and was about to suck him into my mouth when an orgasm hit me as suddenly as if I'd been shot with a pulse rifle. Letting go of him, I doubled over, gasping and groaning in an ecstasy I'd never even imagined. Honestly, the climax I'd experienced when I first saw him smile was a little blip in comparison.

I couldn't imagine how it had happened and stared up at him, quite breathless and completely bewildered by it.

"Joy," he whispered. "Unlike any you have ever known?"

"Yes," I gasped. Then I realized what must have happened. "It's a—a hormone or chemical of some kind in that fluid, isn't it?"

He nodded. "This ability was our greatest gift, but it was also our downfall," he said. "It is how we were able to entice our women, but I believe it was also the reason our race was destroyed."

"Once you go cat, you never go back," I murmured—and it was true. I'd never even been penetrated with that fancy cock of his, but I knew in the depths of my soul that no one—with the possible exception of Trag—could ever even begin to compare. I tried to imagine an entire planet full of these guys let loose on an unsuspecting galaxy, and I knew that their species would have spread, stamping out every other mammalian humanoid variety in the known universe in favor of themselves, simply because, once they'd gotten a taste, the women of any world wouldn't have wanted anyone but them. Someone had obviously decided not to let that happen…

From the perspective of those other species, my own included, it might have been for the best, but still, it was a damn shame.

Chapter 8

FIVE SONGS AND AS MANY SPECTACULAR ORGASMS LATER, I changed into a white gown with a halter top and a floor-sweeping skirt and staggered off in Tychar's wake to have dinner with Scalia, only then realizing that he couldn't have gotten much in the way of satisfaction out of the deal, because, as far as I could tell, I was the one experiencing all the fireworks. It was a sort of win-win situation for me—I'd gotten lots of music out of him, and plenty of joy, too—but I wasn't quite sure how he'd benefited, though he certainly hadn't complained!

Of course, I had an idea he was just biding his time. I knew that if I ever did anything more than just kiss him, it was going to be even better, though to be quite honest, such a thing was hard to imagine.

And the music had been so amazing! The songs were hauntingly beautiful, and Tychar not only had a good ear, but also had a voice that was guaranteed to make any woman swoon. He wasn't short on charisma, either; if he ever got on stage, he'd be a galaxy-class superstar in no time. But, of course, as a slave—and one that Scalia didn't care to advertise—that wasn't very likely.

To my dismay, when we neared the slave quarters, Tychar merely gave me directions on how to find the dining room, obviously intending to leave me to face the dragons alone.

"What? You're not coming with me?" I squeaked. "I have to face a whole room full of Darconians all by myself?"

"They will not eat you," he said with a smile and a glance at the guard who opened the door for him. "They are plant-eaters—remember?"

"But you're my attendant, aren't you?" I said desperately. "Don't you have to go wherever I go?"

"Not if there are outsiders present."

"Oh, yeah, right," I said, feeling slightly confused. All those orgasms must have had my brain in worse shape than I thought. "No one's supposed to know you're here, are they? I forgot."

"Most of the time, we simply keep out of sight, but if there are offworlders visiting—or certain other outsiders—we are locked in. Scalia is not sure who our enemies were, so she keeps us hidden from all of them. She fears that we will be hunted down if we are ever seen."

"Didn't stop her from showing off her cats to the new piano teacher," I reminded him.

"Yes, but Earth is too remote to have taken part in our war," he said with a slow smile, "and you, my lovely teacher, do not appear to be a bounty hunter."

"Hey, I can be tough if I have to," I protested, squaring my shoulders and trying to stand up a little straighter—though, even barefoot, he was still the taller of the two of us by several centimeters. "If it's not too hot… and if I have a decent weapon… and maybe an army behind me. Sure, I could go out hunting bad guys. I'd be good at it, too, because no one would ever suspect me."

If the little chortle I heard as the doors closed behind him was any indication, I don't think he took me very seriously—nor did the Darconian who stood guard at the door.

Looking at me appraisingly, he remarked, "No one would suspect you of being anything but a very beautiful woman."

"Oh, what would you know?" I said witheringly.

Shoulders back and head held high, I marched on to the dining room, and the guards let me in. I was slightly surprised that they allowed me to pass without even giving them my name, but then I remembered that I was the only Terran on the whole damn planet, so even if they'd never seen me before, they would have known who I was. I kept forgetting that…

Upon entering the room, I considered it to be quite fortunate that I'd worked up a bit of courage ahead of time, because the room was positively swarming with lizards. When I entered, all sound and movement stopped as each one of them turned to stare at me.

Now, if you've never faced a large dining room full of Darconians, you may not understand just how I felt at that moment, but Scalia obviously did and broke the silence immediately.

"This is Kyra Aramis, our new music teacher," she said proudly. "She is Terran." Glancing around, she added, "From Earth."

Conversation broke out again instantly, and though most of it took the form of hushed murmurs and words I couldn't catch, I still got the distinct impression that their reception of me wasn't entirely friendly. Remembering what Tychar had said about unrest because of Scalia's progressive ways, I figured it would be best if I watched what I said.

Bowing my head slightly, I bade them all a firm "Good evening," and took an empty seat across the table from Zealon. I thought that adding something along the lines of, "It's a pleasure to meet all of you," might have been a shade on the unbelievable side given the circumstances, and since I didn't want to come across as either fawning or insincere, I left it at that. Actually, I decided that keeping my mouth shut except to put food in it might be my best course of action, but there are times when I tend to blurt out whatever I happen to be thinking, regardless of my best intentions.

As far as I could tell, there seemed to be an even mix of males and females. I was getting better at telling the difference—and the strings of beads some of them wore were a good clue—but there were a few present who could have gone either way—small males or rather large females. Then I almost shouted out loud as the light finally dawned on me, for it was color, as well as size, that distinguished the sexes. The females were green with purple, blue or mauve highlights, while the males had either yellow, orange, or red iridescent tints to their otherwise green scales. Rather pleased that I'd managed to figure that out before having to ask someone—Tychar probably would have charged me a kiss for the information—I must have been smiling to myself, because a large female a few seats to my left demanded to know what I found so amusing.

Just how she knew enough about Terrans to know that I was smiling was a mystery to me. I toyed with the idea that she might have been an anthropologist of sorts, but decided against it when I noticed how many beads and bangles she was wearing—certainly not scholarly attire on any planet! I wondered if she was the wife of one of the government officials, but decided I'd best not ask, since she might have been an official herself, especially given Scalia's statement that the men were too volatile to be in charge.

As always, honesty is the best policy. They might even get a chuckle or two out of my lack of knowledge about their kind. "I just figured out how to tell males from females," I replied. "It's the difference in color, isn't it?"

She appeared to be rather affronted by this. "There are many other differences," she said haughtily. "I would begin with the fact that males are much less attractive than females. We are much more refined than they."

Scalia laughed heartily. "Dobraton!" she said with a wave of her arm that set her own bangles to jingling. "Do not be too harsh with the girl. She had never seen a Darconian before yesterday." Glancing sideways at her daughter, she added, "Zealon was supposed to be educating her in the ways of our world, but I can see that she has omitted some rather pertinent details."

As we had mostly discussed music and Scalia's slaves, I was forced to agree; Tychar had taught me far more than Zealon had. "I suppose it's my own fault for not asking the right questions," I said equably. I chose not to mention that the heat was keeping me from being terribly energetic or sharp-witted—or conscious—long enough to devote myself to the study of Darconian biology. Dobraton would undoubtedly have seen my heat intolerance as a sign of weakness, and my instincts told me that weakness was something I should avoid showing to her at all costs—even if I *was* only a piano teacher!

With that in mind, I decided to make a point of drinking water, rather than wine, unless pressed to do so, since passing out at the table would be a grave tactical error. Hopefully, I wouldn't be asked to attend many of these large gatherings once the novelty of having a Terran in the palace wore off, though it did occur to me that Scalia might not tire of it. She might not be able to show off her slaves to just anyone, but I was fair game.

As the dinner progressed, I noticed that Dobraton's ideas seemed to run counter to Scalia's on most topics, especially with regard to becoming more open to off-worlders. She was extremely delicate in her phrasing when it came to voicing her dissent, but the scathing glances Dobraton sent in my direction led me to believe that if she had her way, I would be among the first to be deported. I wondered what she would have thought of Scalia's slaves and decided that this was one person who Scalia definitely needed to keep in the dark! Another thing I noticed was that several of those present were merely giving lip service to Scalia and didn't seem at all unhappy with what Dobraton was saying. But perhaps the most interesting thing I noticed was that Wazak, who was seated across from Dobraton, was about to explode.

Stupid me, I decided to put my foot in it, if for no other reason than to avoid being caught in the middle of the Darconian version of a cat fight. "So, tell me," I said when there was a brief lull in the conversation. "The government here is a monarchy, isn't it? Not a democracy?"

The arrow hit its mark, and Dobraton recoiled as though I'd actually slapped her, but Scalia was the one who answered me.

"A monarchy, yes," she replied. "But with input from a variety of sources."

"A Queen and her council of advisors, then?" I concluded.

"Yes," Scalia said firmly.

"And these advisors," I said with genuine interest, "are they elected, or appointed?"

Scalia seemed absolutely delighted that I'd asked that question. "They are appointed," she said, beaming at me with frank approval.

"And can, therefore, be… removed, if their advice is unsound?"

"Why, yes," Scalia said, putting a lilt in her voice that I hadn't heard before. "Though I have seldom had to do such a thing."

I nodded and went back to making a careful selection from the platter of fruit in front of me. Wazak looked as though he'd laid a golden egg and was sitting on it at that very moment. I began to think that he actually approved of me.

Dobraton must have decided to fall back and regroup, for she said, in a voice dripping with honey, "Try one of the yellow ones, my dear. They are my personal favorites."

Now, I'd never tasted any of the yellow fruit before, but if the look of pure venomous dislike which Dobraton shot at me just before suggesting it was any indication, she was lying through her big, flat, dinosaur teeth. However, if for no other reason than to prove that the ladies of Earth were not to be outdone by the lizards of Darconia, I picked one up and took a bite of it. As I might have suspected, it was like biting into a lemon—a really old, really sour, really bitter lemon.

"They're a bit sour, aren't they?" I remarked casually, doing my utmost to keep my mouth from going into
a permanent pucker. "I must say, I believe I prefer the
sweeter ones, myself. After all, you are what you eat."
Dropping the sour lemon thingy on my plate, I chose
another kind, adding, "That's an old Earth saying, by
the way." I took a nibble of a purplish plum and added,
"Don't know how true it is, but I believe I'd rather be
sweet than sour."

Dobraton hissed at me, undoubtedly wishing she could
breathe fire like a dragon, though to be honest, I wasn't
altogether sure she didn't exhale a faint puff of smoke.
I'd have to remember to ask Tychar if that was possible.
I'd have imagined that Scalia had probably hissed at him
a few times when she found it impossible to get his dick
hard—which made me wonder briefly what methods
she'd tried. However, having made my point, I kept quiet
and essentially ignored Dobraton after that, thinking that
being locked in with the slaves would have been a lot
more fun than dinner with the council. In fact, the next
time I was invited, I decided to feign some sort of obscure
illness. The Darconians couldn't know very much about
the maladies which might inflict humans; I could invent
all sorts of things, and they'd never know I was lying.

I was toying with the idea of faking one just then, but,
unfortunately, Scalia had other ideas and suggested that
we all go into the Great Hall for our after dinner entertainment—which, as I might have guessed, was me.

Arriving in the Great Hall, this truth became more
evident when I saw that, while we were at dinner, some
enterprising servants had moved the Steinway. It was
quite dark by then, and an intricately carved candelabrum,

which illuminated the entire stage, had been set upon the piano. Upon closer inspection, I discovered that "candelabrum" was a misnomer, because there were no candles; having been carved out of glowstone, it emitted its own light.

I'd never enjoyed performing in front of large audiences, but, deciding that outright refusal was unwise, I sat down and played the "Moonlight Sonata." Somber, but beautiful, I've met very few who didn't like it, and the Darconians were no exception. Taking their seats in the hall—some grumbling, some restless—they became silent with rapt attention once I began. Even Dobraton seemed to be paying attention.

Following a round of enthusiastic applause, I played a few of my other personal favorites, and, as the saying goes, brought down the house—except that this time, it was nearly literal. I discovered that when Darconians are truly excited, they thump their tails on the floor as well as clap their hands—which, as you might imagine, was something along the lines of a hall full of humans jumping up and down. I will also point out at this juncture that Darconian chairs were essentially benches or stools with no backs to them, such as we humans use, which allowed for much freer tail movement.

At the end of my performance, I took a quick bow, hoping I'd done my part to demonstrate that having visitors from other planets wasn't such a horrible thing after all. If the enthusiasm of the audience was any indication, I'd made a few converts—which was quite possibly Scalia's intention all along. She was a tricky old girl…

An odd thing happened after that, though, because Dobraton asked to see The Shrine. Scalia never batted an eyelash—or eye*lid*, I should say, since Darconians appeared to have only a nictitating membrane to protect their eyes instead of lashes—and led the way. If she'd sent word ahead that we were coming and that the slaves needed to vacate immediately, I sure couldn't tell it. Arriving at the entrance, my heart took a plunge toward my feet as the guard pushed the door open; it was not even locked.

The Shrine was quite beautiful by moonlight—Darconia has three moons, by the way—and the sparkling waterfall looked cool and silvery, as did the glistening leaves. No one spoke aloud, but, instead, kept their voices hushed and reverent, as though entering a place of worship—and perhaps that is truly what it was. To the people of this hot, dry land, this was not only the source of the life-giving water, but was also a source of spiritual beauty.

Tychar had said that the slaves slept on pallets wherever they liked, but I didn't see a single one of them anywhere. Apparently, having anticipated Dobraton's request, Scalia had already made a point of sending her slaves elsewhere. Either way, Dobraton seemed rather disappointed—almost as if she'd expected to find the slaves there and would, therefore, be able to criticize Scalia for keeping them in such a holy place. Given this attitude toward the room, it surprised me even more that Scalia would use it to house her slaves, but perhaps it was an indication of just how high the slaves were in her esteem.

The party broke up after that, and I suddenly found myself walking alone down a strange corridor with absolutely no clue how to get back to my room. Completely lost, the triumphant events of the evening now seemed remote, reminding me once again that I was nothing more than a defenseless woman on a strange planet. I'd rarely been one to panic, but I could feel it rising up inside me now, and my chest constricted as I choked back the nausea and quickened my pace. Where was my tiger when I needed him? Tychar had said that even the lizards liked to sleep with something warm, and I would have given an awful lot to be able to check him out of the slave quarters for the night. But if he wasn't in the Shrine, I had no idea where to find him. For all I knew, the slaves might have been locked in the dungeons whenever outsiders visited the holy place.

I tore down one corridor after another as though the hounds of hell were at my heels. My fear was unreasonable, but nonetheless real, and, it being nighttime, doors that might have been open during the day were now closed, with no hint as to what terrors might lurk behind them. Fortunately, the glowstones were listening to me as I silently requested as much light as they could dish out. Taking a left turn at random, I finally found what looked like the doors to my suite, but there was a guard posted at the door, so it couldn't have been mine—unless Scalia thought that Dobraton might be a danger to me, as well as to her slaves. This idea was even more frightening, because I'd probably made an enemy of her now; first, by being an offworlder, and second, by putting her in her place.

I didn't want to talk with another lizard as long as I lived, but this guard was the only one I'd seen, and I figured I could at least ask him for directions. However, as I approached, he gave me no opportunity to speak but promptly unlocked the door and gestured me inside.

And I ran straight into Tychar's waiting arms.

Even in the pale moonlight I could see that they were, indeed, my rooms and not the dungeons. Not even bothering to ask why he was there, I threw my arms around his neck with a sob and then proceeded to break down completely. I hadn't fallen apart like that in a very long time—if, indeed, I ever had—but I knew that out of all the souls in the entire universe who could comfort me, he was the one I wanted most.

"Kyra!" he said with some surprise as I buried my face in his hair. "You're trembling."

I couldn't speak but held on tightly, as though he were my only lifeline in a raging sea.

"Something has frightened you?"

I nodded, though I was feeling better by the second. His warm, strong presence was rapidly dissolving the tension.

"You're safe now," he said, echoing my thoughts. "There is nothing to fear."

He was right about that, because now that I was in his arms, my fear quickly began to evaporate. "I was lost," I said with a shudder. "All alone in a maze of corridors on a planet full of dinosaurs. I know it sounds silly, but—" And it *did* sound silly, especially now that I was safe, but at the time, it had been terrifying.

"No, it doesn't," he murmured, his deep voice acting like a balm to soothe my frazzled nerves. "It is understandable that you would feel strange. I remember that feeling quite well."

Just the fact that he was a slave made his situation so much worse than mine could ever be, and that knowledge made my fears seem even more ridiculous. "You know, it never ceases to amaze me that no matter how bad I might feel, there's always someone else who's a lot worse off than I am," I said with a sigh. "It always puts things in their proper perspective."

"I didn't mean it that way," he said. "Your feelings are just as real as mine—and my life here is not so bad."

"But you're a slave, Tychar! Most people would see that as the worst fate imaginable."

He smiled. "But I have you to care for now," he said. "What more could I want?"

I could think of about a million things he might want, but didn't bother to list them. My fears had dissipated—laid to rest by a few simple words. I had no idea how to reply, so I asked the next question on my mind: "What are you doing in my room?"

"We have to leave The Shrine when outsiders ask to visit. These rooms have always been one of the alternate locations."

"You mean the others are here, too?"

He nodded toward the music room, "In there."

Not quite believing it, I pulled away from him and peeped through the door to the adjoining room. The piano had been returned from the hall and stood on the dais, gleaming in the moonlight, as always, but the rest of the floor was now littered with Scalia's sleeping slave boys. With their pallets scattered all around the room, they looked like a troop of Boy Scouts on a campout. The only thing missing was the campfire.

"Guess the Queen didn't see any reason to change the routine, just because I'm here," I grumbled. "I wish someone had told me."

"The guard didn't tell you?"

"He didn't say a word, and I was so glad to have found my room again, I didn't think to ask what he was doing there." I paused, running nervous fingers through my hair. "You know, that's half of my problem; Wazak made me so leery of asking too many questions, I've neglected to ask anywhere near as many as I should have. I've got to get over that and start asking tons of them! Like to start with, what are *you* doing in here when the others are all camped out in the music room?"

I saw his fangs flash briefly in the moonlight as he smiled.

"Thought you might get lucky, didn't you?"

His response to that was to begin purring. The stones in his collar sparkled as he moved closer, and his purring grew even louder.

"Oh, trying to entice me, huh? Well, it won't work, so you can just go sleep with the other slave boys." When he didn't move, I added, "Go on, now, Tychar. Go."

"I will go," he said. "But have you had water to drink before bed?"

"What?—no—well, maybe a little bit," I said, momentarily thrown off balance by this abrupt change in tactics.

Turning, he poured water from a carafe on the nightstand. "Drink this, and then I will go." It was dark enough that I missed what he was doing, but as soon as I took a long sip and doubled over with an orgasm, I realized what the rascal had done. That fancy cock of his must have been dripping like a leaky faucet, and he'd put some of his joy juice in my water.

"No fair!" I protested, straightening up to stare into his glowing eyes. "If you want me, you're gonna have to do better than that."

He seemed to consider this, blinking a few times, and I watched, oddly fascinated with the way his glowing pupils altered in response to the changing light. As he stood there, his perfect body bathed in moonlight, I felt my anger dissipating even before he spoke. He took a deep breath which came out again in a loud purr.

"Please, Kyra," he whispered. "I need you, and I want you—more than my freedom; more, even, than my life."

How could I possibly refuse him? No one had ever said such a thing to me—not even in jest. Surely even a silver-tongued rogue like Tychar would think twice before telling such a lie—wouldn't he? Tears stinging my eyes, I slipped past him, set the glass on the table, and landed heavily on the bed. Running down the list of the reasons why I shouldn't, I realized that they were all overshadowed by the one reason why I should, which was that I wanted him more than I'd ever wanted anyone, but getting what I wanted—well, asking for it, anyway— was something I'd been unable to do my whole life.

"You can do whatever you want," I whispered. "Just don't make me tell you what to do. I—I have a problem with asking for things."

"And why is that?" he asked. Reaching out, he gently traced the line of my cheek with a fingertip.

I'd been wrestling with the answer to that for most of my life and still hadn't come up with a good reason why. I had theories, of course, but nothing solid. "I don't know," I replied. "Maybe it's because I don't think I deserve anything; that asking for anything, no matter how small, is too much."

"But you are *very* deserving," he countered. "You are kind and good—you should have all that you wish for, and I, I will give you everything I can."

He was a slave; he had nothing—not even himself to give me. "But you can't—"

"I can give you joy," he said, cutting off my protest. "It's the only thing I have to give and is something I can't even give to the Queen—no matter how much she might wish for it."

My tears were flowing freely by this time, and my heart was aching like never before.

"Will you take it?" he asked.

I *didn't* deserve it. There were countless others throughout the galaxy who did—women who were more worthy of him, more beautiful, more talented, more everything that I wasn't. But they weren't there—I was—and he needed someone. I didn't have to think hard to understand how alone he felt, either, for I was in exactly the same situation myself. The only difference was that I could leave if I chose. He couldn't.

I don't remember nodding, or saying yes, or anything, but I must have, because the next moment I was in his arms, falling back onto the bed, and his kiss was melting me like the searing heat of the desert. I felt it all in his kiss—his need, his desire, and, yes, his love—everything I'd wanted from a man. I couldn't believe it was all there. Nothing was wrong, everything was right, and nothing was missing—not one single thing. I didn't care if he was lying, didn't care if he was pretending, because it felt more real than anything ever had before.

His hands caressed my skin as though I were the most precious thing he'd ever touched. He, who belonged to a queen, who was adorned with gemstones, and who lived in The Shrine of the Desert, thought that I was precious! But he was beyond price, and I held tightly to him, never wanting to let go.

Aching with need and wet to my knees, I wanted to beg him to plunge his cock into me. But he didn't even take off my dress, instead caressing my breasts through the thin fabric and leaving a trail of wet kisses down my neck to my nipples. The sound of his purring filled my head, driving out all rational thought as he kissed and sucked them until they were as hard as his cock.

"Mmm," he purred. "I haven't removed a woman's clothing for many years. I'd nearly forgotten how delightful it could be." Skimming his fingertips over my hip, sending waves of warm delight over my skin, he went on to inquire: "There is nothing beneath this dress?"

"Just me," I replied. Okay, so I'd known I wasn't the first—Tychar had "Ladies' Man" written all over him. He might not have been able to get it up for a Darconian, but I had a feeling that he'd been enormously popular on Zetith.

He said nothing further, but began a slow, sensuous striptease with the skirt of my gown. To my surprise, I found that he was moving much too slowly for me. The searing heat between my thighs felt like a wildfire— unquenchable and completely out of control—making me want to rip off my dress and pounce on him.

Lowering his head, he began kissing each place he exposed: the side of my leg, the rise of my hip, the dip of my waist, and the fullness of my breast. By the time he reached my lips, I couldn't stand the wait any longer—if he didn't do something soon, I was going to have another orgasm without him.

"Tell me you love me, Kyra," he whispered against my lips. "Lie to me if you must, but tell me. Let me dream."

Of all the things he could have said, this was not what I expected. That was a woman's line, wasn't it? I'd never heard of a man saying anything of the kind, and for that matter, why would I need to lie, when it was so close to being the truth?

"You want me to lie?"

"If you must," he said. As he kissed me again, I felt not only the heat of his desires and his ravenous hunger, but also an intense longing to have a thing he'd never had before. "But I would prefer that you did not."

"I'd rather not lie to you, either," I said. "Especially about something like that."

"Pretend, then," he persisted. "Make me believe it… for a little while." The kiss he followed that up with was enough to make me shove him back and blurt it out. Maybe I wasn't sure how true love was supposed to feel, but I knew one thing for sure: no one had ever made me feel the way he did—and that was even without the orgasmic joy juice.

"I love you," I gasped. And I wasn't lying; I meant every word.

He must have been very anxious to hear my reply, because I felt the tension drain out of him. "So, Kyra," he whispered, "you have given me your love and now, I will give you joy."

If I thought anything about it being an even trade or an odd ritual, I wouldn't have been able to think it for long, because the things he did after that sent all rational thought straight into oblivion.

My hands were on his shoulders, feeling the strength of his muscles, the perfect symmetry of his body, and the heat of his passion as he nudged my thighs apart. Wrapping my legs around him, I pulled him close, his hot skin soothing the ache, but at the same time, increasing the intensity of my desire for him.

Purring, he kissed me; the taste and feel of him as deliciously creamy as chocolate. His thick cock swept between my thighs, just as his tongue swept my mouth, both teasing and tantalizing, but at the same time, promising even greater delights. When his cockhead found my clitoris, he let out a groan before circling it with his hot, wet heat. Nothing I'd ever felt before in my life could compare as he raked the ruffled edge back and forth across my sensitive flesh.

Sliding further down, he held his cock poised at the entrance and kissed me again. What was he waiting for? Did I have to ask? It was so hard for me, but, like the first time I'd asked for his kiss, the need to have him inside me overcame my usual reticence.

"Tychar, *please*," I begged—and he pushed.

His cock was large and stretched me to the limit, filling me completely. Then heat turned to fire as he began to move, thrusting slowly at first before picking up speed and depth. The ruffle on his cockhead increased the sensation to the boiling point as it raked my inner walls, and I could hear myself moaning helplessly. Then the orgasms began; first one and then another, and another, and another, on into infinity.

Rapture. Ecstasy. Pleasure. None of those words seemed to fit. Joy. Yes, that was it: joy—along with all those other things. For me, it might have been overkill—I'm sure he could have made even the most glacially frigid woman imaginable melt on contact—and I certainly wasn't frigid.

I tried to stay with him, but eventually I had no choice but to simply lay back and take it, to enjoy the ride and savor what Tychar could do. He hadn't been lying—or even exaggerating—and I was right to believe him, for this truly was joy unlike any I had ever known. The other translation was also correct, because he was undoubtedly fucking me senseless. My eyes couldn't focus, and I'd lost all control of my body; all I could do was moan with each thrust.

"Ah, Kyra," he purred. "Does that feel good?"

"Mmm," I replied. I was so far gone, I couldn't even talk. "Ohh," I sighed as he slowed down and altered the angle of entry.

"Better?"

It had been good before, but just that slight change made a difference as great as the distance between Earth and Darconia. "Mmmm."

"It all feels good to me," he murmured, his deep, resonant voice rumbling in my ears. "And do you know why?"

"Um-mm."

"Because I am with you."

Maintaining the angle, but pushing harder and faster, I heard him groan and watched as his back arched, and he drove into me even more deeply than before. Then, with a roar, his climax met one of mine, and we fused. I held my breath as he came, feeling the shot of semen as it hit and delighting in the creamy warmth of it as it flowed into me. I was sorry it was over, but as I waited for the inevitable softening of his penis and his subsequent withdrawal, something else happened. The rest of his body might not have been moving, but his dick never stopped, and I could still feel it swirling deep within me, stretching, pushing, and gliding in the slickness of his semen. It amazed me that he could do that; could stay hard even after he was finished, let alone have control of it.

He'd kept telling me he would give me joy, but euphoria would have been a better word for it because, after that, I was truly gone: lost, blown away completely with fire, explosions, supernovas and then floating, drifting down like a dust mote, falling down deep into myself, into the bed, and into this strange world we were both on. I could feel him breathing, feel myself breathing. I'd almost forgotten I needed to do that…

Purring contentedly, he kissed me with a sweetness that took the rest of my breath away.

"Do you still love me?" he asked.

"Mm-hm," I murmured. "I think I always will."

"You are not lying?"

"Nope," I replied. "I never lie."

Smiling down at me in the moonlight, he whispered, "Then I will give you joy for as long as you wish."

"Even if it's forever?"

"Even if it's forever."

Of course, the real miracle here was that I'd somehow managed to put him off for even the one day I had. As a general rule, I was a cautious person when it came to starting new relationships; the idea of love—or in this case, orgasm—at first sight wasn't something I'd ever put much stock in, but I was beginning to wonder if I hadn't been wrong about that. Tychar had said that the men of his race had to be enticing—which they undoubtedly were—but the question which was bugging me the most was whether or not *any* female would be able to feel what I had just felt, whether she loved him or not—and whether he loved her or not. He'd asked me to say that I loved him—even asked me to lie—but did it make a difference? It was overwhelming, to be sure, but did it truly mean anything, or was it simply a matter of chemistry?

Somehow I knew it would be difficult to separate my feelings and assign a meaning to each of them, but I tried to do it anyway. I liked him—I knew I did. I even liked the sound of his voice—and that had to count for something. I reminded myself that Tychar hadn't been my only choice, and, given the opportunity, Trag would have done the same thing—I think—but he wasn't the one to whom I'd responded. Perhaps that was the best gauge of the situation. Scalia had seen my reaction to Tychar and had acted accordingly. Looking at it that way made me feel better about it—less manipulated, less coerced, less *drugged*…

For Tychar's coronal fluid was essentially that: a naturally occurring drug which virtually guaranteed that the woman of his choice would stay with him. I wondered just how indiscriminate the Zetithian men were with that stuff. For example, did it only work for women they truly cared for, or would it work with any female who happened to stray too close to one of them and become ensnared? Of course, that might go a long way toward explaining what had happened to their people and their planet. Maybe they *hadn't* been very careful—had enticed one woman too many and pissed off the wrong guy. Wars had been started for a lot less, but destroying a planet? Who would be able to pull that one off?

Nobody I ever wanted to meet, that was for sure! I'd leave that part for someone else to figure out, because I was hooked, and now, all I wanted was to find a way to keep Tychar forever. Which apparently wouldn't be too hard, since learning to play the piano takes years and years, and Zealon didn't seem to have the makings of a prodigy. I would stay on Darconia, teaching piano to generations of Darconian royalty, and I'd get to keep Tychar as my personal assistant for the rest of my natural life. Scalia wouldn't mind if we had children of our own—on the contrary, she'd probably be delighted.

And as for her breeding program—whether real or imagined—she wouldn't even have to ask. I was *volunteering*.

Chapter 9

THE SUN HAD REPLACED THE MOONS WHEN I AWOKE TO FIND Trag standing over my bed, clicking his tongue.

"Got lucky, didn't he?" he said when I opened my eyes.

Nodding sheepishly, I said, "What can I tell you, Trag? He's irresistible."

"It's those damned blue eyes of his!" he growled. "Always the blue eyes! I don't stand a chance with him around!"

I shrugged, thinking if he wanted to believe that eye color really mattered all that much, I'd let him. It was easier than explaining the vagaries of the human heart. "He's such a sweetie," I added. "I couldn't help myself."

Trag stared at me in surprise. "You tasted his snard?" he exclaimed. "The first time?"

I stared at him, completely puzzled. "What are you talking about?"

"Snard!" he exclaimed. "It's sweet like candy!" Then he shut up for a second, closing his eyes as though wishing he could correct a blunder. "You didn't mean it that way, did you?"

Shaking my head, I said, "Sweetie is an Earth expression for someone who's very nice. He didn't seem to understand it, either." Then I added, curiously, "Snard?"

"Semen," he replied shortly. "Snard is the Zetithian word for it. One of the few I actually remember."

"And it's really that sweet?"

"Well, so I've been told," he said. "Some guys are supposed to be sweeter than others. Never having tried it myself, I wouldn't know for sure, but…"

"No homosexual tendencies, then?" I inquired, trying not to laugh.

"Not that I'm aware of," he replied.

"Pity," I commented. "You and Tychar could have kept yourselves a lot happier for all these years."

"Very funny," he snapped, making a face at me. Then his expression changed abruptly, and he let out a heartfelt sigh. "Don't suppose you'd reconsider doing us both, would you?"

"I think we've already established that," I replied, throwing back the sheet to get up.

Trag groaned. "Then don't *do* that!"

"Do what?" I demanded. "Get out of bed?"

"No, get out of bed naked—*and* recently fucked!" Grabbing a fistful of hair in each hand, he yanked on it in frustration. "You're killing me here, Kyra!"

"We've gotta get you a girl, mate," I chuckled, noting the raging erection he had sprouted. "Or, maybe you just need to keep out of my bedroom."

"I can't help it if we got locked in with you!" he protested. "It wasn't my idea!"

"No?" I inquired innocently, dropping my nightgown over my head. "Better now?"

"Not really," he replied sadly. "You still smell… well, you smell fuckin' incredible!"

"Thank you, dear," I said, patting him on the arm. "That makes me feel so… appreciated." Glancing down at his rock-hard and dripping penis, I added, "And you look fuckin' incredible, too, by the way. Maybe I'll send a message to Earth to see if anyone back home is interested. I could give them one helluva recommendation, just based on one time with Tychar. You, I'm sure, are every bit as good."

"Liked it, huh?" he inquired with a smug little grin. "It's what we're best at, you know."

"Yeah, I kinda figured that."

"And just imagine what it would be like with two of us!" Trag exclaimed, his green eyes dancing with mischief. I had to admit, his enthusiasm was catching, but I didn't think I could stand having *two* of them after me all the time. I mean, I'd probably never get out of bed, and then Scalia would be pissed because Zealon wasn't learning anything, and then I'd get fired and have to give them both up and go home—and I wasn't about to let *that* happen!

"I'd go insane from all the joy, I'm sure," I said dryly, and trying hard not to think about just how good it would feel. Then I realized that it would probably kill me—but I'd die happy! Taking a look at Tychar, I commented, "Boy, he can sleep through anything, can't he?"

"I'm awake," Tychar said without opening his eyes.

"Oh, just keeping quiet to see if I'd cheat on you with your brother, is that it?"

"No," Tychar replied. "I'm just waiting for you to tell him to go away so I can do it again."

Smiling at Trag, I said sweetly. "There's your cue! You can pack up the other little slave boys and head on back to The Shrine now."

Trag seemed very disappointed and was muttering to himself as he walked away, but he went. A few minutes later, the whole gang trooped out the door carrying their pillows and bedrolls, leaving me alone with Tychar again.

As I gazed at him, lying there in my bed, I knew I'd never seen anything more appealing in my entire life. I could have stood there all day, just looking at him. "You know, I'm going to have to talk to Scalia about letting you stay here all the time," I commented. "And if we have to be locked in, I'm sure she's got a spare guard around here somewhere."

"So," he purred. "You are… pleased with me?"

"You have quite a gift for understatement, don't you?" I said dryly. "And yes, I *am* pleased with you. In fact, I might try to swap you for several years' worth of piano lessons. Of course, that might mean I'll still be teaching Zealon when I'm old and gray, but, hey, I think you're probably worth it."

"Then I will do my best to please you during all of those years," he said, smiling. "I believe it's my purpose in life."

I stood there staring at him, my mouth agape with astonishment, trying to remember the last time I'd heard a man say something like that. Not lately, I decided, and probably never. He was one in about ten billion—and though Trag probably was, too, I would leave him for someone else to discover. With the influx of alien life forms on Darconia, Trag was bound to find one that smelled right eventually. It wasn't my purpose in life to keep *all* of the remaining Zetithians happy, and though I'm sure it would have been a fun job, that was Scalia's business, not mine.

Gathering my wits from wherever they'd been scattered by his last statement, I said, "With lines like that, you should have been able to talk Scalia into setting you up in your own palace by now."

Tychar flicked an eyebrow. "She likes keeping us close—it surprised me that she would assign me to you."

"If you hadn't liked the smell of me, I doubt she would have," I said frankly. "So I'm really glad you did, otherwise, I might have wound up with Refdeck or the guy with the octopus fingers."

"They are not as appealing to you as I am?" His tone might have been all innocence, but the mischievous smile that accompanied it gave him away.

"No, dummy! They aren't!" I snapped. "But they might have gotten up early and brought me breakfast by now. You're still in bed, lazy butt!"

"But I am waiting for you to come back," he said, yawning and stretching in a most languid, sensuous fashion that made me want to do nothing more than to crawl back in and play with him all day long—but I wasn't sure it was such a good idea. The guard at the door had probably heard all of my moans and groans of ecstasy the night before as it was, and if he'd reported what he'd heard to Scalia, with my luck, I could probably expect to be waited on by Refdeck from now on. Besides, there were other reasons to be discreet.

"I think we'd better watch what we do unless Zealon is busy with her other lessons," I said cautiously. "She wandered in here yesterday without so much as a knock."

As if on cue, the door opened, and Zealon entered, followed by Refdeck with breakfast. Tychar made a quick move and now appeared to be straightening the sheets, rather than lying on them. I don't know if Zealon saw him or not, but I was thankful that his normal attire was something he didn't take off while he slept—or made love.

Looking past them into the corridor, I noted that the guard appeared to be off duty. "Anyone else coming?" I inquired, thankful that I'd already put my gown on. "The Queen, perhaps?"

Zealon appeared to be slightly taken aback. "She's having breakfast with Wazak," she replied. "She always does; they go over any security problems from the day before."

"Never mind," I said, waving Refdeck over to the table. "Just set that down and have a seat. I'll be right back."

Disappearing into the bathroom alcove—which was something of a misnomer, because there was no way to take a bath in there—I returned to find all three of them standing around like they didn't know what to do.

"So, what's on the agenda for today?" I asked brightly, taking a seat at the table and hoping they would all follow my lead.

"Well, we're having some other guests for dinner tonight," Zealon ventured.

"Not Dobraton again, I hope!"

"No, some offworld entertainers," she replied. "It's a traveling show of some kind. Mother didn't say, exactly."

"Did she by any chance mention that they are all blue-skinned with red hair?" I asked hopefully. Zealon shook her head, and my heart sank just a bit. I missed Nindala quite a bit, especially since landing on Darconia. *She* would have no qualms about, well... just about anything, actually. Of course, if she ever did show up, I'd have to sic her on Trag, because I didn't want her messing around with *my* tiger. I wondered how she would smell to them—probably even better than a human. Trag would be pleased.

"Well, I'm sure it will be an interesting show," I said, diplomatically, remembering some of the weird things I'd seen during the trip to Darconia. I decided to take the opportunity to be even more diplomatic. "Refdeck, these fruits you brought are simply delicious! Have some, won't you?"

"I have already eaten," he said in an odd, high-pitched voice.

"Oh, well, then. You guys must have really wolfed it down quick, 'cause you haven't been gone very long." Glancing at Zealon, I casually mentioned that the slaves had spent the night in the music room. "It was quite a surprise to get back from dinner last night and find them here. It's fairly obvious that the Queen didn't want Dobraton to see them, but I wish she'd warned me, though Tychar tells me they've been kept here before."

Zealon looked as though she'd have liked to have an answer to that, but couldn't come up with one. "I just came to see how you were this morning," she said hastily. "I hope the slaves didn't keep you awake."

"Oh, I didn't mind having them here," I said with a quick look at Tychar. "Having a guard posted at my door was a little disturbing, but all in all, I passed an excellent night. I might even be adjusting to the heat, finally. I feel almost"—I paused there to stretch and sigh contentedly—"normal today." Actually, I felt better than I had in recent memory—distant memory, too, for that matter. My eyes connected with Tychar's again, and he turned away slightly, barely suppressing a chuckle. "So, when are you coming for your lesson today?"

"The same time as yesterday," she replied. "I'll see you then."

Zealon left after that, followed by an oddly relieved-looking Refdeck, leaving me alone with Tychar again. I wondered briefly if Refdeck was afraid I was being too chummy and would try to get him in bed, too. I toyed with the idea of explaining it to him, but decided against it. Then something else occurred to me.

"The same time as yesterday," I repeated. "Just when *is* that?"

Tychar glanced at the window before taking a seat opposite me. "Not for a while yet," he replied. "You will have ample time to rest before she returns." Judging from his expression, his definition of "rest" was probably a bit different from mine.

"I figured that much," I said, ignoring the innuendo. "I just want to know what time it will be. I haven't seen anything remotely resembling a clock around here. How do the Darconians mark the passage of time?"

He pointed at the window. "With that," he replied.

"That? You mean the sun? No device?"

"No," he said patiently. "That."

I looked at the window again and didn't see anything there to tell me what time it was. "I don't get it," I said, shaking my head.

"The stones around the window," he said. "They're also in the corridors."

Taking a closer look, I saw that part of the design around the window appeared to be highlighted. "Oh, don't tell me they've got clock rocks, too!"

He nodded.

"And how do they work?"

He shrugged.

"So, they're like the glowstones, then?" I suggested. "No one knows?"

"I believe they are similar."

I hadn't seen a calendar yet, but, God knows, they probably had a rock for that, too! "Do they have more portable models? I mean, how did Wazak know when to meet my ship?"

Another shrug. Obviously, with clock rocks on every wall, no one had much use for wristwatches.

"Perhaps the ship contacted him before it landed." I mused. "Maybe they all have to report to him—after all, he *is* the security chief. It's possible that he meets every ship that lands here. I don't suppose there are very many of them."

Tychar apparently didn't know.

"Oh, that's right. You don't ever get out. Do you even remember the spaceport?"

"Vaguely," he replied. "It was a very long time ago."

"Might even be a different building by now," I said. "Tell me something, if you ever wanted to escape, where would you go?"

"The mountains," he replied promptly. "There is water there."

"Not a whole lot, though, I'd expect," I said. "And you'd have to cross the desert to get to it." Then I nearly choked on a piece of fruit as an image of Tychar, in flowing Bedouin garb and riding one of those camel-creatures across the desert, popped into my head. Lawrence of Arabia had *nothing* on him!

Leaning my cheek against my fist, I gazed at Tychar, wondering where he would be and what he would be doing if it hadn't been for the war tearing his world apart. Somehow, pleasing me for a living seemed… inadequate. He was overqualified for the job and should have been off somewhere doing great, heroic deeds—or even singing for a living—but instead, he'd gotten stuck here in a desert palace catering to the whims of a big lizard, just as he was now catering to mine.

"What did you do before the war?" I asked.

He looked up at me as though surprised by my question. "I have never been anything but a soldier," he replied.

"Oh," I said blankly. "Yes, I suppose so." In a world besieged, there was little else for a strong, healthy male to do, was there? I waited a moment, still mulling it over in my mind. "But before you knew you would be a soldier, was there anything else you wanted to do?"

He shook his head. "The war was already being waged from the time I was young. There was never a chance for me to want to do anything else."

"Well, what about now?" I persisted. "If you could go anywhere, do anything, what would it be—or did you think you'd spend the rest of your days here, pouring Scalia's wine?"

"It seemed pointless to think about doing anything else until you came."

It was reasonable that he would think about other things now that I was there, but in all reality, looking after me couldn't be that much different than serving Scalia—except for the sex, that is. "But when you're out there, sleeping beneath the stars, what do you dream about?"

His glowing blue eyes met mine. "You, Kyra," he replied. "I dream about you."

This was a sweet sentiment, but rather unlikely under the circumstances. "Oh, how is that possible?" I scoffed. "You've only known me for two days! How could you dream about me?"

For a moment he was quiet, glancing away toward the window and the brilliant cobalt sky. "Many years ago, I had a vision," he replied, "and I knew that one day, you would come, we would be lovers, and my life would change."

"A vision?" I echoed in surprise. "You have *visions*?"

"Sometimes," he replied. "They are different from ordinary thoughts or dreams—I cannot tell you how. Many of my people have this ability, and though such visions are not common, we know them to be true."

"Uh-huh," I said doubtfully. "And you're saying that you saw me, specifically? You mean, you *recognized* me?"

He nodded, smiling devilishly. "I've been waiting for you for a *very* long time, Kyra."

"That's fairly obvious," I said dryly. "Whether you had a vision or not." I was finding this extremely difficult to believe. I'd run across a few oddities in my day, but certainly no one who ever had visions—especially visions concerning me. "And just how will your life change, now that I'm here? Will you be freed?"

Shaking his head, he replied, "I don't know, but I believe it will be a change for the better."

"That doesn't sound too hard. After all, you *are* a slave!" I declared. "It's no wonder you seemed so glad to see me!"

His seductive smile nearly took my breath away. "I was," he said, "*very* glad to see you."

And Trag hadn't been—which at least partly explained the difference in their reception of me. "Does Trag have visions, too?"

"If he has, he's never told me about them," Tychar replied. "But it is possible. Some of our people have more of this ability than others." Just as Trag had said that some of them tasted sweeter than others. *Interesting…*

"Did you tell him about your visions?"

"No," he replied. "I kept it to myself, only knowing it was true when I first saw you."

"Maybe you should tell him," I suggested. "It might convince him to stop hitting on me."

"He hit you?" Tychar exclaimed, obviously aghast at such a notion—though just when he thought Trag would have done it when he, himself, had been with me most of the time since my arrival, I couldn't begin to guess.

"It's an Earth expression," I said, laughing. "Meaning that a man is *really* interested in a woman and keeps making comments to that effect. It isn't painful, and in this case, it's actually rather flattering. I mean, here I've got two of the most gorgeous men I've ever seen, and both of them are—"

"—hitting on you," he said, contritely. "I'm sorry if I seemed too… anxious."

If it had turned out to be any less fabulous, I suppose I might have been irritated, but, as it was, I had nothing— and I do mean *nothing*—to complain about except, perhaps, that it had taken me this long to find him. Still, he'd been waiting at least as long as I had and had been a slave for many of those years. I tried to imagine what it would have been like to have dreamed about Tychar and then arrive on Darconia to find him there, and I decided that, yes, I would have been quite anxious, to say the very least.

Actually, the more I thought about it, the more I realized that I *had* been looking and waiting for him all my life; I just hadn't had a vision to show me who he actually was. Then there was the fact that, despite a boatload of discouragement, I had come to Darconia in the first place. Me, who rarely left my hometown, had crossed the galaxy to find the man I was destined to meet.

Destiny. Prescience. Kismet. Fate. All these things, which I had certainly heard about before but had never truly believed in, were now proving themselves to be real. Suddenly, I felt the cold, hard finger of fate touch the back of my neck, sending shivers down my spine, despite the growing heat of the day, and I knew that it wouldn't turn out to be as easy as asking Scalia to let me keep him with me all the time. There was more to it than that, even though asking for anything was always a challenge for me. I could have told her about his vision, told her how we felt about one another, but still, deep down, I knew it wouldn't be quite so simple.

Sitting there, staring off into space, I probably would have gone on pursuing that train of thought if Tychar hadn't recalled me to my current surroundings with an uncomfortable-sounding clearing of his throat.

"What?" I said before I remembered that he had apologized for being too anxious—and I hadn't responded. "Oh, an apology isn't necessary," I said quickly. "I was a little… anxious, myself."

Then I realized just how anxious I was. I wanted to get as much of him as I possibly could before he was taken away from me. The reality was that Scalia probably wouldn't keep a piano teacher around forever, and I knew that if I ever left Darconia, it would be without Tychar, unless something else happened to change that. I would have to buy him, or win him, or earn him in some way. Then there was the problem of the bounty on Zetithians. What if we ran into bounty hunters on the trip back to Earth? I was pretty sure he would be safe once we arrived, but there could be dangers along the way.

I hated to admit it, but Tychar and Trag were probably safer right where they were than anywhere else. Perhaps Scalia had the right idea after all.

Tychar cleared his throat once more.

Poor Tychar! My mind had raced away again. Smiling apologetically, I leaned over and kissed him. "Yes, I was anxious. You're pretty hard to resist, you know." Toying with my glass in a nonchalant manner, I said, "So, would you like to sing for me this morning, or would you rather do something else?"

The smile he aimed at me was anything but apologetic. "I don't mind singing, but I would prefer to do… other things."

Which is exactly what I might have expected him to say, the little devil. After all, a guy doesn't break a twenty-year dry spell and then just forget about it for *another* twenty years! "That's right. You *did* say you wanted Trag to go away, didn't you?"

"Yes, I did." He looked at me with heavy-lidded eyes. "And, in case you haven't noticed, he's gone."

"Tell me something, then. Is it true that snard tastes sweet?"

He gazed at me in surprise. "How do you know of snard?"

"Trag told me while you were asleep."

Cocking his head in suspicion, Tychar asked, "He didn't give you some of his own to taste, did he?"

"No, I just said you were a sweetie, and he made that assumption."

"Oh." He sighed, his lips curling into a smile as he purred. "Then I'll give you some of it to taste, and you may judge for yourself."

I just stared at him for a moment as my mind went into a tailspin. Honest to God, if every handsome man on Earth were lined up for my inspection and approval, I would have ignored them all. *This* was the one who drove me wild. This one, and this one, alone. I'd never had much in the way of visions before, but I was certainly having them now! What he would look like on his knees with his buns in the air, his cock and balls hanging below, swinging back and forth when he moved. How his nuts would feel as they bounced against my tush. The way his scrotum would be pulled tight over his balls as he plunged into me as far as he could go. Too bad I couldn't actually *see* all of that, but I could imagine it, and it was making me wet and swollen with desire. So, this was what happened when you got together with a Zetithian!

Then I got a mental picture of his dick firing off in my face and had an orgasm.

Tychar was obviously paying attention, for he was standing by my chair within seconds, the smooth skin stretched tight over his dick; the jeweled cuff around his cock and balls offering them up for me to lick, to suck, to savor... My hands were wet with his fluids as I took his cock and slid my fist up and down his shaft, heard him purr, heard him groan.

"Put it in my mouth," I gasped. "Fill me with your snard... let me... taste it... Make me... scream." It was shocking. I wanted him to do things—wild, erotic, sexual things—and actually had the nerve to ask for them! And at the breakfast table, no less!

He wound my braid around his hand and pulled me closer. "Suck me, then," he said with a purr. "Feel me in your mouth. Taste me."

The ruffled head of his cock pushed past my lips, sliding deeply into my mouth. He tasted good already and felt hot and powerful, as though he were pumping life into me. When my orgasms began, I tried to ignore them and focus only on how he felt, how he tasted, how he smelled. My own body was burning with desire, but I ignored that, too. It was so good, I didn't think I would have needed his orgasmic cock syrup to make me climax—I think I would have done it anyway.

Tychar was still purring, but now there was a groan with every thrust of his dick into my face. I backed off and managed to gasp, "Talk to me. Tell me what you like, how it feels."

"It feels so good," he said. "I like being in your mouth, watching your lips and tongue tease me. You are hot and wet, and your eyes are clouded with hunger." He thrust into me again. "Oh, yessss," he sighed. "Suck harder. I like that."

I nearly swallowed him, stretching the ruffled corona back towards the head on the outstroke. His knees buckled, and he gripped the back of my chair for support.

"Yes, like that," he gasped, his purr becoming more frenzied. "Suck the snard from my cock, Kyra."

Then his breath went in with a hiss, and I swallowed the first shot without even tasting it, but on the second, I let go of him to watch. At point blank range, I saw him erupt, and his snard splattered all over my face. When I gasped in awe, the third round hit me right on the tongue.

And yes, it *was* sweet—sweet, creamy, delicious, and maddeningly euphoric. I watched, fascinated, as the corona began to undulate and then took him back in my mouth, letting the scalloped edge tease my tongue while I caressed his balls with my hands. I'd never felt anything like it—had never even dreamed of such a thing—and soon there were hot tears running down my cheeks.

"Feels so good you could cry, doesn't it?" he whispered.

I nodded and felt his nuts spasm again in my hand when I moved.

He withdrew himself and wiped the snard from my cheek with his cockhead before sliding inside once again. "How does it taste?" he purred. "Is it sweet enough for you?"

Nodding again, I ran my tongue around the corona, tasting his semen, never wanting to let go of him again—ever.

But I did. I backed away and just sat there and stared; it was as though I could get as much pleasure simply by looking. But that wasn't true, of course. He moved closer again, sliding the head of his cock through the snard on my face, massaging my cheeks, my lips, and my nose.

It was hot, wet, slick… I had another orgasm… and another… and another. This was something truly amazing… something I couldn't have ever imagined, not if I'd racked my brain for a million years. He was more than any human lover could possibly hope to be—and Scalia had *two* of them…

Chapter 10

I DIDN'T WANT TO WAIT FIVE OR SIX MONTHS FOR IT TO WEAR off; I wanted an antidote for my birth control pill, and I wanted it *now*. I wanted to have babies—boy babies. Hundreds and hundreds of them who looked just like Tychar. Then I wanted to take them back to Earth and watch women drool over my sons. His sons. *Our* sons. I wanted to save the species; to rescue them from extinction. I wanted his genes to be dominant over mine, so that you could never tell a Terran had given birth to them. I wanted other women to know the joy and pass it on.

Scalia couldn't keep them. The tigers couldn't reproduce on Darconia. They had to go where there were other mammals—humanoid mammals—who smelled good to them and made their dicks hard. And if there *was* a bounty on them—and I only had Scalia's word for that—well, we'd just have to kill anyone who tried to take them. And I *would* kill: to protect my children, and to protect *him*. I would gladly squeeze the life out of anyone stupid enough to make the attempt.

Of course, if there *was* a bounty on Zetithians, the way I was feeling was obviously the reason why. It was doubtful that I was the first to experience it, and I hoped I wouldn't be the last. Something had to be done. My scruples about being used to save a species from extinction had disappeared. Scalia was just sitting on these guys, when she could have bred hundreds of them by now. She should have gotten mates for them years ago.

I wondered if she'd tried. Perhaps she had, and I was just the first one to show up. I was an experiment: she'd needed a piano teacher, so she'd gotten a mammal from Earth. If I was ever granted a moment alone with her again, I would ask her if my suspicions were correct. I wasn't going to be afraid to ask questions anymore, or to make requests; I would decide what I wanted, and I would ask for it—or find a way to get it myself. Having had this brief time with a man such as Tychar had convinced me that I was as deserving as anyone else; God hadn't forgotten me, he'd simply saved me for the right man. Nindala would be proud—if I ever saw her again.

I would ask Scalia if she would book Nindala's troupe at my earliest opportunity. I'd never seen them perform, but if Nindala was anything to go by, the show *had* to be spectacular! The audience the night before had seemed to enjoy my piano recital, so they might be more open to other forms of entertainment now—though I was pretty sure there was a world of difference between the two. Of course, my ulterior motive was to find a mate for Trag. I wondered if he liked redheads…

Nindala might not like Trag, though. I couldn't begin to imagine why, but there's no accounting for taste. Perhaps, being more sexually experienced, she might not be as overwhelmed by the Zetithians as I was—which would be a crying shame…

The entertainers in question turned out to be mammals all right, but they weren't humanoid, reminding me more of goats than anything; they even had horns. So much for finding a mate for Trag. This region of space didn't seem to have much in the way of potential candidates. No wonder Scalia had had to look for one on Earth!

I had dinner with goats and lizards that evening, and we were served by a toad (Refdeck) and the slave with the octopus fingers, but no tigers. I'll have to say, the goats put on a darn good show, but watching goats sing and do acrobatic routines was like watching a circus with talking animals. They had their own musicians, but none of them could play the piano, so Scalia asked me to accompany one of them while he sang. I'd never played for a goat before, and though he had a nice tenor voice, I had to keep my eyes on the keyboard, because I couldn't look at him without cracking up.

Cornering Scalia after the show, I asked her if I could keep Tychar with me in my quarters all the time.

"It is already arranged," she replied with a knowing smile. "I knew you would want to keep him close by in case you needed anything during the night. I do not know why I never considered the matter before."

"Do we get locked in with a guard at the door?" I asked. It didn't matter that much to me, because I would make love with Tychar regardless of whether we were guarded or not, but the guard might get a little tired of hearing me cry out in ecstasy. Then again, it might relieve the boredom of having to stand watch all night.

She seemed to consider this carefully. "I do not believe it to be necessary to lock the door," she replied, "but a guard, yes—for his protection, you understand. I do not believe he would attempt to escape. You have been very good for him."

So, he'd had a few words with the Queen. It must have been during Zealon's lesson, because, otherwise, I didn't think he'd been out of my sight all day—or out of arm's reach—though he *had* been the one to bring me my lunch. At least I thought he had; that whole morning had been one big orgasmic blur, so I may have been mistaken.

I broached the subject of Nindala's troupe then, hoping that Scalia would recognize the possibility of finding a mate for Trag. She never gave any hint that she might have understood why I asked, but did promise to look into it.

Then I got even bolder.

"Any problem with me having Tycharian's children?"

She seemed surprised that I would even consider it. "You would have the children of a slave?"

"Sure," I said with a shrug. "They'd be awfully cute, don't you think?"

Eyeing me unblinkingly, she said, "You enjoy his company?"

"Oh, yeah," I replied. "He's terrific."

"Terrific?" Obviously not one of those words that had made it into the Standard Tongue, at least not in this region.

"Really, really good," I interpreted.

It may have been my imagination, but I believe she turned just a little more green at that point.

"You did say you wanted to breed more of them, didn't you?" I prompted her.

"Yes," she replied, seeming a bit distracted.

"It would take a little while," I added, "because I've got to wait a few months for my birth control pill to wear off. Oh, and I would keep the babies, of course—and I'd like to buy Tychar from you, too, if I could."

I must have been moving way too fast for her, for she just stared at me without comment.

"I could work off his value in piano lessons," I went on conversationally. "A few years' worth should do it, don't you think?" When she still didn't reply, I added, "I could teach some other kids, too. Is Zealon your only child?"

That got a bit of a blink out of her, because I saw her nictitating membrane begin to slide over her left eye. "No," she said, seeming to come to her senses again. "I have other children. All males."

"That's great!" I said enthusiastically. "I could teach them, too."

"Males are not musical," she said flatly.

"Well, they are on my world," I argued. "In fact, I'd be willing to bet there are more male musicians on Earth than there are female."

"Is that so?"

"Oh, yeah! The girls just love them! They sit out in the audience and scream their heads off." Darconians would thump their tails, of course, but the basic principle was still the same.

Something seemed to jog her memory just then, because she changed the subject, stating firmly, "There is a bounty on Zetithians." I knew she'd come back to that sooner or later! "Tychar would not be safe beyond the palace walls."

"He would be plenty safe on Earth," I insisted. "It's a long way from here, and our security is pretty tight. We don't let just anyone land there."

"He might be harmed during the journey." Obviously she didn't want to give up her pets completely, even to me.

"He could wear a disguise," I said reasonably. "You know, a cloak with a hood and a veil over his face? I saw lots of people traveling that way." They must have been really, really ugly, too, because no one ever asked them to uncover their faces. "I know you're very attached to him," I said soothingly, "and it would be *years* before we could leave, but…"

"I will consider the matter," she said regally. "But for the present, you may continue to… enjoy him as you see fit."

I figured it wouldn't do any harm to lay it on thick at that point. "Thank you, Your Majesty," I said, dropping into a deep curtsy. "You are most kind. I will do my very best to make virtuosos out of any students you choose to give me."

"I know you will teach my children to the best of your ability," she said. "And your own offspring, as well."

It wasn't a real obvious, "Yes, and have all the kittens you want," but it was good enough for me. I was chuckling to myself as I walked away, and, if I'm not mistaken, Scalia was, too. I might have sprung it on her faster than she thought I would, but I doubted that I'd said anything she didn't want to hear.

One thing I hadn't reckoned on was just how many other children Scalia would have. Turns out there were five of them, and not one of them had any intention of learning to play the piano. They made me wish I'd been a guitar teacher, instead, because being a rowdy but charismatic bunch of boys, I could have made rockstars out of the lot of them without any trouble at all. Unfortunately, in order to be big enough for a Darconian to play, a guitar would have had to be about the size of a bass violin, which was a bit daunting, and the drums would have had to be really, really sturdy. It was possible that such instruments existed, but I hadn't seen any lying about, and so, after three days of practicing scales, we were down to two boys.

Racknay was the eldest and most pompous of the group, reminding me a lot of Wazak, though I had no idea who his father was. Unfortunately, he had the same problem that Zealon did, which was that his fingertips were wider than the keys, something which caused him a great deal of frustration. Still, he had an octave and a half reach, which was pretty cool.

Uragus was the youngest of Scalia's children; a little bitty guy with the brightest eyes I'd yet to see on a Darconian and was also the first one I'd ever considered to be cute, though I had no doubt that he would outgrow it. He was so tiny that I had to put a cushion on the bench for him to reach the keyboard, and, as a result, there was no hope of him reaching the pedals for a few more years. Still, he was a chipper little fellow and seemed to enjoy playing, working even harder at it than Zealon. I liked him a lot.

With the added students, I had less time to spend with Tychar and saw less and less of Trag. It might have been that he was avoiding me, because I gave him such raging hard-ons, but to be perfectly honest, I wouldn't have minded if he'd come around just to jack off. Tychar might have objected, though, so I didn't suggest it.

But Scalia did.

I guess she didn't want me having all the fun with her cats, and though she made it seem like a spur of the moment idea, I was pretty sure she'd been thinking about it for quite a while.

We were at dinner one evening, and after Zealon went off to bed, she had the Zetithians sent in the way she'd done on my first night in the palace. I hadn't seen Trag for about a week and greeted him warmly. He gave me a half-assed smile and stood by Scalia, serving her wine and feeding her the occasional bit of fruit while we talked. Tychar took up a position beside me, and, as usual, his cock blossomed like a rose and began dripping all over my arm. That and his purring distracted me to the point that I could barely carry on my conversation with the Queen—so much so that, when she asked me if I had the same effect on this one, I didn't know what she meant.

"Excuse me?" I asked. "Effect on what one?"

"This one," she said, stroking Trag's dick.

"Well," I began uncertainly. "I *did* have at one time, but I don't know if…"

"Go stand beside her," Scalia told Trag. "I want to see it for myself."

Damn Queens! I thought. *Always ordering the slaves around…*

Tychar was already making me squirm in my chair, so my scent must have been pretty strong, and if the table hadn't been so large, Trag probably could have smelled me from where he stood. But apparently he needed to be closer, which made some sense, because if they could pick up the scent from across the room, these guys would be hard all the time, and their dicks would probably explode in a crowd of horny women. Trag did exactly as she told him, and if he was trying to control himself, you couldn't tell it, because as soon as he got a good whiff of me, he was as hard as a glowstone.

I tried not to stare, but pretty soon, he was dripping on me, too, which was quite effective at getting my attention. I wondered if that fluid would have the same effect when applied to the skin as it did when it came in contact with a mucus membrane. I thought it might take longer that way, but also knew that this wouldn't have been a fair test, because I was about to climax from the visual stimulation, alone.

"I don't suppose you've ever seen them do that before, have you?" I asked Scalia hoarsely.

"No," she replied, "but it has been a fond wish of mine that I would someday."

"You should taste it, then," I suggested. "It makes me have orgasms."

"Yes," she said. "They have told me of this."

For some reason I could see Trag telling her that, but not Tychar. Trag was a little less... reserved... than Tychar. I could sense that she had never truly believed their claims, for her skepticism was quite evident in her tone.

"It's true," I assured her. "Watch." I took a droplet of fluid from Tychar and tasted it. An orgasm followed swiftly, and I gasped, "See? You should try it."

The table was too wide to reach across, so Scalia got up and came around to where I sat between the two men. I was pleased that when she touched one of them, it was Trag rather than Tychar, because she *did* touch him!— wrapped her big, long, reptilian fingers around Trag's stiff, ruffled dick, leaned down, and licked him.

The fluid appeared to have no effect on her, but what she did certainly had an effect on Trag! The sound he made was almost a shout, though it was unclear as to whether he was in pain or in ecstasy.

The Queen paused, savoring the flavor. "Slightly salty," she remarked, "but it has no effect on me. Pity."

She let go of his cock, at which point Trag gasped, "Don't stop!"

Poor Trag! His whole body was shaking, and his breathing was as harsh and ragged as that of a dying man. He had to be on the edge, because this was a queen he was talking to, and, not only that, he was her slave.

"I haven't come in twenty years!" he exclaimed. "Please, Scalia!" He took in a deep gulp of air, not even able to purr. "I've done everything you've ever asked of me. Please, help me…" His voice trailed off to a whisper, and when I looked up, I thought I could see tears of frustration rolling down his cheeks.

Honest to God, if she hadn't done it for him, I would have! But she did. Using her tongue on the head, she worked the shaft with her hand. Trag looked like he was about to come unglued, and Tychar was rubbing his own cock on my cheek.

"When he ejaculates, catch the semen in your mouth," I told Scalia when Trag appeared to be about to climax. "It's very sweet."

Scalia was in a good position, but when Trag let out a roar, she backed off. He hit her in the mouth with it anyway, shooting out an arc reminiscent of the fountain in The Shrine. It took a few moments, but then…

"Great Mother of the Desert!" Scalia whispered in astonishment. "I feel…"

"Better than you've ever felt before in your life?" I suggested.

"Yes!" she replied with a voice filled with awe. "I have heard of this, but never believed it."

"*Now* do you understand why someone decided to exterminate them?"

Scalia shook her head in wonder. "I have always believed it to have been their beauty which aroused such jealousy and hatred."

"No," I said gently. "I believe it was because of their ability to love. Other men can't compare."

Scalia stood back and looked at Trag. "Yes," she said, nodding. "They are beautiful, and obviously affect females very strongly, but they are also honest and trustworthy. Their emotions run deep, but they are not... belligerent."

I'd known Trag to be a little on the belligerent side, but it had been fairly easy to calm him down, so maybe she was right about that part, too.

"No, they aren't the least bit mean," I agreed. "And it isn't just these potent fluids they secrete; they seem to be natural born lovers. You've always liked them, haven't you—even though you've never been... intimate... with one of them?"

Scalia nodded. "I have always been partial to them. They are my slaves, but they are not cringing or subservient, nor do they whine about their situation here."

I had an idea that this was more due to the fact that she'd treated them with kindness and respect, but I might have been wrong about that. Perhaps they would have maintained the same integrity even if they had been abused.

"No, they don't whine, but they are very... persistent." I glanced up at Tychar, who was smiling at me. Clearing my throat audibly, I added, "Perhaps we shouldn't be having this conversation in front of them. They may become too... arrogant."

"Not a chance!" Trag declared. "Keep talking. I'm feeling better all the time!"

"You see?" Scalia laughed. "Not subservient at all! I like that about them."

"We like you, too, Scalia," Trag said. "And, thank you, for that," he added, with a downward glance at his dick. "That was like giving water to someone dying of thirst in the desert."

Scalia smiled. "I will give you one more gift," she said. "If Kyra will do it for me."

"What's that?" I asked with some trepidation, because if it was sex, I was going to have to decline. Not that I wouldn't have enjoyed it, but I *was* in love with his brother!

"Kiss him," she said. "It would be more... enjoyable... coming from you than from me."

"Well, I don't know if he'd want—" I began, but Trag cut me off.

"I would *love* to kiss you, Kyra," he said wistfully. "If it's okay with Ty."

I didn't see the exchange between them, but Tychar must have given his permission, because Trag pulled me to my feet and into his arms. His kiss was poignant and sweet, making me wish I could have had both of them as my lovers. But I couldn't be that greedy. Somewhere there was another woman who needed him far more than I did, and who would love him all the more because of it. He just had to find her.

Chapter 11

I WRESTLED WITH THIS IDEA FOR SEVERAL WEEKS, BUT other than pestering Scalia to look for more women or to let Trag go find one for himself, I couldn't come up with a way to do it. Scalia did take my suggestion to get Nindala's troupe to come to Darconia, but they were a long way off, and it would be some time before they could work us into their schedule. It was also distinctly possible that Scalia might refuse to let them meet. I reminded myself that Trag had been waiting for twenty years, and, since his dick still seemed to work as well as it ever had, he could wait a while longer.

Not that he didn't become even more persistent. Having all but disappeared for a few weeks, he now found excuses to come to my quarters all the time and even convinced Scalia to let him take piano lessons. He had no talent whatsoever, but must have enjoyed sitting next to me on the piano bench. Which meant that Tychar would sit on my other side—probably just so Trag didn't get any funny ideas. Trag didn't remember very many Zetithian songs, but, having been raised by an uncle who frequented the bars in spaceports, he knew a bunch of drinking songs, which were pretty raunchy and did nothing to diminish his level of arousal.

I loved having them around, but they were driving me nuts, because their dicks were always hot, hard, and dripping with anticipation. As a result, the piano lessons with Trag became more of an exercise in my own self-restraint than any improvement in dexterity on his part. It would have been different if they hadn't both been naked all the time—which was another thing Trag kept trying to convince me was the way to go.

"But it's so hot here, and you look great naked!" he insisted. "And you could wear *something*—a few necklaces… maybe a bracelet or two. I mean, wow!"

I was having enough trouble keeping him at bay as it was, so I told him about Nindala, instead, but it didn't help a whole lot, because he wasn't sure he'd like blue skin and red hair—aside from the fact that Scalia would probably forbid them to meet.

Masturbation was the one thing they both seemed to rebel against doing—said it just wouldn't work without a woman doing it to them—but I just about had Trag convinced to give it a go.

"Or maybe I could get Scalia to do it again," he mused. "She seemed to like the snard."

"Yes, but that was weird," I said. "It was okay on the spur of the moment, but to come right out and *ask* her… I don't know about that. It'd be different if I didn't have to be there so your dick would get hard."

"Yeah, but maybe with you in the room, I could actually *fuck* Scalia—though you'd have to stand pretty close, because my nose isn't all that good. There was a guy in our unit who just had to be *downwind* of a woman to get an erection, but I have to be a lot closer, myself."

"Do you *really* want to have sex with the Queen?" I asked. I mean, she was a lizard! Refdeck obviously didn't mind, but he was reptilian, too.

"Well, no," Trag admitted. "I like her, but you're the only one around here who does it for me—and it isn't just because of the way you smell, either."

"You might remember that the next time Scalia introduces you to someone," I said dryly.

"What?"

"You know, smile? You didn't smile when I first met you. Tychar did."

Tychar smiled smugly. "Yes, I smiled, but I already knew you would be my mate," he said.

"Oh, yeah, right," I said. "Forgot about that vision thing—which I still find hard to believe. Are you sure it wasn't just some line to get me into bed?"

"It's the truth!" Tychar insisted. "And, if you will recall, I had already gotten you into bed."

"Oh, yeah. Forgot about that, too," I admitted. "You see what you guys are doing to me? Addling my brains and making me downright senile! Pretty soon, I won't even be able to play the piano and then Scalia will kick me out, and you guys will have to find someone else to get your dicks hard."

Trag nudged me in the ribs. "But if I get you addled enough, you might actually fuck me *before* she kicks you out." He took a moment to gaze down at my chest. "And I still believe you should rethink the clothing issue. You've got some truly fabulous tits there. Nobody on this whole planet has tits like that. You should show them off more."

"Nindala's are better," I asserted. "Even if they are blue."

"I don't give a damn about Nindala!" he declared. "I'll probably never get to meet her anyway, because I'll bet money that Scalia locks us up if she ever does come around. Jack me off or suck me, I don't care! I just need to get rid of some snard. It builds up, you know."

"For twenty years?" I asked incredulously. "It's a wonder your balls haven't ruptured."

"Well, it's mainly since you've been here," he admitted. "I think it has something to do with the smell thing."

"You mean you don't know?"

"Hey, on Zetith, once a guy was old enough, he was doing his utmost to entice women all the time—the drive to find a willing mate is really strong—which is one of the reasons I went back home. This not having a woman around to catch even a whiff of for twenty years—I don't know if that ever happened before the war."

When consulted, Tychar couldn't remember having ever heard of anything similar to their own particular situation before, either, but thought that perhaps, without a woman nearby to stimulate them, Zetithian males didn't produce any sperm.

"That's interesting," I commented. "Human males produce sperm all the time, and when it builds up, they have wet dreams or just get themselves off if there aren't any women around."

Tychar shook his head. "I just don't understand how that's possible!" he said. "Sex without a woman would be like trying to—" He paused there, as he attempted to come up with something similarly impossible.

"Eat rocks?" Trag suggested.

Laughing, I said, "Well, if that's the case, Trag, maybe you should stay away from me instead of hanging around all the time. Doesn't Scalia have anything for you to do?"

"Aw, we never did much in the way of work anyway," he said. "Mostly, we were just bored out of our minds."

"So, is that all I am? A diversion?"

Trag appeared to consider this for a moment. "Well, you're much more than that, obviously, but I'll have to admit, things have been a lot more interesting since you showed up." He put an arm around me and squeezed. "Thanks for coming, by the way."

"Must have been fate," I replied. "But I'm glad I came, too."

Then I got this vivid mental picture of me lying in bed with two purring, naked tigers and nearly had another orgasm. Why, oh, why, didn't Tychar tell his brother to get lost before I gave in to him? He'd let me kiss Trag but probably drew the line at group sex. Whoa! It hit me then—hard.

"Hey, are you all right?" Trag asked worriedly as I doubled over.

"She's fine," Tychar stated firmly. "She's thinking about having us together."

"And just *how* did you know that?" I demanded hoarsely. "Another vision?"

He smiled seductively. "I know one of your orgasms when I see it."

Trag let out a sort of whimper. "That was an orgasm? Oh, fuck! Do it again!"

"You only know *what* it was," I said to Tychar, "not what caused it!"

"Perhaps," he admitted, "But isn't it logical that you would be thinking such a thing at this time?"

"Does that mean you wouldn't mind if I did?"

Tychar regarded me with a steady gaze from his luminous blue eyes. "You love me, don't you?"

"Well, yeah!" I replied. "That's what this whole thing is about! If I didn't love you, it wouldn't matter that your brother was giving me fits. I'd do you both and never think a thing about it." Which wasn't entirely true, but *still*…

Trag's response to that was a long, tortured groan.

"And you care for my brother as well?" Tychar went on.

"Well… yes," I replied cautiously. "But it's not quite the same way that I care for you. It's hard to explain."

Tychar nodded as though he understood. "On Zetith it would have been very rare for two men to have the same woman," he said. "But the situation is different here."

I was feeling less and less special by the second. "Do you mean that Trag's only interested in me due to a lack of options?"

"No," Trag said firmly. "That's not it at all. It's just that on Zetith, we could be as enticing as we wanted toward a woman we liked—and I *do* like you, Kyra!— but most of the time, they just didn't care—no matter how many of us were after them! Eventually, a man would find a woman who would take him, but finding one woman who would actually want both of us would be—" He paused there, running a hand through his curly locks, trying to come up with an apt simile "—a fuckin' miracle."

"You're kidding," I said seriously. "You have to be. You guys are irresistible."

"To you, perhaps," Tychar admitted. "But not to our females. We were all alike to them."

"Your… um… fluids didn't work on them?"

"Sure they did," Trag replied. "It's just that we all had the same equipment, so they could be as choosy as they liked, and if they weren't in the mood—which they hardly ever were!—they just didn't smell right." I was now being gazed at with luminous *green* eyes, which were every bit as attractive as the blue ones. "You, on the other hand, smell just exactly right *all the time*."

Which explained quite a bit. "Trag," I said gently, "this is a big palace. Why don't you just keep away from me?"

"I should," he muttered. "And I tried! Believe me, I tried! But the scent of you is just so compelling… and that's aside from the fact that I'd like you, whether you smelled good or not." He stopped there, throwing up his hands in despair. "I just plain can't help it."

"Do I leave my scent on Tychar?"

Trag nodded. "Yes. If you've had sex recently, I can smell you on him." He let out a deep sigh. "And you must be doing it an awful lot."

Which was true. If we were alone, Tychar and I were in each other's arms. We must have been feeding off one another's desires; he being enticing and me smelling like sex personified. We must have been driving Trag up the wall—constantly.

My head started to spin as the strength of my emotions and confusion threatened to overwhelm me. I might have had a better understanding of the problem, but the pressure was getting to me. I needed time alone to think without the two of them clouding my mind with desire. Excusing myself, I got up from the piano and pushed past Tychar and, before I knew it, I was practically running from the room. Passing through the doorway to my bedroom, I began running in earnest; out the door into the corridor and continuing nearly the full length of the palace until the stitch in my side became so severe that it forced me to stop.

Leaning out a nearby window, I gulped in the air, which at that hour was hot and oppressive. I would probably faint dead away in another moment or two, thus paying for my headlong flight, which had probably been pointless anyway. Sure, it might have given me a little breathing room, but at best, it had only postponed my inevitable decision. The dilemma I faced was a difficult one; I cared for them both, and being true to the one I loved meant that I would have to deny the other, who I was convinced needed me—which also meant that I would wind up feeling guilty no matter what I did. At that moment, it became almost too much for me to bear, and all I could think of was that I needed to get off of this world and never come back.

Dissolving into tears, I sank to the smooth stone floor, leaning up against the wall. I would tell Scalia to keep her tigers away from me. If I needed a personal attendant, the guy with the octopus fingers would do nicely. I would have to find out what his name was, though, because I couldn't very well call him "Octopus Fingers" forever, and I hoped that he had a name I could at least pronounce—or I could call him Fingerpuss, which sounded a bit kinky, really.

Running a hand through my hair, I felt something I'd rarely felt since I arrived—sweat—and if I was sweating enough to feel it, I was losing way too much water! I was wondering if I could even make it back to my room when Wazak rounded the corner.

Stopping short when he saw me there, he demanded, "You are ill?"

"Nope, just needed to run," I gasped. "Probably ran too far."

Bending down, he scooped me up in his arms without ceremony. "I will return you to your quarters," he said. "Do not run anymore." Having solved any problems I might have had with those few short sentences, he set off down the corridor with his curious, tail-swinging swagger.

"If only it were that simple," I sighed.

"It is not?"

"No." I hesitated a long moment before asking, "Ever been in love, Wazak?"

I didn't think he would ever reply, but, after a bit, he did. "Yes," he said shortly.

"Ever been in love and, at the same time, felt very strongly about someone else, too? Not instead of the first one, but in addition to them?"

"No," he replied. "I have loved only one."

Trust Wazak to keep even something as complex as love simple and straight to the point. "Then I guess you can't help me," I said hopelessly. "Oh, shit! What am I gonna do?"

"You are in love with the Zetithian slaves," he said, correctly interpreting my dilemma.

I looked up at his stoic, impassive face. If he'd ever loved anyone, it certainly didn't show, but perhaps I didn't know the signs. "That's a pretty good guess, Wazak. What was your first clue?"

"You do not appear to love me," he said, as though the slaves were my only other options. This wasn't quite true, because I'd gotten to know a few of the guards, particularly my own and the ones who were posted at The Shrine. However, aside from them and the children I was teaching, I really didn't know very many of the other people who lived and worked in the palace. Perhaps I should try to get on good terms with some of the women, because if I stayed away from the tigers, I'd need someone to talk to.

Thinking back, I decided that Cernada could probably relate to my problem better than anyone. I wondered if she liked Trag, too—of course, she might have had a thing for Wazak—who was turning out to be a pretty decent guy, despite my initial impression of him.

"No, I don't love you, Wazak," I said with a sigh, "though it might be easier if I did."

"No, it would not," he said. "Our species are too dissimilar. It is best that you love the Zetithians."

Suppressing a chuckle, I said earnestly: "Yes, but at least there's only one of you! There are *two* of them, and they're driving me crazy!"

"Your kind does not often have two mates?"

"Well, no, not really—hardly ever, in fact. I mean, I wouldn't mind it myself, but I doubt if they'd see it that way! I have to choose—and I already have, actually— it's just that Trag is so…"

"So—what?" Wazak prompted.

"Well, if I'd never met Tychar, I probably would have been just as taken with Trag, but the fact remains that Tychar is the one I love. The trouble is, Trag wants me, too, and while I'd like to say yes, I know that it would hurt Tychar. But if I deny Trag, then he's going to be hurt, too—and I don't want to hurt either of them!

It could be that I'm feeling sorry for Trag, because he's been without a mate for so long, but I honestly don't think that's the only reason for the way I feel."

If Wazak had any difficulty following my little rant, it didn't show. "So, you would take each of them as your mate if it was acceptable to them?"

"Yes," I said decisively. "Yes, I believe I would." It would probably be the death of me, but I would certainly give it a try.

"You are quite a woman, Kyra Aramis," he remarked.

"Not really," I said miserably. "I'm a big, fat wuss, is what I am." He didn't respond, so I translated it for him. "Coward. I'm a big, fat coward."

Wazak didn't appear to agree with my assessment. "To come alone to this world required great courage," he said. "There are not many who would do so."

He had a point. "But you scared the piss out of me the day I arrived."

"It was not apparent," he said firmly. "You possess more courage than you know."

"Well, I certainly don't feel very courageous," I grumbled. "I feel more like a coward." Yellow-bellied and lily-livered as the saying goes—though what those things have to do with courage is something I've never understood.

"That is often the case with those who possess the most courage."

Eyeing him curiously, I asked, "And just *where* did you hear that?"

It was the first time I'd ever seen Wazak smile. "My first commander," he replied. "I did not believe that I was courageous then." Smiling more broadly, he added, "But I was wrong."

I couldn't imagine Wazak being afraid of anything—ever. "Went toe-to-toe with him, did you?" I prompted.

"With *her*," he corrected me. "My first commander was the Princess Scalia."

"*Princess* Scalia?" I echoed. "So it was before she was made queen, then?"

Wazak nodded.

"So, does Zealon command the guards now? That's funny, I thought *you* did."

"I do," he replied. "The Princess Zealon is still too young, but she will take command when she is of age."

And I'd had no idea. "Well, obviously I need to hang around with you more," I declared. "I've learned more in the past five minutes than I have in all the weeks I've been here."

"The Princess has not been instructing you?"

"Well, yes," I admitted. "But I'd learn more if I asked more questions. The trouble is, I'm never sure what to ask until something comes up. What I mean is, I need to know *everything*, not just little bits and pieces. I need to know your history, politics, geography, culture—all those things."

"I will… speak with the Princess," he said, and I was certain he would. "But I believe you already understand something of politics."

"Really?" I said curiously. "What makes you think that?"

"When you spoke to Dobraton," he said. "You handled her very well."

I grinned at him. "I did, didn't I?"

"You showed courage then," he said. "You were alone among strangers who were at odds with one another, and yet you were able to make your point without being openly antagonistic."

"Thank you, Wazak," I said warmly. "I needed that." I almost felt like hugging him, but he was too big to get my arms around. "You can put me down, now. I'm feeling much better."

He smiled again. "But I wish to intimidate the Zetithians."

I chuckled wickedly. "Gonna march right in there with me in your arms, demanding to know who made me run off like that?"

"Yes," he replied. "It will make them think about what they have done."

"They're probably *thinking* already," I pointed out. "What I want them to do is *talk* about it—with each other."

"I will… suggest it to them."

We were approaching the door to my quarters, which was still standing wide open. I could hear Trag and Tychar talking from the other room.

"It is *not* my fault," Trag was saying. "You could have said something, but you just sat there and let it happen! She's probably gone to tell Scalia to lock us up again."

"We will not force her," Tychar said firmly. "She didn't say she wanted two of us."

"Came damn close!" Trag exclaimed. "Had a fuckin' orgasm when she thought about it!"

They must have heard Wazak's feet slapping on the

floor as we entered, because they shut up after that and rushed over to the door between the two rooms.

Wazak laid me gently on my bed and then turned to face them. He'd obviously had plenty of practice when it came to intimidation, because the pitch of his voice dropped sharply and he cranked up the volume. "You are responsible for her welfare," he said sternly. "You are not to endanger her again by driving her away."

Trag started to say something, but obviously thought better of it, so it was Tychar who spoke. "We did not intend to drive her away," he said. "We will be more cautious in the future."

"See that you are," Wazak said. He glared at them for a second or two longer and then left, his tail sweeping the floor behind him.

Trag was the first to recover, going immediately for the water pitcher. "I think we *all* need a drink," he said, pouring out a glassful—which he gulped down himself before refilling it and handing it to me.

I drank it gratefully, and then gave it to Tychar, who said graciously, "We apologize for our behavior."

Trag nodded in agreement, adding, "And I won't bother you again, Kyra. I'll stay away, if that's what you want."

I could tell just how much it cost him to say that. "Do you have any idea how hard it would be for me to tell you to never come near me again?"

Looking chagrined, he said, "About as hard as it would be for me to have to do it, I'd imagine."

"Well, we've got a problem then," I said. "I hate the thought of depriving you, Trag, but I don't want to be unfaithful to Tychar, either—I do love him, you know!

My biggest fear is that in trying to love you both, I could also end up losing you both—and that's the very *last* thing I want! I want you to think about how you would feel if your situations were reversed." I looked up at my blue-eyed lover. "You two talk about it. I'll do whatever you decide."

They exchanged a meaningful look. "We *have* talked," Trag said. "Talked it to death, in fact."

"And… ?"

"I might not *want* to share if you were mine," Trag said, "but I'd do it for my brother."

"And I would wish for him to share you with me if you loved him, instead," Tychar said firmly. "But I would also understand if he did not." He said this with a meaningful glance at Trag before adding, "I know what he is feeling. I felt that way not long ago, myself."

"Well, for heaven's sake, why didn't you say so before?" I demanded. "It would have saved a lot of trouble—not to mention that mad dash down the hall!"

"But we didn't know what your wishes were," Tychar purred, his eyes already beginning to glow with desire. "You haven't told us—and we have been waiting."

"And not very patiently," Trag put in.

Which was obviously why Tychar hadn't told Trag to get lost. "Well, if I haven't *said* anything, it's because I didn't want to screw everything up by admitting that I wouldn't mind having both of you."

"Wouldn't *mind*?" Trag repeated, looking a bit miffed. "Is that *all*?"

Desperate though he might have been, Trag still had plenty of pride left. "Let me rephrase that," I said. "I would absolutely *love* to have both of you." I hesitated a moment before adding, "But I still think we would all be happier if you found someone else, Trag. I doubt if this could be permanent."

"I can live with that," he said staunchly. "After all, nothing else is—permanent, I mean."

I wasn't sure what to say after that, and it was fairly obvious that they didn't either. I ran a hand through my hair again, noting that the sweat seemed to have dried.

"Boy, that run was a mistake!" I exclaimed. "I feel terrible! I must be in worse shape than I thought."

"You should run with us sometime," Tychar suggested.

"That's how you stay in such perfect condition? You run? In this heat? It nearly killed me!"

"We run at night," Tychar said.

I'd thought they were locked up at night; The Shrine was pretty big, but *still*… "You run in The Shrine? There has to be some sort of law against that!"

"Not in The Shrine," said Trag. "You know the door in the wall around the patio? It's not locked, because it only leads out onto the top of the portico, which has a wall around it, too. Not sure why it's there, unless it's a defensive thing," he added reflectively. "Anyway, it goes all the way around the palace, and we run up there where no one can see us."

"Which one of you is faster?"

Trag grinned. "Me." He rolled his eyes at his brother. "He's older than I am."

"I'd never have guessed. Except for your coloring, you two could almost pass for twins."

"We are littermates," Tychar said, "but littermates are rarely identical." With a withering glance at Trag, he added, "Fortunately."

"I thought you said you were younger?" I said to Trag.

"I am," he replied. "By about fifteen minutes."

Another lull. Obviously this was going to be up to me. "So, how will this work? One after the other? Both at once? Or will you just demand equal time?"

"Any way you wish," Tychar said with a slow smile. "We will not… keep score."

"So, what are you, then? My love slaves? My boyfriends?"

"He's your boyfriend," Trag said with a gesture toward Tychar. "I'll just be the bad little slave boy you like to fuck once in a while."

I experienced a bit of a spasm with that last statement, but it sounded way too good to be true. There had to be a catch somewhere, and I had a feeling that "once in a while" would probably turn out to be a fairly frequent event. "You're sure about this? Both of you?"

They were both nodding and smiling.

"Great Mother of the Desert!" I muttered, mimicking Scalia. I was in deep shit now!

Chapter 12

No one had cleared away the lunch tray yet, and Trag sauntered over and cut up some of those kiwi-like fruits for me. "I thought you might like a little something after your run," he explained.

Tychar picked up a scrail cloth. "This will make you feel better, as well."

Then they converged on me like two hunting cats circling in for the kill; their eyes glowing and both of them purring like crazy. It became quite apparent that they weren't intending to waste any time, and also that they were going to do it together.

Curling up beside me, Trag fed me with his fingers—making sure I had to taste him along with the fruit. After each bite, instead of using a napkin, he licked me right across the mouth, and with every swipe of his tongue drove me further from reality and deeper into the realm of erotic fantasy. Tychar polished me with the scrail cloth, sensuously brushing my skin where it was exposed, exposing more as he removed my clothing, which was one of those long, flowing dresses Trag had told me I shouldn't wear. It hadn't been much good for running, but it was wonderfully sensuous as Tychar slowly moved it aside. Trag gave me more to drink, and this time, when he wiped my lips with his tongue, I captured it, sucking it into my mouth.

His purr became a groan as he leaned into me for the kiss. Tychar was behind me, moving my dress higher, and I could feel his cock, hot and wet against my bare skin. When he pulled me away from Trag and slipped the last of the fabric from my body, his brother fell forward onto my chest, devouring my tits, sucking my nipples, and licking me to a sensuous daze.

"She *is* beautiful, isn't she?" Tychar murmured.

"The most beautiful woman I've ever seen," Trag agreed, backing away from my breast. "She smells of love and passion, and she tastes like desire."

"You have not yet reached the source of those delights," Tychar told him. "She has more."

Leaning against the headboard with his legs spread wide, Tychar pulled my languid body up against his own. I could feel his penis against the small of my back, sweeping back and forth, spreading his fluid, allowing it to glide smoothly. Reaching down, he pulled my thighs apart. "Lick her," he told Trag. "She will feed your desire as no other woman ever has."

Tychar was purring in my ear, nipping at my earlobe as he caressed my nipples, rolling them in his fingers and then teasing them with feathery touches. His touch spoke of his love, and I kissed him in reply, and through that kiss did my best to convey my deep feelings for him. He was so sweet to me, and I loved him so…

But Trag's hot tongue pulled me back to reality, nearly making me scream as my back arched in response. After the first taste, Trag thrust his tongue in for more, sucking the fluid from me, drinking it like wine.

"She tastes like our own women," Tychar whispered to him. "Perhaps even better."

"I never did it with one of ours," Trag gasped. "Women in spaceports—alien women—they were great,

but they never did *this* to me. *Never…*" His voice trailed
off as he plundered the recesses of my body, seeking
more of me to taste. Purring loudly, the vibrations in
his lips and tongue drove me to near madness until,
with a sudden gush of fluid, I climaxed right in his face.
Trag made a sound the likes of which I'd never heard
before, and Tychar placed his hands on my shoulders
and pushed me down, sliding me right underneath his
brother. My head was now pillowed in Tychar's groin,
his hot cock standing like a tree trunk beside my cheek
while his coronal fluids dripped down on my face.

"Bury yourself in her, Trag," he purred. "And we will
both watch as you mate."

What they were doing to me was amazing enough,
but hearing them talk while they did it was even more
of a stimulant than their intoxicating fluids.

Trag licked his lips. "She tastes so good!"

"Mate with her then," said Tychar, "and give her joy."

My body was still screaming from the first orgasm,
but when Trag pushed into me, the look on his face was
almost enough to make me do it again. Wonder, relief,
and passion mixed with awe, he let out a sigh and leaned
down to kiss me.

"Oh, Kyra," he whispered. "You feel like love."

Smiling mistily, I murmured, "But I *am* love," I assured him. "I never felt it before with anyone but the two
of you, never felt so…" I paused there, not being able to
put it into words.

"Laetralent," Tychar said. "That is how you feel, and
the way you make us feel, as well."

"Don't know what that means," I sighed, "but it
sounds very nice."

"*Really* nice," Trag agreed. "The best feeling in the universe."

Then he began to move inside me, and I thought I could come up with an even better feeling, which was that of making love with a Zetithian. His long hair teased my skin while his jeweled collar sparkled in the late afternoon light and his big, ruffled dick raked my inner walls with its wondrous drug and sent me into oblivion.

Though it was something I rarely did, I fought to keep my eyes open, because Tychar was right: I *did* want to watch Trag: wanted to see his face when he came; wanted to watch him lose control. Plunging into the depths of my body, he groaned with each hard thrust, ramming me with an uncontrolled force I'd never even gotten from Tychar. Then he seemed to come to his senses and eased up and moved out slightly, until his cock inside me was all I could feel while his spine undulated as he curled his hips up and down, making me moan with delight.

"Feels really good, doesn't it?" he said, looking rather pleased with himself. "I learned that trick from a Markellian in a spaceport brothel. It was her favorite move."

"I can see why," I gasped, though it was a wonder I could talk at all. "Don't stop."

"I just love it when a woman says that," he said. Taking a quick glance at his brother, he then said to me in a conspiratorial whisper, "Why don't you suck his dick?"

An orgasm hit me just then, but I think it had more to do with the conversation than as the result of any chemical reaction. Then I realized that if I sucked Tychar, I would be getting joy juice from both of them and wondered if it was possible to overdose on the stuff. I had no idea, but I had a feeling I was about to find out.

Tychar seemed to think that having his cock sucked was an excellent notion and shifted sideways so that all I had to do was turn my head to take him in my mouth.

"Mmmm." He was warm, smooth, wet, and delicious. Tychar had tried to teach me to purr, and I believe this was when I came the closest to actually doing it. I couldn't make a sound when I inhaled, but the "mmmm" with each expelled breath was pretty close. Tychar held my head and caressed my face while I sucked him: first his cock, and then his balls. The erotic display must have been getting to Trag, because, after a bit, he forgot about trying to be artistic and raised upright on his knees, scooped up my legs with his arms, and just pounded into me. Letting Tychar's nuts pop out of my lips, I said, "Just keep on going 'til you come, guys. Fill me up with your luscious cream and give me joy."

"No problem," Trag gasped.

Tychar took his cock in his hand and rubbed my face with the head before pushing past my lips again. He fucked my mouth for a short time, then, with a growl, backed off and sprayed not only my tongue but my whole face with his snard. My own orgasm detonated then, seizing Trag's cock with every muscle in my body.

"Oh, fuck!" Trag exclaimed. "I'm gonna come!"

And he did. With his head thrown back and a throaty growl, he thrust into me so hard, I slid up over Tychar's thigh as I felt the gush of his semen. The euphoria which followed was no more intense than it had been with Tychar alone, but with the double dose, the effect seemed to be even more prolonged.

"Great Mother of the Desert!" I muttered when I regained the power of speech. "That was incredible… You know, I think I like that expression—sounds so much better than 'Oh, my God!' or 'Holy shit!' or any of my other standbys. I think I'll start using it all the time, since I'm living in a desert oasis and everything, and 'Oh, fuck!' is something you can't say in polite company— though I *have* been known to let it slip out from time to time. Well, I *guess* you can say 'Great Mother of the Desert' without offending anyone… I'll have to remember to ask Zealon… or Scalia… I don't know which… or maybe Wazak could tell me…"

"She's babbling," Trag said with a chuckle.

"She never did that before," Tychar commented.

"Never gotten it from two of you before," I mumbled from my dazed, but enviable, position between the two brothers. "So, how 'bout it, Trag? Feel better now?"

"Kyra, my dear, you have no idea," he said sincerely.

"Well, actually, I think I might. I mean, if you think you feel any better than I do right now, well, I just don't see how it's possible. It's pretty hard to compare notes on something like that, but let me tell you, it's an incredible feeling! Don't know how I'll feel in an hour—by the way, what *are* the time divisions called here? We call them hours in Stantongue, but what do the Darconians call the time it takes for one stone to go dark and another one to light up?"

"A tourade," Trag replied. "Though it's fallen out of use since the Darconians switched over to Stantongue a few years back. They say hours now, just like everyone else. Hey, would you believe I had to give classes to the palace staff, since I was the only one around who was fluent?"

"That must have been weird," I remarked. I could just imagine the irony of a slave teaching his guards how to say "Get back in your cell" in Stantongue. "No, I never heard tourade, but I guess it just never came up in conversation. I'd still like to find a calendar and figure all this out, though—and, yes, I'm babbling again. I think maybe it's best that I don't do this double-team thing more than once a—what do they call weeks, months, and years here?"

"Weeks, months, and years," Tychar said. "Those are the Standard divisions of time, though the lengths differ on each planet, depending on the time it takes the planet to rotate and orbit its sun."

"Oh… yeah… right. Standard. I knew that."

"Uh, which one were you going to say just now?" Trag asked anxiously.

"Huh?"

"You know, once a… what?"

"Oh, yeah. Once a week, I think."

"But Tychar's been getting it more than once a day," Trag protested.

"You said you wouldn't keep score," I reminded them.

"No," said Trag. "Tychar said that; I didn't."

"Oh, well, shit. He's my boyfriend, remember? So he has to get more."

"There is logic in what she says," Tychar agreed. "And she must be the one to decide." If his expression was anything to go by, he wanted to be the one I decided on—all the time.

"Logic, my ass!" Trag exclaimed. "I think you're just saying that because—"

"Hey, now! No fighting, or the deal's off!" I said severely. "And remember that, because I will *not* have you two bickering all the time!" I was feeling more like myself as the moments passed. Maybe I *could* do it more often—maybe I'd even get used to it. "I'll tell you what, I'll give it a try again tomorrow, and if it kills me, we'll know we have to wait a few days in between."

"If it kills you?" Trag repeated. "I've never heard of sex killing anyone." He looked at his brother. "Have *you* ever heard of it killing anyone?"

"Oh, you know what I mean!" I grumbled. "Right now, I don't even know if I can walk."

Tychar's smile was slow and satisfied. "We will bring you anything you need, or carry you, if necessary, Kyra. It is our pleasure to serve you." The look in his eyes told me he'd like nothing more than to carry me everywhere I went—peel my fruit, feed it to me, rub my feet. Oh, yeah, another foot massage… After all, they couldn't do it continuously—even *they* would have to take a break sometimes…

"Hmmm, that's nice," I said drowsily. "But maybe I should just sleep for a while."

"And I'll go practice the piano," Trag said, sounding far more eager than he ever had before. Guess that's what a little nooky will do for you after a long dry spell.

"I said I needed to *sleep*," I pointed out.

"Oh, yeah," he said, looking a bit crestfallen. "Hey, I know I'm terrible, but at least I'm trying!"

"I will close the door," Tychar said, but I had an idea that he wasn't doing it just to shut out the noise.

Moments later I heard Trag running up and down the scale with more speed than accuracy. "How is it that you can sing so well and yet, your brother is completely tone deaf?"

Tychar shrugged as he closed the door. "We're brothers, not twins."

"True." It occurred to me that by this time he might be regretting having given Trag his permission, and if so, I would withdraw my own consent, whether Trag liked it or not. My first responsibility was to the brother I loved.

As it turned out, I needn't have worried. Tychar got me a drink of water and curled up beside me, purring quietly. "Thank you for allowing my brother to join us," he said. "It was very kind of you to allay his suffering."

"He *was* pretty miserable, wasn't he?" I said. "It was nice of you to let him, too. Not every man would do that."

"Our situation is unique," said Tychar. "In other circumstances, it would not have been necessary."

"Yeah," I agreed. "It's fairly obvious he did a bit of messing around before he was captured. Must not have had much trouble finding willing females."

Tychar grinned. "He used to laugh at the rest of us for being so... inexperienced with women."

"Well, I guess you're one up on him, now," I commented. "But I don't believe you were all that inexperienced, yourself. You didn't get that good just by thinking about it—did you?"

Some other emotion washed over his features—one I couldn't quite identify. "No," he said slowly. "I have known others."

"On Zetith?"

He turned away from me for a moment before returning his bright blue gaze to my own. "We were at war," he began. "A war unlike others, because we were not fighting against each other, but against many worlds, and our defeat was inevitable. No one felt that they could love as was customary—one man, one woman, forever. We mated when we could, but it was seldom with love."

"Those songs you sang for me were love songs, weren't they?"

"Yes," he replied. "They are the only songs I remember—perhaps because they are the only ones to have any meaning for me."

I now thought I understood why he wanted me to love him so badly—even if I lied to him and broke his heart—and also why he had charmed every female in the palace, whether he could mate with them or not. The kind of love he craved had been denied to him all his life, and he was starving for it.

I was beginning to wish I hadn't given in to Trag. Tychar seemed to be far more vulnerable than I would have guessed. Trag didn't love me—he had said nothing of the kind—only remarking that I felt like love. Tychar hadn't said he loved me, either—at least, not yet—but I had a feeling he was simply waiting for the right moment.

"What about Trag?" I asked. "Doesn't love have any meaning for him?

"Possibly," Tychar admitted, "But he is different."

"Well, I did notice that I didn't have to tell him I
loved him before he went ahead with it."

"No," he conceded.

"So that isn't a Zetithian rule of some kind?"

He shook his head. "No," he replied. "I... it was
something I needed to hear."

"Even if I was lying and broke your heart?"

"Yes," he replied.

"But why?"

"Because I needed to feel something," he said. "Anything—even pain."

"You two have been bored to tears here, haven't
you?" When he nodded, I went on, "So you charmed all
the Darconians, just for something to do?"

Smiling sheepishly, he said, "I suppose I did."

"And now you let Trag—? You could have said no,
Ty, I wouldn't have done it if you hadn't agreed."

"Are you saying you didn't enjoy it?"

"Of course I did! And I'm sure he did too, but no
matter how good it feels, getting some out of pity now
and then can't quite compare with being with someone
you love, can it?"

Tychar's lips twitched seductively as he began to purr
"No, it cannot." His fingers trailed over my shoulder and
down to my hip.

"Why is it that I think I'm about to get nailed again?"

"Because you are," he said. "My brother's snard still
fills you, and I am... intrigued... to discover what it will
feel like to mate with you now."

"Sounds kinky," I remarked.

"You may explain that word later," he said as he
turned on his side and pulled my leg up over his hip.

"Mmmm," I sighed as he pushed inside me. "Feels really good, doesn't it? Slick, creamy…"

He nodded. "I like it."

The presence of Trag's semen seemed to diminish the orgasmic effect of Tychar's coronal fluid, but I didn't mind a bit; I just lay back and let my lover rock me to sleep. No dream could have been sweeter than he, but they were still some very nice dreams…

Uragus woke me up bright and early the next morning, saying he wanted to get an early start on his piano lesson. As he was hopping up and down with excitement, I didn't have the heart to dissuade the little bugger. Realizing that I was still nude and had not so much as a sheet up over me, I sent him on to the music room.

"Go for it, big guy," I said sleepily. "I'll be there in a minute."

I sat up and looked around for Tychar, but realized he must have gone to get breakfast. It was then that I decided that one thing they really needed on Darconia was coffee, at least in the morning—and especially those mornings after two Zetithians have had a go at you. Ordinarily, chocolate would have been my first choice of things to add to the menu, but with those two around, I'd probably never crave it again. I could vaguely remember being fed some supper at some point after dark, but that's about all. Scalia's wine had nothing on Zetithian snard for knocking a girl out.

The day was already quite hot, and as I reached for my dress, which someone had laid over the back of a nearby chair, I wondered what would happen if I just didn't put it on. Would anyone notice? I'd always worn clothing up to that point, but no one else around there did. They wore lots of jewelry, though. Maybe if I put on a necklace or two—a string of pearls, perhaps—and some bracelets as Trag had suggested.

I tried it, but it felt weird. There was something strange about being naked with a child in the next room, too, though he'd already seen me once and hadn't seemed to notice. In my dilemma over what to wear, I hadn't been paying attention, but I could hear him playing, and it sounded almost too good to be true. I peeked in on him, and there he was, playing scales to beat the band, his nimble little fingers simply flying over the keys. I stood staring for a moment before exclaiming, "By George, I think he's got it!"

Uragus gave me a quick glance over his shoulder and smiled. "Pretty beads," he remarked and went right back to playing.

Well, obviously *he* didn't give a damn…

I was able to justify it further with the fact that when Nindala's troupe arrived, there would be more skin showing than anyone around here had ever seen before, even if it was blue. I'd never go out of the palace like that, of course, because I'm sure the sun would have fried me to a crisp in minutes. Then it occurred to me that, since my arrival, I hadn't been out at all, except for the occasional venture out onto the portico from the slave quarters. I couldn't imagine running around it at night, let alone in the daytime. The tigers must have been bored out of their minds even to think of doing it themselves.

I wondered what they would do if given the freedom to go their own way, though it was a safe bet that they wouldn't have remained on Darconia. Tychar claimed never to have been anything but a soldier, but with his voice, I thought he might have had a successful career as a singer. Trag had once been a pilot and given a ship of his own, he could roam the galaxy looking for other Zetithians. With any luck, he might even find a female…

Tychar came in with breakfast and smiled his approval of my dress—or lack thereof. I took little notice, however, being more excited about Uragus.

"Would you listen to that!" I said with awe. "He's better than anyone I've ever taught!"

Tychar listened closely for a moment. "He's not playing a song."

"I know, but… wow!" I grabbed a crafnet (which were the closest thing Darconia had to apples) from the tray and hurried into the music room. I had to be sure this wasn't a fluke. He might have been playing scales well, but could he also read the music?

"Play this note," I said, picking one at random on the pad.

Uragus hit it without any hesitation whatsoever and picked up the scale from that point.

I skipped ahead to a short song. "Try this."

His timing might have been off slightly, but he didn't miss a single note.

"Damn!" I exclaimed before remembering the "Great Mother of the Desert" thing. I guess there are some habits you just can't change overnight. I flipped to the left hand scale of bass notes. "Try this." It came as naturally to him as the other one had. "Uragus, how in the world are you *doing* that?"

He shrugged. "I don't know. I... had a dream last night, and the whole thing began to make sense," he said in his squeaky little voice. "That's why I came so early. I wanted to see if it was real."

"Oh, it's real all right!" I assured him. "You've got all the makings of a child prodigy."

"What's a child prodigy?"

"A natural born musician," I replied. "One that grasps the concepts at a very early age—and progresses much more quickly than other children."

He grinned at me. "I'm good, then?"

"You are *very* good," I said, sitting down next to him. My first impulse was to hug him, and I wondered if Darconian children liked to be hugged. Experimentally, I put an arm around him and squeezed. His scales felt surprisingly smooth and warm—not like hugging a lizard at all.

He smiled up at me, but asked me why I'd done that.

"That, my little prodigy, is called a hug," I replied. "Humans do that when they're glad to see someone, or happy for them—that sort of thing."

"I have never been hugged before," he said. "But I like it."

"I like it, too," I said. "So you can expect plenty of hugs from me from now on." I scrolled ahead in the tablet and found the song I was looking for. "Now, try this one. It's pretty easy, but you have to use both hands to play it."

He stumbled in a few places and didn't quite get the timing then either, which was something I felt could be easily corrected, but still, he was nothing short of amazing.

I couldn't quite believe it myself. Here I was, a bazillion kilometers from Earth, and I had finally found my prodigy—and he was a lizard, of all things! My excitement was tempered by the fact that, as he grew, his fingers would widen, and he wouldn't be able to strike the keys individually, which made it most unfortunate that the folks at Steinway hadn't had Darconians in mind when they constructed this particular instrument. Then it occurred to me that his mother *was* the Queen, and as such, had the wherewithal to commission someone to make a piano with wider keys. In fact, considering the trouble that Zealon and Racknay were having, I ought to suggest it right away. I would have to measure Racknay's fingertips to get an idea of just how wide they needed to be, but I thought it was possible. For all I knew, such a thing might have already been made, for there were keyboard instruments all over the known galaxy. Just because I had never seen them didn't mean they didn't exist.

I hadn't noticed a *Musician's Friend* or a *Zzounds* catalog lying around anywhere—the interplanetary versions, that is—which meant that I'd have to get on a computer and check out the Net. I hadn't seen many computers since my arrival, but I knew Wazak had one in his office. The funny thing was that after being so intimidated by him on that first day, I now had no qualms about cornering him in his den and asking him. I couldn't remember where his office was, though, so I'd have to get Tychar to take me—or one of the guards. I wondered what they would think of my new wardrobe.

I left Uragus playing his little fingers to the bone, and Tychar and I went down to find Wazak. On the way, we passed Dragus, who was guarding The Shrine. I must have been there long enough to change my opinions about Darconians, because while Wazak was just plain big, I thought Dragus was a hunk. Now, I know he was a lizard, but he was still a handsome devil in his own way.

"You have adopted our manner of dress," he remarked. "I approve."

"Thanks, Dragus. I wasn't sure it would work for me. I may need a few more beads, though," I admitted. "I've never been one to wear more than one strand at a time, so I don't have many. By the way, what does it mean when you wear a lot of them? That you're rich, or what?"

He smiled. "It means that you have many admirers."

"Ah," I said archly. "So they're like Mardi Gras beads, then."

Not surprisingly, he didn't know what I meant, so I had to explain, but anyone from Earth would have understood the reference right away. Women had been flashing their boobs at men to get a string of beads on Bourbon Street in New Orleans for nearly as long as the city had been in existence. It was a great city for musicians, too, and I thought Uragus would fit right in with all the jazz pianists, though he'd have to learn from someone other than myself, since I'd always tended toward the classical or pop styles. I could just picture him playing the blues in some backstreet café—he would give the term "lounge lizard" a whole new meaning.

We arrived at Wazak's office to find that he did indeed have a computer with which we could access the Net. It was an older model, but usable. When I told him what I was looking for, he seemed pleased that I would consider the needs of the male children.

"It is good of you to teach them your music," Wazak said. "Males are not considered to be… musical… on this world."

"I've heard that before, but it's a bunch of Saturnian bunk, if you ask me," I declared. "I mean, you should hear Uragus! That little bugger would make a believer out of anyone, and I think Racknay would be a decent pianist if he had a piano that fit him."

Actually, Racknay tended to lean more toward the hard rock end of the music spectrum, as did most Darconian music, though it was performed exclusively by females. I had played him some songs from my collection and discovered that he liked Aerosmith a whole lot better than Mozart.

Wazak seemed even more pleased by this and offered the use of his computer without hesitation.

The connection was slow, but I finally got *Zzounds* online, and yes, they had a keyboard with extra-wide keys, though it was a synthesizer rather than a grand piano. The price wasn't bad, either—only fifty credits. Shipping was pretty pricey, and even though it wouldn't be coming all the way from Earth, it would still take quite a while to reach Darconia. I had no fears that Uragus would outgrow the one we had before then, but the price was a lot more than I had in my pocket. Someone else would have to pay for it.

"I will authorize the purchase," Wazak said, punching in some numbers. "I believe the Queen will be pleased that you have suggested this." Wazak, himself, appeared to be tickled to death by the notion, and I could only assume that it was because I was helping to dispel the myth that Darconian males were good for nothing but being grumpy.

On the way back to my quarters, I discovered that Darconian males were good at something else, too: they could make a Zetithian jealous.

As we passed The Shrine, Dragus smiled and waved us by, but after a moment, he called me back. I thought he might have looked a bit sheepish, but, being a Darconian, it was difficult to be sure.

"I would like for you to have this," Dragus said, holding out a string of beads. "And I would be honored if you would wear it." As he focused his attention on the necklace, I saw that some of the beads were beginning to glow. I stared at it in awe, realizing that fully a third of the beads were glowstones! What the other stones were, I couldn't have said, but his gift was easily worth far more than my pearls—on Darconia or any other world.

"Why, th—thank you, Dragus," I stammered. "It's very beautiful, but are you sure you want me to have it? I mean, isn't there someone else you'd rather—"

"No," he said, drawing himself up to his full height— which was considerable—his earlier sheepishness seeming to have vanished completely. "It would look best on you."

I didn't know whether to take it from him or let him put it around my neck, so I just stood there, staring back at him.

"Will you wear it?" he asked.

I peered up at him suspiciously. "This doesn't mean we're sweethearts, does it?"

"No," he replied. "Only that I find you to be as lovely as the stones."

I wasn't sure, but I thought that maybe on Darconia, comparing someone to a stone was a compliment. "That's very kind of you," I said. "Yes, I will wear it."

With that, he placed it around my neck with an almost ceremonial reverence. I got a little choked up there for a second, but then I remembered all the jewelry Dobraton wore and almost laughed out loud, for I couldn't imagine anyone, Darconian or otherwise, doing this same thing with her. The exchange with Dragus was sort of romantic, and Dobraton was anything but. No, what I *could* picture was Dobraton snatching the beads and then giving the man in question the boot for taking liberties.

As we walked on, I was fingering the beads, wondering if they would be worth as much as Tychar. Considering how much it had meant to Dragus for me to wear them, it would probably be tacky of me to trade them in for Tychar, but I was toying with the idea when he spoke up.

"He may expect favors from you now," Tychar warned.

"Favors," I echoed. "You mean like free piano lessons?"

"No," Tychar replied. "Sexual favors."

"But he said it didn't mean we were sweethearts!" I protested. "If it had, I wouldn't have accepted it." I couldn't begin to imagine what sort of sexual favors a Darconian might ask for—and didn't want to, either. Still, if he only wanted to have his tail tickled, I thought I could probably handle that, but if it was something more intimate… well, let's just say I wasn't any more interested in the Darconians than the Zetithians were.

I felt a pair of hands grab my ass and thought Dragus might have started already, but it turned out to be Trag. "Where you been, babe? My dick hasn't been hard all day!"

"It isn't even lunchtime yet," I said witheringly. "You've still got plenty of time."

"Don't need it," he said. "All I need is a whiff of you and a glimpse of that ass. Wow! See, I told you you'd look great dressed like a Darconian!"

"I'm still not sure I care for it myself," I admitted. "But I did get a necklace from Dragus, so I guess we can consider it a success."

Trag rolled his eyes. "I wouldn't consider it a complete success until you get one from Wazak."

"A hard man to get in the mood?" I ventured, remembering that I had just been in his office, and he hadn't mentioned anything about the fact that I seemed to have lost my dress.

"Something like that," Trag agreed. "Now, Dragus, on the other hand, is a real slut."

"Takes one to know one," I quipped.

"Look who's talking!" Trag sputtered. "You've done two of us at the same time. I'd say that was pretty slutty myself."

"Careful now," I cautioned him, "or I might decide to reform."

"Wouldn't want that," he grinned. "Guess I'd better shut up."

"Yes," Tychar said. "That would be best." He walked on for a few steps before adding, "And never call her a slut again."

Trag laughed. "He's so... *Zetithian*. No sense of humor at all."

"Tell me something, Trag," I said. "Are you the *only* Zetithian ever to have a sense of humor?"

"Well, no, probably not," he admitted. "It's just

that he's so... stiff, don't you think? I'm a whole lot more fun."

"Ah, trying to get me to switch brothers, are you?" I said knowingly. "Well, you can just forget it, Trag. I'll ease your pain now and then, but you won't make me fall in love with you."

Trag shrugged and draped a casual arm across my shoulders. "Can't blame me for trying, can you?"

"No, but your brother might beat the shit out of you if you don't knock it off."

Trag looked at Tychar questioningly. "Any idea what she means by that?"

"Not really," said Tychar. "But it sounded like a warning."

"Uh-*huh*," Trag said uncertainly.

Tychar slipped his arm around my waist and pulled me close to him. My God! If Nindala could only see me now! The timid little piano teacher had been completely erased, and a woman unafraid to walk through the palace wearing nothing but some jewelry and two naked tigers had taken her place. This new woman wasn't even afraid of Wazak!

"So, when are we getting together again?" Trag asked eagerly. "You *did* say you would try it again tomorrow, and, in case you haven't noticed, it's tomorrow now."

"I think I've created a monster," I groaned.

"No," Tychar said gloomily, "he was already a monster."

"Why didn't you warn me?"

"It was foolish of me not to," he agreed. "But he *is* my brother."

You'd have thought Trag would have objected to being called a monster, but he actually seemed proud of it and made the most terrifying, snarling face, just to prove how monstrous he could be. The tigers were beautiful, but they could look pretty fierce, too: a pissed-off Zetithian probably could have put the fear of God in a Darconian. I wondered if Scalia had ever thought about letting them take care of Dobraton for her, but then I remembered that she was trying to keep the tigers a secret.

"Tell me something," I said, changing the subject completely. "Ever hear of anyone by the name of Dobraton?"

"You mean that tough old lizard who gives Scalia so much trouble?" asked Trag.

"That's the one," I said with a nod. "Ever meet her?"

"No," Tychar said. "But I believe she knows we are here."

"What makes you think that?"

"Scalia has said so," he replied. "She believes that Dobraton has spies in the palace."

"That wouldn't surprise me a bit," I remarked. "She doesn't seem to like Scalia very much—or her policies. Any idea who the spies are?"

"No," said Tychar. "We've tried to figure it out, but all the guards and staff seem to be loyal to Scalia. They could be lying, or the whole thing could just be our imagination, but sometimes… I wonder."

"Well, if Dobraton ever comes skulking around the music room instead of the Shrine," I said, "we'll know she's been tipped off."

"You're using too many Terran speech patterns," Trag complained. "Even *I* don't understand what you say a good part of the time."

"You'll get used to it," I said, patting him on the shoulder. "I'm going to be here for a very long time."

Unless Dobraton had her way and threw all the off-worlders off the planet, which would have meant that the slaves would be free to leave—or that they would all be dead. The tigers had escaped execution before, but they might not be as lucky this time—and I might not be, either. Shivering slightly, I thought I'd like to put my dress back on. Perhaps the new me wasn't quite so different from the old one, after all.

That night, I awoke from a dream with something calling out to me, beckoning me to come to it. Unable to resist, I rose from my bed, leaving Tychar sleeping in the moonlight. The night air was chilly, and I slipped into a robe as I stole silently into the music room.

The three Darconian moons were conjoined—surely a good omen—and shone down on the planet below with a brightness that cast shadows as though daylight had come early. The piano sat silently on the dais, but I could feel the pull and knew that this was what had been calling to me. The ancient instrument was ready at last; to tell me its story and to share its secrets.

Sitting down on the bench, I began to play one of the Zetithian love songs at first, but then the melody changed, seemingly of its own accord, to become something different, yet similar, as though inspired by the original song. I'd never played like that before, and the music seemed to come through my hands straight from my heart. It was my love song to Tychar: how I felt when I was in his arms, how I knew he was my one, true love—forever and always.

A fleeting thought told me that I should be recording this so I wouldn't forget it, but I knew in my heart that it would be indelibly placed in my memory. No, I wouldn't forget it, and the melody would grow with each day I spent with him, for this was his song: the expression of my feelings for him. I had never been inspired before, but I certainly was now.

Something moved within the shadows, taking the shape of the one I was playing for; the one I loved. Moving nearer, he placed his hands on my shoulders, and their warm strength inspired me even further. The melody changed again, becoming two songs, somehow blended into one. Was this how the great composers had worked their magic? Had they had such a love to inspire them, to carry them far beyond their usual talents? How else could one explain why the occasional mediocre composer could suddenly bring forth a piece of music that survived the ages?

I played on, letting his love be my guide, and when the song reached its conclusion at last, I was reluctant to break the spell and waited silently for him to speak.

"That was the most beautiful thing I've ever heard," he said gently. "It reminds me of you."

"No," I whispered. "It is my love for you, nothing more."

His grasp on my shoulders tightened. "Do you truly love me that much?"

"I do," I replied. Taking his hand from my shoulder, I kissed it softly. "Can you doubt it?"

"No," he said in a somber tone. "My vision was a true one. You are here, we are lovers, and my life will never be the same."

"Or mine."

I knew it was true, because for better or worse, it had happened; he was the one great love of my life—and he was a slave.

Chapter 13

THE EDRAITIANS ARRIVED FOR THEIR PERFORMANCE ABOUT A month or so later, and since I didn't see any point in advertising the fact that I was pale all over when they were such a beautiful shade of blue, I went back to wearing a dress for the duration of their visit.

We decided to have a short piano recital before the main event, and Uragus had been practicing like mad. Zealon and Racknay would also be performing, but it was a safe bet that their little brother would be the star of the show. Tychar had urged me to play my own composition as a part of the program, but I wasn't quite ready to share it with the world. It was still too personal, and besides, I didn't want to appear to be trying to upstage the children. This was their night, and I didn't want anything to overshadow their accomplishments.

I met up with Nindala in the Great Hall the day they arrived, and we spent the next two days exchanging news and girl talk. She hadn't changed a bit since I saw her last: still tall, still stately, and still spectacularly beautiful. If only Trag could meet her! I had asked Scalia's permission to introduce them, thinking that she might like the idea of finding him a mate, but it was fairly obvious that Trag had been talking, because she seemed to know just how much "help" I had been to her lonely slave boys.

"They do not need another female if they have you," she said with a regal wave of her hand. "Do not forget the bounty on them, Kyra! These entertainers may mention their presence here to the wrong people."

"Yes, but Trag needs his own mate," I argued. I hated to tell her this, but after that one joint encounter, Trag hadn't broached the subject much at all. Oh, he teased, and he flirted, but nothing more, and I had an idea his conscience was bothering him. "If you're worried about the money, maybe they could buy him from you."

I could tell that this suggestion was not at all to Scalia's liking. "I do not wish to sell my cats," she said flatly. "Not to anyone."

Which included me. While I *had* mentioned the idea of buying Tychar from her, Scalia had never actually agreed to it, and it was now quite apparent that she wanted to keep things just the way they were. This meant that I would certainly never willingly leave Darconia, but whether Nindala would want to stay remained to be seen. She was more of a free spirit than I was, though given what I knew about the Zetithian brothers, Trag might be enough incentive for her to stick around for a while—if they ever met, that is.

Of course, if I couldn't tell Nindala about the tigers, any time I spent with her would be time spent without them, which made me wonder if I would go into withdrawal from the lack of joy juice. I hadn't reckoned on Scalia being so possessive, though I probably should have—after all, she'd been keeping her slaves a secret for a very long time. Nindala probably posed no threat to their safety, but people *do* talk, and a band of entertainers who traveled the galaxy were bound to spread the news of the Zetithians far and wide—news which might come to the attention of bounty hunters, who would then converge on them.

If there still *was* a price on their heads. It had been twenty years since Scalia had bought the two brothers, and in that time, any bounty on them might have been forgotten or revoked. It was a difficult thing to keep tabs on, especially since, the best I could tell, even Scalia didn't know who had been offering that bounty.

Scalia would undoubtedly find the Edraitians fascinating, because she liked diversity, and their coloring would make them stand out in any crowd. I didn't know if there would be any men in the show, but there were presumably some of them working behind the scenes, and I hoped that Scalia wouldn't try to add one of them to her slave collection. Not being an endangered or hunted species, I wasn't sure just how she would justify it, though she might simply invite some of them to settle on Darconia.

I spent as much time as I could with Nindala, and while she may have appeared to be the same as when I'd last seen her, she was of the opinion that I had changed considerably.

"You are wearing jewels," she observed.

"Local custom," I said with a shrug. "You know, when in Rome, and all that?"

Not surprisingly, she didn't understand the reference, but thought that my glowstone necklace was quite remarkable—especially after I lit them up for her.

"This must be very valuable," she said, inspecting it carefully. "Where did you get it?"

"Oh, one of the guards gave it to me," I said in a nonchalant manner. "I think he thought I was underdressed."

Her skepticism was evident, for her red eyebrows both disappeared into the lock of hair which was draped dramatically across her forehead. "Do you mean to say that you have taken to dressing in the Darconian fashion?"

"I'd hardly call it 'dressing,'" I said dryly. "More like *un*dressing."

"I find it difficult to imagine," she confided. "You are not… comfortable with such things."

A lot had happened to change that about me, but I couldn't very well explain it without mentioning Trag and Tychar. I still wore my hair in a braid, though, so at least I hadn't gotten into the "big hair" habit. Maybe that would come next, but I doubted it. Not wearing clothes was easy enough, but the hair thing would take more time than I was willing to devote to it. Besides, Tychar seemed to enjoy undoing my braid.

Changing the subject before I slipped up and told her about the tigers and their own lack of clothing, I went on to tell her about my students, Uragus in particular.

"He's a genuine prodigy," I said excitedly. "It's been hard keeping up with him. I mean, he's already playing Beethoven!"

"I do not know Beethoven," she remarked, "but this means he is showing progress?"

"Oh, yeah! I've never had a student this gifted before. It's like a dream come true!"

"So, you are happy here then?" she ventured.

"Much happier than I ever thought I'd be. The Darconians took a little getting used to, but really, most of them are quite nice."

Which was true, if you didn't include Dobraton, and I hoped that Nindala would at least be spared having to meet *her*. Having met Tychar and Trag on my first evening hadn't hurt my opinion of Darconia, and I was very glad I'd decided to take on the job, because it had turned out to have more perks than I could have possibly imagined. I was dying to tell Nindala, too, because I was certain she would have been very impressed. I also wanted to tell her that Garon had been wrong about the possibility of finding love on Darconia, and it really griped my cookies not to be able to tell her any of my juicier stories. That left only my students and maybe Wazak—or Dragus. Actually, Dragus was the best story, so when Nindala seemed skeptical that any Darconian could be nice, I played it up a bit.

"But they *are* nice, Nindala! I protested. "Especially Dragus—the guard who gave me the necklace—though I was told that he'd be asking for sexual favors after I accepted his gift."

"And has he?"

"Well, no," I admitted, "but things have been a little hectic around here lately. I've been working with my students nonstop, trying to get them ready for the recital, and I don't see Dragus very much—he's usually posted in another part of the palace—but he's quite good-look-ing for a reptile."

Nindala's expression was openly skeptical. "They are egg layers," she reminded me. "There is no future in such a relationship."

"Who said we had a relationship?" I countered. "But I do like him. He made quite a ritual out of giving me those glowstones, too. It was almost romantic."

"These Darconians cannot begin to understand ro-mance," she scoffed. "They are crude and inelegant."

I'd almost forgotten what a snob she could be, and the best I had to show for my stay on Darconia was an amorous guard! If she could only see the tigers! Now, *they* were elegant!—even without their jeweled collars. She would have been terribly impressed with their cocks, too. Not telling her about them was going to be even harder than I thought.

"And they do not appear to have anything remotely resembling a penis," she went on. "How do they have intercourse?"

Somewhat exasperated, I grumbled, "I don't know, Nindala! I haven't had sex with one of them—never even seen one who was aroused." Remembering the Zetithians and the problems they had with reptiles, I added, "Maybe they can't get it up for a mammal."

"But one of them gave you a valuable necklace," she reminded me. "That must mean something."

"Like I said, he probably just thought I needed more jewelry and took pity on me for appearing to be so poor and lacking in admirers."

"But even Garon admired you," she persisted. "These lizards might do so, as well."

Nindala had a severely overinflated view of my attractiveness to alien species. I wondered where she got the idea and couldn't come up with any reasons other than what she thought about Garon, unless she'd overheard some of the other passengers talking. I still didn't believe any of it myself.

"And here comes one of them now," she said, keeping her voice down.

I turned around to see Dragus approaching. It just had to be him, didn't it?

"Pardon me, Kyra," he said politely, "but your presence is requested at The Shrine."

It didn't take much imagination to figure out who was doing the requesting. The only mystery was how they'd persuaded him to come after me.

"I am to escort you there," he added.

I wondered who was guarding The Shrine with him gone, though I thought he might have gotten Hartak, who usually guarded my door, to cover for him. Hartak really liked being my guard, too—said he wouldn't give up his post for anything. I wasn't sure why, exactly—though it was an easy job, and I was always nice to him—but I was beginning to believe that he liked hearing all the noise I made when the tigers were on the prowl. Delorian, who was posted there at night, seemed less enthusiastic, but perhaps it was because we kept him awake.

Making my excuses to Nindala, I went off with Dragus. As soon as we were out of earshot, he said, "I see you are wearing that… *thing* again."

"Thing?" I said blankly. "Oh, you mean my dress?"

Nodding, he added, "It does not become you."

"Well, I *am* wearing the necklace you gave me," I pointed out, rattling the beads around my neck. "And it's very pretty. Nindala thought so, too."

"Yes," he conceded, "but the stones look best against your skin." Since the dress I was wearing had a relatively low neckline, I had an idea that the "skin" he was talking about was the skin on my tits. Men! They're the same everywhere!

"What is so wrong with wearing clothes?" I demanded. "Do you have any idea what would happen to my skin if I stuck my nose outside the palace for an hour?"

"It would burn?"

"You're damn right it would burn! I'm not covered in scales the way you are. I've got some pretty sensitive hide under this dress!"

Dragus cast a sidelong glance at me. "I know."

At that point, I decided it might be best to change the subject. "Mind telling me who's requesting my presence in The Shrine?"

Another sidelong glance. "I believe you know who it is," he said.

"And just how did he manage to persuade you to deliver the message?"

Dragus smiled. "Tycharian has promised me a favor," he replied.

"Yeah, right!" I said skeptically. "What sort of favor could a slave possibly do for you?" Unless it was cleaning chamber pots—though I doubted this was one of Dragus's duties, either.

"There is a lady I would like to get to know better."

I prayed to God he wasn't talking about me. "Oh," I said carelessly. "And who is that?"

"Her name is Cernada," he said. "You may have met her."

"Yes, I have," I admitted, greatly relieved. "Are you saying that Ty is going to fix you up with her?"

"Fix me up?"

"Get you a date," I said with an impatient wave. "You know, put it a good word for you?"

Dragus nodded. "If I cannot have you, then I must look elsewhere."

"Oh, come on, now, Dragus! We're too different to ever get together, and you know it! Do you want the beads back?" I was rather fond of my glowstones, but I would have given them back in a heartbeat if I'd been the lady in question. Don't get me wrong; I liked Dragus, but dating a Darconian was *not* what I had in mind, aside from the fact that I was in love with someone else.

"No, I have given them to you," he said graciously. "I will not take them back."

"That's very sweet of you, Dragus! You're not such a slut, really—now, are you?"

He shrugged. "I would have liked to be as fortunate as the slaves, but—"

"Stop right there, Dragus," I warned. "I don't think I want to hear any more."

"But I have studied Terran culture," he protested. "Your species… turns me on."

"I wouldn't have thought that," I commented. "After all, we're quite a bit different, and the tigers aren't the slightest bit interested in Darconians." I chose not to mention the fact that I considered Dragus to be rather handsome for a Darconian, since he didn't seem to need any further encouragement.

"Perhaps not," he conceded. "But I find your soft skin very… stimulating."

"Stimulating, huh?" I echoed. Then something else occurred to me "And just *how* do you know my skin is soft?" I inquired. "I can't recall ever having been touched by you."

Since we had arrived at The Shrine, he didn't reply, but his appreciative glance was enough to assure me that he'd at least thought about trying. The guard posted at the door opened it without comment, and I wondered if he knew why we were there. If he did, I could only assume that *someone*—probably Hartak—had been talking—which wouldn't be too surprising, given the nature of palace gossip.

As usual, the abrupt change in the humidity level upon entering The Shrine hit me like a wet blanket. Thus far, I'd never done much in the way of physical activity while I was in there, and while I would have preferred the drier heat in my quarters, with Nindala visiting, my rooms were now off-limits to the slaves. Scalia was taking no chances with her slave boys.

The tigers met us just inside, and one whiff of me had their dicks stiff almost immediately. Dragus made no move to leave, but, instead, turned and leaned against the door.

"I have missed you," Tychar purred as he took me in his arms. "It has been two entire days since I last saw you."

"What? No visions?" I teased.

"Now that I have had the real thing," he said with a smile, "visions are not nearly as satisfying as they once were."

"I wouldn't take a vision over you, either," Trag said, though his compliment sounded a little forced. He backed away slightly, with the air of one who was admitting defeat.

"I don't know," I said, scrutinizing him carefully. "Seems like you must be doing just that."

"How do you mean?"

"It's just that after that first time, I figured you'd be more… demanding, but you haven't been."

Trag looked acutely uncomfortable, and it was several moments before he spoke. "It isn't that I don't like you—because I do, Kyra, it's just that… well, you and

Ty…" Throwing up his hands in a gesture of futility, he said: "Do you love me?"

"A little," I admitted. "But it's not the same as what I feel for Tychar, and to be perfectly honest, I don't think you love me at all."

Trag took a breath as if he was about to say something, and then looked away.

"You don't, do you?" I persisted.

He was having a very hard time admitting it, but finally, he did.

"No, I don't love you," he said. "—though I probably should—I loved the sex, and you still smell fabulous, but—"

"You want a girl just like the girl that married dear old dad?"

He'd never heard that old song, of course, but he did understand the sentiment. "I risked going back to Zetith to find a mate," he said. "I didn't get one."

"And now that you've had a little nooky, you're good for another twenty years?"

"Probably not," he admitted, "But you and Ty—I know you love him, not me. It makes a difference."

"Planning to hold out for a Zetithian?" If he did, I had an idea he'd probably be waiting until the day he died.

"I'd sure like to," he said, letting out a pent-up breath. "But I could go the rest of my life and not find one—even if I wasn't stuck here playing slave boy for Scalia."

"Well, you never know what might happen," I said. "Things can change just like that," I added with a snap of my fingers.

"I sure wish they would," Trag said wistfully.

As Tychar began purring again, I got the idea that he hadn't sent Dragus after me to listen to me comfort his brother. "So, now that you've got me here, what did you have in mind?"

The answer to that was fairly obvious, because it *had* been two days since I'd seen him, and before that, Tychar had been with me almost constantly. I ought to have been suffering from withdrawal, but it was also possible that I'd needed the rest. Still, the sight of him fully aroused and purring was having its effect on me: my clitoris was tingling as it became engorged, and I was probably pumping out just as much juice as he was.

Tychar moved in close behind me and ran his fingers under the straps of my gown. "Why are you wearing a dress?"

"We have visitors to the palace," I replied, "so I thought I should."

"It is odd that you would feel that way," Dragus piped up, "for even they do not wear clothing."

"But I feel, well… naked," I said, trying to explain. "You know, vulnerable?"

"Let me tell you something, Kyra," Tychar murmured in my ear. "Seeing you naked makes *me* vulnerable, not you. It makes me want to mate," he purred. As his hot tongue slid across my neck, my resolve began to weaken along with my knees. "And when I wish to mate, I become your slave. You are free to do anything with me, and I will do whatever you ask."

I glanced over at Dragus. "I'm not so sure I can feel 'free' with Dragus lurking in the corner," I said. "Think we could get rid of him?"

"That was not part of our agreement," Dragus said. "I was told I could watch."

I looked up at Tychar in frank disbelief. "You devil!" I exclaimed. "You told him that?"

Tychar shrugged. "I was desperate."

"Yes, but—"

"You did *not* have to come, and you don't have to do anything you don't want to do," Tychar reminded me. "You aren't a slave, Kyra."

"Oh, yeah, right!" I grumbled. "But tell me something: have *you* ever said no to a Darconian—one of the big ones who could knock you over with one swing of his tail?" I heard Dragus chuckling and turned to glare at him. "And don't you go getting any funny ideas, Dragus!"

Still laughing, Dragus shook his head. "But Kyra, I can think of nothing I would like more than to watch, if I cannot have you myself."

The thought of Dragus being anywhere other than the other side of the door when I was making love with Tychar creeped me out completely. "Forget it, big guy! It's not gonna happen!" Eyeing him with suspicion, I added, "Is this your way of getting your necklace back? Do I have to bribe you with it?"

Dragus shook his head, but it was Tychar who spoke. "Just forget about him," he suggested, which was a bit ridiculous, since Dragus was entirely too big to miss, "and come over by the fountain. I have a bed all ready for you."

Against my better judgment—which was rapidly evaporating—I was just about to comply when I spotted Refdeck. "Oh, come on! Not all the other slave boys, too!"

"Well, they *are* locked in with us," Tychar said reasonably. "And they promised to be quiet."

"But they aren't invisible, and they aren't blind!" I protested. "I don't think I can—"

Tychar silenced me with a bone-melting kiss. "Just close your eyes, my love," he whispered against my lips. "And I will give you joy unlike any you have ever known."

My eyes were already closed—I could no more have kept them open than I could have kept from responding to his soft, wet kiss. Sighing as his hands caressed my back, I felt his fingers as they combed the braid from my hair. Knowing that all was lost, I wrapped my arms around his neck and returned his kiss, forgetting everything else as his tongue teased my own, sending tendrils of fire curling through my body. Oh, yes, focused on him, I could forget just about anything—until I felt my dress begin to slip away.

"Leave it on!" a shrill voice squeaked. "It's better that way!"

Opening one eye, I could see the guy with the octopus fingers jumping up and down at the head of the pack of slaves who were all gathered around to watch.

"You are supposed to keep quiet, Sladnil!" Tychar said severely. "One more word, and I'll throw you over the wall!"

"So, he *does* have a name," I murmured. "I was wondering what it was." Chuckling softly, I added, "Imagine that! One of you who actually *likes* my dresses!"

"He likes a lot of weird things," Tychar said.

"Such as?"

Tychar cleared his throat uncomfortably. "You really don't want to know."

I tried to imagine what weird things a skinny little guy with bulbous eyes, fish lips, and octopus fingers might enjoy and decided that Tychar was absolutely right. "No, I probably don't."

I did my best, even kissing Tychar again, but having Sladnil standing there watching was creeping me out even more. "Come on, you guys," I protested. "I just can't do this with you around."

"I'll get rid of them," Trag offered. "Seeing as how I'm not getting any, I'd just as soon not watch, either." Motioning for the others to follow, he said, "Come on, guys, let's go outside and… pound sand or something."

The slaves all trooped morosely to the door to the portico. It was hot as hell out there at that hour, even in the shade of the dome, but I hoped they were used to it. Dragus, however, didn't move a muscle. "You, too, Dragus," I said severely. "I'm not doing another thing until you're out of here."

Dragus laughed. "I will leave," he said, capitulating at last, "but you must admit, it was worth a try."

"You can listen," I conceded, since I was fairly certain all of the guards did just that. "Though how you could hear anything through those doors is beyond me."

Dragus shrugged. "There are other ways," he said casually. "And you may keep the necklace," he added.

I had no idea what he meant by "other ways," but didn't care as long as he left.

As the door closed behind Dragus, Tychar began purring again, making me forget everything but him. He'd gone to a lot of trouble to get me there, and I wasn't about to disappoint him. After all, I'd missed him, too.

"You handsome devil," I whispered, running my fingers through his hair. "You know I can't resist you."

He smiled knowingly. "You haven't forgotten me, have you?"

"Impossible," I vowed. "I couldn't forget you in a million years—well, I might, if Dragus conked me on the head—but I wouldn't forget you only because Nindala was here! It's just that I've been really busy getting ready for the recital, and you guys have been locked up more than usual. That's got to be hard for you."

Tychar smiled, and his purr deepened. "It gives me more time to think of ways to please you," he said. Picking up where he left off, my dress was on the floor in moments. The only sound was the splashing of the fountain. We were alone and naked in the Garden of Eden—and I felt like Eve with the apple.

"I've been thinking of ways to give you pleasure, too," I said mysteriously.

"Such as?"

Using his hair to pull him closer, I licked his lips and then bit him lightly. Hearing his low growl, I took it further and wrapped my fingers around his cock, giving it a hard squeeze. "You'll see," I whispered. "Lie down."

I was treated to the vision of my shockingly handsome, blue-eyed tiger as he lay back on the pallet, his hair fanned out behind him and his jeweled cock waiting for me to gorge myself upon. Down on my hands and knees, I crawled up between his legs and licked him, but avoided his hot, dripping cock, fully intending to tease him mercilessly and make him *beg*…

Running my tongue up his inner thigh, I felt pure delight as his cock pulsed, sending a river of fluid cascading from the head. The mere sight of it nearly sent me over the edge, but I controlled myself—somehow managing not to succumb to temptation and suck him. Hooking a finger under his jeweled cock ring, I pulled it up so that the skin of his scrotum was drawn tightly over his balls. I'd never known how much I would like such things until I met Tychar, but I was certainly hooked on it now. The fact that he was naked all the time probably helped, but just knowing that I could grab his balls anytime I liked was empowering for me. I wasn't timid anymore; I liked looking at my sexy tiger and didn't bother to hide that fact.

"You like it when I've got you by the balls, don't you?" I teased.

"I like everything you do," he said. "You could beat me, and I would enjoy it."

"Ooo, kinky," I commented approvingly—which was odd, because until I met him, half of what we did together would have seemed kinky. "Better not give me any ideas. I just might try it someday."

Thrusting his hips up, he spread his legs further apart. "I'd rather have you eat me."

"Not yet, slave boy," I growled. "I'm gonna make you suffer."

His cock seemed to quiver with anticipation as he pointed it toward my mouth. "Kyra, *please*!"

I shook my head. "No, not yet."

Groaning, he reached down to take my head in his hands and force me down on him.

"Nooo," I said, backing away. "No hands! You're my slave, remember? I get to do whatever I want with you, and if that includes tormenting you, then I will."

"You have tormented me for years," he said. "I have seen your face in the stars, laughing at me, telling me to wait—and I have waited."

"Then you can wait a little longer," I said. "Right now, I'm not touching your dick. I want to enjoy you without the orgasms interfering."

"How?" he whispered hoarsely.

"I'm going to suck your balls, and then, when I can't stand it anymore, I'm going to 'mate' with you every way I can think of."

Coronal fluid erupted from his cock, and his eyes glazed over. I was *definitely* getting to him! As his testicles slid up higher in his scrotum, I pulled harder on the cock ring, making the skin over his balls so tight, it was as shiny as his dick. Leaning down, I licked him and watched him squirm.

"You're killing me, Kyra," he moaned.

Laughing wickedly, I sucked one testicle into my mouth and bit down on it gently. It was hard to tell whether it hurt him or not—his subsequent gasp and explosive purr could have been from pleasure or pain—but he'd said I could beat him, and he'd like it…

I certainly liked it; I was unbelievably wet, and my clitoris was so engorged, it hurt. But I kept on sucking his balls and licked underneath them, pulling him up off the floor with the cock strap. His dick was always huge, but I'd never seen it like this before—he was so hard, it was a wonder the skin didn't split.

"Please, Kyra!" he begged.

With a slow shake of my head, I twisted the jeweled strap to tighten it and said: "No."

His roar of frustration was loud enough for Dragus

to hear. "I don't care what you do," he gasped. "But do *something*!"

"Aw," I said tauntingly. "Does my naughty little slave boy want more?"

His breathing became erratic and ragged. "Yes, Kyra, yes," he said desperately. "Do something… *anything*…"

Letting go of the cock ring, I backed away. "Turn over," I said, remembering a fantasy I'd had before. "Get up on your hands and knees."

Tychar flipped over so fast, I almost didn't see it, giving me a full view of his fabulous buns and his balls hanging down between his thighs.

"Now, aim it at me."

Where another man would have had to use his hand, Tychar effortlessly did what I asked, forcing his cock back as far as he could so that his balls were draped over each side of the shaft.

"Oh, yeah," I sighed. "Just like that. Now move." I slapped him on the butt, and he rocked back and forth, letting his cock and balls swing freely. "Great Mother of the Desert," I swore, letting out a pent-up breath. "That is *so* hot!" Then I got another idea. "Lie down on your stomach and spread your legs."

The sight of his perfect body spread-eagled on the mat, his huge cock framed with his ass and testicles, was too much for me, and another spontaneous orgasm hit me even harder than the one I'd had when I'd first laid eyes on him. It took a few moments to recover, and then I crawled up between his outstretched legs and bit him on the ass.

"You bad boy," I scolded him. "That's what you get for driving me wild."

His response was a low growl as his penis gushed again. "Just lick me," he pleaded. "Please."

I did as he asked but continued to avoid his cock, licking only his buns and his balls until he was writhing and dripping with sweat, and his penis was a deep shade of slick purple.

"Kyra," he said, sounding quite dangerous.

"What?"

"Do you have any idea what you're doing to me?"

"I believe I do," I replied. "Don't you like it?"

"No!" he roared. "No—yes—I can't take—"

"Had enough? Should I leave now?"

"If you ever leave me again, it'll be the death of me," he said breathlessly.

"Well, we can't have *that*…" I said, biting him again. "Should I lick your dick now?"

"If you *don't*, I'll…"

"You'll do *what*, slave boy?" I taunted, slapping his ass again. "Tell the Queen on me?"

"I'm going to fuck you *so* hard…"

"Oh, promises, promises," I taunted him. "Even Trag fucks harder than you do."

With a roar, he came up off the mat and, pouncing on me with a snarl, pulled me up against him, nearly drawing blood with his kiss. "You evil woman," he growled. "I will show you no mercy."

"That's the general idea," I gasped.

Throwing me down on my back, he got on his knees beside me and ran his cock over my breasts, teasing the nipples with the serrated corona until I was writhing in anticipation.

"I can torment you, too," he gloated. "*And* make you beg."

"Ha!" I said weakly. "You can't possibly wait that long. Look at your cock—it's about to go off all by itself."

"Then suck the snard out of it," he said thickly, as he pressed it against my lips.

My lips slipped over his cock as Tychar thrust into my mouth and his fingers tangled in my hair. I was becoming intoxicated with him: his heat, his strength, and his overwhelming sexuality. He was so... *male*, and try as I might, I hadn't enough wits left to come up with a better word to describe him.

The mere sight of his hard, wet cock was enough to drive me insane, but the taste and feel of him, as well as the orgasms his coronal fluid gave me, soon had me helpless with ecstasy.

"I like seeing your lips around my cock... I don't think I'll ever get enough of that." He thrust harder, and his balls tightened. "No," he groaned, "I must have more."

Backing away, he pushed me back, pulling my legs apart with an abruptness that both shocked and excited me. Gazing down at me, he growled again, revealing his fangs. "You temptress," he said in a voice made even deeper with passion. "You tease me and drive me insane with desire. You are mine, Kyra. You can belong to no other."

His head dipped down, and his tongue plunged into me, licking deeply until his face was wet with the evidence of my desire. Reaching up to tease my nipples with his hands, he then went after my clitoris with his tongue, drawing a long torturous moan from my lips.

"Omygod," I groaned, my hips rising up to meet him of their own accord. "You're the tempting one, Ty, the one I can't resist. I can't—stand it."

Sweat was trickling down my back as every muscle in my body tightened to reach orgasm. Then I felt it; the searing, piercing note that heralded my climax. The moment my body began bucking against his mouth, he switched his position, placing his cockhead against my clit. His cock syrup added its own magic, prolonging and intensifying my orgasm until my body could take no more.

I lost all track of time, but it seemed as though days were passing, rather than mere minutes—days filled with endless pleasure. My moans mingled with his purring, becoming almost a roar in my head. Through the mists of joy, Tychar leaned down to give me a taste of his warm, delicious lips.

Then his purr became a growl as he thrust into me with a fury I'd never imagined. My body lay open for him as he filled me with his hot shaft, and I used my legs to urge him on, kicking my heels against that fabulous ass.

"Do you want more, Kyra?" he purred.

I didn't see how there could possibly be more; his cock was slamming into me so hard, I could feel his nuts bouncing off my butt. My response was a half-scream, half-gasp as he stopped completely and altered the angle of entry and hit… something… and the whole world turned upside down. A deep growl issued from my throat as I raked my nails down his arms.

His glowing eyes and satisfied smile assured me of his delight, and I knew I could search for the rest of my life and never find anyone for whom I felt a greater love than I did for him right then. He was mine, no matter who his rightful owner was. "You're mine!" I screamed. "All mine!"

"You won't leave me?"

"Never! They'd have to kill me first." I felt him moving inside me, his hips undulating as he gave me his love, and we merged into one.

"You won't ever torment me like that again, will you?"

"Every day for the rest of my life," I promised, crying out in wonder as he pulled my legs up, locking my ankles on his shoulders before he began rotating his cock inside me.

His fangs gleamed as his smile intensified. "Good."

Then I remembered my intention to do it all. "Do it from behind," I gasped. "I want you in every possible way."

As he rolled me over onto my stomach, I expected him to plunge inside as before, but Tychar took his time, teasing me relentlessly: pushing, withdrawing, and pushing again, getting me primed with the syrup dripping from the ridges of his cockhead. The more he teased, the more orgasms shook my body, the more I wanted to rock back into him and take him inside me. But I felt so weak; I didn't think I could do it.

At last, summoning up what little strength I had left, I caught him on the instroke and impaled myself with him—and let out a gasp as my eyes nearly popped out of my head. I had no idea anything could feel so good and heard myself crying out in a way I'd never done before.

My mind shouted, "Don't stop!" though my mouth was incapable of forming the words. Unable to speak, I held my breath waiting for what would come next and then let out a scream as he began grinding his cock inside me, evoking a sensation that went beyond mere pleasure into the realm of erotic fantasy and beyond.

Tears poured down my cheeks as my passion for him reached new heights, but I couldn't do anything, couldn't say anything, because I had lost nearly all control of mind and body. I had no idea that the human body was capable of feeling so much pleasure.

"Do you like it, Kyra?" he purred.

"Yes!" I shouted, finding my voice. "Don't stop—oh, *please*, don't stop."

"I like it, too. The view from here is quite… delectable."

I was trying to remember if my backside had ever been called delectable before when his movements became increasingly erratic as he lost all control. "Oh, Kyra," he sighed, "What you do to me…"

Groaning as his cock erupted, he drove in deeper to fill me with his euphoria-inducing cream. His climax persisted long after it ordinarily would have ceased, and the undulation of his corona took me to a new level—a higher plane, where the whole world seemed to stop and I could see stars suspended there before me; shimmering, tantalizing stars floating just beyond my reach. Straining toward them, I was about to touch one when they all suddenly winked out.

Chapter 14

THE SKY WAS BEGINNING TO DARKEN WHEN I AWOKE, AND my first thought was that if Scalia had ever experienced what I just had with Tychar, she'd have never let me anywhere near him, though perhaps that sort of total loss of control was a risk that a queen could not afford to take. But still, waking up in Tychar's arms was something even a lizard queen—and perhaps even a female toad—could appreciate. Purring softly, Tychar lay sprawled on his back with my head pillowed on his chest and his arm draped over my back. I hated to move—wasn't even sure I could—but I had a recital to prepare for, and if Dragus had let me oversleep, I was gonna stomp on his big, fat Darconian tail!

"What time is it?" I said hoarsely.

"Don't know," Tychar murmured. "Don't care, either."

"Well, I do!" I said. "I've got that recital tonight—remember?" Sitting up, I took a quick look around and saw no one. "Anybody there?" I called.

"Just us slave boys," Trag replied from behind a thicket of palms. "We figured it was safe to come back in—I mean, you two couldn't possibly have gone on *this* long."

"Not much to see after we've fallen asleep, is there?"

"I disagree," Refdeck said. "You are still very beautiful, even when you are asleep."

Laughing out loud, I said, "What is it with you guys?

One human female comes along and you're all panting like a pack of wolves! On Earth, I'd only be considered moderately attractive."

"Well, around here, you're the hottest thing anyone's ever seen," Tychar murmured, giving me a squeeze.

"Well, you guys just need to get out more," I said roundly. "I mean, when the *toads* start thinking I'm beautiful, it's time for a change!"

"Uh, just in case you haven't noticed, we *can't* get out, and you *are* the change," Trag said. "For all of us."

Tychar's purring ceased abruptly. "She is mine," he said sternly. "Do not forget that."

"No one's forgetting that, Ty," Trag said soothingly.

"Just one little touch," Sladnil said in his shrill voice.

"No!" Tychar roared. "You will not!"

Sladnil muttered something I didn't quite catch, but it piqued my curiosity.

"What happens if he touches me?"

"He, uh, sucks with those things on his fingers," Trag explained. "They leave a mark—even on a Darconian."

Sladnil chuckled. "The Queen likes it," he said smugly.

"Yes, but what do you get out of it?" I asked him.

He laughed again. "I can taste her essence."

"Her essence?" I echoed. "And that does something to you?"

Sladnil went off into a long peal of laughter after that.

"It makes him come," Trag said informatively. "And from what I hear, he can fuck really hard. Those suction cups help him hold on."

"And just how would you know that?" I scoffed.

"Scalia told me," Trag replied.

"Did she? She can't do it with you, so you get to hear all of her stories, is that it?"

"Sort of," he admitted.

His tone of voice suggested that she wasn't the only one who would kiss and tell. "And do you report to her on what the three of us have been doing?"

"Well… yeah," he said. "It's part of the deal I made with her—you know, to take piano lessons?"

"I *knew* someone had been telling tales!" I declared. "Really, Trag! You should try for a little more discretion!"

"Well, shit, Kyra!" he said. "I mean, she is the Queen! Should I lie to her?"

Rolling my eyes, I got to my feet. "No, you probably shouldn't," I agreed. "But that's enough talk for now. We've got a recital tonight. Wish you guys could be there. Uragus is gonna bring down the house."

"He *is* very good." Tychar agreed.

"Yes, he is—and so are you. Too bad you can't get out there and sing," I said wistfully. "But Scalia would have a conniption fit for sure."

"Conniption fit?" he echoed.

"Get royally pissed," Trag translated. "As only a Queen can do."

It would have been a very bad idea, especially since I knew Dobraton would be in the audience. What she would have thought of me and Tychar doing a duet, I couldn't begin to imagine, though getting Uragus on-stage would be novel enough, since if Scalia didn't consider Darconian males to be musical, it was a safe bet that Dobraton didn't either. She had a lot to learn—actually, they both did.

I kissed Tychar good-bye and then retrieved my dress from the bench by the fountain. I wondered what Sladnil thought was so sexy about a Terran in a dress, but when I put it on, he sighed dreamily, and his thin little body shuddered. Best not to ask why, I decided, and went and pounded on the door for the guard to let me out.

As it happened, it was Dragus, and he was smiling like a cat who'd been in the cream.

"Have fun?" he asked.

"Yes," I replied shortly, thinking I'd best change the subject as quickly as possible. "Are you going to move the guys tonight?" I asked. "Dobraton is going to be here, and the last time she asked to visit The Shrine."

"We will be prepared," he said. "The Queen's guard sends me the alert. We've never been caught yet," he added proudly.

"Sends you the alert?" I echoed. "So you *do* have a way to communicate with one another then! I've wondered about that." I'd never seen anybody use a phone or a comlink of any kind, so whatever they used must have been pretty unobtrusive. Then again, given where I was, they probably had a stone for it. "Back home, *everyone* carries a communication device. There's no such thing as being out of touch." I hadn't missed being out of touch myself, but the guards would find it useful, especially given the size of the palace.

As I might have expected, Dragus pointed to a small stone on the left side of his chest armor. "This activates the link," he said. "And then we can converse over it."

As I looked up at him, it occurred to me that he seemed slightly overqualified for his job of guarding slaves who never tried to escape. "Tell me something, Dragus, how do you feel about having to guard the slaves and all?"

"The Queen rewards me well," he said with a smirk.

"Must be a boring job, though," I reflected. "Not much in the way of danger or excitement."

The look he gave me spoke volumes.

"I probably shouldn't have asked that," I mumbled. As I crossed the threshold, I slipped and would have fallen if Dragus hadn't caught me by the arm. "What's that slippery stuff all over the floor?"

Dragus' sheepish expression was all it took to tell me just how it was that he alleviated the boredom of being a guard.

Trying very hard not to smile, I advised, "Better ask the slaves for a scrail cloth and get that cleaned up before somebody breaks their neck!" When he didn't move I scolded, "Hurry up, now!" before heading off to the Great Hall. Biting my lip in a valiant effort to keep from laughing, I had rounded the next corner when finally I lost all control.

"It's not funny!" Dragus called out, obviously having heard my giggles.

With a shout of laughter that brought tears to my eyes, I didn't reply but hurried on to the recital. I couldn't wait to tell Tychar that story!

Thanks to Dragus and the boys, I'd managed to miss dinner but grabbed a bite or two backstage. The kids were playing before the Edraitians, and one nice thing about Darconian piano students was that I didn't have to worry about them being dressed appropriately, so our preparations mainly consisted of making sure they went onstage in the right order.

The Great Hall was packed with lizards of all sizes and colors and ablaze with light emanating from elaborately carved glowstone sculptures, which had been placed in niches high in the walls. Peeking past the curtains, I spotted Dobraton in the audience, and even she seemed excited. Scalia was beaming with pride at the prospect of her children performing onstage.

Zealon went first, and her competent performance drew thunderous applause. Racknay followed, but his performance was a bit spotty and was met with a polite response. The smug expression on Dobraton's face as he exited the stage told me that she undoubtedly saw this as positive proof to support the widely held belief that males were worthless as musicians. However, I still had my ace in the hole, and Uragus was bouncing up and down before going out onstage, barely able to contain his exuberance.

"Do you think they'll like me?" he asked anxiously.

"Are you kidding?" I scoffed. "They're gonna love you! And you won't believe what they'll do after they hear you play!"

"Really?"

"You bet, buddy," I assured him. "You just get on out there and knock 'em dead! They won't know what hit them." Giving him a big hug, I aimed him toward the stage and tweaked his tail.

Grinning at me over his shoulder, Uragus scampered over to center stage and climbed up on the bench while the audience waited in silent anticipation as the lights dimmed.

I'd given Uragus three pieces to choose from, and he'd picked "Für Elise," a Beethoven composition, which was one of my own personal favorites. I'd been skeptical at first because, though it isn't terribly difficult, it is played with both hands and isn't your usual beginner's first recital piece, but the way he played it gave me goosebumps.

Halfway through it, I looked out at Dobraton. Her expression was neutral, but she *had* to be impressed. Even a bunch of tone-deaf Darconians couldn't help but realize that his performance was outstanding—for anyone, and not just a tiny little guy who couldn't even reach the pedals. Scalia looked so proud of him, and I was happier than I'd been in a very long time. Sometimes being a teacher has its rewards.

As the last notes died away and Uragus took his bow, the applause and tail-thumping was positively deafening. Standing just offstage, I was watching Dobraton, trying to gauge her reaction, so I was staring right at her when she raised a pulse pistol and shot Scalia point blank.

I never heard the shot, and, given the noise level, it was doubtful that anyone else had, either, but when Scalia hit the floor with a loud thud, it got everyone's attention. Uragus was crossing the stage toward me at the time, and I knelt down and held out my arms. He ran to me, oblivious of what had just happened, and as the curtains closed, I gathered him up in my arms, turned, and ran. Zealon and Racknay were waiting in the wings, so they hadn't seen, either. They both stared at me in surprise.

"Run!" I shouted as I hurried past them. "We've got to get out of here!" It didn't take a student of history to know that when a queen is deposed, her children are in just as much danger as she. I had no idea which direction we should take, but away from the Hall seemed best. The Shrine seemed like a good place to go, but for the life of me, I couldn't have said why I was thinking that, other than the fact that Tychar was there.

I knew we'd have to get out of the palace somehow, but Dobraton undoubtedly had followers, and I had an idea that any conventional entrance would have been blocked by then. They were probably swarming all over the palace, killing off anyone loyal to Scalia. But how to get out? The Shrine was high up, but the portico went all the way around the palace…

Rope. We needed rope to scale the wall. Surely backstage there would be something! The Edraitians were all milling around back there, doing stretches and practicing their leaps, and I ran to Nindala screaming for help. "You're in danger!" I yelled. "Dobraton hates offworlders! If she's taken power, she'll probably have the whole lot of us executed!"

Stately Nindala seemed taken aback for once. "What are you talking about?" she demanded. "Who has taken power?"

"Dobraton!" I shouted. "With any luck, all you'll be is deported, but I wouldn't count on it. Dobraton would just as soon kill you as look at you."

"She would not dare!" Nindala said with all the conceit of her kind evident in her tone.

"She just killed the Queen, Nindala!" I snapped. "I'm sure killing a bunch of blue acrobats wouldn't bother her a bit. We need food, water, clothes, and a way out of here, and we need them now!"

The Edraitian manager looked at me aghast. "They have killed the Queen?"

"Either that or stunned her real good," I said in a grim voice. "We've got to get moving. Bring anything you can carry. Don't suppose you've got a gun or two in your bags, have you?"

"We are entertainers!" he insisted, sounding rather prim. "Not soldiers!"

"Are you people stupid, or what?" I yelled. "This is a coup, and if we don't get going, we're all dead!"

Still holding Uragus, I looked around wildly. We needed rope and lots of it. Zealon and Racknay just stood there, apparently struck dumb by the news. Then I remembered the curtains! "Cut the lines to the curtains!" I shouted. "Bring the rope!"

No one moved. They all just stood there, staring at me like I was insane. Then the sound of screams and pulse-rifle fire from the Great Hall became more audible. "Believe me now?" I yelled. "Let's go!"

If he wasn't off duty by then, Dragus was probably still guarding The Shrine. I was sure he would let us in, and we'd go out on top of the portico and climb down the wall. And then go where?

"The mountains!" I said aloud, echoing Tychar's reply to my question as to where he would go if he ever left the palace. "We've got to head for the mountains!" It seemed like eons ago when I'd asked him that. Perhaps he and the other slaves had already escaped. If so, I'd find him there—that is, if he lived after crossing the desert wearing nothing but a collar! Oh, God, we needed clothes! And I was the only one who had any. The trouble was, my quarters were nowhere near The Shrine.

One of the Edraitians, presumably their pilot, said, "We should go back to our ship and leave this world."

I wondered how organized this coup was and decided that it had to be pretty well planned, because if Dobraton killed Scalia and didn't intend to sacrifice herself in the attempt, she had to have backing. "They've probably got control of the spaceport by now," I warned. "It might not be safe."

Zealon and Racknay may have been momentarily speechless, but Uragus was not. "My mother is dead?" he asked.

I'd almost forgotten he was still in my arms. Looking down at his bright little eyes, I said gently, "I'm not positive, babe, but it sure looked like it to me."

"Put me down," he squeaked. "I want to see."

Wriggling his way out of my grasp, Uragus ran to the edge of the stage and peered through the curtains. "They are fighting!" he reported. "I can't see my mother."

Just then, Wazak came storming across the stage with six guards and Scalia's other three boys. "We must flee!" he shouted, scooping up Uragus. "There are too many of them for us to fight."

"Do you believe me now?" I shouted at Nindala, who still appeared to be in denial. "That's what I've been trying to tell you!" With Uragus no longer in my arms, I looked around. There was a tablecloth where the food was laid out for the performers—presumably their own, because I'd yet to see one during my sojourn on Darconia—and I gathered up the corners and handed the bundle to one of the guards. "Take this," I said. "We'll need it. Got any water?"

"We will get it when we reach The Shrine," Wazak said. "It is the only way out."

"That's what I thought," I agreed. "We should bring the curtains. We may have to shred them to make rope."

"No time," Wazak said tersely. "Besides, there is a way down from The Shrine."

"Really?" I said. "There's a way out from there? How do you keep the slaves from escaping?"

"They do not know of its existence," he replied.

So, the tigers had lived there for twenty years without knowing they were sitting on an escape route from the palace. I stared at Wazak in frank disbelief.

"They are slaves," he reminded me. "We do not tell them everything."

"Oh, yeah, right," I mumbled. "But couldn't you have at least told me?"

Wazak herded us out into the corridor. If he thought this was a ridiculous question for me to have asked, he didn't let on. "There was no need," he said simply. "Now, run!"

With the possible exception of their stage manager, the Edraitians were all in prime physical shape, as were the guards. I was probably the weakest one there, and I wished I'd done some running with the tigers, but I'd never been in The Shrine at night, so I'd never had the chance. Still, I was in better condition than I'd been when I arrived and somehow managed to keep pace with Zealon and Racknay. My only hope was that Wazak wouldn't mind carrying me again if I crapped out, because I had no desire to be left behind to become Dobraton's slave. I could imagine just how much she would enjoy torturing me to death, and it made escape seem that much more imperative.

Of course, staying alive without Tychar was... well, simply not acceptable! It occurred to me then that with Scalia dead or at least deposed, the slaves were now freed, which was one obstacle out of the way, but her death also created at least a dozen others.

We sprinted on through the corridors with Wazak and half of the guards in the lead and the other three bringing up the rear. I'd have felt a lot better if we'd all been armed, but all we had to rely on was the safety in numbers. Then I heard shots behind us. We were being pursued.

One of the Edraitians fell, and we kept right on running. Wazak barked out an order, and the guards fell back slightly and opened fire on our pursuers. I didn't look back, but, after a moment, I noticed that the shots being fired at us had stopped.

It was hard to believe just how fast those Darconians could run! Wazak was setting a blistering pace, and I wasn't sure I'd be able to go the distance, but I'll have to say, being chased by a bunch of trigger-happy Darconian rebels will put wings on your feet.

We passed through an intersecting corridor and—thank God!—met up with Hartak, who must have just been relieved by Delorian at my quarters for the night. Wazak bellowed out another order—presumably in Darconian—and he joined up with us.

A squadron of the rebels met us at the next corner, and Wazak and the guards fought a fierce battle while the rest of us waited further down the corridor for the outcome. It was apparent that Wazak resented the slowdown, because

after several shots, which demonstrated that the battle
would end up in a standoff, he fired wide beam stuns and
took them all out at once, and then covered us while we
ran on to The Shrine. I heard Wazak trying to call ahead
to someone called Jataka, telling him that the Queen had
been overthrown and to open the passage—whatever that
meant—but he received no reply.

Arriving at the doors, we saw why. As Zealon gasped
in surprise, I was horrified to see a dead Darconian lying
there, and the doors to The Shrine standing wide open.
Realizing that it wasn't Dragus made me feel much better, but I had no idea who it was, though Wazak would
certainly know. Running past the dead lizard, I realized
that he must have been the night guard on The Shrine,
but I'd seldom seen him and didn't even know his name.
Still, he was dead, and with the doors unlocked, I was
terrified at the prospect of what we might find inside.

Whoever he was, he must not have been down long,
for when we passed the fountain and headed for the door
to the outside, we caught up with Dragus and the slaves
who were running for the portico.

"Jataka was the traitor!" Dragus shouted at Wazak. "He
tried to kill me but slipped and fell. I have the keys."

Dragus saw me in the pack, and our eyes met. I had
no difficulty imagining why Jataka had slipped, and just
exactly what he had slipped on. It would make a great
story, if either of us ever lived long enough to tell it.

"Good," said Wazak. "Open the passage."

Dragus continued on to one of the pillars which supported the domed roof of the patio and pulled out the
keys. Inserting one of them into the intricate carving,
he turned it. A large section of the pillar then detached

itself from the whole, revealing a hollow interior with a spiral stair leading downward.

"Arrgghh!" Trag shouted, tearing at his hair in frustration. "After all these years of being locked up in here, do you mean to tell me that we could have gotten out that way?"

"Yes," Dragus said with a grin. "Ironic, isn't it?"

Trag appeared to be speechless for once, and Tychar appeared at my side, slipping his arm around my waist and pulling me into his embrace. He didn't say a word, but kissed me fiercely. Just knowing he was still alive was enough for me.

"I'm glad to see you, too," I whispered. "When I saw that guard, I thought you were all dead."

"But we are not," he said. "Stay close."

"This passageway has always been a closely guarded secret," Wazak said, "but Jataka knew of it. We may meet opposition at the exit."

I was hoping that the rebels had counted on Jataka being in control of the keys, though it seemed rather stupid of them to underestimate Dragus that way. I'd have sent more than one man, myself, though if Jataka hadn't fallen, things might have turned out differently. It made me wish I hadn't told Dragus to clean it up, because all that semen in the corridor would have brought down an entire squadron. As it was, he must have missed a spot.

Wazak sent Hartak back with the keys to lock the main doors to The Shrine. It wasn't much, he said, but it might slow down anyone else who might have been following us. Then he chose four of the guards to send down the stair first.

"Hey, Wazak?" I asked tentatively as I peered into the dark stair. "Where does that stairway come out?"

"Below here on the portico."

"Well, can you see it from here? Like if you lean out over the wall or something? You know, to see who might be down there waiting for us?"

"The wall is very high," he replied.

"Yeah, I know, but we do have a bunch of acrobats with us," I reminded him. "They could probably climb up there to take a look."

"And we could then spray any of the rebels standing down below with a wide stun beam." Wazak rubbed his chin thoughtfully. "Yes, that would be helpful."

"Hear that, Nindala?" I said eagerly. "See if you guys can climb that wall."

The Edraitians had all been running and were undoubtedly as tired as the rest of us, but they were still quite nimble, and several of them formed a pyramid with Racknay and two of his brothers joining in to form the base. Even so, they still weren't high enough to top the wall.

"Hey, Sladnil!" Trag shouted. "Why don't you take your sticky fingers and climb up those guys and take a look." In an aside to me, he added, "So, these are the blue redheads you were telling us about, huh?"

"Yeah," I replied. "Pretty cool, aren't they?"

"Well, maybe," he said, not sounding terribly enthused. "If you like blue."

"You don't like blue?"

"Not particularly."

I thought this was a rather odd prejudice for him to have, but then I remembered the crack he'd made about

Tychar's blue eyes and wondered if that had anything to do with it.

Sladnil was climbing up the pyramid of blue-skinned acrobats, who were getting completely weirded out whenever his fingers sucked onto one of them. He slowed down when he got to Nindala, seeming to savor her "essence" just a bit before moving on.

"He'll come all over himself if he keeps that up," Tychar muttered. "Stop that, Sladnil!" he called out to him.

"Oh, all right!" Sladnil said, his voice even more shrill than usual. "But if I am to die anyway…"

"You won't die," Tychar called back. "You're too ugly to die! Heaven wouldn't let you in, and hell would probably spit you back out!"

"Known each other for a long time, have you?" I commented as I watched Sladnil reach the top of the wall. Crawling on his hands and knees, he crept toward the outer edge.

"Too long," Tychar said. "He's the strangest one of the bunch—but also one of Scalia's favorites."

I wasn't quite sure how to tell them. "Um, you guys, about Scalia. I think, that is, I'm pretty sure she's…" I stopped there, hating to say it aloud again. In the heat of the moment, I'd spat it out at Nindala—and in front of the children, too—so I don't know why I was finding it so difficult to tell her slaves, but for some reason, I did.

"Dead?" Tychar gasped. "So that's what's going on here? Someone else has taken the throne?"

Nodding, I went on, "It was Dobraton, and she doesn't like offworlders one little bit!"

"In deep shit, aren't we?" said Trag.

"You bet," I agreed. "Along with any of the royal family and anyone else loyal to them."

I could see the slaves were having trouble grasping this. I wondered if they realized that Scalia's death would probably set them free—most slaves would see the death of their master as a blessing, but this was an unusual situation, one which could just as easily result in their own deaths, in addition to hers.

Of course, Dobraton wasn't the only thing we had to fear, and I abandoned that line of thought as another problem occurred to me. "Hey, we shouldn't be standing around here watching," I exclaimed suddenly. "You guys need clothes! You won't last long naked outside the palace, especially if we're heading across the desert to the mountains! Get a sheet and make a poncho out of it, at least. Bring one for me while you're at it—and some pillowcases, too. Wish I could have gone back to my quarters," I grumbled. "I hate being unprepared."

Tychar came back with some sheets and asked, "What's a poncho?"

"I'll show you," I said. "Got a knife, Dragus?"

The one he handed me looked like something out of a museum with a curved blade and an ornately carved handle. It was sharp as a razor, too, and I cut a slit in the middle of the sheet and slipped it over Tychar's head. Then I knelt and ripped a strip of fabric from the bottom. "Here, tie this around your waist," I told him. Ripping open a pillowcase, I made a headdress out of it, tying another strip of cloth around his head to hold it in place. "Wow!" I said softly, looking up at him. "It's freakin' Lawrence of Arabia! With darker skin, you'd look like a real Arabian sheik."

"It would be better if we looked like Darconians," Tychar pointed out. "Even dressed in this manner, we still look like offworlders."

"Well, unless you want to go skin what's-his-name over there," I said, "this is the best we can do in a pinch. At least the sun won't burn you to a crisp." I ripped up some more sheets and donned my own desert attire while Trag made his own.

"I see them!" Sladnil reported from his perch on the wall. "There are six of them down there."

"Here!" Wazak called out, tossing him a pistol. "Shoot them."

Catching the pistol effortlessly with his sticky fingers, Sladnil hissed incredulously, "*All* of them?"

"It is set for a wide stun beam," Wazak said dryly. "You will not miss."

"There may be more that he can't see," Dragus muttered. "It's a wonder they haven't heard us up here and taken cover."

"They will not have the chance," said Wazak, and then sent the four guards down the stairwell with orders to unlock the door at the bottom and come out firing on his signal. He gave them time to descend, and then called up to Sladnil. "Have you got a clear shot?"

"Yes," Sladnil called back.

Wazak muttered something into his comlink and then waved at Sladnil. "Fire!"

I heard the pulse pistol fire, and Sladnil let out a squeal. For a second I thought he'd been shot, but it was a shout of triumph.

"He's really enjoying that, isn't he?" Tychar muttered, shaking his head. "Strange fellow…"

"The way is clear," Wazak said, motioning us on down the passage. The children went first, followed by me with Trag ahead and Tychar behind. Inside, the air was stuffy and stale, and I wondered how long it had been since anyone had been through there. Given the political climate, I wouldn't have been surprised if it hadn't been checked out fairly recently, but it felt more like we were descending into an Egyptian tomb that had been sealed for eons rather than a secret passage to the outside.

And suddenly, we *were* outside. It felt strange enough for me to be leaving the palace, though I'd only been in residence for a couple of months, but the slaves must have been feeling very peculiar, indeed. So near the source of the oasis, I could feel the moisture in the cooler air as my flowing garment was caught by the wind. Looking about, I felt a frisson of fear pass through me as I caught sight of a number of shadowy shapes in the distance. At first I thought they might be the vanguard of some alien army, but then I realized that they were only the fruit trees, growing in neat ranks on the fertile plain surrounding the oasis.

The tigers were like two ghosts walking beside me in their light-colored robes, while the blue-skinned Edraitians seemed to almost disappear into the shadows. I ought to have been relieved that we had escaped the palace, but it was still likely that the desert would consume us in the end. I couldn't understand why there hadn't been more in the way of survival gear in our escape route—something to carry water in at the very least. Wazak had said we would get water at The Shrine, but if we had, I'd missed it in all the excitement.

The Darconians searched the fallen rebels, collecting their weapons and passing them on to those of us who weren't armed. Surprisingly, the first rifles Wazak gave out were to the two Zetithians. He must have trusted them more than the Edraitians, but they had been slaves to his queen, and it seemed to be a rather strange and ironic turn of events. After ensuring that the older children were armed, Wazak then checked the settings on a pulse pistol, after which, he handed it to me.

"That is set to kill," he said evenly. "Do not hesitate to use it should the need arise."

I took the pistol without protest, though Dobraton's men were the least of my worries at that point, since dying of thirst seemed far more likely. "Wazak?" I began in a hoarse whisper. "What about water?"

"There are secrets to this palace that many do not know," he said. "Follow me."

I had no idea what he meant by that—and neither did anyone else—but we followed him anyway. What we would have done without him I couldn't begin to guess, and if Dobraton had had any sense at all, she'd have killed him even before she shot Scalia.

It was still hard to believe what I'd seen. In the events which followed, I hadn't had much time to think about it, but the horror of watching someone be killed was now creeping into me like a chill, and I shuddered in spite of the heat. Then something took my hand, startling me to the point that I nearly screamed.

Looking down I saw two shining eyes blinking up at me. It was Uragus. "Kyra," he whispered. "I would like a hug."

Gathering him up in my arms, I gave him a squeeze. "Are you scared?"

"Yes," he replied.

"Me, too," I said.

Then he asked the most surprising question. "Was it because of me?"

"What do you mean?"

"Was my mother killed because I played the piano?"

"Oh, no, sweetheart!" I said, giving him another hug. "Your playing was marvelous! Dobraton had other reasons for doing what she did. What you did had absolutely nothing to do with it!"

But even while I was saying it, I knew it wasn't true—at least, not completely. Attitudes toward males on Darconia could be just as prejudiced as they were against offworlders in some respects, and he was not only male, but he'd been playing music written by a human, on an instrument which had been manufactured on Earth, and had been taught to play it by a Terran—and did it remarkably well, which was possibly the greatest offense of all. Perhaps it was symbolic that Dobraton had chosen that particular moment to assassinate his mother.

"Is she going to kill us, too?" he asked.

"I don't think so," I replied. "Wazak is a good leader. He'll keep us safe."

To my surprise, Wazak heard that. "I did not protect his mother," he said bluntly. "I have failed in my duty to her."

"I wouldn't exactly call that failing, because there was no defense against what Dobraton did," I said briskly, "but if you're looking for redemption, Wazak, now's the time to do something about it! You just keep the rest of us alive, and I think even Scalia would forgive you."

Zealon spoke up just then, but if I'd have expected tears from her, I would have been disappointed. With barely contained anger, she said, "Yes, I forgive you, Wazak, but I will not forgive Dobraton. She will pay for this."

Racknay was close by as well, and if looks could have killed, Dobraton would already be dead.

"I'm so sorry for your loss, Zealon, Racknay," I began. "I know—"

"We have no time for sorrow," Zealon said, cutting off my expression of sympathy. With a defiant lift of her chin, she added: "And Darconians do not cry."

Wazak didn't comment, but led us on through the portico a little way before stopping at a perfectly blank place in the wall. Taking a small key from his breastplate, he inserted it into yet another lock which would have seemed invisible if we hadn't watched him do it. A moment later, a heavy section of stone swung out from the wall.

"In here," Wazak said.

It was dark inside, but I could hear the sound of flowing water. Illuminating the glowstones on my necklace, I held them up. Though their light was dim inside such a large space, I could see that this must be the oasis source, for there was a dark pool inside with a cascade of water erupting from the center.

"Put down your stones, Kyra," Wazak said. "They will not be necessary."

Then he focused his gaze on the ceiling, and the whole place lit up—so brightly that I had to close my eyes and wait a moment for them to adjust from the darkness outside. Looking up, I saw that the entire room appeared to be lined with glowstone—not just a few of them set into the ceiling here and there, mind you, but forming every surface, with the exception of the floor. Even the catchbasin for the water was glowing.

"This is the true Shrine of the Desert," he said quietly. "It was closed off long ago by a ruler who feared it might be desecrated." He glanced around briefly, and the light dimmed to a more comfortable level. "I disagree. It is only water, and the walls are only made of stone. Life is far more important than either of these things."

He was obviously referring to Scalia, and though she might have been no more than his queen, her death must have affected him deeply—as it had affected us all. I was no more than a visitor to her realm, but I already missed her. She had been a strong ruler, but, unlike the usurper of her throne, there was no malice in her, nor had she been corrupt—at least, not beyond her penchant for exotic slaves. The people of Darconia had been fortunate in their queen, and they would feel the effects of her loss soon enough. My only hope was that they would choose to do something about it. Up until this moment, we had simply been running for our lives; the will of the people of this region would determine what would happen next.

Chapter 15

DARCONIANS HAD NEVER STRUCK ME AS BEING A FLOCK OF docile sheep to be herded wherever their queen chose. Scalia's policies toward offworld trade had been gradually introduced to her people, not forced upon them. She had brought in offworld culture in an effort to demonstrate the advantages of contact with the rest of the galaxy. There were also disadvantages to this, which Dobraton had been quick to focus upon—the dilution of their own culture, the loss to their own people of planetary resources, not to mention the influx of radical ideas—but there were many advantages, which included advances in science, technology, and medicine. These things, when managed wisely, could be of great benefit to a world that had always been focused entirely upon itself. Scalia, who saw it as progress, understood that; Dobraton, who clung to the old, isolationist ways, did not.

If the other shrine had been a tribute to the beauty which water could bring to a dry and desolate world, this was a shrine to the water itself; an altar to the life-giving liquid. In the past, Darconians must have been allowed to come here not only to see the miracle of the oasis source, but also to partake of the waters, for there were containers in niches near the doorway for carrying the water. This had been what Wazak had meant when he'd said we would get water at The Shrine—*this* shrine, and not the place where the slaves lived. I agreed with

Wazak; it should have been reopened. Scalia should have done it herself. In a place where water was at a premium, it would have been a gesture that would have solidly united the people in her support. Dobraton would then have been unable to recruit many followers, and the coup would never have taken place. Promising your people a McDonald's was one thing; opening this shrine would have been something else altogether.

Having overcome our initial sense of awe, we filled the empty bottles and slung them over our shoulders with the carrying harnesses hanging nearby. Unfortunately, these had been made with Darconians in mind and were too big for most of us, so we had to make a few modifications. The bottles themselves were surprisingly light and strong—like glass in some ways, but like plastic in others—undoubtedly having been intended for carrying water over long distances.

I'd never been part of a band of refugees before; I'd always been as solitary as Dobraton wanted their planet to be, but already I could feel a sense of camaraderie beginning to develop. We all knew the danger we were in, and we also knew that there was no hope for our survival if we didn't stick together. Wazak, it seemed, was of the same opinion as Tychar had been about escaping to the mountains, though what we would do after that was unclear. It was possible that we could round up enough support there and in the city to take back the palace, but before that, some regrouping was necessary—as was the time for the people to become discontented with their new ruler.

And discontent was something which I was quite certain would arise from Dobraton's rule—and I hoped it would come quickly. I had known them both, and even without Dobraton's prejudice against me, I believe I would have chosen to follow Scalia's banner, for she possessed the character of a good leader, which Dobraton did not.

Dodging a few patrols, we melted into the trees, moving quickly. The need for speed was understood by us all; we needed to get as far as we possibly could under cover of darkness.

The Darconians were tough, but we did have some children with us. I carried Uragus for a while, but it soon became apparent that I was no tougher than he was—probably less so—and I handed him off to Racknay. We snatched a bit of fruit as we passed through the trees, and it wasn't long before I was wishing for some pockets and a backpack. I tied my headdress to the harness for my water bottle, making a pouch of sorts, and collected what I could, but there was a limit to what I could carry and still keep moving.

The tigers stayed close beside me, as did Dragus. I must say that, at a time like that, it was very nice to have a surplus of big, strong, male admirers! The only thing they didn't do was try to pick me up and carry me, though Dragus *did* make the offer, which I promised to keep in mind.

Reaching the edge of the farmland by midnight, the city streets were quiet as we passed down roadways that were completely deserted at that hour. Alert for any signs of pursuit, we moved stealthily from shadow to shadow.

At length, we passed by a stable, and I whispered to Wazak. "What about stealing a few camels?"

"Camels?" he echoed.

"Oh, you know, these things," I said, pointing to one of them. "I don't know what you call them."

"Drayls," he said with disdain. "I would prefer to steal some hovercars."

"Yeah, well, I'd bet even hovercars would break down after a bit—and they're kind of noisy. These guys look like they were made for the desert." Looking up at Wazak, I knew he wouldn't have a bit of trouble crossing the desert, but I wasn't so sure about the rest of us. "I don't think I can make it across that desert on foot, and I'd be willing to bet the rest of these offworlders can't do it either."

The Edraitians who heard that exchange didn't seem averse to riding rather than walking, but I knew for a fact that a Darconian couldn't ride a drayl, because for one thing, they were nearly the same size. The ones I'd seen had been used as pack animals, rather than for personal transport. I'd have traded my glowstones for a good speeder, but during the limited tour of the city I'd been given upon my arrival, I hadn't seen one.

Wazak still seemed reluctant, but it was getting on toward morning by this time, and to be perfectly honest, I was just plain tired and wanted a camel to ride.

So I took one.

None of the drayls tried to bite me when I entered their pen, though one of them seemed to find me quite fascinating, sniffing at me as though trying to identify my scent.

"He must smell your desire," Tychar commented.

"Well, he might if I was feeling any desire at the moment, but I'm not," I said frankly. "In fact, I don't think

I've ever felt less desire in my life." Which wasn't quite true; I'd felt less when I first met Wazak. Now that I was surrounded by males most of the time, my "desire" was probably automatic. Unfortunately, for the first time since I'd met him, I couldn't just look at Tychar's cock and know for certain.

"Guess I ought to pay something for him," I said reflectively. "Stealing a drayl probably isn't the best way to gain support among the locals." I had about decided to leave my pearls as payment when Tychar stopped me.

"No," he said as he began removing his collar. "I will leave them this. It's no more than a pretty trinket, but someone might value it, and I have no need of it now."

So, he *did* realize he was free! It seemed fitting to me that he get rid of his collar to symbolize that freedom, but Dragus was incredulous.

"You're trading *that* for one drayl?" With a snicker, he added, "And I always thought you were fairly intelligent for an offworlder."

Tychar appeared somewhat bewildered. "What d'you mean?" he asked. "These aren't real jewels, are they?"

"I guess Scalia never told you," Dragus said, "but what the two of you have been wearing around your necks and cocks would just about buy a space cruiser. One stone for the whole herd would be too much."

"Hear that?" I said, giving Tychar a nudge. "Better hang on to your jewelry, big guy! It's a boy's best friend, you know."

Turning them over in his hand, Tychar stared at the sparkling stones in wonderment. "Why would a queen put something of such value on a slave?"

"Could be that she valued the slave even more than the stones," I said gently. "Scalia was very fond of you guys."

Tychar nodded absently, and I wondered if he realized that he now was not only free, but filthy rich on top of that.

In the end, Tychar left one of the smaller stones out of his cock ring, which he then decided to wear as a bracelet so he would be less apt to lose it. At least, that's what he said, but I had an idea he also thought it might be uncomfortable to wear it while riding a drayl. Trag wanted to know if Tychar's blue stones were worth more than his green ones, but Dragus wasn't sure.

"They are the same mineral and are therefore of equal value," Wazak said in a firm voice, obviously not wishing to hear any further discussion on the subject. "The only difference is in their color."

That said, the Edraitians were quick to follow my lead, and pretty soon we had quite a caravan. The Darconians helped us tack them up—I'd never even saddled a horse back home—and though they were on foot themselves, they seemed to have no trouble keeping up with those of us who were mounted. Much more mobile now and reasonably well-armed, we blew through the city like a sandstorm.

I rode double with Tychar—well, actually triple, because I had Uragus, too; he'd conked out a good while back and lay curled up in my arms. Nindala rode with Trag, but if he smelled any desire coming from her, it wasn't obvious. The tigers looked really cool in their flowing robes, but I did miss being able to see their dicks.

The streets were completely deserted, as if the entire city had gone into hiding. It was likely that the residents of Arconcia had heard about the government upheaval and were staying inside their homes—or had been warned to stay off the streets—but whatever the reason, we saw no one.

Reaching the fringes of the city with the dawn, we now faced the desert crossing by day. I was all for holing up somewhere to sleep until it got dark again, but Wazak insisted we push on. Riding a drayl was a lot easier than running, so I couldn't really complain, but I would have thought that even Wazak would have to rest now and then. I kept waiting for some of the younger ones to start grumbling, but they never did. Zealon and Racknay ran side by side, never slowing their pace for a moment. As marathon runners, they'd have beaten the pants off of anyone else—especially any humans—and they had their anger at Dobraton to sustain them.

Then the sun came up, and the temperature began to rise. Fortunately, it wasn't as far to the mountains as I had imagined, and after I thought about it, I remembered that from the shore, you could only see about eighteen kilometers out to sea on Earth. Darconia was a much larger planet, which meant that its curvature was less and you could see farther, but still, the base of those mountains couldn't have been much more than thirty kilometers away. Even so, it was thirty kilometers across a very hot desert strewn with rocks and boulders.

From a distance, that is. Up close, there was a whole lot more to it, and I saw plenty of tough-looking plants and the occasional scuttling bit of wildlife. I'd also forgotten that there were mines in the mountains, and, consequently, there was a road of sorts leading in that direction with stone shelters built along the way. Of course, anyone looking for us would have checked those places first, but as the morning wore on, I began to wonder if anyone was looking for us at all. It was possible that our enemies would assume that we would disappear into the desert and die off, one by one, but I found that hard to believe, because the pursuit in the palace had been pretty determined.

If Wazak had heard anything over his comlink, he didn't mention it, but kept us moving, though we did have to stop twice to let the drayls have a rest. Riding had its obvious advantages, but the swaying gait of the drayl was rather hypnotic and, having been up all night, I kept nodding off and was afraid I'd drop Uragus, so I wound up handing him off to Racknay and Zealon again. Tychar, however, stayed awake and held me steady when I would have fallen. The journey would have been much more difficult without him, and his arms around me helped keep me strong. We spoke very little, and I was left to wonder how he felt about being free after so many years of slavery. It could have been that he hadn't come to grips with the idea enough to talk about it yet. Or perhaps he didn't consider being on the run much different from being a slave.

I kept those thoughts to myself, however, because talking would have made us that much more thirsty, and even while riding drayls and wearing our Bedouin garb, it was still hot as hell. I was sparing with my water, and I hated to think how quickly I would have wilted had this flight to the mountains taken place a few months previously.

The more we rode on without any pursuit or opposition, the more convinced I became that we had to be riding into a trap. Dobraton had to know we'd head for the mountains, but since the mountains were the chief source of the wealth of that region, she would undoubtedly have done her best to seize control of them along with the city. Leaving the mines to us made little sense, though it was possible that she was just plain stupid and hadn't figured that out yet. Well, no, I decided. Closedminded she might be, but she wasn't stupid—at least not altogether.

We were about halfway across the desert when this notion seemed to occur to Wazak, as well—either that, or he was finally getting tired, because he began slowing down.

I pushed my drayl to catch up to him.

"Getting tired?" I asked casually. "We could all use a break, you know."

"Perhaps," he replied. "I have been… thinking."

"Yeah, so have I, and I smell a rat."

"A rat?"

"Mm-hm, either that, or something's rotten in Denmark."

"Denmark?" he echoed. "Why is Denmark significant?"

"Oh, stop being so dense!" I said, becoming exasperated. "You know very well what I mean! Something's just not right about all of this! Someone should be coming after us, and they're not!"

"I concur."

"We got chased out of the palace, and now, nothing! It doesn't make any sense."

"This is true," he agreed. "It has been far too easy."

"So, do you think we're heading into a trap?" I inquired. "Or does Dobraton just not care what we do now?"

"I do not believe she considers us to be a threat to her any longer," he said.

"Possibly," I said hesitantly. "But is that true? *Are* we a threat? I mean, could we plan a counterattack and be successful?"

Wazak appeared puzzled by this notion, almost to the point that I thought he was only planning to get us to the mountains and stay there, hiding out for the rest of our lives.

"You are thinking about fighting back, aren't you?" I demanded. "Surely you're not just going to take this lying down!" When he didn't reply, I went on to ask, "Tell me something, Wazak, has there ever been an overthrow like this before?"

"Not for many centuries," he replied.

"Hmm, well, maybe Dobraton just doesn't know how to organize a decent coup. You know, killing off the royal family is usually a pretty effective means of destroying a monarchy, but she's left the job undone—or does she think the desert will do it for her?"

"For the offworlders, perhaps," he conceded. "But we Darconians would not perish in the desert."

"Well, maybe that's it, then. She's just waiting for the rest of us to die off, and then she'll strike again."

"She may be waiting for us to retaliate," Tychar suggested. "In an open battle, if their numbers were greater…"

"They could just mow us down," I finished for him. "Be a lot easier than chasing after us, I suppose."

"I think Wazak's right," Trag said. "I think she doesn't consider us to be a threat and isn't wasting any time on us."

"It wouldn't be the first time a small band of rebels was underestimated," I remarked.

"Meaning you think we *should* try to fight back?" asked Trag.

"Well," I said reasonably, "do *you* want to spend the rest of your life hiding out in the mountains?"

"Kyra, dear," Trag said sweetly. "I've spent most of my life doing light housekeeping in a palace full of lizards while wearing nothing but a collar and a cock ring and *still* didn't have sex for twenty years! Hanging out in the mountains sounds like a fucking vacation to me! At least I've got you and the redhead to make things interesting."

Nindala's spine stiffened visibly. "I would rather consort with one of the Darconians!" she said with evident disgust.

This was a rather tactless thing for her to say, seeing as how Dragus and Wazak were both walking alongside us. I was thankful that the younger ones had fallen back into their own little pack and probably couldn't hear what we were saying. "I could arrange that," I said promptly. "I know Dragus would be interested. He'd probably kill you, though. If his dick is anything like the rest of him, it's probably huge."

"Aw, Dragus is a slut," Trag said dismissively. "You should try me. You might even like me."

"I thought you didn't like blue," I reminded him.

"I don't," said Trag. "It's just that now we're out and about, I've got more options, and Ty never did like the idea of sharing you, anyway."

"You *shared* her?" Nindala was clearly aghast at such wanton behavior on my part. "*Kyra*?"

"Things have changed quite a bit since I saw you last," I admitted. "These guys belonged to the Queen, but she assigned Tychar to me as my personal…"

"Slave," Tychar said bluntly. "We were slaves."

Trag gave Nindala a nudge, and she jumped as though he'd bitten her. "Sex slaves, actually. Only we never had any sex. Reptiles just don't smell right to us."

"Does *she*?" I asked curiously.

Trag leaned forward and sniffed at Nindala. "Nope," he replied. "Not getting a thing."

"If you don't smell of 'desire,' they can't get it up," I informed Nindala. "Now, Dragus likes humans very well, and the way you smell probably wouldn't matter to him. Don't know how he feels about blue, though."

Dragus looked up at me and grinned. "I like blue just fine."

"You see!" Trag said. "What did I tell you? He's a fuckin' slut! You can insult him all day long, and he'll still fuck you."

"Or get himself off," I chuckled. "At least, I *think* that was what was all over the floor in the corridor yesterday."

"Yesterday?" Wazak said, pouncing on that pertinent detail. "*That* is how Jataka slipped and fell?"

"Well, I *did* tell Dragus to clean it up," I said, "but he must have missed a spot."

Wazak actually stopped and pulled my drayl to a halt. Looking me right in the eye, he said, "Do you mean to say that we escaped from the palace only because there was semen on the floor outside The Shrine?"

"Well, I hadn't thought about it that way," I admitted, "but now that you mention it, yes, I suppose that's true."

I had never heard Wazak laugh before—and it took a moment for the humor of the situation to sink in— but his serious mask of a face finally cracked, and he doubled over, laughing hysterically.

Trag was cackling too. "We're all alive because Dragus is a slut!"

Dragus just shrugged his big shoulders and grinned in a completely unapologetic fashion.

Tychar was laughing too. "We must have been better than I thought," he whispered in my ear.

"We were better than all three of us put together, actually," I whispered back. "I know I made plenty of noise, but still, he must have really good ears to be able to hear through the door like that."

Dragus glanced up at me with a guilty expression— the acuity of his hearing becoming even more evident.

Tychar saw it, too. "What was that look for, Dragus?" Tychar demanded. "Is there something you aren't telling us?"

"I promise not to use it again," Dragus said quickly.

"Use *what*?" Tychar asked, sounding quite dangerous. So, my charming rogue could be a tough guy when the need arose. *Interesting…*

"The comstone," Dragus replied reluctantly. "There's one in the necklace."

"Do you mean to say you've been listening in on us?" Tychar demanded.

"Well, not *all* the time," Dragus said, hedging just a bit. "Just… sometimes."

Growling, Tychar plucked my necklace from around my neck and inspected it closely. "Which one?"

"The green stone," Dragus replied in a sulky voice.

Twisting the link, Tychar removed the stone and threw it at Dragus. "You may keep that and be thankful that I am not one to hold a grudge." Tychar may have been a slave, but his commanding tone was enough to make anyone think twice before crossing him—even a Darconian.

"Good thing he *doesn't* hold a grudge," Trag said meekly. "He'd probably kill me for doing what I did with you. Glad I decided to quit bugging you before we wound up being freed."

"No kidding!" I agreed. "But remember, you're out and about now and have more options."

"Well, I may be out and about," he admitted, "but I don't think it'll do me much good, because Miss Blue-butt doesn't like me—and I'm not so sure I like her, either. She smells all… blue."

"Well, who knows what we'll find in the mountains," I said in an effort to cheer him up a bit. "Maybe there'll be some other offworld refugees who smell even better than I do."

"Not unless there's a Zetithian woman hiding out there—or another Terran," Trag grumbled. "And somehow, I doubt that."

"Well, just give her a little time," I suggested, with a gesture toward Nindala. "She might warm up to you, and then you'll be able to smell her desire."

Trag mumbled something I didn't quite catch, but the gist of it was that he was expecting hell to freeze over before that happened, and Nindala's expression did nothing to suggest otherwise. Then I remembered that Nindala only liked rich men, and thought perhaps that Trag ought to remind her that he was wearing the value of half a space cruiser. I didn't suggest it, though, because I've always been of the opinion that women who required pretty baubles to stimulate their interest in a man weren't worth having, and a man who had to resort to bribery wasn't worth much, either. Trag shouldn't have to stoop to buying a woman's favors; he deserved much better than that.

Even so, the need for scent notwithstanding, I didn't see how any man, Zetithian or otherwise, could have ridden double on a drayl with Nindala and not wanted to screw her silly, whether she smelled right or not. I mean, she was beautiful, and she was naked, for heaven's sake! Trag had his hands resting on her hips and could have easily reached up to fondle her spectacular tits. There was only the sheet he was wearing between his cock and her ass, and, sure, we were running for our lives, but *still*...

Experimentally, I shifted my weight backward and felt Tychar's hard cock pressing against my tailbone. You couldn't hide anything from those guys: if you were in the mood, they knew it, no matter how much you might try to deny it.

"And when we reach safety," Tychar whispered in my ear, "I will do my best to make you very pleased that you chose me instead of my brother."

If there was anything he hadn't already done to convince me of that, it must've been some minute detail that I'd never have missed. "I think you already have," I said. "But I have no problem with being convinced again."

Leaning back against him with a sigh, I sincerely wished every dire fate anyone could imagine to befall Dobraton for making this trek across the desert necessary. I would have been waking up in my bed after a night of love with Tychar right about now if it hadn't been for her—the bitch! Still, her actions had made it possible, however unintentionally, for the two brothers to be free. It seemed ironic that they had been enslaved by a queen who had admired them greatly, but were subsequently freed by someone who would prefer that they had never set foot on her planet.

By this time, Wazak had recovered from his bout of mirth and got us moving once again, and it was surprising just how much better I felt. It hadn't been a very long rest—a couple of days wouldn't have been amiss—but a good laugh will often do wonders for morale.

Purring softly, Tychar settled me against his chest, secure in his arms. His cock was getting wet, and I could feel it sliding up my backbone with every step the drayl took. I wondered idly if he would ejaculate at some point, and if he did, I wanted a taste of it; a little euphoria would have been nice after the kind of night we'd had. Maybe that would be what it would take to get Nindala interested in Trag. So far, I hadn't had the opportunity to explain to her just how fabulous my tigers were. She was stupid not to want Trag on sight, though—they were both irresistible! Then again, she had been admired by men all her life, and perhaps it would take more to sway her than it had with me. I couldn't begin to imagine why, though, because even the most jaded beauty would have to admit that they were devastatingly attractive—especially Tychar.

"Sleep now, Kyra," he purred. "And when you awaken, the desert will be behind us."

Relaxing against my purring tiger, I fell asleep thinking about what truly was behind me, and it certainly wasn't the desert!

Chapter 16

My dreams were wild and fitful as we rode on. One moment I was safe and warm in my lover's arms, and the next, I was watching Dragus ejaculate all over Dobraton. Then I dreamed that Trag was fucking Nindala for all he was worth, groaning as sweat dripped from his body, his balls slapping hard against her ass as he pounded into her. She was screaming for more, but he was all played out. When the inevitable happened and he lost his erection, she hissed at him like a snake and struck him full across the face.

I awoke with a shout forming in my throat, but the mountains looming ahead of us terrified me more than any dream could have done. There were huge boulders among the foothills that could have concealed any number of enemies, and the mountains themselves seemed to be closing in on us as though they couldn't wait to lure us in for the kill.

"Spooky place," I said to no one in particular.

"And to think, *this* is where I would have gone if I ever escaped from the palace," Tychar said grimly. "There isn't a drop of water anywhere."

"The water is on the other side," Wazak said. "It is the mountains which stop the rains from reaching the desert."

"Are you saying we have to climb *over* these mountains to find water?" Trag gasped in horror. "We'll never make it!"

Despite the fact that they were acrobats and could have made mountain climbing look easy, the Edraitians began grumbling, too.

"We do not have to climb the mountains," Wazak said patiently. "There is a tunnel through them, though it may be defended against us."

"Well, that's just great, isn't it?" Trag said in a voice heavily laced with sarcasm. "We've somehow managed to cross this cursed desert and we still aren't safe!"

"I thought there were mines," I said, looking around in bewilderment. "If that's the case, then where are the miners?"

I had no more gotten the words out of my mouth than what seemed like hundreds of heavily armed Darconians emerged from behind nearly every rock—and there were a *lot* of rocks—completely surrounding us. No wonder I'd gotten so spooked! "The next time I feel like I'm walking into a trap," I muttered, "somebody be sure and kick me for going blindly forth."

As I've said before, one Darconian looks much like another, and without uniforms to distinguish one sort from another, it's difficult to tell just who you're dealing with. I'd gotten better at recognizing palace guards by their insignia, but this was virgin territory as far as I was concerned. These could have been Dobraton's soldiers or the miners, either one.

"Do not move," one of our captors shouted.

As none of us had so much as blinked, this order was completely unnecessary.

Moving closer, he added, "Throw down your weapons."

"Great Mother of the Desert!" Trag mumbled as he pulled off the pulse rifle he had slung over his shoulder.

"I finally get a gun and have to give it up before I've even had a chance to use it!" Tychar handed over his own pulse rifle, but since no one could see my own pistol, I opted to keep it right where it was until someone insisted that I give it to them.

"Silence!" the Darconian shouted. "You, there," he went on, with a gesture toward Wazak. "What business do you have here?"

Obviously, these had to be the miners, since it was a given that anyone in Dobraton's army would have opened fire on us without bothering to ask.

"The Queen has been overthrown," Wazak said. "We have fled the city."

"Scalia overthrown?" the man scoffed. "By whom?"

"Dobraton," Wazak replied. "The Queen was assassinated last night."

There was some muttering among our opponents following that revelation, though I had an idea it merely confirmed some suspicions they already had. "Yes," the Darconian said, "Soldiers came yesterday in an attempt to take over the mines."

"So, you're miners, then?" I asked impulsively, forgetting I should probably keep my mouth shut. "How did you escape?"

"We did not *escape*, offworlder," he spat out contemptuously. "We defeated them."

"Oh," I said, duly impressed. "Cool! Think you could do it again?"

Wazak threw me a look that said in no uncertain terms that I should shut up and let him handle the negotiations. Still, if Dobraton had sent soldiers to take over the mines, obviously this was why we hadn't been pursued, for, had her forces been victorious, we would have been captured and undoubtedly executed once we reached the mountains. She must not have sent enough, though, keeping the bulk of her force to take the palace. Her mistake…

I wondered what else Dobraton had targeted and decided that the spaceport would have been my first choice, and, if so, there might have been others who had also headed for the mountains. "Are there any off-worlders with you?"

In reply, a small group of men—who were obviously *not* Darconians—stepped out, all bristling with weapons. They were some of the scariest-looking guys I'd ever seen in person—and I'd not only traveled halfway across the galaxy, but I'd also met plenty of Darconians! Each one was decked out in weapons, boots, and bits of garb that had probably once belonged to soldiers in someone's army, along with plenty of scars and tattoos. Their dress suggested the military, but, unless I missed my guess, I was looking at a band of interplanetary mercenaries—or arms dealers.

"Oh, let me guess," I said wearily. "Gun runners?" So, *that* was how the miners had won out against an army! They'd been warned—and subsequently armed— by these guys. I wondered how many glowstones it cost them. "Always out to make a credit or two, aren't you?" I chided them. "What'd you guys do? Sell weapons to both sides?"

One of them, presumably their leader, who was hooded and cloaked against the sun, stepped forward. From what I could see of him—and I could only see the lower half of his face at the time—he appeared to be at least partly human. What the other parts were, I couldn't have said, because he had a tail like a lion's that was twitching from beneath his robes with barely concealed anger, frustration, or irritation—or perhaps all three. He shrugged contemptuously and said with a smirk, "Which is why we always demand payment in advance. That way, it doesn't matter who wins."

I thought it mattered a great deal—and, being off-worlders, it should have mattered to them, as well. It wouldn't have surprised me if Dobraton had bought weapons from them and then had them either killed or booted off the face of Darconia. But perhaps she'd tried, which might have been why, out of spite, they'd sold weapons to the miners.

"Well, if you've already been paid, then why are you still here?" Without waiting for a reply, I taunted, "Aw, what's the matter? Can't get to the spaceport?"

"And just who are you, woman?" he demanded angrily. "The Queen's handmaiden?" Obviously he wanted me to shut up just as much as Wazak did. I happened to catch a glimpse of Nindala just then, who was staring at me as though I'd suddenly sprouted horns, obviously thinking that this wasn't the same meek little woman she'd met on the cruiser.

I almost called him a sexist pig out loud, though I doubted he would have understood my meaning. Even if he had, I figured the worst they could do was kill me—but this was another of those times when I couldn't seem to keep my mouth shut. "Well, no," I replied, completely unperturbed. "Actually, I'm the piano teacher."

Pushing back his hood with an angry gesture, the man glared at me with dark, flashing eyes. He was quite handsome, really; dark-skinned with high cheekbones and a sharp, aquiline nose. There was some sort of rune tattooed on his left temple, where, even from where I sat upon my drayl, I could see his pulse beating. This man might have been a ruthless weapons dealer, but things hadn't gone so well for him this time, and he was *upset*. It was probably unwise to press him much further, since the weapon he was holding looked as though it could have launched a missile and blown up the palace from where he stood.

"The piano teacher," he repeated, as though he didn't quite believe me. "And just who were you teaching?"

"The Queen's children," I replied.

Nodding dismissively, his eyes then swept over our group, landing on Uragus.

"One of your students, perhaps?"

"Yes, and quite the little prodigy," I said proudly. "You should hear him play!"

While the man didn't quite roll his eyes, he was obviously not one who cared much for music. "What about them?" he went on, with a gesture towards the Edraitians. I waited for their manager to speak and then realized he wasn't with us anymore. He must have been the one shot down in the palace.

It was Nindala who spoke up. "We are performers," she said haughtily.

"Well, you certainly *look* like you could perform," he remarked dryly, which prompted a rather forced laugh from his companions, who were obviously just as upset as he was by the recent turn of events. "And the others?" he added, looking pointedly at Sladnil.

"We were slaves to the Queen," Tychar replied.

"I see," he said. "And now you are free?"

"Not really," Tychar admitted.

"How so?"

"Well, you're the one holding the bazooka," Tychar said reasonably. "You tell me."

Tipping his head to one side, I could see that this guy was just about to decide to trust us and lower his weapon. "What about the Darconians among you?" he asked finally. "How do we know we can trust them?"

"We are palace guards, loyal to the Queen and the remaining members of the royal family," Wazak said with a gesture toward the children. "Dobraton is now our enemy."

The weapons dealer appeared openly skeptical. "Loyalty can be bought, my friend," he knowingly. "That coup was an inside job."

"Yes, and Dragus killed at least one of them," I piped up. "Well… *sort* of…"

"My loyalty cannot be bought!" Wazak said angrily. "I was Chief of Security for the Palace." He sounded as if he might have said more, but stopped himself there.

"And…?" our opponent prompted—obviously having felt there was more to it than that, as well.

Wazak took a deep breath and stood up a little taller— if that was possible. "I was also the Queen's consort," he replied. "And these," he added with another gesture toward the young ones, "are my children."

"Ah," the other man said, and though he didn't exactly lower his weapon, he seemed to relax his stance ever so slightly.

Our captors might have relaxed a bit, but everyone else just about had a cow.

"You're our father?" Zealon gasped in surprise. "I never knew!"

"You were not supposed to know," Wazak said shortly. "It is… traditional, and also the Queen's wish."

"Wow!" I said admiringly. "All six of 'em? Way to go, Wazak!"

I could see he was having a very hard time trying not to smile. It was becoming increasingly clear that Wazak had disapproved of Scalia's slave boys on grounds other than the usual moral objections to slavery. He was understandably jealous of them, but Scalia had been Queen, and there wasn't a damn thing he could do about it.

Then I remembered that the Queen was dead, and Wazak had probably watched her die. "Oh, Wazak!" I whispered. "I'm so sorry! You loved Scalia, didn't you?"

"That is no longer important," he said gruffly, but didn't bother to deny it. "What is important now is to protect the children."

"Well, then," I said briskly, "the way I see it, there are two ways to do that. We can retake the palace and establish Zealon as Queen, or retake the spaceport and leave this planet."

"Leave Darconia?" Zealon exclaimed. "We can't do that!"

"Okay, then," I said with conviction. "We retake the palace."

Our captor laughed. "What is your name, piano teacher?"

"Kyra Aramis," I replied. "Hopefully soon to be Kyra—" Suddenly, I realized I had no idea—I didn't even know if the tigers *had* surnames. Twisting around to look at Tychar, I asked: "What's your last name?"

"Vladatonsk," he replied with a wry smile.

I stared at him for a long moment before I could speak. "You're kidding me, right?" I said. "Your name is Tycharian Vladatonsk?"

"No, he's not kidding," Trag assured me. "You've never heard my full name, either, have you? It's Tragonathon Vladatonsk."

"Great Mother of the Desert!" I exclaimed, feeling thankful that at least my first name was reasonably short.

"While we're making introductions," the arms dealer said with an expression of amusement, "my name is Lerotan Kanotay." Lowering his weapon at last, he stepped closer to Wazak, holding out a hand. "And you are…?"

"Wazak," he replied, shaking Lerotan's hand. "Just Wazak."

"Thank God!" I said roundly. "The rest of these names are about to choke me."

A murmur of laughter went through the ranks of the Darconian miners, who were lowering their weapons as well.

"So, Leroy," I began. "Ever try to infiltrate a palace?" Then I laughed as I remembered an important fact. "We've got the keys."

"That would be helpful," he said, "but not required. And no, I have yet to try to infiltrate a palace."

"Think you can?" I asked.

Lerotan grinned delightedly. "Without question."

"How about overthrowing a would-be queen?" Tychar put in.

"No problem whatsoever."

"Cocky fellow, aren't you?" Tychar observed.

Lerotan shrugged. "I have been called that."

"Don't happen to need a pilot, do you?" Trag piped up.

"Not at the moment," Lerotan replied. "Our ship has been impounded."

"I'm surprised that would stop a resourceful fellow like you," I said dryly.

"Let's just say that's next on my list of things to do," Lerotan said. "However, if I get the rightful queen reinstated, that problem will solve itself."

"True," I agreed. "So, Leroy, are we friends now?" This might have been a bit of a stretch, but at least we were fighting a common enemy.

"I suppose so," he said with a shrug.

"Then can we *please* go someplace and get out of the sun?"

With a smile, Lerotan beckoned us on to their mountain stronghold. Our numbers were growing by leaps and bounds. Maybe we had a chance after all…

We spent the rest of the day sleeping in the relative coolness of the mines. Wazak and Dragus took turns standing guard—I suppose even with an agreement reached between us and Lerotan, Wazak still felt responsible for our safety.

And for his children, too! I was still having some difficulty remembering that. I'd never really thought much about who might have fathered Scalia's offspring—or even wondered if they all had the same father—but if I had, I probably should have suspected Wazak, especially after the way he'd talked about her having been his first commander. What a pair they must have been!

Even on the stone floor of the mines, curling up with Tychar was heavenly compared with all we'd been through in the past day or so. So much had changed in that time, making it seem far longer than that since life had been normal. Scalia was dead, we were hiding out in the mountains, but at least the slaves were free. It was difficult to grasp the concept that Tychar really could be mine now, and not just a personal attendant on loan from the Queen. It crossed my mind that he might decide to go looking elsewhere for love, but what he'd said about making me glad I'd chosen him was very comforting. Tychar might not have been able to do quite what he'd promised under the circumstances, but just being in his arms while he purred made me feel very much loved and made me very glad that I had, indeed, chosen him rather than his brother.

Not that Trag wasn't a great guy—and I certainly didn't regret anything I'd done with him—but while it's often been said that you can't help who you fall in love with, sometimes you get it right anyway.

As I lay there with Tychar, I remembered the vision he'd had that I would come to him, and his life would change as a result. I hadn't thought about that for some time, but now, it all seemed to be coming true. The one thing I hadn't considered was just how much everyone else's life would change—or end—along with his.

"You are not sleeping," he murmured.

"Wish I could," I grumbled. "Must be that nap I took on the drayl keeping me awake."

He laughed softly. "I can think of many other things

which might keep you awake," he said. "Much better things," he added.

"You're probably right about that," I admitted. "But there are some not so good things keeping me awake, too."

He seemed to hesitate a moment before saying carefully, "What will you do if we are able to secure the throne for Zealon? Will you stay here or return to Earth?"

"I don't know," I said frankly. "I suppose that depends on whether or not she wants to keep on taking piano lessons."

"And also if she wishes to keep slaves as her mother did."

Obviously he wasn't completely convinced that his freedom was real. "I don't think she would," I said. "Besides, I've always gotten the impression that you guys were Scalia's own personal possessions, not government property, so her death should free you. But if you're concerned about it, you should talk to Zealon, since she would probably stand to inherit anything of Scalia's. I don't think she'd feel any need to keep you as slaves—though she might employ you at the palace—but I seriously doubt she'd want to keep you locked up, even for your own protection."

"She didn't question it when I used one of the stones to pay for the animals we took," he said reflectively.

"No, if you're truly free, then I'd say those stones are yours now—as sort of a reimbursement for your years of service. So you've got enough money to do just about anything—you could stay here or leave Darconia altogether, if you liked."

"And if I was to do that—travel to another world— would you go with me?"

Since I had already decided never to leave Darconia in order to stay with him, I'd have liked to see anyone try to stop me from following him clear across the galaxy! "Yes, I would go with you," I replied. "If you wanted me to, that is."

"Kyra," he said gently. "How can you imagine that I would not?"

"Well, you've got plenty of money now, and you aren't a slave anymore," I reminded him. "Any woman would want—"

"I have no interest in what 'any woman' would want," he said. "Your wishes are the only ones that matter to me." He paused as he kissed me again, his soft, warm lips sending my senses reeling. "So, tell me, Kyra: what do you wish for?"

My mind went blank as I realized there was only one thing I'd ever really wanted enough to ask for it in my whole life. "You," I sighed. "Just you. You're all I've ever wanted."

"Then from this moment forth, I am yours," he said. "You have my body, my soul, and, most of all, my love."

With tears welling up in my eyes, I could barely speak through the tightness in my throat. "I love you so much, Ty," I whispered.

"No more than I love you, Kyra, and I will love no other," he promised. "We will be together forever."

Tychar had once said he wanted me to break his heart, but it was mine that was breaking as our lips met again. Here we were in the middle of a war, talking about forever! Losing him was something I didn't ever want to have to face. He might vow to fight to the death to save me, but it was up to me to keep *him* safe, too—and I promised myself I would do just that—even if I had to fight to the death myself.

"Sleep now, my love," he whispered in a voice which promised even greater delights yet to come. "I will be here to keep you safe."

And send shivers down my spine for the rest of my life. I was looking forward to that…

As I began to drift off to sleep, I heard the strangest sound—almost like that of a donkey braying.

"Oh, God!" Trag said morosely from where he lay on my other side. "Sladnil's upset!"

"Upset?" I repeated. "About what?" If I seemed skeptical, it was because, out of all of Scalia's slaves, Sladnil struck me as the least likely to cry about anything.

"Scalia," Tychar replied. "He was very fond of her."

"Oh, my Scalia!" Sladnil moaned. "Where will I ever find such a lover again? I loved her big, scaly body."

"This is grossing me out," I muttered, wondering why Wazak didn't just up and flatten him on general principles—one consort to another, as it were. "I don't suppose there's any tactful way to shut him up, is there?"

"Guess we could find him another woman," Trag suggested. "But I don't know if we'll find any around here. All of the miners I've seen so far have been men."

It was hard to comfort someone like Sladnil—I mean, he wasn't the sort you'd want to hug or anything—but surprisingly, Nindala murmured to him, and he quieted down. When I got up later on, I saw why. They were lying side by side, and Sladnil was sound asleep with the tip of one finger sucked onto her nipple. Nindala appeared to be sleeping, too, but she had a smile on her face.

That evening, we had dinner with the miners, who were surprisingly subdued—undoubtedly due to Zealon's presence; either that, or Wazak had them all too scared to open their mouths. They seemed like a decent bunch of guys to me, though I still thought Dragus was better looking.

After the meal, we talked strategy. Going in under cover of night seemed the best plan and, if the passage hadn't been blocked, we knew we could get into the palace through The Shrine—though it was anyone's guess what we'd find once we got inside. With Lerotan's weaponry, we had plenty of firepower, but it would be so much more effective to get to Dobraton and take her out without killing anyone else. Being a peace-loving piano teacher, this plan appealed to me, not only because Dobraton was the one responsible for every-thing, but because so many people had already died as a result of her bid for power. Nineteen of the miners had been killed in their battle alone, and we could only guess at how many had died inside the palace and at the spaceport—on either side—though if anyone had counted the number of fallen in Dobraton's army, I hadn't heard of it, which made me wonder what had become of the survivors.

"What happened after the battle?" I asked Lerotan. "Did Dobraton's men retreat, or did you capture them, or what?"

"They are being held captive in the mines," he replied.

"Think we could persuade them to come over to our side?"

Lerotan laughed mirthlessly. "Would you trust them?"

"Well, to be perfectly honest, Leroy, I'm not sure I trust *you*."

His smile indicated that he didn't really blame me for that, nor did he seem to mind the nickname I'd given him. Nice smile, too. Charming fellow.

"I have no reason to trust you, either," he said equably. "When everyone in your group was told to throw down their weapons, you didn't."

"Noticed that, did you?" I said with a grin. "Hey, it seemed like a good idea at the time. I'm new to this being taken prisoner thing."

"Not a typical day in the life of a piano teacher?" he suggested with another killer smile.

Oh, yes, he was *definitely* charming! In fact, I thought I might have to revise my initial impression of him; he might not be such a sexist pig after all, and the tail might prove interesting, too. I wondered if he liked blue redheads.

"Not really," I admitted. "But to answer your previous question, no, we probably can't trust them, but we could still use all the help we can get. What about it, Zealon?" I asked, with a nod in her direction. "Think you could drum up some support?"

Never having done much in the way of public relations as yet, Zealon wasn't sure, but said she would give it a try. It would be helpful to know what Dobraton had promised them—money, power, prestige?—because if they truly agreed with her beliefs, it would be difficult to convert them. Mercenaries, however, were a different story and could be bought. It was possible that they might hold out, thinking that someone would come and rescue them, but Dobraton was undoubtedly too busy to worry about what had happened in the mines and was putting off dealing with the problem until things settled down a bit. For my part, I hoped her situation never did improve; in fact, I hoped things were going really rotten for her. An open rebellion would be best, but an attitude of noncooperation might cause her enough headaches to keep her from dealing with the miners—before we got around to dealing with her, that is.

Wazak was all for storming the palace and going in with guns blazing, and I was afraid Lerotan would agree. To prevent further loss of life, I felt we should be more subtle than that, and besides, we *did* have the keys! The trick would be to get into the palace to organize a counter-rebellion. There had been far more guards in the palace than we could count among our group, and there had been scads of other workers who had been loyal to Scalia, as well. Dobraton couldn't have killed them all—though it was possible that she'd simply had them expelled from the palace. If that was the case, we might be able to find them in the town, get them together, and then retake the palace by force, if necessary. And if we could gather enough support among the civilian population, our numbers would be even more imposing.

Unfortunately, no matter how we went about it, we still had to cross the desert, and out there in the open, a large army could have defeated us quite easily. Therefore, it was agreed that our return had to be as stealthy as possible, using Lerotan's weapons as a last resort. We didn't want to reduce the palace to rubble to take it, either, which was something Tychar pointed out. He knew a little bit about that, and though he wasn't completely sure that the destruction of Zetith had been intentional, the timing had been entirely too opportune for it to have been mere coincidence.

The funny thing was, the former slaves were the ones who seemed to be the most excited about retaking the palace. The Edraitians just wanted to get on to their next gig and the arms dealers to their next sale, but Sladnil and Refdeck were practically jumping up and down with excitement, and they weren't the only ones—Tychar and Trag both had a bit of a gleam in their eyes, as well. Having been slaves for so long, they probably welcomed the opportunity to kick some Darconian ass—either that, or they truly were fond of Scalia and wanted to avenge her death—but the simple truth was that they were all bored to tears and were craving a little adventure. Aside from that, the palace *was* their home, and they had nowhere else to go—and if the spaceport never reopened, neither did I.

More out of curiosity than anything, I went along with Zealon and Dragus to visit the remaining members of Dobraton's forces. I wasn't sure how they would respond, but apparently a little time spent locked up in the darkness of the mines had been enough to make a bunch of sun-loving lizards willing to swear an oath of fealty to the devil himself.

They made a brief show of belligerence, but it passed pretty quickly when Dragus made some comment about leaving them there to rot until Dobraton decided to come to their rescue. Zealon asked them a number of good questions, but the one that had been plaguing me was one she omitted.

"So, just what was it that Dobraton promised you guys when you joined up with her?" I asked curiously. "Money, glowstones, or what?"

There was a bit of foot shuffling and some averted eyes, which meant it had to have been something other than money and possibly something not quite kosher—spoils of war and such.

"Favors," came the reluctant reply from one of the group, though I didn't see who had actually spoken.

"Favors," I repeated. "What kind of favors?" Searching their faces, I finally singled out one who was actually making eye contact with me. "You there, what were you offered?"

He looked at me for a long moment before he replied. "Those loyal to Dobraton would be paid well," he said at last. "And then given their choice of the females taken prisoner."

"I see," I said slowly. "Well, I guess that's what happens to prisoners of war," I admitted, though I wouldn't have thought they'd be that desperate. "But a handsome bunch of guys like you shouldn't be so hard up for women that you'd have to resort to taking prisoners!"

Another of them cleared his throat in a very human gesture. Carefully avoiding Zealon's eyes, he said, "We were promised a chance at the Princess."

I laughed out loud. "Well, to do that, Dobraton will have to catch her first, and somehow I can't see Wazak letting that happen."

"Nevertheless, that is what we were promised," he said stiffly.

"Well," I said in as matter of fact a tone as I could under the circumstances, "if any of you have a desire to become the consort of a *queen*, rather than a princess who's been taken prisoner, you might consider helping her regain her throne."

This was an aspect of the situation which had obviously not occurred to any of them. Perhaps it was a good thing Zealon had come to recruit them herself, though she seemed awfully young to be choosing consorts. She handled it well, however, showing more poise than I would have at that age. Perhaps growing up as a princess made you mature faster—and suddenly becoming Queen when your mother was assassinated would tend to have a sobering effect on anyone.

In the end, the men swore an oath of loyalty to Zealon, which probably wasn't as believable and binding as one coming from men who were not behind bars, but circumstances can't always be as perfect as one would wish. Zealon then conferred with Dragus on whether we should release the prisoners or keep them where they were until we were ready to leave for the palace. Not surprisingly, he wanted Wazak's input before releasing anyone.

"In his capacity as the Chief of Security, you understand, Princess," Dragus added courteously. "His advice in this instance would be beneficial."

I'd always known Dragus to be a smooth talker, and perhaps the men of Dobraton's army weren't the only ones interested in becoming Zealon's consort. There seemed to be some competition going on here, but it was subtle, and I wondered just who she would choose. Given that the females of this world considered their males to be too rowdy, I had no idea what they might have valued in a man. Scalia had seemed to value honesty as much as a cooperative attitude, but there was no asking her about it now.

I also wondered just how much courting any of the other palace guards had done with Zealon even before this—with the attitude that if they were good to her while she was Princess, they would have a better shot at becoming her consort. This train of thought led me to Scalia and Wazak, which must have been a very interesting courtship! The fact that Scalia hadn't been what you'd call exclusive—at least, not lately—meant that if Wazak truly was the father of *all* of her children, she'd obviously been quite taken with him. Funny how she'd never let on...

When Dragus and Zealon left to confer with Wazak, I opted to stay behind to talk with the prisoners to hear more about their side of the story. The man I had been talking with introduced himself as Falah, and he seemed quite willing to enlighten me.

"So, did you really intend to fight a battle here?" I asked. "What I mean is, what were your orders?"

"We were to take over the mines," Falah replied. "Any way we could."

"And since these miners were ready for you, you had to fight," I said with a nod. "What would you have done if they hadn't been warned?"

"That would depend on how reasonable they were willing to be," he replied.

"Hmm," I said reflectively. "And Lerotan sold Dobraton the weapons you carried?"

"I believe so," he said.

"Tell me something, Falah, if you were to choose—that bit about getting Zealon notwithstanding—which side would you be on?"

"Whoever paid the highest price," was his prompt reply.

"Well, that certainly sounds like an honest answer," I said with a chuckle. "You didn't really believe what Dobraton was selling, did you?"

Several of them exchanged meaningful looks. "We did not know what she intended."

"You just took the money and didn't ask questions?"

Falah nodded.

"Were you that hungry?"

"No," he replied.

"Well then, why do it?"

They looked at each other again and shrugged.

"Honest to God, this world is as bad as any other!" I said, stomping my foot in sudden anger. "I've never understood why men are so willing to go to war! I've often wondered just what would happen if a government decided to wage a war and the soldiers on both sides simply refused to fight it!"

There was a bit more foot-shuffling, but no one commented.

"Nothing was so bad here," I went on. "Oh, it could be argued that getting a McDonald's might raise your cholesterol levels a bit—but really, what's so wrong with visitors from other worlds? Granted, some of them—and I think we can include Lerotan in this group—aren't the most peace-loving, law-abiding citizens in the galaxy, but most people are! You just have to be careful who you let land. This isn't the

first planet to be visited by offworlders, you know!
Space travel has been going on for a long time, and
most societies are just interested in trade, not planetary conquest."

I might have continued with my little antiwar tirade,
but I soon realized that, for all intents and purposes, I
was talking to myself. These guys hadn't a clue. Apparently, along with being volatile, being stupid wasn't far
from the mark either.

When I rejoined the others, it appeared that Wazak
wasn't about to set Dobraton's men free until we were
on our way. "They must not be allowed to escape to
warn of our attack."

If they hadn't already.

"Hey, how far away do those comlink stones of yours
work?" I asked. "Seems to me that they could have reported back to Dobraton a long time ago."

"They only function effectively over less than a kilo-
meter," Dragus said. "Beyond that, reception is poor."

"You guys definitely need some better technology!"
I declared. "On Earth that would be like something out
of the Stone Age."

Lerotan got the joke, though I'm not sure anyone else
did. "I *tried* to sell them better equipment," he said with
a shrug. "But their budget was too tight."

"Which side do you mean?" I asked with a chuckle.

"Both," he replied. "Neither of them bought any communication equipment whatsoever."

"Their loss," I said. "Don't suppose you could sell us
some of that stuff now, could you?"

His grin was downright diabolical. "What were you planning to use as payment?"

"Well," I began, "Trag and Tychar have some really nice jewels, and I've got this glowstone necklace… and my pearls. Zealon and Nindala have lots of nice beads, too."

For a moment there, the gleam in his eye suggested he might be more interested in getting something else as payment, but he only said he'd think about it.

"You don't have anything with you to sell, do you?" Tychar said shrewdly.

"On my ship," Lerotan said with a regretful sigh. "We only have our personal comlinks with us," he added. "And since they're implanted, we can't sell them to you."

"They would still be useful," Tychar said. "If we are divided into groups, we could maintain communication with each other through them."

A long silence followed, which was finally broken by Wazak. "One of Lerotan's men with each squadron," he said thoughtfully. "Yes, it might work."

It might make them more trustworthy, too, and though I doubted I was the only one to be thinking that, nobody said it aloud. I thought we should split up Dobraton's former soldiers in the same way, but I didn't say anything, because I was pretty sure Wazak would figure it out on his own. Of all the Darconian males I'd ever met, he was certainly among the least volatile, nor was he one bit stupid.

Chapter 17

IT WAS PROBABLY THE FIRST TIME IN THE HISTORY OF DARCONIA that a member of the royal family had spent any time at all with miners, acrobats, and mercenaries, but Racknay was definitely intrigued. I wondered just what a prince who would never take the throne had to keep himself occupied besides taking piano lessons. Since they were supposedly too "volatile" to do much else, I could only come up with a military career. Actually, the more time I spent among them, the more I decided that the bit about them being too volatile was ridiculous; they were no more so than the males of any other world. I wondered what queen in the past had decided to keep them off the throne—though undoubtedly it had been the daughter of a man who'd been a bit of a warmonger. Still, Dobraton was proof positive that having a female in power could be every bit as bad as a power-hungry king.

I wondered just what Dobraton was calling herself now. Queen? Prime Minister? President? I also wondered if she was intending to maintain control until her death, which would mean that the new government would essentially be a dictatorship, which was bad news for everyone. Besides, if there had ever been any misuses of power by Scalia, they weren't readily apparent. In fact, the best I could tell—aside from the harem she kept—she was more progressive than many of our elected officials back home. While it was true that I'd only spent time among those who worked in the palace—or were slaves there—I hadn't heard even a whisper of discontent beyond the trouble Dobraton had stirred up. They all seemed to be as loyal to Scalia as they could possibly be. Even her slaves liked her!

The miners were another good example. They could have surrendered to Dobraton's forces with no loss of life if they had supported her bid for power, though Lerotan might have scotched that plan by warning them ahead of time and selling them weapons. Being well-armed and warned, the miners might have decided to shoot first and ask questions later.

Still, I couldn't help feeling a personal grudge against Dobraton for messing up everything. When I lay down with Tychar that night on a hard pallet in a chamber carved out of a mountain, surrounded by a multitude of other people when I would have very much liked to have been alone with him, I found myself feeling quite murderous toward her. My mind was seething with irritation, frustration, and plain, old anger! Things had been going pretty well; granted, I was still only a piano teacher, but I *was* working for a queen and had fallen in love with a wonderful man, and now this! Needless to say, when Trag nestled up behind me, I was feeling a bit crabby. I stood it for a while, but finally spoke up.

"Trag," I whispered. "What are you doing?"

"I would have thought that was perfectly obvious," he whispered back. "I'm just lying here enjoying your scent—since that's about all I can get these days."

"Guess we're right back where we started, aren't we?"

"Yeah," he grumbled. "It really sucks to be me."

"You have my sympathy," I said kindly.

"I'd rather have… well, just about anything besides that!" he declared.

"Go to sleep," Tychar told him.

"I can't!" Trag protested. "I'm lying here wondering if we'll all live through this adventure, and I—"

"Don't start that!" I warned, cutting him off abruptly. "I'm having enough trouble sleeping as it is!" Sighing irritably, I added, "Honest to God, if I could get my hands on Dobraton right now, I think I'd kill her."

"You could try," Trag amended. "But I doubt if you could do it with just your hands."

"Oh, you know what I mean!" I muttered. "I'm just mad, that's all." I blew out another exasperated breath. "Don't suppose either of you has any joy juice flowing, have you? I could use a little of that right about now."

"Got lots of it," Trag said eagerly. "I've been smelling you, remember?"

"How could I possibly forget?" I asked dryly. "You've only been breathing down my neck for the past hour! Look, Nindala isn't the only Edraitian woman we've got camped out with us. If she doesn't like you, why don't you go sniff one of the others?"

"Sorry," he said meekly. "But none of the other blue girls smell good, either."

"Go commiserate with Dragus, then," I suggested. "He hasn't had much luck lately."

"I don't want to talk to that slut and hear about all the women he's had," Trag grumbled. "I've had to listen to that crap from him for years!" Pausing briefly, he took a deep, fortifying breath before continuing, "Actually, I was hoping you would—"

"No," Tychar put in firmly. "She will not."

"See, you've even got Tychar irritated now," I whispered fiercely. "And that's pretty hard to do. Go to sleep!" With that, I snuggled in closer to Tychar, who leaned down to kiss me. It was dark, but I found his lips anyway—and had an orgasm.

"Why, you sneaky little devil!" I exclaimed. "There was some joy juice in that, wasn't there?"

"Well, you *did* say you wanted it," Tychar said in a frankly seductive voice that, surprisingly enough, could still send shivers down my spine, even in mid-orgasm.

"No way am I gonna kiss her now," Trag said miserably. "D'you suppose I could find some nice, blue Edraitian girl to do me real quick?"

"Don't even mind the fact that they're blue anymore, do you?"

"No," Trag said. "Doesn't look like I can afford to be too choosy." I heard him shift on his pallet. Calling out to the others, he said: "Hey, there! Any of you acrobats want to spend the night with a Zetithian? We're so good that lesser men tried to exterminate us."

I heard a few groans—mostly from the men—but, surprisingly enough, a female voice replied. "Sure it wasn't because you were a bunch of boastful jerks?"

"Uh, no," I said, raising my voice a bit. "I believe I can vouch for him on that. It's pretty incredible— well, it is for humans, anyway. Don't know about Edraitians."

"Hey, what's that line again?" Trag whispered to Tychar.

"I will give you joy unlike any you have ever known," Tychar whispered back.

"Yeah, that's it," Trag said. Calling out again, he said, "I'll give you more joy than you can stand."

"I don't think he got that quite right," I said to Tychar.

"Doesn't matter," said Trag. "I think she bought it."

I heard movement in the darkness and the sound of footsteps coming closer. My glowstones must have picked up on my thought that it was too dark to see, for they slowly illuminated. It was one of the Edraitians, all right, but it was a male.

"Be quiet, Zetithian," he warned, "or other 'lesser' males will finish what someone else began."

"Okay, okay," Trag muttered under his breath. "I'm just kidding," he said aloud. "Your blue girls are safe from me."

"I will hear of it if they are not," the Edraitian said menacingly before returning to his own pallet.

"Now, let's all be friends," Lerotan said, speaking up from where he lay. "We all need to get plenty of sleep."

"Or sex," Trag muttered, none too quietly. "You know, we could have one hell of an orgy here."

"Which would do wonders for interplanetary relations, I'm sure," I chuckled.

"Dibs on the Terran!" someone else called out. Not surprisingly, it was Dragus.

"Oh, be quiet, Dragus," I said witheringly. "There are children present, you know."

"I'm not complaining." It took me a moment to place the voice, but then realized it was Racknay. He was growing up pretty fast, it seemed.

Of course, the next voice I heard was Wazak's, and he wasn't anywhere near as nice as the Edraitian had been. We all quieted down after that.

It took three days to organize our supplies and plan our attack. We had no idea what Dobraton might do, so an open battle strategy, along with a plan for infiltrating the palace, had to be hashed out. Wazak took charge of most of this, but Lerotan claimed to be good at stealth and secrecy, and he'd been on the occasional battlefield, as well, though, as he later informed me with an infectious grin, it had only been in an advisory capacity.

I smiled back at him. "Didn't want anyone to jerk a knot in your tail, huh?"

"That has been attempted," he said suggestively, "but never during a battle."

Rolling my eyes, I went back to packing. He might have been in a few fights, but the "advisory capacity" stipulation rang true, for I had an idea he didn't want his handsome face messed up any more than he did his tail.

Later that night, with the sound of the deep, even breathing of those around us, my lover kissed me. Melting into his embrace, I returned his kiss with a fervor that went beyond what it had before. I might not have been deserving of him, but he was mine, nonetheless. I'd never known it could be possible to love one man as much as I loved him. He was the breath of life itself to me; my lover, my friend, and my solace in times of trouble. I did my best not to think about the fact that one or both of us might die tomorrow. We had this one, last night together, and we didn't waste it.

With a minimum of noise, I was able to slide down to take his cock in my mouth. He smelled good and tasted even better; delicious dick, succulent balls, fabulous body—and all this was aside from the fact that I loved him—what more could anyone want in a man? I could have lain there all night until I sucked him dry, but he had other plans for me. Pulling me back into his arms, Tychar rolled me over onto my back and slid his hot, thick cock into my wet, aching body.

I could see his eyes glowing from out of the darkness that surrounded us, isolating us from the others lying nearby. While they slept, we loved. He rocked into me, filling me with rapture with each stroke as the serrated edge of his cockhead raked my inner walls, coating me with his elixir of joy. I lay back in an orgasmic haze and watched as he climaxed but noted that his eyes stayed open, and he didn't stop, but kept on. The lack of euphoria told me he hadn't ejaculated, but was continuing on as though this orgasm was only his first of the night. He kept going; I could feel the sweat dripping from his body as he drove into me harder, deeper, slower, then faster, then stopping to sweep inside me with his cock, using every muscle he had to control its movement.

I wanted to scream in ecstasy, having to clamp my hand down hard over my mouth to stifle my cry lest I wake the others. I could scarcely believe what was happening and knew that any better feeling simply could not exist in this life or any other—but I was wrong. Gathering up my legs in his arms, he locked them nearly over my head as he continued to rotate his cock inside me. I was helpless to resist. He pushed me over the edge, and I felt the orgasm come, not from any chemical effect, but from the sheer stimulating action of his penis.

This time, I actually saw my own orgasm appearing as a flash of rippling blue light against a background of complete darkness. Whether it originated inside my brain or was something my eyes could actually see, I have no idea, but it reminded me of the image of a raindrop falling into a pool of water when slowed sufficiently for the human eye to visualize; that first undulating drop, which then expands out in circular waves. It was beautiful to behold just as it was, but with his own climax and the euphoria which followed, the color changed from blue to deep purple before slowly fading from sight.

As his kiss touched my lips—salty with the sweat of sweet love—and our bodies slowly parted, I knew that such a thing might never happen again in my lifetime. And it was fitting that it had occurred on this, of all of our nights together—this one night that could very well have been our last.

Chapter 18

WHEN WE WERE FINALLY READY FOR BATTLE, WE LOOKED like the motliest crew of brigands you've ever seen in your life. As usual, the Darconians looked fierce without any help whatsoever, but with weapons and supplies strapped onto their dinosaurlike bodies and stones glittering on their breastplates, they appeared even more deadly than usual. The miners had cannibalized some of their equipment and were carrying various objects that looked pretty nasty, but I had no idea what they were planning to do with them. Perhaps intimidation was their only intention.

Lerotan and his men looked like they would just as soon kill you as look at you (which was nothing new for them), and the Edraitians were all carrying spears and shields which they had made out of whatever the miners had handy. In addition to that, one of them must have been carrying their theatrical makeup when we escaped from the palace, because they had put it on like warpaint and had banded sections of their hair near the scalp so that it stood up in bristling, red bushes above their heads. Suffice it to say, they looked pretty scary.

Scalia's former slaves (aside from the tigers) were equipped with weapons from Lerotan, body armor which they had fashioned for themselves out of some kind of flaky stones, and they'd borrowed some warpaint from the Edraitians and had written "Down with Dobraton!"

on their shields. Sladnil had painted white circles around his bulbous eyes and had used his little sucker fingertips to put red and white dots all over himself. I took one look at him and screamed.

I opted for the Joan of Arc look, myself, wearing a lightweight vest over my flowing desert robes. Lerotan had given me the vest—swearing that it would stop anything short of a bomb—along with a helmet which didn't fit too badly. I couldn't see a damn thing when I had it on, but I'm sure the overall effect was as intended. The two tigers were similarly dressed—envision Lawrence of Arabia meets Spartacus—appearing simultaneously sexy and dangerous. With pulse pistols and rifles slung across our backs, we were ready for anything Dobraton could throw at us—short of a missile attack, which was something Lerotan assured us she did *not* have.

"Nice to have the arms dealer on our side," I commented to Tychar as I donned my armor. "Too bad we can't get to his ship and get even more of this stuff."

"Aw, we don't stand a chance, anyway," Trag said cheerfully. "This is what you call a desperate battle against overwhelming odds. What good would more guns do?"

"My, aren't we confident?" I said dryly. "Are you saying we should just hole up in the mines forever?"

"Naw, that's not what I meant," he replied. "That was just a little prebattle black humor. You know, something to break the tension."

"Well, then, here's another one for you," I said, getting into the spirit. "'I think it is a good day to die.' That's straight from Sitting Bull or some other chief, I

forget which one—he was Native American, anyway—
and I believe it's appropriate in our case."

"Ooo, I *like* that!" Trag said appreciatively. "I think
I'll paint it on my shield real quick."

Lerotan, who was eavesdropping on the conversation, commented, "Too many words. How about: 'Die,
Dobraton! Die!'?"

As I had written "Kill the Bitch!" on my own shield,
I thought this was much more appropriate, as did many
of the other refugees who had straggled in over the past
couple of days. Just having to escape with little more
than their lives and then cross the desert had made them
mad enough, but they brought with them tales of perse-
cution and oppression. It appeared that Dobraton was
not making many friends; at least, not among those who
joined up with us.

This was good for our side, because we certainly needed
all the help we could get, and, as anyone who is any good
at taking over command of anything will tell you, the one
thing you need to avoid doing at the outset is making any
changes that will turn your constituency against you. Be
nice, give them plenty of support and perks, and then later
on, when you start initiating other, less popular policies,
they won't mind quite so much—theoretically, that is.

Dobraton had obviously never taken that class in
basic leadership. Not wasting any time, she'd rounded
up as many offworlders as she could find and had them
executed, along with a few Darconians who had been
harboring them. As you might guess, this was *not* a
popular move!

To Dobraton's credit, I believe she intended these actions to instill fear in her new subjects and guarantee their

submission. However, I had done a bit of study since my discussion with Wazak the day he'd scooped me up off the floor, and I knew that the people of Arconcia had enjoyed a very satisfactory life under Scalia's rule; the crime rate was low, no one went hungry, there was medical care and education for all, and everyone was entitled to the same basic freedoms and opportunities. Scalia had added contacts with other worlds to the simple life in her realm, but most of her subjects had seemed to welcome this change.

Unfortunately, those who had supported Dobraton must have had a fair amount of clout—possibly wealthy merchants who didn't want offworlders horning in on their business, as well as ministers in the government who, like Dobraton, wanted to keep things just as they had always been—because seizing control the way she had done wasn't an easy thing to do. It took lots of money and planning to pull off something like that, and it also took a certain amount of gall. Running against an incumbent in an election was one thing, but killing someone to take their place was quite another!

We began our desert crossing about an hour after it was fully dark—though with three moons and rarely any clouds, it was always light enough to see where we were going. The desert was quiet, though there was nocturnal activity wherever you looked, and distant Arconcia gleamed in the moonlight. Some sort of night-flying bird or bat flew overhead in varying numbers, occasionally swooping down from the sky, as if trying to encourage us to turn back. We marched on in spite of them, some of us on drayls, some on foot, and a few of the later arrivals in hovercars, which they had brought with them—though whether they'd been stolen or not, I didn't know and didn't care. Hardly anyone spoke as we traveled, which might have been due to fear or a desire for secrecy, but it also added to the eeriness of the journey.

Never having gone marching off to war before, I couldn't have predicted the way I would feel, but, surprisingly, the thought that I might not live to see another day wasn't first and foremost in my mind. I was more concerned with the danger to my friends, and the fact that Tychar or Trag might be killed terrified me more than anything Dobraton might do to me. I did my best to put such thoughts out of my mind, but they kept creeping back to torment me.

While our preferred plan might have been to retake the palace from within, with the coming of dawn it became apparent that engaging in a desert battle was to be our fate. As we drew nearer to the outskirts of the city, we could see Dobraton's army massed out on the plain, ready to advance. There was no hope of infiltrating the palace now, and unless Dobraton was leading her own army, there was also no hope of taking her out without killing anyone else. We should have sent a party ahead, I thought ruefully, sending them circling around to the opposite side of the city to get to her. It might have taken longer with the more circuitous route, but that way they wouldn't have known which direction we were attacking from. As it was, we were marching right straight into the jaws of doom.

I could hardly believe just how large an army it was. How had Dobraton managed to amass such a force?

Surely not all of those men could have wanted the Princess as a prize! The city itself had a population of only about two hundred thousand and comparatively few of them were military men. Who *were* these guys?

Lerotan had some really cool binoculars, and while I was pretty sure I could see Dobraton at the center of the column, I could see nothing else which would provide a clue to their identity.

I handed the binoculars to Wazak. "That *is* Dobraton, isn't it?"

I'll swear he smiled. "Yes, it is she," he replied.

"Well, this doesn't look a bit good," I remarked to no one in particular. "Guys, are you *sure* about this?" No one said a word. I'd been gung ho enough earlier, but my enthusiasm was fading fast. "Well, what do you want to do? Keep on marching, or try for a parley?"

"Parley?" Wazak inquired, as if he'd never heard the word before.

"Oh, you know," I said. "You ride out carrying a white flag and then discuss terms of surrender or a truce—or give your opponent one last chance to back down."

"I don't think they're gonna back down anytime soon," Trag remarked. "We aren't *that* terrifying."

"But we have better weapons," Lerotan pointed out while patting his grenade launcher—or whatever it was. He'd never said, exactly, and I'd yet to see him use it, but he never seemed to want to part from it, either.

"Maybe so," I admitted, "but unless we can kill them all from here, I don't think it'll do much good."

If Lerotan's smirk was anything to go by, he was just waiting for the word from Wazak to do just that.

"How did they know we would be coming today?" Tychar mused.

"Well, we're not invisible, you know," Trag said reasonably. Glancing around at the surrounding tumble of boulders, he added, "Dobraton probably has a bunch of spies out here somewhere."

"But we came in the middle of the night!" Zealon said. "And we have seen nothing."

"It is the business of spies to remain invisible," Tychar pointed out.

"Either that, or somebody ratted on us," I said darkly. "And I'd sure like to know who it was, too!" I figured it was probably some of the men we'd recruited from Dobraton's gang, though I didn't suppose any of them would confess.

Of all people, Wazak was the one who spoke up. "I wished to engage Dobraton in an open battle."

"You did it?" I exclaimed in disbelief. "Wazak, are you insane? It's suicide! They'll kill us all!"

"I do not believe so," Wazak said evenly.

"What? Which part?" I asked. "That you aren't crazy, or that they won't kill us?"

I received only a speaking glance in reply, but knowing Wazak, if he didn't have some tricky little plot up his sleeve, I missed my guess, though putting his children's lives at risk seemed downright foolish to me.

"Well, I'm not going to go marching on to my death just so Dobraton can go ahead and be queen," Trag said, echoing my own thoughts. "Making Zealon queen is what we're here to do, and we won't do it just standing around talking. I say we blow them up from here."

I looked over at Lerotan, who appeared supremely confident in spite of the large army massing in the distance. "Can you do that, Leroy?"

Lerotan nodded. "Yes," he replied. "But do you really *want* to do that?"

"Well, to survive this ordeal, it would seem that our only other option is to go out under a flag of truce." I said tentatively. "We should try to talk with them." I glanced at Wazak. "How did you tell them we were coming?"

Tapping his breastplate, he just gave me another look.

"Your comstone? Who were you talking to?"

"You will see," he said mysteriously.

"You left someone behind, didn't you?" I said accusingly. "Someone to contact?"

He said nothing. We kept on moving. Dobraton's army was advancing.

"So, what do we do?" I asked nervously. "Hold our fire until we see the whites of their eyes?"

"Uh, in case you haven't noticed, Kyra, Darconians don't *have* whites to their eyes," Trag said informatively.

"We may not get the chance to fire at all," said Tychar, pointing to the left of the city. "Look there."

Following his gesture, I looked to the north, and in the growing light, I could see that another army was now exiting Arconcia, and this one was even larger than the first.

Chapter 19

"WE WILL MARCH ON," WAZAK SAID DECISIVELY.

"You're not serious!" I exclaimed. "We're outnumbered a thousand to one!"

"Have faith, Kyra Aramis," he said.

"Faith?" I echoed. "*Faith*? Great Mother of the Desert!" I urged my drayl onward in an effort to keep pace with him. "We're all about to die, and you're talking about faith?"

"It's a good day to die, remember?" Trag said cheerlessly.

"I take it back!" I said with fervor. "It's *never* a good day to die! Sneaking back into the palace to nab Dobraton is one thing, but are you saying we should just march right up and let them blow us to bits? Or capture us? They might not kill any of the natives, but Dobraton already doesn't like me on principle and doesn't like me much personally, either, so I'm dead meat. Guess I should have thought about that sooner," I added reflectively.

"I will fight to the death to save you," Tychar said, leaning forward to kiss me on the neck. Thrills of desire might have rippled over my skin, but there was no time for that now.

"Yeah, but what good will that do me?" I grumbled. "I mean, if you're dead—and I'm sure Dobraton wants you dead on general principles, too—why would I want to go on living?"

"Aw, isn't that—what is it you Terrans say?—sweet?" Trag said. "They really do love each other!"

"Yes, we really do," Tychar said stiffly. "It is nothing to laugh about."

"Well, if you say so," Trag grumbled. "Now, me, I just want to f—"

Tychar silenced him with a gesture. "We will not speak of that now," he said.

The two brothers kept on talking, though; bantering back and forth and distracting me to the point that it was some time before I realized that we were, indeed, still moving forward. Gazing out at Arconia, to my horror, I saw another army of Darconians begin to emerge from the southern reaches of the city.

"*Now* can we turn back?" I pleaded, any brave notions I'd ever possessed evaporating with the increasing heat of the morning. "We don't stand a chance in this battle, and, you know, the mountains weren't so bad, were they? We could stay there a while longer, and in the meantime, Dobraton might die from… oh, I don't know… a—a bad cold or something. You never know."

"She's babbling again," Trag commented to Tychar. "I thought she only did that when we—"

"Enough!" Tychar said in commanding tones. "Her fear is understandable."

"And your *lack* of fear isn't!" I said roundly. "What about you, Zealon? Aren't you scared to death?"

"No," she replied. "I am angry."

"Well, I *was* angry," I said, "and it sustained me for a good, long while, but it's all gone now! Somebody better make me mad again real quick."

"You're a really terrible piano player," Trag said promptly.

"You'll have to do better than that," I said witheringly. "I've heard that one before, and I didn't believe it then, either."

"You are even uglier than Dobraton," Lerotan said.

"Okay, that did it, Leroy!" I said, laughing. "I'm hopping mad now! Put down the bazooka, and I'll jerk a knot in your—er, I mean—Dobraton's tail."

It might not have made me feel any more courageous to laugh, but it did divert my mind from my imminent death. While we were talking, we were continuing to draw nearer to the city, and it was fairly obvious that Trag was just itching to shoot something. Tychar was very quiet, but as we rode upon our drayl, his arm around my waist spoke volumes. Wazak's swagger became even more pronounced as Dragus and about a hundred of the miners, along with one of Lerotan's men and Racknay, split off to the left. A similar group divided from our main force and formed a line to the right, led by Hartak, Zealon, and the Edraitians. Even spread out like that, our force was paltry compared with what we were facing. All of the other offworlders, myself included, were divided up among the three groups, with Trag, still riding with Nindala, opting to stay near Tychar and me. If Dobraton was aiming to target all the aliens, she'd have to take a few Darconians along with us—which, unfortunately, wasn't something she'd ever considered to be much of a deterrent.

"We're in range," Lerotan said quietly to Wazak. "Just give the word."

Wazak nodded, but cautioned, "Not yet."

Lerotan seemed surprised at Wazak's reluctance to open fire, but the more I looked at what we were up against, the more I realized that we were facing not just Dobraton's army, but what had to be the entire population of Arconcia. We couldn't possibly kill them all—and wouldn't have wanted to. What good was getting Zealon's throne back if there were no subjects left for her to rule?

It was a subtle move, but I saw Wazak tap his comstone and mutter something.

Then, as if on his command, the two factions on either side of Dobraton's central force closed in to form a buffer zone between the new "Queen" and her guard. Wazak then picked up the pace until we were about a hundred meters from the enemy and stopped. From where I sat on my drayl, I could see that these must have been the ordinary citizens of Arconcia we were now facing, because they were brandishing every manner of homemade weapon imaginable. Despite their numbers, Lerotan's arsenal could have taken out most of them before they ever reached us, and I thought it was pretty sad that Dobraton would sacrifice them in such a callous manner.

"Dobraton!" Wazak called out. "Lay down your weapons, and you will not be harmed."

"He wants *them* to surrender to *us*?" Trag whispered in disbelief. "That's pretty cocky of him, don't you think?"

"Extremely," Tychar agreed. "If nothing else, you can't deny he's got balls."

As you might expect, Dobraton's response to Wazak's demand was a sharp bark of laughter.

"You will not retake the throne with your pitiful little band," Dobraton jeered. "We will not surrender, nor will you surrender to us. Whether you stand and fight or run for the mountains, we will destroy you."

"*And your mangy little dog, too!*" I muttered with a grim smile, though, to be honest, Dobraton made the Wicked Witch of the West seem downright grandmotherly in comparison.

"You have given us your answer then," Wazak said gravely. "So be it."

Again, he spoke quietly into his comstone as he motioned for our front line to advance. We'd just about halved the distance between us and our opponents when the buffer zone of Darconian citizens all turned to face Dobraton, leaving an open space of desert in front of where she stood.

If I was surprised, I'm sure Dobraton was completely dumbfounded.

"Again, I ask you to lay down your arms," Wazak called out.

Dobraton looked at him, and then at the force of citizenry who now appeared to be ranged against her. She was completely mystified but didn't back down for an instant.

"What is this?" she demanded angrily. "I will not tolerate such disloyalty! You will *all* be destroyed!"

"I don't think so," Zealon called out. "You made one small mistake when you took power."

"And that is?" Dobraton sneered.

"The people of this city are not as opposed to change as you are," Zealon said, stepping forward. She looked and sounded quite royal; she would make an excellent queen. Scalia would have been proud. "As Queen, I will give them the changes which they, themselves, decide upon."

A cheer went up from the crowd, evoking a glare from Dobraton. Zealon waited a moment for silence to prevail before she continued. "What my mother began, I shall continue," she said. "The will of the people shall determine our future, not your small circle of followers. Such a small minority cannot control the entire population of a city if they do not choose to cooperate."

Undaunted, Dobraton shot back, "We control the water, and when the water no longer flows from The Shrine of the Desert, the people of this city will see that I, and I alone, am in control. Thirst and hunger will bring about cooperation."

I almost laughed out loud as it occurred to me that Dobraton probably didn't know about the true Shrine of the Desert—and Wazak had the keys…

"You may attempt to maintain control in that manner, but it would be a serious mistake," Zealon stated firmly. "The people would not stand for it."

She was right about that, because Dobraton's plan was sure to backfire on her. She might try to maintain her death grip on the city, but it wouldn't last. On any world, oppression breeds discontent, and discontent breeds rebellion; we would only end up fighting this battle again at a later date. The trouble was, some of us might not be left alive to fight it. This had to end bloodlessly, or too many would die.

"There is knowledge which you have not been privy to," Zealon went on. "The water cannot be stopped at the source."

"Perhaps not," Dobraton conceded, "but we could control who received it."

"You could *try*," I said with a chuckle. It was said more under my breath than anything, but Dobraton must have had excellent hearing.

"Why do you laugh, *Terran*?" Dobraton demanded, putting an emphasis on the word "Terran," which made it sound like an insult. "If I have my way, you will be among the first to die—along with those… *cats*."

If the way she'd said "Terran" was insulting, the word "cats" sounded downright obscene, and it brought my anger back in full force. She could threaten to kill me all she liked, but the tigers were off limits.

"Yeah, right, *bitch*!" I snarled. "Go ahead and kill us all! That's your answer to everything, isn't it? Somebody doesn't agree with you, you kill them—just like you killed Scalia." I took a deep breath and added, "And you know something, sweetheart? You should fuckin' *fry* for that! And speaking of fries, have fun telling all these people they'll never get to eat at a McDonald's as long as they live. *Then* see how happy and cooperative they are."

A murmur went up from the throng. "McDonald's?" they whispered.

"Yeah, that's right!" I shouted. "A McDonald's! Every planet in the known galaxy probably has at least one—except for Darconia! Think about it, now—crispy, salty fries and hot, juicy hamburgers—but you'll never get a taste of them. Ever."

As a rallying cry, it was a bit odd, perhaps, but I waited while the whispers grew, then someone began a chant in a loud voice that sounded decidedly female—

and surprisingly human. In a matter of seconds, the chant became a tail-thumping, weapons-clashing roar.

Zealon gave it a few minutes and then held up a hand for silence—and she got it, too. Immediately. "This is but one example to demonstrate the desire for change," she said, her voice ringing out across the sand. "Contact with other worlds and other cultures will enrich us all, and we shall take our place among the great planets of the galaxy." She paused there, taking a deep breath for emphasis. Oh, yes, Scalia had taught her well. "As Queen, I shall reopen The Shrine of the Desert. No longer will it be open only to the privileged few, but to all comers." Pausing again, she smiled. "Our people want a McDonald's, Dobraton. And since you are not willing to give it to them, I will."

The cheer that went up from all sides was deafening, and the crowd—her "guard" included—backed away from Dobraton to leave her standing alone in the middle of the desert floor. Dobraton was overthrown.

Never underestimate the power of the golden arches.

Chapter 20

IN THE WILD DISPLAY OF JUBILATION WHICH FOLLOWED, IT'S a wonder no one got squashed. The Darconians themselves probably weren't in any danger, but being part of a mob of happy, tail-thumping, back-slapping dinosaurs is not something I would recommend to anyone less sturdily built than they are. Tychar and I wound up getting thrown off our drayl when one of the Darconians bumped into it, and when a hand reached down to pull me to my feet, I was astonished to find myself looking up into the dancing eyes of a tall, broad-shouldered, dark-haired human female.

"Captain Jacinth Tshevnoe, at your service," she said gaily. "Though my friends—and some of my enemies—call me Jack. And this guy here is my husband Carkdacund, also known as Cat. You must be the piano teacher." Taking a quick glance at the general revelry going on all around us, she added, "Damned if I know when this melee will end, but it seems kinda dangerous for us Terrans right now. We should probably get the heck outta Dodge while we can!"

I stood up and stared back at her in surprise, but my jaw dropped when I saw the man standing behind her. With his waist-length black curls and devilishly fanged grin, he was undoubtedly Zetithian.

My gasp might have been lost in the tumultuous cheering, but I believe Tychar heard me screaming at him. "Hey, Tychar!" I yelled as I spun around to locate him. "Take a look at this guy!"

Tychar was still in the process of extricating his flowing robes from the drayl harness and at that moment, obviously decided to dispense with them altogether. Backing away from the drayl to pull it off over his head, he turned to face us wearing nothing but his collar and a pulse rifle.

"Ooo, *nice* one!" Captain Jack said approvingly as she gave him the once over. "Not scarred up at all! Not anywhere near as handsome as Cat, of course, but still pretty nice. And I *love* the hair!"

Tychar seemed puzzled for a moment before he finally saw the man she was referring to and let out a yell even louder than that of any of the Darconians.

"Wazak said there were two of them," Jack commented as the two men hugged each other like a pair of long-lost friends. "They're brothers, right?"

"Yeah," I said, still staring at the one called Cat in disbelief. "Trag's around here somewhere."

"Holy shit!" Trag exclaimed as if on cue. "It's Cark!"

Leaping from his drayl and nearly knocking Nindala off in the process, Trag joined in the group hug.

"And not just him, either," Jack said, laughing. "I believe you know Leo, too!"

"Great Mother of the Desert! There's *another* one?" I screamed as a Zetithian man with golden-brown hair approached and, to the shouts of "Lecarrian!" from the tigers, joined in the reunion.

"Yeah," Jack replied. "Picked him up on Utopia, along with his wife." Putting a hand up beside her mouth, she added confidingly, "And she's a real witch, too."

"Oh, stop it, Jack," said Leo's wife as she swept a lock of her thick, dark hair from her lovely face. "And yes, I'm a real witch," she admitted, "but one with actual powers, mind you—not just a bitchy woman."

"Yeah, so watch out what you say to her," Jack advised. "Those pretty green eyes of hers can set you on fire."

I wondered if the withering glance she shot at Jack was capable of setting her to smoldering, but the witch apparently had better control of her powers than that. "I'm Tisana," she said, holding out a hand. "You must be Kyra."

"Yeah," I replied absently as I shook her hand, still mystified that these people were not only standing in the middle of the Darconian desert as if they belonged there, but seemed to know a whole lot more about what was going on than I did.

"We've been in touch with Wazak ever since the coup," Jack said in answer to my puzzled expression. "I'm a trader," she explained. "We were here to check out some of their stones when Dobraton decided to get uppity." She grinned engagingly, adding, "Nothing for it but to organize a counter-rebellion!"

"And how did you do that?" I asked faintly, though it shouldn't have surprised me, because "Captain Jack" looked to be capable of just about anything.

"Oh, you know, give them a little taste of this and that," she said with a casual wave. "I'm not sure, but I think it was the Hershey bars that did it, wouldn't you say, Tisana?"

The witch nodded but added dryly, "That, and the fact that you told them I'd roast them alive if they didn't join up."

"'Course, it could have been the video games," Jack added reflectively. "Would you believe they'd never seen any?"

"Hey, these people are vegetarians and they don't even make fruit salad," I remarked. "And in all the time I've been here, I've only seen one computer, so the video game thing doesn't surprise me either—and I *know* they don't have chocolate!"

"They were a bit iffy about the White Castles, thinking that McDonald's hamburgers would be better," Jack went on. "'Course, that's a matter of personal taste. I like them both, myself," she confided with a shrug. "Even the vegetarian versions."

"Don't mind Jack," Tisana said with a roll of her sparkling eyes. "She'll eat anything."

"That is not true!" Jack exclaimed. "I'm just not as picky as you. Now, Cat, on the other hand, is partial to sweets, which for a member of an obviously carnivorous race has always seemed a bit odd to me."

"It's only because they were slaves and never got any," Tisana put in. "Your Zetithians were slaves, too, I believe?"

She had directed her question at me, but the sight of four Zetithians standing together—especially when my own was naked—had me slightly distracted, so it took a moment for me to reply.

"Yes," I said. "Queen Scalia owned them, but they were more like pets than slaves. She treated them very well."

"Cat and Leo were pretty beat up when we found them," Tisana said fondly. "But they recovered quickly."

"Yeah," I agreed. "They look great." And they did—breathtakingly so.

The din had begun to subside slightly as the Darconian hoards began to move back toward the city. I saw Dobraton being marched off to God knows where— didn't really care, either.

Jack moved closer. "So, which one is your boy-friend?" she asked.

"That one," I replied, pointing to Tychar. There was no point in denying it, because if all Zetithians were like my tigers, Jack and Tisana had to know firsthand just how irresistible they could be. Quoting Trag, I added, "Trag's just a bad boy I like to—" I broke off there, for some reason deciding that it might be best not to say anything further. Didn't want to ruin his reputation—or mine.

"Oh, come on, now!" Jack urged. "Don't leave us hanging. We know what our guys are like. Tell us about yours."

"Well," I began tentatively, "they were coming off of a twenty-year dry spell, so I… had to… you know… I mean, there *were* two of them…"

"Oh, my God, you did them both!" Jack exclaimed.

"At the same time?" Tisana squealed.

"Well, yeah, but only once—"

Jack started to say something else, but the guys were heading our way.

"They have been talking about us again," Cat said with a knowing nod. "Whenever they are alone together, they talk about us."

I shook my head sadly. "You poor, unfortunate guys," I mocked. "It must be awful for you."

The one called Leo smiled. "But we retaliate by talk-ing about them."

"Comparing notes?" Tychar remarked. "Well, your Terran women are lovely, of course, but my Kyra—" Pausing for a moment, he smiled at me, sending delightful shivers running up and down my spine. "—looks and smells and feels like love."

Trag groaned, pulling at his hair. "Stop reminding me! I've *got* to get off this fuckin' planet!"

"You could hitch a ride with us," Jack suggested. "We'll head back to Earth eventually, and I'm sure you could find a woman there. You might not believe it, but I know of some ladies who are putting their daughter's names in a pot for a chance that they'll get one of our sons."

"A lottery?" I scoffed. "They aren't that—" I broke off there, because I knew she was right. It would be the only way to thin out the multitude of women who would want one of them. It was a bit like breeding rare and highly prized dogs, and everyone wanted a puppy of their own—except the Edraitians, of course. They seemed to be immune to Zetithian charm. Their loss…

"I might just do that," Trag was saying. "You don't happen to need a pilot, do you?"

"Still insisting that you can fly anything?" Cat asked with a wry smile.

"Well, yeah," Trag said defensively. "I mean, I'm sure I still can. After all, I'm a natural!"

"You couldn't get that old freighter off the ground," Leo reminded him. "Which is why we were captured."

"You don't still blame me for that, do you?" Trag said, aghast. "Shit! I make *one* little mistake…"

"And if you had not, then we would not be here," Tychar said gravely. "If we had been able to launch, we would have been shot down, not captured."

"So, essentially, he saved your lives," Tisana observed.

"Yes, I believe he did," Tychar said, his smile displaying the warm affection he felt for his brother.

"So, I'm a hero, then?" Trag said brightly. "A real hero?"

Leo rolled his eyes. "He always did have delusions of grandeur."

"But only about flying!" Trag grumbled. "And at least I didn't go around waving my sword yelling, "I am the greatest!" all the time."

"You did that?" Tisana said to Leo with surprise. "I don't believe it! You've always seemed so... modest."

"Once," Leo insisted grimly. "I did that *once*— after winning a tournament. He never *would* let me forget it."

"Well, you're all heroes as far as I'm concerned," I said roundly. "And I do mean all of you! Even Sladnil."

"Who's Sladnil?" asked Jack. "One of the Darconians?"

"No," I replied. "He's one of the slaves, actually." Glancing around, I finally spotted him hobnobbing with Refdeck. "There he is, over there with the little guy who looks like a toad."

Jack, who struck me as being just about the toughest woman I've ever met in my life, took one look at Sladnil and turned as white as a glowstone.

"Oh, God!" she said with a shudder of revulsion. "He's a Norludian! If there's one thing I can't stand, it's one of them! They really creep me out!"

Nindala, who had remained silent up until that point, lifted her elegant chin and said haughtily, "He is my lover!"

While we all watched in astonishment, Nindala turned

her drayl and rode out across the desert, her bushy red hair waving in the wind. When she stopped to pick him up, Sladnil made her a sweeping bow before climbing up to ride behind her, his suction-cup fingers gripping her bare, blue arms. As they rode off toward Arconcia, Sladnil looked back at us and grinned.

"So long, suckers!" he yelled.

"Interesting choice of words," I remarked to no one in particular. "Norludian, huh? So, tell me, Jack, why do they creep you out so much?"

"You don't want to know," she said with another shiver. "I mean, you *really* don't want to know!"

As I gazed out at the two of them riding off across the desert, knowing that I couldn't even *begin* to imagine a stranger couple, I said, "You're right, I probably don't, at that. So tell me more about Cat."

Regaining her color, she grinned wickedly. "I found him in the slave market on Orpheseus Prime wearing nothing but chains."

This mental image alone was enough to make me choke on my own spit, but I knew I could top her story. "Tychar and Trag were wearing nothing but collars and cock rings when I first saw them," I said. "And I had an orgasm when Tychar smiled at me."

Tisana shrugged. "I think you've both got me beat," she said. "Leo was about half dead and in rags when I first saw him."

"They are talking about us again," Cat said to Leo.

"Better get used to it," I said, slipping an arm around Tychar's waist. "Of course, you guys know how to shut us up."

"Yes, we do," said Tychar. Gazing after the dwindling

crowd of Darconians, he added, "We should return to the palace."

"It's funny hearing you say that," I remarked. "After all, you were a slave there."

"But not anymore," he said. "I belong to you now, Kyra. No matter where we go, I am your lover, your protector, and above all, your slave." Drawing me close, my tiger kissed me gently, melting my very bones, just as he always did.

And still does.

Epilogue

CHANGES HAVE BEEN RAMPANT SINCE THE BATTLE OF Arconcia—though a lot of people will tell you it wasn't really a battle at all, since there was no loss of life, not even Dobraton's. Having been there, I disagree, for it was as much a battle of wits as any war. As far as Dobraton was concerned, I was of the opinion that if she had been killed, it would have been no more than she deserved, though I thought a more fitting punishment would have been to teach her to say, "Would you like fries with that?" and have her serve each and every customer who walked in the door of the new McDonald's for the rest of her life. While this may not sound like a particularly harsh sentence, it probably would have killed her in mere weeks because they did more business in that first month than any McDonald's in history—and it's *quite* a long history! Still, I would have liked to have seen it—and I *did* suggest it—but was forced to admit that it probably would have caused a riot, because the lines would have been moving too slowly.

After a great deal of soul-searching, Trag left Darconia with Lerotan, whose pilot had been killed in the take-over of the spaceport, rather than with Cat and Leo. It was hard for the guys to split up after finding each other again after so many years, but though Jack comes back now and then on trading runs and we stay in touch with them, we've seen Trag very seldom since he left.

It was difficult enough for me to say good-bye to him; I couldn't imagine what it must have been like for Tychar. Having been together for so long would have made it hard enough, but *they* were brothers! I suppose it wasn't that much different for me to part with my own family when I left home for Darconia, but they had been through war and slavery together—not to mention me.

"Jack was right," Trag said. "I need to go out and find my own woman."

"Still holding out for a Zetithian?" I asked.

"Maybe," he replied. "Or a Terran—might even have to go as far as Earth to do it—and then my dick will be hard for the rest of my life." Grinning at Tychar, he added, "Can't let you have all the fun, and besides, I have to make up for lost time!"

Which was something that Tychar seemed to be bent on doing himself. They didn't have what you'd call a marriage ceremony on Darconia, but we didn't need it. Our mutual bond is far more binding than any legal contract could ever be.

Although it has taken a few years to finally happen and neither of them has admitted to it, I'm pretty sure that Dragus is the father of Zealon's first child. It isn't as though the baby actually resembles him—at least, no more so than she would any other Darconian—but he seemed to be entirely too pleased with himself following the birth. Come to think of it, he's been pretty cocky ever since he took over as security chief when Wazak became Regent.

No one guards The Shrine of the Desert anymore—or my door, for that matter, though Hartak does admit to missing my cries of ecstasy. Actually, I think he hangs around sometimes to see if he can hear me, because every now and then I run across him prowling the corridor outside my rooms. The Shrines (both of them) as well as the secret passageway are now open to all comers at all times, as any good shrine should be.

I've gone on with my teaching, and though Zealon has less time for such things now that she is Queen, I still have plenty of other students—along with my own children.

It came as a bit of a surprise to give birth to three of them at a time, but I'm not complaining, because they're all adorable little fellows who look just like their father. I still hope that more mammalian offworlders will settle on Darconia, because unless they do, our kids will all have to leave home to find mates the way Trag did. I must say, the idea of scattering them like seeds all across the galaxy appeals to me. Jack laughed when I suggested that we start a registry for Zetithians so they can find each other, and the more I thought about it, the more I decided it was a bad idea—especially if that bounty is still on them. I can see no point in making it easier for anyone who might try to exterminate them again.

Jack tells me I should watch out for something called Nedwuts on principle, since they were apparently the ones who destroyed Zetith, and though I haven't run into any, I stay ready for them. If anyone ever tries to collect the bounty on my tiger, I've still got my pulse pistol, and Lerotan left me his grenade launcher. He never bothered to teach me how to use it, but I'm sure the mere sight of such a weapon would be enough to frighten off even the most determined bounty hunter. As you can see, I'm not the same meek little piano teacher that I once was. Not any more!

As for my career as a composer, my Zetithian sonata was published and seems very popular among the younger pianists—and a few of the older ones. It's difficult to get new music onto the classical scene—there hasn't been another Beethoven or Mozart in a thousand years of waiting—but interest in it has already grown substantially. I may be a one-hit wonder, but that's okay. Inspiration doesn't always strike on demand.

Uragus has turned out to be as much of a prodigy as I could have hoped, though the classical style didn't hold his fancy for long. I suppose it was my own fault for playing a few rock songs for him, and there's been no stopping him ever since!

Racknay went wild on the synthesizer and decided against a military career in favor of becoming a rockstar. He and Uragus got together to form the first all-male rock band in Darconian history and, after some debate, they asked Refdeck and Sladnil to join—which meant they had to change the name of the band from *Princes* to *Princes & Slaves*. As it turned out, Refdeck is a pretty decent guitar player and Sladnil, interestingly enough, can play drums—haven't seen him drop a drumstick yet! He's taken to painting his face for performances the way he did before our last battle with some rather terrifying results. He's got a lot of rabid fans—most of them just as weird as he is—but Nindala doesn't let any of them get anywhere near him.

Tychar was reluctant at first, but he finally agreed to be their lead singer. He wears more when he's on stage performing than he did when he was a slave, but he still wears nothing but that jeweled collar above the waist, and his pants are cut so low that women have been known to faint at the mere sight of him—and you already know he can sing! Imagine that! The hottest act in the quadrant—and he's all mine.

**Escape to the world of
the Cat Star Chronicles,
by Cheryl Brooks**

SLAVE

WARRIOR

ROGUE

OUTCAST

Read on for a sneak peek...

SLAVE

Chapter 1

I FOUND HIM IN THE SLAVE MARKET ON ORPHESEUS Prime, and even on such a godforsaken planet as that one, their treatment of him seemed extreme. But then again, perhaps he was an extreme subject, and the fact that there was a slave market at all was evidence of a rather backward society. Slave markets were becoming extremely rare throughout the galaxy—the legal ones, anyway.

I hitched my pack higher on my shoulder and adjusted my respirator, though even with the benefit of ultrafiltration, the place still stank to high heaven. How a planet as eternally hot and dry as this one could have ever had anything on it that could possibly rot and get into the air to cause such a stench was beyond me. Most dry climates don't support a lot of decay or fermentation, but Orpheseus was different from any desert planet I'd ever had the misfortune to visit. It smelled as though at some point all of the vegetation and animal life forms had died at once and the odor of their decay had become permanently embedded in the atmosphere.

Shuddering as a wave of nausea hit me, I walked casually closer to the line of wretched creatures lined up for pre-auction inspection, but even my unobtrusive move wasn't lost on the slave owners who were bent on selling their wares.

"Come closer!" a ragged beast urged me in a rasping, unpleasant voice as he gestured with a bony arm.

I eyed him with distaste, thinking that this thing was just ugly enough to have caused the entire planet to smell bad, though I doubted he'd been there long enough to do it. On the other hand, he didn't seem to be terribly young. Okay, so older than the hills might have been a little closer to the mark. Damn, maybe he *was* responsible, after all!

"I have here just what you have been seeking!" he said. "Help to relieve you of your burden! This one is strong and loyal and will serve you well."

I glanced dubiously at the small-statured critter there before me, and its even smaller slave. "I don't think so," I replied, thinking that the weight of my pack alone would probably have crushed the poor little thing's tiny bones to powder. I know that looks can often be deceiving, but this thing looked to me like nothing more than an oversized grasshopper. Its bulbous red eyes regarded me with an unblinking and slightly unnerving stare. "Its eyes give me the creeps, anyway," I added. "I need something that looks more…humanoid."

Dismissing them with a wave, I glanced around at the others, noting that, of the group, there were only two slaves being offered that were even bipedal: one reminded me of a cross between a cow and a chimpanzee, and the other, well, the other was the one who had first caught my eye—possibly because out of all the slaves there, he was the one seeming to require the most restraint, and also because he was completely naked.

I studied him out of the corner of my eye, noting that the other prospective buyers seemed to be giving him a wide berth. His owner, an ugly Cylopean—and Cylopeans are *all* ugly, but this one would have stood out in a crowd of them—was exhorting the masses to purchase his slave.

"Come!" he shouted in heavily accented Standard Tongue, "my slave is strong and will serve you well. I part with him only out of extreme financial need, for he is as a brother to me, and it pains me greatly to lose him."

His pain wasn't as great as the slave's, obviously. I eyed the Cylopean skeptically. Surely he couldn't imagine that anyone would have suspected that his "brother" would require a genital restraint in order to drag him to the market to part him from his current master!

Rolling my eyes with disdain, I muttered, "Go ahead and admit it. You're selling him because you can't control him."

"Oh, no, my good sir!" the Cylopean exclaimed, seemingly aghast at my suggestion. "He is strong! He is willing! He is even intelligent!"

I stifled a snicker. The slave was obviously smart enough to have this one buffaloed, I thought, chuckling to myself as it occurred to me that no one around here would even know what a buffalo was, let alone the euphemism associated with the animal.

I blew out a breath hard enough to fog the eye screen on my respirator. Damn, but I was a long way from home! Earth was at least five hundred long light-years away. How the hell had I managed to end up here, searching for a lost sister whom I sometimes suspected of not wanting to be found? I'd followed her trail from planet to planet for six years now, and had always been just a few steps behind her. I was beginning to consider giving up the search, but the memory of the terror in her wild blue eyes as she was torn from my arms on Dexia Four kept me going.

And now, she had been—or so I'd been informed—taken to Statzeel, a planet where all women were slaves and upon which I didn't dare set foot, knowing that I, too, would become enslaved. The denizens of Statzeel would undoubtedly not make the same mistake that the slave trader had, for I was most definitely female, and, as such, vulnerable to the same fate that had befallen my lovely little sister. That I wasn't the delicate, winsome creature Ranata was wouldn't matter, for a female on Statzeel was a slave by definition. Free women simply did not exist there.

Which was why I needed a male slave of my own. One to pose as my owner—one that I could trust to a certain extent, though I was beginning to believe that such a creature couldn't possibly exist, and certainly not on Orpheseus Prime! I was undoubtedly wasting my time, I thought as I looked back at the slave. He was tall, dirty, and probably stank every bit as much as his owner did. I was going to have to check the filter in that damn respirator—either that or go back and beat the shit out of the scheming little scoundrel who'd taken me for ten qidnits when he sold it to me. I should have simply stolen it, but getting myself in trouble with what law there was on that nasty little planet wouldn't have done either my sister, or myself, a lick of good.

As I glanced at the man standing there before me, he raised his head ever so slightly to regard me out of the corner of one glittering, obsidian eye. Something passed between us at that moment—something almost palpable and real—making me wonder if the people of his race might have had psychic powers of some kind. That he was most definitely not human was quite evident, though at first glance he might have appeared to be, and could possibly have passed for one to the uneducated. There weren't many humans this far out for comparison, which was undoubtedly why I'd been able to get wind of Ranata's whereabouts from time to time. She seemed to have left a lasting impression wherever she was taken.

Just as this slave would do, even with the upswept eyebrows that marked him as belonging to some other alien world. His black, waving hair hung to his waist, though matted and dirty and probably crawling with vermin. I had no doubt that his owner hadn't lied when he had said that the slave was strong, for he was collared and shackled—hand, foot, and genitals. I'd been through many slave markets in my search, but I'd rarely seen any slave who was bound the way this one was, which spoke not only of strength, but also of a belligerent, and probably untrainable, nature. The muscles were all right there to see, and while they were not overly bulky—appearing, instead, to be more tough and sinewy—their level of strength was unquestionable.

This man had seen some rough work and even rougher treatment, for jagged scars laced his back and a long, straight scar sliced across his left cheekbone as though it had been made with a sword. He had a piercing in his penis, which appeared to have been done recently, for the ring through it was crusted over with dried blood. A chain ran from the metallic collar around his neck, through the ring in his cock, to another metal band that encircled his penis and testicles at the base. The pain that such a device could inflict on a man was horrifying, even to me, and I'd had to inflict a lot of pain in the course of my travels—though never to someone so defenseless and completely within my power as a slave. My never-ending search for Ranata had left me nearly as tough and battle-scarred as the slave was, and I'd often had to fight to the death in order to stay alive. So far, however, I'd never stooped to torturing a slave, and sincerely hoped I never would. This slave owner obviously had no such qualms, and it made me want to take a shot at him, just on general principles.

Call me an old softy if you will, but I must admit that I considered buying this slave, if for no other reason than to set him free of his restraints. I might feed him first, though—and perhaps buy him some clothes.... I cocked my head to one side as I considered him again. You're a fool if you think feeding this thing will tame it, I told myself. A bona-fide fool...

WARRIOR

Chapter 1

HE CAME TO ME IN THE DEAD OF WINTER, HIS BODY
burning with fever. Even before he arrived on my doorstep, bound, beaten, and unconscious, I knew my quiet
life was about to change forever. And I was ready.

As I stirred my potion, I heard the creak of saddle
leather and the muffled thud of a body falling into the
snow outside my isolated cottage, followed by Rafe's
grunt of effort as he dragged the unconscious offworlder
through the drifts. With a gust of cold air and a swirling
cloud of snowflakes, he pushed my door open and burst
inside without so much as a knock.

The evening had begun tranquilly enough. I had just
brought in extra wood from the shed, but it was snowing
so hard, I decided to go back out into the wintry darkness
for more. I can conjure up fire better than any other witch
I've heard of, but it helps to have some fuel. Besides, I
love the cozy warmth and smell of a wood fire.

From her place by the fire, Desdemona gazed up at
me with narrowed eyes, nodding her agreement. I trusted
her feline intuition to alert me to danger, but Desdemona
had given me no warning. Yawning, she stretched and
let out a loud purr before curling up once more.

Reassured, I pushed open the heavy wooden door
and peered out into the thickly falling snow. Big, fluffy
flakes drifted by in the beam of light, floating gently but

inexorably to the ground. It was already a handspan in depth and more was on the way. But there was something else in the air tonight—a strange feeling, heralding something altogether new and unexpected. Not a feeling of dread or fear, but something that whispered of the fulfillment of a promise. It hung there, on the edge of awareness, teasing me with its elusive aura. Just what—or who—it was, only time would tell. Time and the gods.

My woodshed was only a few paces from the door, though with the snow it seemed farther than usual. Treading softly, I sank into the snow with each step, feeling my way through the darkness. The door to the shed creaked open on its rusty hinges and I glanced up at the lantern, shooting fire into the wick, instantly illuminating the interior with a warm glow.

I had plenty of wood stored there for the winter; the people of the forest saw to that. I was too important to their well-being for them to ever let me freeze or starve, and offerings appeared almost daily on my doorstep—sometimes openly, sometimes covertly, but still they came without fail. I reminded myself frequently that one day they might not, and was, therefore, frugal with whatever I had. I knew full well that my honored status could vanish on a whim, and I wouldn't have been the first of the chosen ones to be cast out to starve. It was a tenuous existence, to be sure, but one for which I had been born and bred.

Stacking the new logs on my arm, I made my way carefully back through the snow to my house. Although the right to own property was denied most women on this world, it was *my* house and had been my mother's

before me, and her mother's before her, time out of
mind—never once having a male to claim ownership.
Our children had fathers, of course, but we seldom married—at least, not in the traditional sense—and therefore traced our lineage through the female line. The one
child we were granted was of the utmost importance,
for it was she who would continue our work and our
traditions—and that child was always female. Always.

Desdemona purred her greeting as I came back inside
and dumped the logs by the fire. I had three days' worth
of wood there already, but the snow was deepening
quickly, so I thought I might as well bring in more. Pausing by the door, I listened. There was barely any wind,
and the snow fell silently until, just on the fringes of my
hearing, I was at last able to hear what I'd been waiting
for: hooves in the snow, and heavily laden, by the sound
of them. A rider was coming, but that was not all.

I could hear the effort the horse was making as he
strained to climb. He was coming from the east, and I
could place him now. It was Sinjar; I sent a greeting of
thought out to him and heard him nicker in reply. We
knew each other well, for his master, Rafe, had been my
lover once. Too arrogant now to trouble with the likes of
me, he'd been charming enough in his youth. I'd known
that Rafe wasn't the one—had always known, even from
the beginning—but loneliness sometimes drives one to
seek out solace in places where happiness can never be
found. It had been over for many years; Rafe had a wife
and sons now and had never once strayed back to my
bed. That it was for the best, I was well aware, because
he had become too powerful and had too much to lose
by consorting with a witch.

Sinjar's thoughts reached into my mind. *"I'm tired and hungry,"* he said. *"They are heavy."*

"They?" I asked.

"The master and another," he replied. *"Sick and hurt. A slave, I think. He is...strange. An offworlder."*

"I'll have food and water waiting for you, Sinjar," I promised.

"Good. It's not far now. I'll be glad to see you again, Tisana."

"And I, you."

Returning to the shed, I gathered up buckets and feed and carried them back to the house, filling one of them with water from the pump by my door. Rafe might want food and drink as much as his horse did, but he would have to ask for it when he arrived.

Rafe and I had not parted company on the best of terms, though he did use my talents when it served his purpose. He must need my help very badly to come out on a night like this—and for a slave, no less. An offworlder, which didn't bode well, for my skills and medicines were sometimes useless with other species. My knowledge had grown with time, but there were still those whose physiology was too different to respond to my treatments. Many of the basic principles were the same, but they were usually strangers, and often didn't trust me completely, which was half the battle. This one might already be beyond my aid, for I could sense something ominous about him, a life-force on the wane. Rafe may have been too late.

I set Sinjar's food and water down and went inside, leaving the door unlatched, and gathered what herbs I thought I might need. Water was already hot in the kettle hanging from a hook over the fire, and I mixed the pungent potion in an earthenware bowl on a heavy wooden table that was probably as old as the cottage itself. Powdered comfrey root mixed with sage and rosemary tea would help to heal his battered body, but an infusion of thyme, lavender, rosemary, and vervain would help restore the will to live, which I could tell even from a distance was the chief problem afflicting my newest client. I doubted that many slaves would prefer death to slavery, but some might. Rafe was a stern man and could be an exacting master. On the other hand, Rafe would presumably have paid good money for him, and see him as an investment to be protected. He wouldn't be coming at such a time if it didn't matter to him.

Putting my fingertips to my temples, I wished for perhaps the millionth time that I could read the thoughts of humans as well as those of animals. My grandmother had had that gift. My mother had had both, though to a lesser degree, but I could read only the beasts of the forest and farm. It was a useful skill, for very few others could ask their horse which foot was hurting them, or if the girth was pulled too tight. I always knew where to find the juiciest berries and the lushest patches of wild rosemary, because the rabbits knew, and their minds were much occupied with these matters. Animals had a feel for weather, too, and were a much more reliable source of information than your typical village sage.

Still, with sick or injured humans, you can ask what the trouble is—if they're conscious enough to reply— but it's a given that they will sometimes embellish upon the truth. Rafe had lied to me—many times. I sometimes let him think I believed him, but I wasn't fooled.

Taking a deep breath, I put my thoughts of Rafe firmly aside. I couldn't afford to let them, or anything else, interfere, because I knew this one would require all of my concentration.

OUTCAST

Prologue

WHAT BEGAN AS EVERY MAN'S DREAM SOON BECAME one man's nightmare, and though he earned his freedom in the end, his quest for inner peace was a long and tortuous one.

Lynx was only seventeen when he was taken prisoner in the war that destroyed his planet. Slated for execution, he and the other members of his unit were sold into slavery instead. Thrown into the hold of a ship with no food and very little water, the new slaves were smuggled half-way across the galaxy to a slave auction on a distant world.

Dragged onto the auction block, the terrified boy almost wished he'd been executed. To be bought and sold like an animal was unheard of on his own planet of Zetith, where the world had been green and beautiful and the people were free. On this planet, whose name he never knew, he was sold to a trader who then sold him to an owner whose face he never saw.

Stowed in the hold of yet another ship, exhaustion outweighed his fear and he fell asleep on the journey, only to be rudely awakened by two men. As one held him down, a flexible tube was painfully injected into the soft skin of the inside of his left upper arm.

"Take that out, and you die," he was told, then was given a drink and left alone again in the darkness.

Lynx lay sobbing with fear and pain and hunger. Even war had not terrified him like this. He had no idea where he was, or where he was going, and he believed that death would have been preferable to the life he now faced. He felt completely and utterly alone. Not knowing if the journey lasted for days or weeks, he lost all track of time, and was fed at odd intervals, which served to disorient him that much more.

At last, the ship landed and the bright light nearly blinded Lynx as he was pulled into the harsh sunlight by his captors, who marched him down a dusty street and into a large, palatial building.

"Pretty, isn't he?" the ugly, harsh-voiced man remarked to his cohort as they stripped him of his bonds and his clothing.

"He'll fit right in!" the other man laughed. Unlocking a large, ornate door, he pushed Lynx inside. "You're their slave now," he said with a nod. "You do whatever they tell you."

The light inside was much brighter than the corridor through which he had been brought, and it took a moment for his eyes to adjust as the scent of perfume wafted forward and curled into his sensitive nose. Green was the first color he saw: lush, tropical plants growing in profusion. Then he saw the women—scores of them, all beautiful and all as naked as he was himself. They smelled of desire, and, despite his fear, that desire aroused him instantly.

Not knowing what to do, Lynx simply stood by the door, but was beginning to feel somewhat relieved by what he saw. Being the slave of women wouldn't be so bad; he was fairly certain they wouldn't beat or torture him. But Lynx had never understood women. Most of the time, he felt intimidated by them—never knowing what to say or do—and remained alone in the background while his friends found lovers. Granted, he was young, but the concepts of enticement were something that Zetithian males generally grasped at an early age; Lynx, however, was mystified.

As he stood there waiting, the women ignored him at first, but his erection eventually elicited a few stares, and soon he was being touched by several soft hands—hands which soon found his hard cock, and played in the fluid which had begun to ooze from the scalloped edges of the wide corona on the head. Lynx gasped as they fondled him before pulling him down onto the soft cushions on the floor. He'd never felt such pleasure before in his life. Then one of the women licked him, savoring his fluids until her body contracted in a powerful orgasm. Then another tasted him, and another, and another. He had the same effect on all of them, and they marveled at his attractive feline features and his sexual prowess.

He was the slave of other slaves, and he did whatever they asked, though his own needs were never considered. Not even given food of his own, to survive he had to scavenge what he could from what the women left behind, and if they ever felt the need to punish him, they made sure that there was nothing left for him. When they finally gave him permission to eat, they laughed at the way he wolfed down his food.

Still, it was easy at first, for he was young and his sexual desires were at their peak. Day after day he fucked them, fed them, licked them, and massaged them. He catered to their needs and overheard their conversations, but more than anything, they craved his body, for he affected them in a way that no other man had ever done.

He was both lover and slave to each of them, who were, in turn, the slaves of a man who owned far more women than he could possibly service.

At first, Lynx didn't understand their language very well, but as he learned, he discovered that the women's greatest fear seemed to be bearing his child. Whenever one discovered her pregnancy, he saw the terror in her eyes as the others reassured her that Lynx couldn't possibly be the father. This puzzled him greatly, for he could never understand why having his child was such a horrible thing—or why they never did—but he heard it constantly, and his heart grew bitter. They would take what pleasure he could give them, but wanted nothing more; not his children, and certainly not his love.

And so, for many years, he lived with them, at first only watching as their children were born, then later assisting with the births and caring for the children. He liked the babies and never held it against them that they weren't his own. He could never understand why none of the children ever resembled him, though he'd had intercourse with each and every one of their mothers. After a while, he came to realize that he must have been unable to father children, and this weakened his self-esteem even further.

His sleep was seldom undisturbed, for there was always a woman seeking his attention—whether it was to bring her food or to make love to her—and before long, it all began to seem the same to him. What he had initially considered to be a blessing now became a curse. The sound of female voices began to grate on his nerves and the constant bickering among them irritated him almost to the point of screaming. There was no respite, no

time to himself; they were always there, always demanding his undivided attention, and the sexual gratification
he could give them.

His bitterness grew, and his exhaustion was never-
ending. As time went on, his erections began to diminish, becoming infrequent before finally ceasing
altogether. Then one day, three men marched into the
harem, seizing Lynx and dragging him out to be resold.
He heard some of the women laughing, and, knowing that they must have complained about his impo-
tence, any feelings he might have had for them turned
to dust.

Marched naked to the auction block, Lynx was sold
again, but this time, his companions were all male,
which was a welcome change. The men might have
been rough and crude, but they were undemanding, and
Lynx slept well for the first time in many years. His
new owner, a just man who didn't believe in slavery,
told Lynx that after five years of service, he would be
freed. Seeing hope for the first time since he was enslaved, Lynx put in his time, working hard and learning what the men could teach him, after which he was
freed. He stayed on for several more years, working
and saving his pay, for he had heard of a new colony
on a planet called Terra Minor where he could be his
own master and live out the remainder of his days in
peaceful solitude.

Peace and quiet were the things he longed for most
of all, but to find that peace, Lynx needed money, so he
saved his own and watched as other men gambled away
their pay or wasted it on the favors of women. As a free
man, Lynx saw women and could smell their desire, but

he was never aroused by them, and he avoided them whenever he could, for, having been used and betrayed by women, he now despised them all.

But their voices still haunted his dreams, and he would wake up in a cold sweat with the sound of their laughter as he was dragged away echoing through his mind—not one of them even whispering goodbye.

Acknowledgments

My thanks to my family and friends for their support, and to Earl Grey for his life-sustaining tea.

About the Author

Cheryl Brooks is a critical care nurse by night and a romance writer by day. She is a member of the Romance Writers of America and lives in Bloomfield, Indiana, along with her husband, two sons, five cats, and four horses. *Rogue* is the third book in The Cat Star Chronicles series, following *Slave* and *Warrior*. You can visit Cheryl's website at http://cherylbrooksonline.com or email her at cheryl.brooks52@yahoo.com.

SLAVE

BY CHERYL BROOKS

"I found him in the slave market on Orpheseus Prime, and even on such a god-forsaken planet as that one, their treatment of him seemed extreme."

He may be the last of a species whose sexual talents were the envy of the galaxy. Even filthy, chained, and beaten, his feline gene gives him a special aura.

Jacinth is on a rescue mission... and she needs a man she can trust with her life.

Praise for Cheryl Brooks' *Slave*:

"A sexy adventure with a hero you can't resist!"

—Candace Havens, author of *Charmed & Deadly*

"Fascinating world customs, a bit of mystery, and the relationship between the hero and heroine make this a very sensual romance."

—*Romantic Times*

978-1-4022-1192-8 • $6.99 U.S. / $8.99 CAN